AN ABIDING
LEGACY

Chris Piechowski

IndePenPress

First published in Great Britain by IndePenPress

All paper used in the printing of this book has been made from
wood grown in managed, sustainable forests.

ISBN13: 978-1-78003-437-9

Printed and bound in the UK

Indepenpress Publishing Limited
25 Eastern Place
Brighton
BN2 1GJ

A catalogue record of this book is available from the British
Library

Cover design by Jacqueline Abromeit

This book is for Becky

Your unwavering patience, insight and enthusiasm are wonders to admire. If only I could match them. You are a true marvel in so many ways and deserve the utmost praise and gratitude. I have been truly blessed.

Chris Piechowski was born and raised in England. The son of a Polish father and and English mother, he served for over thirty years in the police force. Now retired, he lives with his wife in a small village on the edge of Salisbury Plain.

An Abiding Legacy is the second in a trilogy beginning with the critically acclaimed *Poles Apart - From Darkness, Fire and Chains*. The final novel, *Footprints in the Labyrinth* is expected sometime in 2013.

www.chrispiechowski.co.uk

CONTENTS

Clouds

They say that the Dead die not, but remain
Near to the rich heirs of their grief and mirth.
I think they ride the calm mid-heaven, as these,
In wise majestic melancholy train,
And watch the moon, and the still raging seas,
And men, coming and going on the earth.

Rupert Brooke 1887 – 1915

Also in memory of **Johnny Klimenko**
A True Veteran - 20.2.1925 – 30.12.2011

Pro libertatem nostra et vestra

Prologue

CALL OF DUTY

Salisbury – 3rd November 2009

I opened the brown paper parcel and read the note inside:

Dear Mick,

I thought you should know that Dad passed away last month. I'm so sorry that I haven't told you before now, but it was purely an oversight on my part and I know that he would have been most annoyed at my negligence. He died peacefully in his sleep and only a few days before, he had told me that the last year had been the most joyous and rewarding passage in his long and challenging life. He was true to his word and spent no end of time with his brothers and their families and his obvious happiness and contentment was in itself a source of great comfort to Mary and me. The positive change in him was incredible and his enthusiasm and energy was an inspiration to us all. We will miss him so very much.

Yesterday I started to put his affairs in order and I came across the enclosed sealed package in his desk. It had a 'post-it' attached on which Dad had written, 'I've kept this for 70 years and when I'm gone, I want Mick at Salisbury to have it. I'm sure he'll know what

1

best to do.' I have not opened it and have no idea what it is. I must admit I'm intrigued. It's so typical of Dad to have his fun and keep us guessing, even at a time like this, so please let me know as soon as you can.

With kind regards and grateful thanks for everything,

David.

I cut the string, opened the package and found a small diary wrapped inside an oilskin cloth. It measured five inches wide by six inches long by three inches thick. The fold-over leather cover was dirty, water stained and fraying at the edges, but the clasp still worked and inside the tiny but immaculate copperplate handwriting was clearly legible. Inscribed on the first page were the following words:

Duty bade me fight.
The Life of Dominik Dabrowski:
A Polish Soldier.

I remembered who he was. Jan Nowaski, David's father, had spoken of him several times during our conversations about his own wartime exploits – always with respect, admiration and warmth. Jan was thirteen when war broke out on 1st September 1939 and with his mother and three brothers he was evacuated east; away from the German assault on Poland through Pomerania to the relative safety of the countryside just outside Luck, a city in what was then the Polish Ukraine. Dominik owned the farm where they stayed and shortly after their arrival, the Red Army invaded from the east and they were all besieged by hostility and intimidation. For a few terrifying weeks the two families shared the humiliating privations caused by total war as both the German and Soviet invaders tightened their grip on the civilian population. They experienced constant hunger as their meagre supplies ran out and were stunned and brutalised by the pernicious occupation.

Jan and his brother, Tomek, were caught stealing food from the Russians and were about to be shot. Just as the machine gun was primed, an officer intervened to save them. Jan was fortunate to eventually escape to England, but his parents, sister and a brother perished during the conflict. In subjugated Poland life became very cheap and survival a matter of chance.

I had no idea what had become of Dominik, although Jan suspected that he had been amongst the thousands of farmers in eastern Poland that had been rounded up by the Russians and summarily executed or transported east as slaves. Most of the latter also perished, either in the Gulag or worked to death down the mines, in the factories or in the fields and forests of Siberia. It was curious that Jan had never mentioned the diary to me and I had no idea of how it came to be in his possession. I pictured him at our last meeting with his friendly, weathered face; wrinkled old eyes, yes, but still bright with the joy of life and the flash and sparkle of mischief. His smile was warm and welcoming and even well into his eighties he still stood proud and upright. His mind was sharp and incisive and he carried his history of hurt and suffering with an admirable dignity, acceptance, and lack of malice. I smiled as I remembered him and spent a few moments happily reminiscing our short association and firm friendship.

I first met him a year ago when I returned a number of letters, photographs and personal possessions which he had abandoned in mysterious circumstances and had then remained forgotten for decades. In the course of my enquiries I also traced his long-lost brother and this led to a wonderful family reunion with relatives who had not been seen for 70 years. I had been privileged to listen to the heart-wrenching stories of their epic journeys home. This diary, however, was a new and surprising development. I was intrigued as to why he had given it to me and not to his son, but knowing him as I did I suspected that he had another task for me and if past history was anything to go by, it would not be straightforward. Why else would he have been so secretive and cryptic? I would have to read it to find out. Little did I know then that I was about to embark on a memorable voyage of my own. It would be a passage of discovery and wonderment, full of twists, turns and surprises, as I was navigated through the amazing lives of a small group of remarkable heroes. A few ordinary men and women who, by the chaos of the time and a twist of fate, were thrown together, destined to struggle against the greatest evil of the twentieth century. Perhaps we only exist today because they and a few other like-minded individuals managed to prevail.

It was not a diary in the traditional sense but a carefully written narrative and as I settled down at my desk, I had absolutely no idea what to expect. When I started to translate, however, it became obvious that Dominik was an intelligent, well-educated and observant man. His prose style was easy to read, engaging and concise but very descriptive and colourful in its use of imagery. After just a paragraph or two I was hooked. I read on and nothing could have prepared me for the revelations to come...

Chapter One

THE LEGEND OF VIENNA FOREST

Kalisz, Central Poland – 4th December 1899

My earliest recollection is that of my grandfather sat in his large, upright wooden chair by the fire recounting, in his soothing, sing-song voice, the many stories of the hero Knights who fought through the generations for Poland's freedom. Every tale started with the same words: "Pray to God that he makes truth be your master, duty your friend and justice your endeavour. Honour is everything!" By ritual I would always answer: "Above all, I will uphold our noble traditions and protect those who cannot protect themselves. This I so swear." Only then would he speak in 100 voices and let the enchanting stories unfold.

I would stare into his weather-beaten face and try not to look at his right hand which was missing three fingers, lost in his youth to a sabre slash when fighting the Russians. I listened in wonder and joy as he spun his magic and drew me into a courageous world of weapons, chivalry, battle and pride. His flowery language, continuous, sweeping gesticulation and his captivating use of dialect and intonation brought the characters so alive that they were ever present in my infantile world, where all things were possible.

Throughout my childhood I was constantly reminded that we were very privileged to live in Kalisz, the oldest city in Poland, set astride the Amber Road and even mentioned by Ptolemy. My father, his father and their ancestors were all fiercely proud of their military history and achievements. Their loyalty and duty to the Motherland was unswerving, especially during the many decades when it had been divided up and ruthlessly occupied by its powerful neighbours. But our family story starts with legendary significance, during a time of Polish prominence; a tale repeated so many times that it's etched into my memory.

In the early morning light of 12th September 1683 Jan Sobieski, the King of Poland, looked out from the 1,300 foot summit of the high Kahlenberg and surveyed the great plain stretching far into the distance. A clear strategic advantage was his reward for the slow and difficult struggle, climbing up the rocky mountain track through the forest. He enjoyed a 120° panoramic view, framed by the impressive, meandering sweep of the Danube. This precious ribbon of blue cradled Kara Mustafa's massive crescent shape encampment and his vast army, which was laying siege to the Habsburg capital, Vienna. He could now walk the escarpment, scrutinise the enemy positions surrounding the city below and prepare his battle plan.

The vizier had made a serious tactical mistake in not securing the heights during his two month siege and now he made another by disdainfully dismissing the approach of his enemy. He believed that only a small, lightly armed force could have successfully scaled the mountainous terrain. Being preoccupied with the breaches in the city walls and the extreme vulnerability of the 10,000 weakened, diseased and desperate defenders inside, he was diverted from the real danger. His sappers had placed a massive mine under the already weakened fortifications and he felt certain that the city would now fall within hours and the relief army would be too late to prevent his victory. He vastly outnumbered the enemy forces, and was convinced that once the city was his, he could attack the relief column at a time and place of his choosing and prevail by sheer force of numbers. Unbeknown to him, the mine had already been discovered by an Austrian tunneller and had been defused. The weakened, embattled garrison, boosted by this reprieve and the sudden arrival of allies on the heights, was determined to maintain their disciplined, effective and obdurate defence. They would not surrender.

Overconfident with hubris and eager to increase the pressure on the depleted city garrison, the vizier dispatched only a small force towards the hill to intercept and harry the approaching relief column. He then carried on with the bombardment, massing his troops for a final full-scale assault. He would not be deflected because he reasoned that once he controlled Vienna, then its power, wealth and prestige would be his alone. The population would become prisoners and hostages and he would hold all the bargaining power. He commanded over 120,000 fighting men and they came from every province of the Ottoman Empire. His camp contained a similar number of slaves, herdsmen, armourers, sapper/miners and general camp followers, with thousands of horses, camels, buffalo and baggage wagons. The vizier's luxurious quarters were in the very centre of the tented city. Made from the finest green silk, embroidered with gold and silver thread and bedecked with jewels, his tent was so large and imposing that extraordinary rumour spread across the land. It was said to contain many exotic, oriental luxuries such as baths, fountains, a harem, bizarre animals and even a sumptuous garden.

It also secured his most treasured item: the Noble Banner – the Sacred Standard of the Prophet. It was a holy relic, second only in importance to the Blessed Mantle. When not in use, the flag was safely protected alongside the latter, securely locked inside a pair of golden chests. They were housed under a latticed silver canopy, inside a special pavilion chamber off the Throne Room in the Fourth Courtyard of the Topkapi Palace in Constantinople – the capital and the power base of the mighty Ottoman Empire. Only the sultan held the keys and occasionally he released the banner to be carried into battle to embolden his troops and drive them on to victory. Koranic chants had been read aloud and incense burned at a special historic ceremony as the sultan had handed it over to the vizier. It had been carefully removed from the chest by the sultan who then fixed it to a royal staff, before carrying it personally to the Throne Room, while officials and guests called out "Allah Akbar!" All then stood in reverential silence as the sultan kissed the Holy Banner and solemnly assigned it to his grand vizier, with the traditional words, "I entrust the Sacred Standard to you and you to God. May He be your helper." It would be returned the same way, with a formal ritual of acceptance, culminating in the sultan personally carrying it back to its chamber and securing it in the golden chest. Here it would remain, until the next major threat to the vast empire.

That afternoon the Hussars emerged, a few at a time, from the shade of the trees on the heights, into the bright and burning late summer sunshine. Their infantry had driven the last of the advance guard of Turks from the gullies, outcrops and vineyards on the slopes, and now it was their turn to enter the fray. As their numbers increased and the size of the force became clear, the vizier, still unable to take the city and with time running out, finally realised the imminent danger and potential catastrophe. He ordered his massive army to reform, into full battle order, to defend their camp against the new infidel threat. He demanded, "Every man must hold his ground at all costs, or die in the effort."

The gloomy forest backdrop on the hill suddenly glittered with light and colour; dazzling reflections of silver and gold in a sea of red and white standards, as the squadrons of heavy cavalry formed for battle. The finest horses from the Holy League (Polish–Lithuanian Commonwealth), the Holy Roman Empire (based in central Europe) and beyond, bore the szlachta (Poland's nobility and the privileged elite) whose posture, dress and weaponry were the hallmark of aristocracy, wealth and power. Their steel helmets and armour were adorned with gold, amber and plumes and over one shoulder they wore cloaks of leopard, wolf, tiger or bear skin. Each man carried an array of fearful weapons designed for every battle situation, and also richly decorated to display the rider's affluence. They included an ornate and bejewelled shield, a modified Eastern slashing sabre, which by its unique combination of length, weight and curve, gave considerable cutting power for a minimum of effort. He also carried a straight stabbing rapier with a six-foot blade, which could also be used as a short lance. At his waist or attached to the horse's harness he would have another sword, two pistols, a short carbine, a small bow, a quiver of arrows and a dagger. Some preferred the czekan, a long steel hammer of personalised length and weight that could smash through helmets and heads as if they were eggshells.

Strapped on his back was a wooden, leather and metal frame, adorned with twin parallel sweeping arches of several dozen eagle, or more rarely ostrich feathers, that rose up like wings. Finally, he carried the most imposing of his weapons: an eighteen-foot, steel-tipped, gold leafed, and brightly painted lance, decorated with a six-foot-long flying red and white pennon. Such a long reach meant that the Husaria could easily penetrate a square or any other defensive formation and then, leaving the lance embedded in the front rows of defenders, they could charge on through the formation using their other weapons. The Polish eagle and the white cross of Christendom was emblazoned on many of their huge flags and pennants; for this was a Holy war and as they faced the Jihad of the Sultan of Sultans, Mehmed IV, both sides were convinced of their divine right of victory.

The Polish mounts, sporting crimson and gold velvet saddle cloths or embroidered silk caparisons were seventeen hands high; huge, strong and fearless beasts, trained to ignore the noise of battle and hold formation at full gallop. They set off downhill, audaciously crossing in front of the Turkish camp lines at 45 degrees, to arrogantly display their strength, splendour and discipline. They trotted, slowly at first to preserve their horses, but relentlessly and economically they built up speed until the air was filled with the roar of 14,000 hoof beats – more intimidating than a massed army of ancient Roman warriors beating their shields as one.

The ground vibrated to the rhythm of the charge of ten regiments of Husaria. When the steel clad, winged lancers were at full gallop they mesmerisingly and effortlessly changed direction, instantaneously turning half right. This was a wondrous and awe-inspiring sight, akin to a flock of half a million starlings weaving as one in the early evening, against the dramatic background of a late autumn sky. The hussars skilfully used the lie of the land to gain that final vestige of added momentum, and in doing so they threatened the very heart of the enemy formation. The terrified defenders were tempted to run, to save themselves from the inevitable onslaught and it took immense courage and discipline to stand fast but hold they did.

Then they heard an eerie humming noise, the murmuration growing ever louder until it could be heard above the beating of hooves, the Polish battle cries and the sounding of trumpets. It grew in pitch and intensity until the 100,000 feathers 'sang out' as the wind rushed through them. The flapping of countless pennants and flags that festooned this seemingly unstoppable formation bearing down upon them, added to the ramping cacophony which spooked the Turks' horses. This hellish, demoralising sound was the last ever heard by hundreds on the battlefield that day as the solid mass of heavy horses carved effortlessly through the front ranks of Ottoman cavalry and then on into the infantry beyond. Row after row they died underfoot or were swept aside as the Poles surged on through the defenders. Even the lines of elite Janissaries, the sultan's personal and household guard, could not stop them but turned and fled as the leading Polish lancers charged towards the very heart of the enemy encampment, threatening the grand vizier's personal quarters.

Despite their success, the Polish king and a handful of his retinue suddenly found themselves in imminent danger. Their impetuous charge and incredible feat of arms left them some 100 yards ahead of the main body of lancers who were now losing momentum as their horses faltered amongst the piles of enemy corpses and they began to tire from the immense physical demands of fighting in armour under a baking sun. The enemy ranks immediately behind Sobieski suddenly found open ground and room to manoeuvre as they were displaced sideways and backwards into the gap, by the sheer compacted pressure of their own comrades facing the main thrust of the attack. The sight of the king's growing isolation also emboldened the Janissaries who rallied and then attacked from the front and sides. The king was now surrounded by fifty to sixty fierce, battle-hardened Turks, all lunging and hacking their way towards the prize of their hated and suddenly vulnerable, enemy chief.

His retinue had already abandoned their lances and were now fighting with sabre and pistol in an attempt to force a way through the horde and extricate themselves from the deadly mêlée. Enemy cavalry then rushed in to drive home their advantage and one by one the lancers were overwhelmed. They were brought down by arrows and musket fire or pulled from their horses and impaled or beheaded by the turbaned warriors, effortlessly wielding their scimitars and cutlasses and already relishing the taste of victory.

Marek Dabrowski, my forefather, saw his king's plight and at the head of half a dozen knights, and closely followed by a supporting squadron of Bavarian light cavalry, he charged forward. He knew he had to be quick and so he dug his spurs into his mount and the animal reared, almost unseating him, before surging through the enemy infantry. Marek abandoned his rapier and continuously hacked to left and right with his sabre, slashing and cutting through the foot soldiers. He was covered in blood and gore and the battle lust, which I have also known, enveloped him. He screamed at the top of his voice and the remaining infantry in front began to scatter to avoid being trampled by the massive horse, or cut down by its crazed and high-winged rider. The king, now totally isolated and surrounded, heard the approach of his knights as he desperately fought on to save his own life and press home the attack. He twisted and turned in the saddle and continuously spun his horse to strike down infantrymen closing in. He managed to beat them off and created a few yards of clear ground all around, but a Turkish light cavalryman took advantage of the opportunity and closed in, striking down at the kings head with his sabre.

Marek clearly heard the resounding clash as the king managed to parry the blow with his shield, but as they fought another mounted Turk attacked and when he raised a wide scimitar, to cleave the king from behind, Marek covered the last few yards and drove his horse straight into him. The Turk momentarily lost balance but Marek, braced for the impact, had the advantage and thrust his weapon through the Turk's throat with such force that he almost severed his head. Arterial blood shot high into the air, spraying both Marek and the king, before the body fell to the ground. The first Turk took flight as the other Polish knights arrived to form a protective screen around their king. Before they had even recovered their breath the King was urging them on, "Forward my bothers. They will not stand now. On, on into the city and free those poor souls who have suffered for too long. This battle is done and the day is ours."

The rest of the winged lancers caught up with their king to find the whole Ottoman army in full retreat. The battle-weary garrison poured from the breaches in the walls, and cheering and jeering, they too fell upon the enemy and the rout was complete. The king rode into the centre of the tented city and although a man used to wealth and opulence, he was astounded at the vast range and quantity of riches, equipment and baggage that had been abandoned. Inside the vizier's extensive tent it was like a ghost town; everything in situ except the people. A half-eaten banquet was spread across the floor, surrounded by swathes of silk and brightly coloured, luxurious cushions. Dozens of strange musical instruments had been discarded in the central area. Personal possessions and the impedimenta of war littered the floor, jettisoned by the Ottoman high command and their entourage in the panic to lighten their load and escape.

Off to the side, the orders of battle, the siege plans and campaign maps were scattered across a low table, surrounded by a hoard of treasure. It included gold and silver quivers encrusted with precious stones, ceremonial swords and daggers, tapestries, rugs and artwork, jewels and plunder, all in addition to the vizier's own household riches. His prized and personal standard of horse tails and the holy banner of the Prophet had also been captured. The victory was so complete and the sultan's camp such a treasure house that the king wrote home to his wife, "God be forever blessed! He has given our nation victory; He has given it such a triumph as no past centuries ever saw. All artillery, the whole Muslim camp, all its uncountable riches have fallen into our hands. The approaches to the town and neighbouring fields are covered with the infidel dead, and the remainder is in flight, and stricken with panic. In Vienna all the common people cheered and many kissed my feet and my clothes; others touched me, saying, let us kiss so valiant a hand!"

The following day, inside the vizier's tent, the king addressed his generals and senior commanders. They had all been summoned to attend: to report upon their actions and account for their losses of men and equipment. Their mood was exultant and euphoric and they applauded, cheered and lauded their king as he entered. He allowed them to settle and then, with his first words, he added to their sense of victory and historic achievement by paraphrasing Julius Caesar's famous quote. He fervently and loudly proclaimed, "Venimus, Vidimus, Deus vincit" – We came, We saw, God conquered.

He openly acknowledged that both the bravery of the entire relief force and the endurance, sacrifice and resourcefulness of the city garrison had together forged their triumph. After congratulating them all on their impressive achievements he dispatched a number of cavalry units to pursue and harass the enemy right across the plain and then he called forward Marek Dabrowski. The king placed his hand upon his vassal's head as he kneeled before him and said in his loud and booming voice, "I can stand victorious before you today because at the height of the battle my life was saved by a brave and loyal knight, who came to my aid with such speed, vigour and strength, that he struck fear into the very hearts of mine enemy. Above all else, it was his charge that turned the day and started their collapse. It is such selfless action as this, which will drive the Turks from our lands

13

forever. I freely acknowledge that I owe this man my life and I will forever be in his debt. Everyone here must salute him. I swear before God that throughout his life and in perpetuity, through his sons and heirs, our motherland and all its institutions are by honour and duty, warranted to provide all manner of succour and comfort to him and his issue. Whenever called upon to do so, aid must be proffered without reservation. This I order by Royal Proclamation, binding on all Monarchs, Courts, Governments and Citizenry, both present and future. I demand obedience on this matter, without question or qualification. By my hand and my sword: so be it."

Later that day, in private audience, the king presented Marek with an illuminated parchment containing the Royal Warrant of Privilege, the state's reward for his actions. He then thanked the knight personally, kissed him on both cheeks and smiling broadly, bestowed upon him a private gift, a captured Ottoman ceremonial dagger and sheath, in recognition of his own enduring respect and gratitude.

That short and decisive battle marked a turning point in European history. At a stroke, the sultan's expansionist ambition to drive west and carry Islam into central Europe and beyond was reversed and he never recovered from the humiliation and huge loss of men and equipment. Over the following years the Ottoman Empire fell into decline as Austria and her allies, strengthened and emboldened by their success, expanded ever further south and east. On the personal order of Mehmed IV, the vizier was publicly put to death for his failure. As custom demanded he was strangled by a long silk scarf, a gift from the sultan, being slowly pulled tight around his throat by four specially chosen executioners.

A week later, as Marek and his squadron waited in Vienna for their orders, they watched the hundreds of labourers clearing and grading rubble for the masons. They were already repairing the fortified walls and buildings that had been so badly damaged by the prolonged bombardment. As they relaxed and talked of the anticipation and comforts of home, they were able to enjoy some unexpected but abiding cultural by-products of their victory. The sacks of strange looking beans recovered from the vizier's tent led to the creation of the very first Viennese coffee house and to celebrate the resounding victory over the sultan of the East, captured flour was used to bake small, crescent-shaped loaves. And so the croissant was conceived, introduced and devoured by the victors.

∞∞∞∞∞∞∞

My eyes were beginning to ache from the strain of reading the tiny writing and so I took a break, but I couldn't stop thinking about what I had read. I was aware of some of the famous exploits of the Polish cavalry throughout the eighteenth and nineteenth centuries, but I had never heard of the winged lancers and knew very little about the siege of Vienna. How true was Dominik's account, bearing in mind it related to events some 250 years before and had probably been told dozens if not hundreds of times? Even if it was based on fact, surely it would be full of exaggeration, embellishment and misrepresentation. I found the events surrounding the king's rescue, and the presentation of the scroll and dagger, particularly colourful and dubious. On the other hand, I had no proof either way but it would certainly encourage me, and probably help my future translation and overall understanding of the entries, if I knew whether or not I could rely on the veracity of his account.

I spent the next four hours researching the events of that day so long ago and I was very surprised to find that, historically, the action unfolded exactly as described by Dominik. The protagonists and their various military units were correctly portrayed, even in minute detail, and the winged lancers had indeed carried the day in the manner described. All the weapons, armour and equipment proved authentic and I also found a couple of references showing that the king and his guard had become isolated during the battle and had to be rescued. Incredibly, virtually everything checked out precisely as stated. I was, however, disappointed but not surprised that I could find no reference to Marek Dabrowski or the presentation, but the descriptions of the valuable treasures seized matched up and did include a number of bejewelled ceremonial daggers. The standard of the Prophet was indeed captured and sent directly to the Pope. Even the references to coffee and croissants were mirrored in the contemporary accounts. Frankly, I found the overall accuracy and detail of Dominik's account quite staggering.

Although, as an investigator I must always strive to remain objective, I am by nature somewhat sceptical, some would say cynical, but even so I found myself warming to the Dominik persona that was just beginning to emerge from the pages of the diary. It seemed that he was credible, well informed, possessed almost total recall and had a real eye for detail. Although I was no nearer to finding out why Jan wanted me to read the diary in the first place, I was certainly now very eager to learn more. With luck I might discover what had happened to the author or even find proof, or otherwise, of the existence of the scroll and the dagger. I had to read on.

∞∞∞∞∞∞∞

My grandfather explained what happened in the years after the battle, telling me that future generations should always remember the many centuries of Poland's splendour and greatness, and not dwell on what it had become. He was convinced that such days would return and this is what I learnt as a young boy. In the euphoria of victory the king was lauded throughout the royal houses of Europe, as their own gallant, legendary hero and saviour. In turn, Poland and her armies were honoured and courted by her neighbours, everyone wishing to bathe in the reflected glory of their triumph. Nevertheless, such gratitude and mutual appreciation were short-lived as political expediency and a hostile alliance of neighbours once more contrived to halt Polish ascendency. No, it was not Poland – then the largest state in Europe – but Austria that prospered, taking full advantage of the injection of power, wealth and newly conquered lands to the east and the south.

Within a few years, as the Ottoman Empire shrivelled back, severely weakened by a combination of further military defeats and internal political strife, Vienna was transformed from little more than a frontier town to the central hub of the new Austrian Empire. To the north and north-west of Poland it was the Brandenburgs and Prussians that held sway, to the west and south-west, the Habsburgs and to the east, Russia was also looking to expand. The Commonwealth of Poland fell apart and proper government became impossible as the Sejm parliament was riven by petty rivalries, disputes and personal greed. Even the most minor deputies from the outer reaches of Lithuania or the Ukraine could veto any proposal. This traditional throwback, ensuring consensus and enshrined in the Polish constitution, led to the strangulation of all the organs of power, as her neighbours continually exploited the weakness. Willing to pay vast sums to their client deputies, they simply purchased a veto to anything that they felt threatened their own national interests or their future aspirations to grab a share of the Polish prize.

Internally, every attempt to change the system failed as many saw any move to reform the right of veto as a direct attack on their hard-won freedoms and heritage, and as time passed Poland slowly disintegrated. My forefathers continued to faithfully and proudly serve in the army but as Poland inexorably grew weaker and they grew poorer, they were forced to spend increasing periods of time abroad in the pay of foreign generals. Within a century of the battle of Vienna, a declining Poland was simply removed from the map by a coalition of Russia, Austria and Prussia and as our country diminished, so too did my family's wealth and standing. In the end they lost everything, when what was left of their impoverished home, possessions and estate was confiscated by the Prussians and they were expelled south.

They sought refuge in Krakow where they now had to earn their living and so my grandfather subsequently followed the relatively new family trade as a cabinet maker. My father was also a skilful carpenter and in turn, he took over the family business. We were not wealthy but neither were we poor and I could afford to go to university but then, as the Great War loomed and the depression struck, our business failed and we were once again indigent. Along with a few of my single friends I immigrated to America and, as I left, my father gave me what he proudly called my birthright: the scroll and dagger. I was totally unaware that my father had them and it was the first time I had ever seen them. Throughout our recent history, generations of my family had resolutely held on to them, even when the temptation to sell, and at least temporarily improve their lot, must have been overwhelming.

As his father had done before, he made me swear that in due course I would hand them on to my son. I couldn't even imagine having a family. I was exclusively focused on my quest for freedom and betterment, but I was soon to learn how elusive such naïve dreams could be. When repeatedly telling me of the legends of Polish knighthood and chivalry, my grandfather always spoke to 'his dear boy' of the honour, glory and splendour of war but when, as a very young man, I experienced the bitter reality, it was one of horror, hatred, brutality and shame.

Chapter Two

Welcome to Hell

The Trenches, East of Reims – 18th June 1918

I arrived in the trenches of war as a volunteer in Haller's Blue Army.
Under cover of darkness, and in the immediate aftermath of the
French mutiny, we were among the very first of the newly formed
Polish units to be deployed straight into the weakened line. And
what a shock it was. Our sector was designed for defence in depth:
a complex, subterranean system comprised of both traditional
trenches and separate redoubt positions that were strategically
sited to support each other. Even without the fighting, life was so
hard to endure. There was the constant physical labour of repairing
and extending the massive, mile-wide trench system every night
or patching up the shell damage to the acres of barbed wire
entanglements. Every time we dared to move around in daylight
we risked being picked off by enemy snipers. We cowered and
suffered under the heavy artillery bombardments and gas attacks
and an air of fatal resignation pervaded the trenches. There were
so many ways to die that your number could be up at any moment.

The heat, garbage, squalor and vermin in the lines, the
overpowering smell of flyblown, putrefying bodies abandoned
in no man's land and the obnoxious stench from the primitive,
leaking latrines, all combined to grind down our resolve. Every

night teams dressed in dark clothing set out towards the enemy. Snipers crept forward at a snail's pace to find suitable laying-up positions to attack the German sentries and officers, once daylight broke. Repair teams left to inspect the shell damage and restore the wire or erect new barriers. Fighting patrols were dispatched, intent on capturing prisoners, gaining intelligence or taking an isolated enemy position. Raiding parties regularly tested the enemy strength and probed their weak points. But the Boche did the same, all potential cannon fodder, straining every nerve to keep silent and avoid detection, trying to gain the merest advantage. At the slightest noise or hint of movement, flares would go up and the machine guns would home in on the source of alarm. We called them 'suicide sorties' and death did not discriminate.

It was not uncommon for these patrols to run into each other in no man's land, resulting in fierce hand-to-hand fighting and a general alarm on both sides. Sometimes, when surprised, one side would simply turn and run for their line, in the hope that they would survive, while desperately wishing that their own gunners could catch the enemy in the open. In any event, the number of bodies of the dead and severely injured left abandoned between the lines, mounted day by day. This brutal, repetitive and attritional ritual, played out across a few hundred yards of ground in front of us, was replicated across the entire front line. It was an alien and dehumanising ribbon of misery that snaked across a once benign and pleasant landscape, stretching from the Swiss border in the south, to the North Sea coast of Belgium. Despite the stalemate that existed between the armies, there was no stagnation; the killing continued unabated.

The contrast between the wide-open spaces of field, hill and sweeping plain across which the wind-borne, winged lancers had charged and the morale-sapping, claustrophobic atmosphere within our tiny section of zigzag trench could not have been greater. We were trapped inside a Dantesque reality, surrounded by enemies who took many forms, all conspiring to rob us of our sanity and destroy our souls. The lice caused trench fever and could drive a man crazy. They were in our hair and in our uniforms. They used our body heat to breed and our blood to survive: laying eggs and secreting themselves under our arms, in our crotch and in our clothing, until it felt like the 'seam squirrels' were eating us alive. We scratched ourselves raw in an attempt to alleviate the constant itching. We were also plagued with swarms of flies, attracted to the rotting corpses, trench waste and our rations. And in addition to being a constant irritant, they also spread disease and illness. Scattered bodies and body parts were regularly stumbled upon, seemingly alive, possessed of a writhing mass of millions of fat, gorging white maggots: cleansing the crop of carnage like locusts. Dysentery and sickness and diarrhoea became a constant affliction, adding to the cycle of infection that swept through our tightly packed, undernourished and filthy army.

There were very large rats, both the black and brown varieties, everywhere. They too fed off the waste and the bodies. Those seriously wounded and abandoned in no man's land sometimes took several days to die from their injuries. No one could go to their aid: to do so was certain death. Their cries for help and their moans and screams still haunt me today. After so much suffering in life, then again in death they were desecrated, their decomposing bodies set upon by hordes of rats. Sometimes they were not quite dead. They ate the eyes first, before gnawing into the stomach and chest cavity seeking out the heart and liver. Even the buried were not spared this final indignity. They were constantly being unearthed by the shelling. Some had been killed fairly recently and emerged virtually intact; others surfaced in various states of decomposition and those dating from the first battles were mere skeletons, covered with patches of leathery skin, clumps of hair and scraps of uniform. Often the rounds that unearthed them also blew them apart. Sadly, irrespective of their condition, the remains were immediately assailed by these ugly, bloated, bald-faced vermin that we knew as corpse rats. So abundant was their food supply and so aggressive and fearless their behaviour that they grew to twice the normal size. We even took terrier dogs down into the trench and although they killed dozens, sometimes hundreds, every day, they continued to multiply.

However, the horror of horrors, the most vivid of mordant memories for me always has been and still remains today, the appalling and sticky stench of death. That is war! We were soaked and cloaked in it: the sharp, all pervading smell of decomposing bodies and the haunting, distinctive stink of shell-shattered and roasting human flesh. That is war! The only escape for us was death. Even then it lived on with the survivors as crippling tears of guilt, triggered in the day by the most innocuous of sights, a sudden sound, taste or sensation. Sleep was constantly chased away by the fever of repetitive and explicit nightmares in the dark. That is war! There is no honour or glory in any of it: simply shame and despair, but it remains the fate of every soldier and my duty is to tell you of it – warn you of it. This is the stark truth of war!

We could only see along the trench for about 20 yards before it changed direction and during the day our biggest enemies were isolation, hunger, fatigue and boredom, all of which could cause carelessness. It was difficult if not impossible to sleep and many a jaded soldier lost his life by taking an inquisitive look through the loophole. The German snipers were very good and even used armour piercing bullets to shoot right through the metal spy-hole flaps and covers at their unsuspecting target. I was always tired and hungry. Food supplies were erratic because, as with everything else, they could only be delivered at night and could be destroyed or delayed by heavy shelling. The individual rations were poor, the bully beef tainted and the biscuits were either as hard as bullets, covered in mould or infested with small brown weevils.

The veterans of these trenches told us that we were lucky because the generals had finally started to get their act together, after their early madness and reckless leadership, which had needlessly killed millions of their own men. Improved tactics, better weaponry and the recent impetus provided by the deployment of hundreds of thousands of fresh American troops had tipped the balance in our favour. We were not convinced by what we had seen so far and believed that if we managed to endure the enemy, the vermin and the disease, then that in itself was a victory. However, no such survivor could escape the madness of the guns. The almost constant report of heavy weapons, the daily witnessing of the devastation caused by just one shell, let alone salvo after salvo and seeing your friends literally being blown to pieces, left you in fearful apprehension of when your turn would come. The noise, perpetual fear, hours spent hiding in dug outs and shelters that could collapse on you at any time and the trauma caused by such alien sights of slaughter, could destroy the spirit and sanity of any man. Shell shock was a real threat.

Often the first sign of this scourge was a fixed expression of fatigue and confusion or 'the 1,000-yard stare' as it became known, but if the man was left in the line then madness could follow. Some such terrified men had been known to run from their post or refuse to go back into action following their period on 'stand down'. Accused of cowardice, a number had been taken back at gunpoint; others had been shot for desertion. Our predecessors in the trenches had seen strong, sturdy, heroic men blind with terror, shaking, slobbering and convulsing, like someone suffering from epilepsy. Some would rant and become violent and uncontrollable and have to be strapped to a stretcher before they could be carried away. Others became speechless figures of dreadful fright, clawing at their mouths and cringing and cowering, hiding behind their hands at the sound of a rifle shot, the appearance of an officer, or even the very mention of the front. I discovered that hundreds of such men sat in field hospitals, dazed and unresponsive as though deaf and dumb, paralysed and besieged by their demons. We were told we were lucky because we were new to the trenches, too green to fall victim to shell shock, but every soldier's life was just to fight and suffer – suffer and fight.

We had come to war full of patriotic enthusiasm, proud and eager to fight the Germans and free Poland from the iron grip of foreigners and to see her reborn as a free nation state. All through our young lives we had dreamt of such an opportunity and we wanted so much to be part of that miracle, but we soon lost our bravado, our dignity and our naivety. I'm not ashamed to say that within a matter of days, I longed to be anywhere other than in the unrelenting misery of such a degrading and dismal ditch.

A few prisoners captured during one of our dreaded and costly night patrols revealed that a large enemy offensive was imminent and so we rushed to make our final preparations. The fire trench was fully manned at all times and we were 'stood to' far more often than had previously been the case. Reserves, munitions and supplies were massed to the rear in preparation for action and our physical defences repaired and reinforced. Extra saps were excavated as listening posts and we also dug two blind dummy trenches and mined them as a welcome for our future guests. We knew just how deadly this tactic could be. We had heard the accounts of the suicidal, see-saw battles for the strategically vital Hill 60 near Ypres. Although it was called a hill, it was not a natural feature but man-made some 50 years earlier: just a huge mound of earth which had been excavated to form the nearby railway cutting. It provided a perfect military position from which to look down on and dominate all the surrounding flat areas including the view of Ypres.

We had been told how massive mines had been placed right under the German trenches, under the hill itself and then far beyond, stretching out in both directions: first by the British engineers in 1915 and then by the Australian miners in June 1917. On the last occasion they had tunnelled 90 feet below the enemy lines, making huge chambers in the clay to accommodate nineteen massive mines, containing 500 tons of explosive. They were detonated at the start of the battle of Messines, just as the Germans had massed their troops in the trenches, ready to repel the expected attack. Thousands were killed and it was said at the time that it was the largest explosion in history, which was felt as far away as London and Dublin. So, as prepared as we could be and less than a month after we had arrived, we faced a desperate German onslaught in what became known as the second battle of the Marne: their last offensive on the Western Front. It turned the tide of war in our favour and the Germans never recovered from the defeat.

The first shell burst in the trench about 30 feet away, right alongside our Vickers machine gun position instantly killing the team. It atomised the closest men and sent shrapnel, body parts, skull fragments, bone splinters and gore whistling along the trench towards me, at the speed of a bullet. The side of the trench collapsed. I was knocked off my feet and left deafened and disorientated by the shock wave of the detonation. I landed on my back in about six inches of faeces and urine contaminated water and the panic induced by it splashing and sloshing across my face made me spring upright, coughing, spluttering and frightened witless. Miraculously still in one piece, I staggered around and as my hearing returned, I became aware of the continuous sounding of the gas gong.

I grabbed for my mask but immediately dropped it in horror as I saw the dismembered and eviscerated torso of one of the gunners splattered across the top of the dugout right next to me. I recoiled from the sight and looked away in disgust towards the fire step opposite, only to be confronted by a blackened severed head with brain matter oozing from the shattered crown and running down the side of the face. A two-foot tail of skin and raw flesh draped down from the throat towards the bottom of the trench. It looked as if it had been placed there, in isolation, like some macabre ornament. I froze. I had never known such shock and fear and this time I couldn't avert my eyes. I was transfixed, wide-eyed, as the image was seared into my memory.

Nothing had prepared me for this. Then, as if a switch was turned back on, I took in the full significance of what had happened in my trench – to my friends – and I panicked again at the gruesome sight. If the sergeant hadn't picked up my mask, grabbed me by the shoulders and shouted at me to get it on, I know I would have run headlong from the trench, right back along the supply line. If not fatally gassed I would probably have been shot for cowardice. I have repeated his words to stir myself from shock or apathy many times since: "Snap out of it! Remember your drill, focus your mind, and protect your friends. Now move!" I soon learnt that inaction is just as much a killer as recklessness, but once moving, the adrenaline always kicks in and your training and self-preservation take over.

There was little time to brood, because within an hour of the gas attack we were under full infantry assault. It started when one of our lookouts spotted an enemy flamethrower unit creeping towards a break in the wire. I had heard the blood-chilling stories about this fearful weapon and I knew what it could do. A dozen of our own men had recently been trained on the Schilt model, the French equivalent of this hated, German-invented and potentially devastating weapon and I had seen it demonstrated. Each machine was normally worked by one or two men and was deployed in a unit of six or so. It consisted of a steel cylinder tank that was strapped to the back and attached to a seven-foot-long rubber tube and nozzle. The tank was divided into two, with one reservoir containing a compressed gas to provide the pressure and the other holding the oil. The gas propelled the liquid down the hose, which was ignited at the end of the nozzle by a wick. Flame could be continuously shot forward for about two minutes and up to a distance of about 60 feet.

It was very effective at clearing out trenches and reinforced bunkers, but the operators needed to get really close before they could cause panic in the line and so they became very exposed and prime targets. Their life expectancy was extremely short, limiting its operational effectiveness. Nevertheless, its psychological impact was so great that it outweighed the risks to the operators. Now, those out in front of us didn't get very far past the wire before they were brought down by concentrated and accurate fire. A machine gun continued to pour rounds into the bodies until one of the tanks exploded, incinerating the whole unit.

The huge ball of fire reminded me of the stories I had heard about a British secret weapon, which had supposedly been used in the front line around Mametz in 1916. Apparently, it was a terrifying experience, even for the British, or so the story went. It was a giant flamethrower they called 'the Dragon of the Somme' (officially known as the Livens Large Gallery Flame Projector, named after the engineer who invented it). I was told that it was over 50 feet long and weighed over two tons, and needed hundreds of men to carry all the components along the trenches and then down into the sap stretching out right across no man's land. It was then assembled underground and finally, when all was ready, the nozzle was forced up through the last foot or so of earth onto the surface by using compressed air. A pressurised jet of blazing fuel oil was then fired through the nozzle which raked along the enemy lines for a distance of about 100 yards.

The molten, sticky mixture rained down into the defences, pooling and then streaming along the trench floors, burning and destroying everything in sight. It was said that the Tommies then went over the top and reached the enemy trenches, incredibly without losing a man. When the German survivors – those lucky ones who had occupied their deepest underground dug outs – finally emerged, they found their trenches already taken by the British. They were so traumatised by what they saw that they immediately surrendered. Apparently, the British had made spectacular territorial gains in the specific areas where this weapon had been deployed, but they failed to make any progress elsewhere in the line. I don't know whether the rumours were true or not but as I watched the enemy approaching, I earnestly wished that we had something similar to protect us.

Their attack grew in intensity and it soon seemed as if the whole German army was in front of us, but they too had learned the lesson from the mindless slaughter of the early years. They didn't come over the top and charge in a line, offering themselves up to the withering fire of our heavy machine guns. No, they advanced cautiously in groups, desperately seeking whatever shelter was available and putting down covering fire for each other as they moved forward. Mortars started to rain down on our lines as their artillery shells slowly began to creep back, away from us, towards our support trenches and beyond. When our spotters scrambled back from the saps our own artillery and machine gunners opened up, maintaining an incredible rate of fire, concentrated on the forward groups.

Notwithstanding their initial caution, dozens of enemy infantry were brought down. Apart from shell craters there was precious little cover across the open ground which, at great cost to the fencing teams, had been strewn with 15-feet-high by 12-feet-wide walls of barbed wire and other obstacles. These were strategically placed to funnel the enemy into the prepared arcs of fire and predetermined artillery coordinates. Although the enemy gunners had destroyed much of the wire, it still slowed them down and forced them into the gaps. They became bunched together in these bottlenecks while they attempted to infiltrate and widen the breaches; and then the real slaughter started as the machine gunners in the fortified forward redoubts could attack with destructive enfilade fire. It was hideous to witness but eventually, as their sappers cleared a way through the formidable maze, they managed to destroy several machine gun positions with mortars and grenades. Slowly, and at an increasing cost, they managed to make progress towards us.

By now we could make out individual targets and I fired round after round, concentrating on those directly in front. I saw several men go down, but it was impossible to say whether I actually hit anybody. We were also taking a great deal of incoming fire: bullets were peppering the parapet and flying over the top of the trench, and mortars were falling to our rear. The enemy were gathering momentum as they poured through the new breaches in the barriers and it became perfectly clear that this was no feint attack. If we stayed where we were, there would soon be a hand-to-hand battle right inside the trench and I knew we couldn't hope to hold them. There were just too many and we would certainly be overrun. To my immense relief and as I later learnt, in accordance with our plan, when they were within 50 yards we were ordered to fall back to the support trenches. We left a dozen dead comrades behind, but we were drawing them into a trap.

They poured into our now empty fire trench and I could hear them shouting and cheering above the noise of battle as we raced the 200 yards back down our communication trenches. We passed more redoubts and bunkers that continued to hammer fire into the ranks of the enemy, still streaming through the wire towards their own targets. No sooner had we arrived and taken cover than there was a massive explosion as the mined trenches were detonated. The ground shook with the energy released and the sky was obscured from view, as a cloud of smoke and debris sent huge clods of earth and rubble cascading down all around us. I imagined the enemy soldiers pumped full of adrenaline and high on the exhilaration of their success, pouring into the trenches, seeking cover underground. They would have been mightily relieved that unlike hundreds of their colleagues, they had made it unscathed across no man's land but also wary and fearful of what lay ahead.

They were regrouping when the explosions hit them; the tremendous force excavated massive craters and rolled along the trenches with the destructive power of a tsunami. The enemy attack faltered and those approaching the wire turned and ran for their own lines and at that very moment our artillery opened up: four batteries of 155mm field guns, each firing at a rate of two rounds per minute. Thirty-two 90lb, high explosive shells landed on those exposed troops every minute. When nothing was left standing between the lines, the guns moved on, tracking forward into the German trenches and then on again, beyond the front lines right into the heart of their reserves.

We soon learnt that the Germans had attacked on a broad front and although they had been held on the first day in our sector, they had been much more successful further along the line to the west of Reims where they had broken through. Reserves were still pouring in behind us and while we prepared for a counter-attack we had to endure further shelling and gas attacks. As we waited, so once again the tension, fear and apprehension started to mount, but fortunately we didn't have long to fret. The German breakthrough across the Marne at Dormans was stalled on the 17th July and we moved forward the following day, fighting our way across the same small piece of land where the German army had first been stopped on its drive for Paris, almost four years previously. Many of the original trenches had been in use ever since. Millions of lives had been lost in the early years of the intervening period as both armies sacrificed regiments of their finest young men in meaningless battles, for just a few yards of mud and wire. Their only achievement – mindless slaughter and deadlock. What a waste!

Once our artillery bombardment ended we attacked and this time we were supported by tanks: half a dozen Renault FT 17's, the first type to be fitted with a fully rotating turret. It was a real breakthrough in armoured warfare with a modern shape, effective armaments and the capability to consistently traverse trenches and obstacles without stalling or becoming bogged down. All future tanks would follow the same basic design. We assaulted the enemy trenches one at a time, mostly using hand grenades and shotguns. The latter was my favourite weapon: unlike the unwieldy rifle and bayonet it was easy to turn quickly in the confines of a trench and shoot repeatedly along either axis. Mine was a Winchester M97 slide/pump action, 12 gauge assault weapon, with a short twenty-inch barrel. It fired military grade cartridges, each containing nine double 0 calibre, antimony-hardened, buckshot pellets. Although I never used the modification, it could also be fitted with a bayonet and a heat shield so that the barrel could be gripped when charging. It became known as a trench gun but we preferred the much more descriptive term of 'trench broom'. We had managed to obtain a box or two from the Americans and they were much in demand. They were so destructive that one shot could literally take a man's head off. They had such a detrimental effect on the morale of front-line German troops that their government issued a diplomatic protest. They claimed that their use was prohibited by the Hague Convention on the laws of war. Although their allegations were quickly rejected, they still threatened to execute any soldiers captured in possession of one but as far as I know, they never did.

I also used a trenching tool as a weapon. We honed the edges until they were razor-sharp and because of the short handle on the shovel, it could be wielded for slashing or stabbing, as we slowly and methodically cleared out the Boche. At first I was repulsed by the frightful killing but as time passed it became easier, particularly at long range, either with a machine gun, rifle or grenade. Up close it was always much harder to deal with and when in action I was always totally exhausted by the sheer physical exertion of simultaneously running, fighting, stabbing and blasting my way along a trench. It was a lottery. Could I kill them before they had time to finish me? I learned to live with fear, but it was always simmering away inside of me, feeding on the sights, smells and sounds of carnage. Then malignantly it spread and seethed during 'stand down', until it could be contained no longer and erupted into anguish and temper when I rested, and haunting nightmares if I slept.

On the fourth day of our advance I dropped down into an empty section of enemy trench just ahead of three or four colleagues. As I ran around the first corner I saw half a dozen German soldiers charging in line straight towards us. Before the first could raise his rifle, I started to 'slam fire' my broom gun. The six shells could be fired one after the other simply by working the slide whilst holding the trigger down. This was possible because the gun had no trigger disconnector. I fired five shells and the effect was devastating. The first man took the full force of the first shell in the chest from about 15 feet. The next two were brought down by a combination of the second and third shots. By this time the others were turning to run, to save themselves but two were struck in the side and back as they did so. One man managed to escape around the next bend in the trench just as my fifth shell blasted harmlessly into the side of the trench right behind him. I stopped to reload before we continued forward.

About 20 minutes later as I turned another corner, I literally ran straight into a German as he was firing up towards the top of the trench. Startled, he spun towards me swinging his rifle butt around and aiming for my head, but he was a big man and I managed to duck down underneath and inside the weapon. I could smell his foul breath and the stench of his body as he gripped me in a bear hug, and started to squeeze. I was helpless as he increased the pressure, driving the breath from my lungs. My arms were pinned, but in desperation I clawed at the dagger in the trouser pocket, on the outside of my right thigh. I was becoming frantic and gasping for air. As soon as I had shaken the weapon free from its sheath, I used every limited inch available to me to stab at the outside of his left knee. I felt the dagger strike and pushed downwards and inwards with all my strength. He screamed and I broke his grip as he reached down towards his badly slashed leg. I tried to move back to bring my shotgun to bear, but he sensed the danger and whip-like, grabbed me, pulling me in again. I was still panting for breath and despite his painful injury, I was no match for his speed and strength.

I was held so close to him that I didn't have enough room to swing my right arm. It was trapped against his chest and I couldn't use the dagger. I knew that I wouldn't survive long, locked as I was in his iron-like grip, as he literally squeezed the life out of me. In extreme despair I kneed him in the groin as hard as I could and as he instinctively bent forward from the pain, I twisted my wrist and pushed the point of the dagger into his chest. There was still insufficient space between us to stab at him so I used both hands and kept forcing it in using all my faltering strength. I felt the blade glance bone as I drove it in right up to the hilt towards his heart. He made squelchy sucking noises as he tried to breathe and then nothing, as he started to crumple at the knees. With his considerable weight falling against me and pushing me back, I had difficulty in pulling the knife out and the blood soaked handle twisted in my grip. I let go completely, stepped back and let him fall to the floor. I was left gasping for breath and badly shaken by the brutality and animalism of this close-quarters bloodshed. But then I remembered my sergeant's words and tried to refocus. It was fortunate for me that by this time the trench had been taken, and was quickly filling with our own troops.

Relieved and thankful, I retrieved my dagger and sheath and moved forward with my unit, but I couldn't get the incident out of my mind for a very long time. My life wasn't saved by a weapon of modern war: the miracle of the tank or my trusted shotgun, not even by my rifle, bayonet, or modified trenching shovel but by a small, unauthorised and antique ceremonial heirloom. I had been lucky and logically, I knew it had nothing to do with destiny, legend or a king's blessing and that one day my good fortune would run out but I couldn't help wondering.

Our success did not come cheap and over the next three weeks the butcher's bill mounted. Several of my close friends were killed and one died in my arms, begging me to stop the pain. Another lost a leg and an eye to shrapnel and eventually went mad and killed himself. There were also moments of redemption. As I passed a group of apparently dead German soldiers one of them called out for water. I'm ashamed to say that I kept on going. I hadn't time to nurse the enemy. I was there to kill them. Then he called out again, this time in his native tongue, Polish – and I stopped in my tracks. He had severe leg wounds and I doubted he would survive, but I gave him a drink and made him as comfortable as I could. In a weak rasping voice he told me his story. It was not dissimilar to my own and I lamented that Poland's arbitrary partition meant that our roles could so easily have been reversed. So what, I pondered, was either of us really fighting for?

He knew he wasn't going to make it and he asked me to make sure his parents were told of his fate. I was allowed to stay with him until, now barely conscious, he was evacuated from the line. The futility of that war was so clearly defined for me in these last two incidents. There was no righteousness, credit or triumph to be found in those muddy fields and bloody ditches. All that mattered was survival. Shortly after, we were moved into reserve and then rested, and despite the continuous sound of artillery, I slept for three days. Thank God my unit never returned to the front line.

When the war ended and millions of battle-weary but relieved servicemen were being shipped across the world, back to their homes in every continent, our own struggles continued. Within a year the Blue Army was at war again: this time in Poland, Ukraine and the USSR!

Salisbury – 4th November 2009

My maternal grandfather had also fought in the trenches but after being captured and 'sent down the salt mines' for the duration. He had said little of his experiences, preferring to take his secrets and his horrors to the grave. Until now I had only a distant, general and purely bookish understanding of how terrible the conditions actually were and I was both shocked and moved by Dominik's vivid, emotional and personal account. As I reflected on the enormity and futility of the suffering and the unprecedented loss of life, I unconsciously flicked through the diary, when suddenly a few lines of script on the antepenultimate page caught my eye and shattered my musings. It was clearly in a different hand and was even addressed to me! Although, like the diary entries, it was written in Polish and in blue ink and there were quite a few blank pages left between the end of the narrative and this short, additional entry, I still kicked myself for not having noticed it before. Some detective I was!

Dear Mick,

What you saw before, when you helped my family, has now been confirmed by Dominik. Life was always hard and much demanded of us in those times of war. If you're going to do what I ask then it is vitally important to me that you firstly understand the terrible events that shaped his young life. Only then can you move on and discover what happened to him when he entered the dangerous and shadowy world of the resistance movement and espionage. You will soon learn of incredible and frightening events and experiments that, even in the technological and sophisticated world of today, would probably be classified by most as pure fiction. Yet they are still, some 70 years later, shrouded in secrecy and denial by governments and agencies alike.

I assure you that what you will hear and discover is true and the consequences of this story helped to define the nature of post-war Europe in the 1940s and beyond. Furthermore, Dominik's life was one of bravery, fortitude and courage and he saved many lives. There is no hyperbole when I say he helped to change the course of history: away from tyranny and oppression towards tolerance and democracy.

Only a handful of us know the full story and now I'm gone there will be just one left. Time is running out and so the task of putting things right falls to you. You helped me in life and now I reach out from the grave and ask that you bring comfort to another, long since gone: a man who will make you proud. So take this letter to Stanislaw Pawłowski at Swindon and he will tell you what you need to know. He has been expecting you for a while now. I will say no more.

Thank you my friend. Pray for me.
Goodbye and Good Luck!

Jan – 4th August 2009

It felt as if my mind was on overload. I couldn't think clearly. Even before I had the chance to absorb the detail or check the authenticity of Dominik's account of his time in the trenches, I had been hit by another broadside that left me reeling. I read the note again but still felt no sense of clarity as to what it really meant. It was mostly insinuation, assertion and enticement, lacking specific details but certainly not short on drama and intrigue. In the broadest of terms it was all there: spies, secrecy, danger, the influencing of world affairs and finally the captivating prospect of 'putting things right'. I realised I was slowly being drip-fed a few key bits of information and felt uncomfortable and annoyed that my participation in their plans was being carefully manipulated.

My experience told me that these were honourable men, but nevertheless, I didn't like the way I was being drawn in so deeply on the basis of so few facts, and with absolutely no idea of where it was all leading. On the other hand, what choice did I really have? Jan knew I admired and respected him and would certainly have helped him if I could and he recognised what made me tick, and so all he had to do was present me with a challenge. When facing his own mortality he had certainly done that and by offering up just that one piece of direct evidence – Stanislaw Pawłowski – then, not for the first time, he had me well and truly snared.

I thought for a while and then made up my mind. The diary could wait for a day or two but I couldn't. I had been passively receptive for too long and I needed to hurry things along and take some control. As stimulating and tantalizing as this situation was, I was already fed up with being led along slowly by the nose. I was going to find out, once and for all, what this was really all about and it seemed obvious to me that the quickest way to do so was to see the Swindon Pole, whoever and whatever he might turn out to be. Decision made, I felt better already and then I found him listed in the telephone directory and a quick check of the electoral roll showed that he lived on his own in sheltered accommodation in the Old Town area.

I called him, introduced myself, and explained that I would like to see him regarding Jan Nowaski, Dominik Dabrowski and the diary. He didn't seem surprised to hear from me and somewhat strangely asked not a single question; he merely suggested that I should meet him the following day. I spent the next hour or two skimming through the rest of the diary to make sure there were no further hidden surprises and then I made a few notes and planned my interview.

Chapter Three

A DIFFICULT BIRTH

Swindon – 5th November 2009

Stanislaw Pawłowski opened the door and I saw that he used a stick to walk. Before a word could be said he leant against the jamb and looked me straight in the eyes, holding the stare: seemingly searching for a reaction to his unsettling facial appearance. I had the impression that this had become his habit, honed and perfected over the years. By almost challenging me to comment or avert my eyes, he could ensure silence, until the moment of initial shock and awkward embarrassment had passed. At first it was very difficult for me not to stare at the disfiguring half-inch-wide, ragged and swollen scar. It ran, grey and zip-like, from his left temple almost straight down across his cheek and neck until it disappeared underneath his old woollen jumper. When his gaze finally shifted, I felt able to introduce myself and as I followed him inside I could see that although slightly bent with age, he was still a very tall man, well over six feet with broad shoulders and a barrel chest.

We were soon sat in a pair of old-fashioned fireside chairs, facing each other across a coffee table in the small lounge of his ground-floor flat. The room was quite dark with thick, dusty brown curtains drawn across the only window. The doors to the passage and kitchen were firmly closed, creating a sombre, twilight atmosphere which was in keeping with the rather drab and shabby 1950's decor. But there was nothing dull about my host. Although physically slow he was mentally very sharp for a man well into his eighties. He didn't repeat himself once and gave no indication of any confusion or absent-mindedness. He was genial, easy to speak to and appeared relaxed and confident in my company. I was struck by the total absence of photographs or pictures in the room. Many elderly people live surrounded by such memories. Important moments forever frozen in time, reflections of childhood, education, family, military service and employment: but his clutter consisted of newspapers, magazines and books. They were everywhere. On every raised surface across the room and also haphazardly piled up in three-foot-high stacks, balanced precariously on the floor in all four corners. His love of reading was reinforced by the two pairs of spectacles and a magnifying glass on the coffee table. They sat haphazardly on top of that day's completed *Daily Telegraph* cryptic crossword and next to a thick A4-sized, hard-cover notebook. As far as I could see all the publications in the room seemed to be in English and there were no obvious reminders of Polish life on view, but some old habits always linger.

He took glasses from the oak sideboard next to his chair and poured two generous measures of Polish spirit vodka, used his stick to stand up and in a soft and familiar Polish accent said, "Please call me Stan. I've lived in England since the war and absolutely love the place and now I can't remember being called anything else. I've been naturalised you know, so officially this is my home. Now, we've got a great deal to discuss, but first we should raise a glass to my dear friends Jan Nowaski and Dominik Dabrowski – Na zdrowie."

To be polite and respectful I had joined in the toast and took a small sip of the incredibly strong liquor and then replaced the glass on the table before asking, "Tell me then, why have the three of you conspired to bring me here?"

He chuckled to himself and smiled before answering, "Jan and I decided it should be you. Dominik was already a long time dead, but I'm sure he would have approved because Jan was mightily impressed by your investigative ability, your sense of honour and integrity and, of course, your Polish background was also vital. We decided that the last one of us left alive would set the ball rolling by handing everything over to you. The diary was the bait and thankfully here you are."

"But how do you know Jan? He last saw Dominik at the farm near Luck in Poland in 1939 and I'm pretty sure he never mentioned you, not even once, when he was telling me his life story."

"I was hoping you'd pick up on that, otherwise I'd be questioning your detective credentials and wondering whether you're the right man for the job after all. Anyway, I found out about Jan last year when the story of his family reunion and your part in it, was all over the local papers and on the radio. During the war Dominik had told me about the Nowaskis and he was pretty sure that Jan had taken his diary with him when he left the farm. So I went to see him. He agreed to help and as they say, the rest is history."

"What do you want me to do then?"

He stood up, picked up the notebook from the coffee table, slowly shuffled towards the kitchen door and said, "I'll keep this with me. I've been jotting things down over the years and I'll probably need to refer to it from time to time. You know, just for dates and small details. I'm not quite as sharp as I used to be. Anyway, that's not important. So let me show you something that is. I think we've waited long enough and it's time to get down to business."

He lifted the lid on an old, battered metal chest which was large enough to almost cover the entire surface area of the small dining table.

"Dominik's whole life is here, inside this chest, and before I tell you our story and explain how you fit in, I'll show you proof of our good faith; then you'll have no reason to doubt what I say or to question my motives." He turned the chest around on the table so that when he opened the lid it blocked my view of the contents, and then took a ceremonial dagger and sheath from inside and handed it to me. "This is what you've read about and it's as real as you and me. Its history dwarfs us all and whenever I touch it I think of Dominik and his family. You've also got to take a look at this!"

He then closed the lid and handed me a small buff file but I couldn't take my eyes off the dagger and so I put the file straight back down on the table while I turned the weapon over in my hands and closely examined it.

It was a beautiful object: a work of art in the guise of an Islamic, ornamental kard. It measured just over a foot long with the hilt and sheath in gold, studded with rubies, emeralds and crystal, in identical and matching spiral patterns, so that once sheathed there was no discernible join. I marvelled at the craftsman's skill. Only the most talented and creative of artisans would have been able to design and fashion such an enduring, visually stunning and opulent object, without in that process losing the perfect balance and feel of a lethal weapon. The sharp and still unblemished steel blade was about seven inches long, tapering down the last three inches and curving slightly just before the razor-sharp tip. There was an inscription running along the blade, but I had no idea of what it said.

Stan saw me frowning and provided the answer, "Dominik told me that it's written in Old Ottoman Turkish rather than classical Ottoman, which means it's sixteenth century or perhaps even earlier. It says something like: 'A Lion sleeps in the heart of every brave man.' I think it's an ancient proverb."

"It's absolutely magnificent, and in immaculate condition, considering it's 500 years old. What do you think it's worth?

"Well a rather plain Ottoman dagger of that era could fetch a £1,000 or more. This one, with its precious stones, inscription, scroll and provenance would certainly cost tens of thousands or even six figures because it's so unique. Truth be known, you could probably name your own price, so we'd better look after it!"

It certainly felt special, almost religious and mystical, as I slowly rubbed my fingers across the sparkling jewelled patterns of the handle and sheath. Reluctantly, I handed it back and picked up the file. Inside, preserved in a plastic cover was the illuminated warrant on parchment. The writing and the coloured inks were as crisp and clear as the day the document had been produced. It was a painstaking work of art and had probably been created by a monk or other religious scribe employed within the royal household. Few others would have possessed the necessary skills and experience to produce so fine a document. I read it slowly and found that the rights and privileges bestowed upon Marek Dabrowski and his heirs were exactly as described in the diary. I felt a great surge of relief and excitement that, at last, I was making real progress and had now entered their world in a very tangible sense.

Stan placed the items back in the chest and then surprised me once more, "If you agree to listen to everything I've got to say and then do your best to help us, you can take this box home and go through the contents in your own time but first of all tell me, have you finished reading the diary yet?"

"No, I've just read about his time in the trenches but being perfectly honest, I was getting annoyed at being inveigled into your schemes without knowing what I was actually committing myself to. I needed to find out what's really going on, so I dropped everything and came straight to see you and I'm very glad I did because I've still got so many specific questions that need to be answered. For example, what happened to Dominik? Why are his possessions here? What else is in the box? How did Jan fit in and what's your role? I could go on and on."

As I looked at him for a response other questions became foremost in my mind, such as, "How did you get that horrendous scar? And is that why there are no photographs?" Perhaps they would be answered in due course, if he ever decided to open up a bit more but until then, politeness and tact demanded that they would have to go unasked.

"Okay, you've got a point, so I'll try to fill in some of the blanks for you. My father and Dominik, my godfather, were the best of mates. They first met on the Praetorian, the boat that took them from Hamburg to the States when they emigrated just before the Great War in 1914. Three years later they crossed into Canada and joined the Blue Army together and then fought in France but in different units. Even before the armistice was signed Haller was planning for the future and sent them (and other members of his personal staff) on ahead, back to Poland. The general followed when an Allied and German agreement authorised the repatriation of his entire army and equipment. Then they fought alongside each other in the 1918-20 wars against the Ukrainians and the Red Army. That's the point where the diary would have taken you next." Suddenly, he winced several times and shifted in his chair, flexing his legs, trying to find a more comfortable position.

"Are you alright? Can I help?"

"It's my sciatica; it comes and goes but can be quite painful. It's just another cross I've got to bear but it'll pass in a minute or two. Take it from me, Mick, as one who knows: getting old is a real bastard because half of what you've got doesn't work, and what does hurts! Then again, I'm lucky in a way because I've still got it all up top. It's the poor souls with Alzheimer's I feel most sorry for. I've seen it up close and personal in my old neighbour, God rest her soul. It's a pitiless and dreadful affliction, leading to a life just like Shakespeare described – second childishness and mere oblivion – but only towards the end. There's a lot of suffering first. For the families, the carers as they're called today, it can be even worse. It's a constant struggle for them to cope with the extreme mental, emotional and physical demands. All the while they must look on helplessly as their loved one's personality, ability and very essence disintegrates right in front of them. It's a hard place to be for everyone concerned, so for now I count my blessings."

He took some painkillers and then continued, "Anyway, that's enough digression, so let's get back to dealing with your questions. If I were to answer them one at a time I'm sure that every response I give will immediately lead to a host of further queries and comments from you and we would be jumping about all over the place. Confusion would reign and all context would be lost. So I suggest I save both of us a great deal of time and tell you, in a logical and methodical way, everything that has happened. As we go, I'm sure you'll get most of the information you want and then, right at the end, we can deal with any outstanding matters. But let's have a cup of tea first."

As he struggled to stand up to put the kettle on, his stiffness, old age and frustration, were all too obvious, but he immediately shrugged off my attempt to take his elbow. His offer to tell all, seen alongside his disfigurement, infirmity and stubborn independence reminded me of Dominik's grandfather and their storytelling ritual. I dwelt on those thoughts for a while, realising that control of the meeting had been so easily wrested from me by this intelligent and mentally agile old man. As a consequence, my interview plan had gone clean out of the window but surprisingly, my irritation had now completely passed and I recognised why. Having spent just a few minutes in his beguiling company I had come to accept that these few characters now dominated my life and I was content, even enthusiastic, to be drawn further in. I thought it could easily become an obsession for me. I looked forward to hearing what else he had to say and I would agree to help in any way I could. Then the tea arrived and Stan began his account.

He set the background by giving me a very short history lesson. He explained that following the Great War, Poland was not alone in simultaneously facing both golden opportunities and potential disasters. With the collapse of the Russian, Austrian and German occupying authorities, virtually all of their newly independent neighbours began fighting over their borders. Romania fought with Hungary over Transylvania; Yugoslavia with Italy over Rijeka. Lithuanians, Estonians and Latvians fought against each other and against the Russians, who were just as divided. Bolshevik doctrine and social unrest spread westward and resulted in communist revolutions in Munich, Berlin and Budapest. These conflicts were fairly short-lived, but Poland was drawn into a much longer and very violent confrontation on her eastern borders with the Ukraine. It was started by the Ukrainians in Lwów in Eastern Galicia on the morning of 1st November 1918 and it would lead to a full-scale war with Russia.

All this was happening whilst Poland struggled to form a national army from disparate forces that had recently been fighting each other. Their leader, Pilsudski, was presented with an almost impossible task. He had to quickly and efficiently amalgamate those who fought either under him for Austria in the Polish Legion, or for Germany in the Polische Wehrmacht or in the Poznan regiments, or with the Czarist forces in Russia, or with the Blue Army in France. They had little in common except an allegiance to the recreated Poland. Then he told me about Lwów.

∞∞∞∞∞∞∞

Joanna Adamska was awoken from a deep sleep by her father vigorously shaking her shoulder, "Come on child, wake up! The Ukrainians have taken over. They've been creeping about like thieves in the night and the Austrians must have colluded with them. How else could they have seized control right across the city? It's an absolute and diabolical outrage. They've even taken down the Eagle and put their own flags up. Come on get up! God only knows what will happen next. We could all be in great danger now."

His twenty-two-year-old daughter suddenly sat bolt upright as his words finally broke through and their momentous impact registered. Now she realised why the two regiments of so-called Austrian Empire troops, consisting almost entirely of Ukrainians, had arrived the previous month. "They must have been planning this for ages. It makes sense now. That's why all the Polish soldiers were transferred away and those Ukrainians sent in to replace them."

"I'm sure you're right. To take over so easily and totally unopposed, it must be part of a bigger plot. I expect that devious bastard, Archduke Wilhelm will be behind it all. He thinks he's a Ukrainian patriot now and there's none so committed as the converted. They're probably planning to take over the whole of Galicia and stop us in our tracks because they don't want to see a unified Poland. Their empire's falling apart and they want to take us down with them before we get our independence back. It looks like our fight to exist is starting all over again. It will be war. You mark my words, child."

"You're frightening me, father. You've got to think of mother and our safety. Anyway, what can we do against trained soldiers? You're too old to get involved in any fighting and I wouldn't know where to start. Perhaps some of our own troops will be sent from the west. Anyway, let's hope you're wrong and it will all blow over very quickly without too much trouble."

"I don't think so. Ever since the battle of the big fish ended and the victors decided to reshape Europe and punish Germany, we minnows have been left to sort out our own differences. There's been fighting and border skirmishes all around us ever since. Every country wants to gain maximum political and territorial advantage while they've still got the chance. I predict Poland's birth will be a very difficult one."

Even as they were talking, posters were going up all around the city proclaiming the founding of a new Ukrainian state. The Austrian governor handed over power to the Ukrainian National Rada (council) and Colonel Dmytro Vitovsky became commander-in-chief of the Ukrainian forces in Lwów, numbering some 1,300 personnel. The city was declared the capital of the West Ukrainian People's Republic, which now claimed absolute sovereignty over Eastern Galicia. Almost 60% of the city's population were Poles, 20% Ukrainians and 20% Jewish, but in the surrounding countryside ethnic Poles were in a minority. Nevertheless, they could not countenance what they saw as further foreign occupation. Their conviction was reinforced by the general momentum towards autonomy across the whole country. Further west, the Austrian authorities were already handing power back to the Poles and so Krakow and Warsaw were on the brink of freedom at long last. Moreover, Poland's declaration of national independence and democracy was only days away.

Against this background the wider Ukrainian citizenry were enthusiastic supporters of the takeover and the Jewish population understandably declared themselves neutral, but about 200 Polish military veterans in Lwów decided to fight. They took up positions in a school to the west of the city, armed only with one old rifle for every three men. The noise and news of battle spread throughout the city like wildfire, kindling a spirit of Polish nationalism and patriotism, particularly among the youth. School students as young as ten, scouts and young workers rushed to join the fight. Within hours the numbers swelled to over a thousand and the newcomers brought with them an assortment of hunting and sporting weapons.

Although outgunned and outnumbered the Poles used their local knowledge to good effect. They exploited the fact that the enemy, not used to street fighting, often overreached themselves, becoming isolated and vulnerable to counter attack. On the second day the Poles, boosted by their early success and captured weapons, started to push the Ukrainians back towards the city centre. Hundreds of university students, including an initially reluctant Joanna, a postgraduate mathematics student and several of her friends, motivated by the bravery of the young fighters, overcame their innate fear and rallied to the cause.

Joanna and many of the other volunteers, including her closest friends, were issued with weapons captured from a police station in the Horodok suburb and then briefed for an attack on the railway station. They had been warned that a regiment of crack Ukrainian Sich Riflemen from Bukovina were trying to break into the city in the suburb of Klepariv. It was imperative to obtain a significant quantity of weapons and ammunition for issue to the hard-pressed defenders in that district if they were to stand any chance of holding them off. The force of about 100 students was led by 20 fully equipped and experienced members of the PMO (Polish Military Organisation) and their objectives were an ammunition depot and a Ukrainian supply train. Although the enemy were regular troops, they were mainly conscripted country lads with minority local support, few personal ties to the city and little combat experience. On the other hand the Poles were fighting for their own families, their homes, schools and neighbourhoods and they were well led by a small group of professional, military veterans. They knew every inch of the battleground, were highly motivated and could count on the support of the majority of the population.

Joanna was frightened. She was shivering, despite her hands being wet with sweat, as she gripped her pistol tightly and crouched down behind a wall. They waited for the two specially selected and most battle-hardened soldiers to silently take out the sentries at the goods yard entrance. She saw a figure suddenly emerge from the darkness and the flash of a blade in the moonlight and then the first guard was slowly lowered to the ground. She was amazed that he had been completely taken by surprise and dispatched so quickly. Then almost immediately, she felt a surge of overwhelming remorse and sadness as her thoughts automatically flew to the inconsolable grief and suffering of his poor mother. She was quickly sparked back into action when the second guard was also silently and similarly eliminated and the signal to move forward was given. Crouching low, they all ran for the gateway. Suddenly, there was gunfire from the station about 300 yards away, as their sister group attacked the armoury. They ran on, through the gate onto the sidings and then left towards the dark shadow of the engine. As planned they split into two groups, the smaller to spread out in a skirmish line to protect their rear and the other sprinting forward to take the train.

Joanna was struggling to keep up as she gasped for breath and stumbled over the uneven ground. She was out of condition and not used to physical exertion. She had never been much of an athlete, always giving games, gymnastics and sports a wide berth, preferring a sedate academic life. Her friend Hannah, some 40 feet ahead, noticed that she was no longer alongside and looked over her shoulder. She saw her trip and immediately ran back to help. This probably saved both their lives as the first half a dozen front runners were suddenly cut down by a volley of shots from several Ukrainians who appeared from the shadows behind the rear of the train. The rest dived for cover and returned fire, most of which was wildly inaccurate. The students, already fearful and highly stressed, had never experienced combat, and the shock of seeing their young friends mown down, some writhing and screaming from the excruciating pain of their wounds, was enough to destroy any vestige of self-control. In such a state they were just as likely to shoot their own people as the enemy. Fortunately, the two Polish soldiers who had disposed of the sentries anticipated an ambush and had therefore approached in a wide arc and outflanked the Ukrainians, killing them with a flurry of captured grenades.

Further volunteer units helped to secure the perimeter before the horses and wagons were brought forward and the train's vital cargo of weapons, ammunition and supplies transferred. This one small action, and the simultaneous and ultimately successful raid on the armoury, cost fifteen lives but ensured the survival and fighting capability of the Poles within the city. Word and evidence of its success acted as the best possible recruiting sergeant for their cause. Within hours their numbers had risen to over 6,000. Over the next few days the Ukrainians were driven out from the western part of the city and the Poles prepared for an assault on the city centre. Slowly Joanna, Hannah and the other recruits gained in military confidence and under the control and guidance of the veterans they melded into a reasonably competent and disciplined fighting force.

Just before the Polish attack was to take place, several units of the Ukrainian Sich Riflemen finally succeeded in breaking through. Together with their reinforcements from surrounding towns, they were able to substantially strengthen their defence lines and once more outnumber their enemy. The Polish offensive was beaten back and with neither side having heavy weapons or the manpower to force a victory, the situation settled into stalemate. A permanent front line only existed in the centre and both sides tried to avoid civilian casualties and damage to the city's infrastructure. Many areas around power plants and other important civic and industrial buildings became designated as demilitarised zones. Local ceasefire agreements were signed on an almost daily basis. It was common for fighters from both sides to play sport or party together, whilst their commanders used the truce to evacuate casualties, or iron out local threats to the water supply or other utilities and hospitals.

Joanna was not too surprised to witness a Ukrainian officer waking up blind drunk in the local Polish command post. He had spent the night of a ceasefire in conference with his counterpart, trying to arrange a protection agreement for staff at the nearby gas plant. Having drunk far too much, he passed out and missed the end of the ceasefire period. But instead of the Polish officer taking him prisoner, as he was entitled to do, he simply signed another so that his enemy could sober up and then return safely to his unit. For these reasons, and the relatively low casualty rate on both sides, the battle has often been referred to since by historians as, 'the last civilised conflict'. However, the aftermath was anything but proper or decent and was to become a stain on Polish nationhood.

On 11th November, 1918 Poland declared her independence and a relief force set out for Lwów. The Ukrainians, feeling that they were running out of time, prepared a full-scale attack on the Polish positions. The battle raged for a week, but the Poles held their ground and another ceasefire was signed on the 18th. A Polish force of some 1,400 men, equipped with artillery, finally broke the siege on the 21st November and the Ukrainians withdrew from the city that night.

Newly promoted Dominik arrived in Lwów on General Haller's personal order on the 22nd (with his friend and now full sergeant, Konrad Pawłowski) in charge of a small detachment of Polish cavalry, attached to the relief force. Dominik and about two dozen of his comrades, who had performed with distinction in the trenches, had been summoned by the general whilst still in France. He was looking for suitable officer material which was untainted by military service in any of the three occupying powers. He used them to bring fresh blood into a new national army being formed in Poland: men that would also owe him a debt of personal loyalty. Two major politicians were vying for the control of Poland and there could only be one leader. And so, preparing for the inevitable rivalries and power struggles that lay ahead, Haller wanted to dispatch his own 'trusted eyes and ears'. He feared being politically and militarily outmanoeuvred by his rivals, who were already assembling back home and debating who they should support.

Roman Dmowski, who headed the Polish National Committee in Paris and had control of the Blue Army and direct access to the western Allies, fervently believed that Poles should abandon what he described as their foolish romantic nationalism and rigid social traditions. He urged them to modernise, using reason, logic and a strong work ethic to succeed in business, science and trade. He was tired of nostalgic patriotism and noble gestures of defiance against their powerful neighbours. Raised in a poor urban family he became an accomplished biologist and deeply disliked his rival Pilsudski, whom he regarded as a privileged product of the old Polish-Lithuanian Commonwealth. He favoured good relations with Russia and sought an accommodation with them over disputed territories, being prepared to offer up land for guarantees of autonomy. He recognised Germany as the real threat to Poland's aspirations for independence. Although he supported the 'Triple Entente' against the Central Powers and was favoured by France, he was disliked by a handful of influential diplomats and politicians in the western alliance, particularly America and Great Britain. This was mainly because of his overt anti-Semitism, often railing about 'Jewish conspiracies against Poland' and his unrelenting and excessive territorial claims against Germany.

General Jozef Pilsudski was a fervent patriot, leader of The Polish Socialist Party, a scholar, a linguist, and a man of noble birth. He was a strident nationalist and having been born in Wilno under strict Russian rule, he was convinced that Poland's independence would have to be won by force of arms. After becoming involved in organised resistance to the Russian occupation and serving periods of imprisonment and exile for plotting revolution against Czarist Russia, he formed the Polish Legion. In 1914 he also established its secret intelligence arm, the PMO. Its mandate was to gather intelligence by all available means and to sabotage the political and military capability of the enemies of the Polish people. Its first targets included the Russian Empire during the early phase of the war and the German Empire later on. It was formed with less than 500 members but by 1918 this had risen to 30,000 and it had also developed a formidable counter-intelligence capacity. Many of its members were then absorbed into the new Polish intelligence Service.

Pilsudski predicted the outbreak of The Great War; the Russian Empire's defeat by the Central Powers and in turn, their defeat by the western alliance. With his Legion, he fought alongside the Austro-Hungarian and German Empires to ensure Russia's defeat. In 1917, with Russia on the point of collapse and gripped by revolution, he withdrew his support from the Central Powers looking to use his military experience and the Polish Legion to lead Poland through the political turmoil and into independence.

Dmowski and Pilsudski were so diametrically opposed – personally, militarily and politically – yet both claimed to govern Poland. Many feared that their antagonism would lead the country into civil war and that Poland would be consumed from within, even before it could be formally established. In a final bid to avert disaster, the world famous pianist and composer Paderewski met them both and persuaded them to form a coalition, with Pilsudski acting as provisional head of state and commander-in-chief of the armed forces (including the Blue Army) while Paderewski became Prime Minister and along with Dmowski he would represent Poland at the Paris Peace Conference. At the signing of the Treaty of Versailles on 28 June 1919 Poland was formally recognised as an independent and sovereign state.

It was against this turbulent background that at Dominik's personal interview, General Haller had told him that he had been recommend for special duties by his Regimental Commander and he quoted from the assessment report: 'when fighting in the trenches Dabrowski has grown into an ideal soldier, a professional killer who can control his emotions, think clearly in a crisis, take the lead and inspire others. For such an inexperienced man he has shown surprising skill and leadership qualities when in action and I have no hesitation in recommending him for a transfer to your staff. He will not let us down.' Dominik was completely taken by surprise because he thought that he had done nothing special and he had no idea that his conduct had been noticed or reported upon. Neither could he imagine what such a move would mean, but he was pleased with the compliments.

They also discussed their national military history and their own ancestry and being gripped by Haller's friendly, infectious enthusiasm and the sense of occasion, Dominik showed the general his Royal Warrant. He read it carefully, thanked Dominik and then handed it back. He stood up and contrary to protocol, saluted first then shook Dominik's hand and said, "You are indeed someone special and I must make good use of your talents. I think it's best that for the time being, in these uncertain times, that we say nothing further of your document. Guard it well. I'm totally satisfied that you have what it takes to be a first-class officer under my command. Congratulations, Lieutenant Dabrowski! And now I have a vital mission for you, but there will be no written orders. You will leave for Poland tomorrow and enter secretly through Gdansk. This is what I want you to do..."

Dominik's contingent received a hero's welcome from the Polish citizens inside Lwów, even though they had only been involved in a brief skirmish with the Sich Rifleman as they had withdrawn from the siege to new positions in the countryside. The Ukrainians then surrounded the city to the north, east and south, but the Poles secured their lifeline, a supply route westwards. Inside Lwów the newcomers soon discovered that law and order had totally broken down.

Before leaving the city the Ukrainians had absurdly released all the prisoners from the city's prison. Hundreds of criminals from all three ethnic communities along with Austrian army deserters roamed the town, taking advantage of the chaos: robbing, looting and many looking to settle old scores. The Jewish population had formed a militia during the battle in order to protect their own people. The Ukrainians had respected their neutrality, but many Poles resented this fact and felt betrayed because the Jews had not helped when they were really needed. Moreover, once the fighting ended many Polish inhabitants, based on a few exaggerated examples of so called collaboration, openly accused the Jews of being on the Ukrainian side. This antipathy and anti-Semitism was also fuelled by the fact that for years the Jews had been the scapegoats for the woes of both sides in their long-standing struggle for supremacy in the western Ukraine, or the Polish Ukraine as the Poles called it.

As crowds rampaged through the streets and rumours spread that the Jews would be made to pay for their collaboration, the Polish authority disarmed the Jewish Militia and interned its leaders. Arguments still rage today as to whether this was to prevent a major escalation, as the Poles maintain or as the Jews see it, to render them defenceless. Overt prejudice, mob rule and the participation of violent criminals and military deserters, some now armed once again as they had volunteered to fight for the Poles, was an explosive mix. Ignition point was finally reached when Jewish Ukrainian sympathisers resisted the Polish forces trying to take control of the Jewish quarter. As news of the confrontation spread, the mob gathered to attack and their target was the Jews. Their businesses, homes and synagogues were ransacked, looted and set alight and anyone who resisted was beaten or worse. The madness also spread to the Ukrainian areas and groups of soldiers joined the mob in an orgy of violence, hatred and revenge. For two days anarchy reigned, as the innocent and helpless endured an onslaught of violent contempt and murder.

The next day, in this atmosphere of civil disorder and riot, Dominik sent his first secure report back to General Haller.

1. Primary.

Route in via Gdansk now secure and relevant personnel set in position to control and facilitate further traffic. Lwów safe but besieged. Relief force can hold. From travel across length and breadth of country I report no shortage of volunteers or enthusiasm – recruits flooding in for national army. Given time – then no shortage of combat troops. Logistics are a nightmare. Most equipment pre-war and consists of heavy guns made in five countries and rifles manufactured in six, each using different ammunition. Example – 1st Legion Infantry Division comprises three regiments – one armed with German Mauser rifles – second with French Lebel carbines – third using Russian Mosin-Nagants. Each make needs ammunition of different calibre. Repeat no shortage combat troops now 200,000 and rising rapidly but lack of seasoned and experienced personnel at all ranks. Coordination and strategic command is patchy. Chronic shortage of uniforms, kit, vehicles, tanks, planes and heavy weapons.

2. Secondary.

Contact made at university. Confirmed at least three possibles. All specialists in prescribed areas – with optimum coverage across critical subjects. Internal recommendations and security clearance obtained from Head of Department. Making contact shortly for full assessment from PMO.

3. Additional.

Contact established with Captain Merian Cooper of American Relief Administration in Lwów. A true friend to Poland and keen to assist Polish Air Corps with a squadron of American Volunteers. He says to repay us for the American debt to General Tadeusz Kościuszko for his unstinting aid to George Washington during their own war of independence! Prepared to fly with the Blue Army Air Corps and looking to obtain new French aircraft.

Summary – 1. Chaos but improving – 40% combat ready but insufficient for major theatre.

2. Positive progress – recruitment of team on schedule.

3. Cooper en route Paris (where he will recruit and equip) via Warsaw. He will establish Kościuszko Squadron.

Ends DD.

Within 24 hours he was on anti-riot patrol in Lwów city centre with Konrad and six troopers. They fired into the air in an attempt to drive a mob away from a damaged and looted bakery and shop. The group of about 100 were still throwing stones and shouting abuse at the owner and his two sons, as they vainly attempted to stop wholesale theft from their property. Dominik saw a drunken Polish soldier at the front of the baying mob pull a revolver from his belt and point it at the old baker, "You stinking Jewish traitor. You won't be robbing us blind anymore. You're about to meet your maker, you thieving piece of shit!" He then shouted at the crowd, "Come on! Let's set fire to the place and build a pyre for the bastards."

One of the sons ran in front of his father to protect him with his body as the drunk stumbled towards them pointing his wavering pistol. Dominik screamed out, "Put that gun down now or I'll shoot." The crowd around the drunk, suddenly aware of the risk that he posed to their own safety, started to back away. He was too far gone to hear, or Dominik's voice was drowned out by the noise of the riot; either way he did not react. There was now only a yard or two between the gun and the baker's son and Dominik felt he could hesitate no more. He aimed carefully and shot the soldier in the side of the head: a brain shot intended to prevent any reflex discharge of the offender's weapon. As he fell, those nearest the body turned towards Dominik in surprise, disbelief and anger. Konrad and the whole patrol turned their weapons on the mob and Dominik again fired his pistol, this time into the air and he shouted, "You've caused enough trouble. One man is dead already and many more of you will certainly follow if you don't go home straight away and stay off the streets. You're a disgrace to your country and you make me sick. Bugger off, before I shoot someone else. Now I've seen exactly what you're capable of, I consider it my certain and absolute duty to rid the streets of vermin like you." It was no idle threat, but nevertheless, he breathed a sigh of relief when the crowd immediately started to break up and disperse, away from the city centre.

He approached the baker and his sons, "I'm sorry for what's happened here. I'll make sure that you have a guard posted outside until proper order is restored to the neighbourhood. I'll also try to get you some compensation for what you've lost but please be careful. I'd stay inside as much as possible. This place is a tinderbox and we're nowhere near getting it under control yet."

The baker's distraught wife emerged from inside, supported by Joanna and her friend, Hannah, who explained that they had been helping her aunt inside the bakery when the riot started and they had been trapped inside ever since. They came every Thursday evening to help with all the extra work before the Sabbath and earn a few coins which helped to pay for their studies. Joanna introduced herself, modestly explained their limited role in the defence of the city and said, "I saw what you just did. It took a great deal of courage to stand up to that rabble like that and rescue us so gallantly. You're just the chap I need."

Dominik carefully and admiringly examined the attractive young women and declared, "So you are two of the brave eaglets who flew the nest to save your city at its time of peril." He took a pace back, bowed dramatically and came to attention, smiled broadly and then saluted them. "Ladies, you have earned my respect and devotion. I am but your humble servant and I willingly offer my services in any way you may deem necessary." The exchange momentarily lifted the tense and dangerous atmosphere that had surrounded them and the young women both broke into laughter at his exaggerated sense of theatre. Dominik and the rest of the patrol joined in before Joanna went on to explain Hannah's predicament.

Dominik arranged for the removal of the body and instructed the patrol to remain in the area, before he took Joanna and her friend straight to the military headquarters at the Uhlan Barracks. He demanded to see the officer in command of the Jewish prisoners. They were kept waiting for two hours before Captain Waligorski, an ex-Austrian cavalry officer introduced himself. Dominik wasted no more time; indicating Hannah he said, "This young woman's brother, Aaron Silberstein, has been arrested for being a member of the Jewish militia. I want you to release him into my parole."

"Don't be ridiculous. I can't possibly let him go, certainly not while these riots are going on. For all I know he could be one of the organisers."

"Look, Hannah his sister here has risked her life, time and time again over the last few weeks, trying to drive the Ukrainians out. She is a Jew and yet she fought for our shared city and our independence. She battled around the clock, alongside young Joanna here and their other friends from the university. Yet shamefully, at the same time many adult Polish men, with everything to fight for and a duty to the flag, stayed in their homes, too afraid to step outside. It was these brave students, the eaglets as we now respectfully refer to them, who answered the call and took up arms. We all owe her a debt of thanks and her religion has nothing to do with it. You also have my assurance that her brother is no threat to us; he was only protecting his family, friends and community, just as we are doing now."

Joanna joined in, "Has he been charged with anything?"

"No, he's being held with the others to prevent them from attacking our forces. It's precautionary."

Dominik pressed his point home, "So what better guarantee could you have for his future conduct than the word of a brother officer. Surely to refuse now, would be callous and a slight on the honour and tradition we both share."

"Alright, don't overdo it! You've made your point, but I want your assurance in writing."

Aaron was in his mid-twenties, about six feet tall, handsome and dark haired with a swarthy complexion and a muscular physique. Dominik could see that he would indeed be a handful if he ever turned against them. Hannah had already explained that he was a linguist and worked as a researcher in the university library. He was also well known as the city's chess champion. He was active in Jewish politics and although he was not a hardliner, he was sympathetic to the Ukrainians as he identified with their minority status. She did the introductions and brought him up to date with events, emphasising Dominik's role in obtaining his release.

Once outside the barracks Aaron offered his hand to Dominik, "Thank you for your kindness to my sister and for obtaining my release, but I can take care of things from here on." He started to shepherd his sister away.

Dominik followed, "I'm sure you're more than capable of looking after your family but that's not the issue here. Whether you like it or not, you've been released into my charge and I'm personally answerable for your conduct. I take my responsibilities just as seriously as you do and so as I see it, we've got to work together, at least until the rioting ends."

"You've got a bloody nerve. There wouldn't be any rioting if you Poles had left us alone in the first place. Your fight with the Ukrainians has nothing at all to do with us. What we did was both necessary and sensible, but your lot come steaming in, throwing your weight about, beat us and arrest us. Do you honestly expect us to sit on our hands when we are attacked and our homes are burnt down?"

Hannah could see that her brother was getting very angry and was about to launch into one of his anti-Polish diatribes. She knew that Dominik certainly didn't deserve it and that such accusations and confrontation would get them nowhere.

"Aaron! That's enough! For goodness sake get a grip and calm down. I can assure you that we're all friends here. Just be grateful you're out and now shut up. Let's get home before you say something you really will regret."

As usual he took her advice, reluctantly perhaps, but he put his arm around her shoulder, gave her a squeeze and they started walking towards home. To his surprise Dominik strolled up alongside and said, "No Aaron, no I don't expect you to do nothing when you're attacked. I expect you to fight to defend your home and your family and I would fight alongside you. We are on the same side you know."

When they arrived at the Jewish quarter they found things had quietened down, but it was now surrounded by Polish troops. Dominik found Konrad and the rest of the patrol and they passed through the checkpoint, but the civilians were warned to stay inside after dark as a curfew had been imposed. Inside they were greeted by a scene of destruction. Dozens of the wooden buildings had been burnt right down to the ground. Others of a more solid construction had fared better but even so, some survived only as skeletal monoliths, their chimney stacks brazenly finger-pointing, thrusting accusingly towards the heavens. They towered, proud and resolute, over a site of charred desolation and each one, like a giant headstone, signposted the exact location of a family's sudden and violent demise. With increasing anxiety they hurried on towards the tailor's shop and as they turned the final street corner their relief on seeing the building intact soon turned to alarm. Two men ran off in the opposite direction, away from the front door and into the labyrinth of side streets.

Dominik immediately grabbed Aaron's coat to stop him sprinting forward in an automatic response to a possible threat to his family. They both instinctively sensed a real danger inside the building and so Dominik signalled for silence and sent three men round the block to cover the rear. He gave them five minutes which seemed like an age and then they crept forward. It was slow progress because there was smashed glass and debris everywhere and they were desperate to keep the element of surprise. Dominik led the way in, followed by Konrad, Aaron and one soldier. Two troopers were ordered to stay outside and protect the women. They passed through the already forced and open shop door at the front, moving on towards the living quarters at the rear, where they heard raised voices. The men inside were obviously unaware that their lookouts at the front had run off at the first sign of trouble.

"Come on you old goat, this is your last chance. Where's the money hidden?"

When Aaron heard his father's sobbed response, it made his blood boil, "Please don't hit her again. We have given you everything. On my life, there is nothing left. If you must make someone suffer then take it out on me but let her go. Please – I beg you."

Then a third voice added, "Jesus Christ! This is getting us nowhere. We've been here too long already. Let's take what we've got and finish them off. We can burn the place down and nobody will ever know."

"No, it's here somewhere. He's just a tight Jewish asshole trying to hang on to his fortune. Smack her about some more and if that doesn't work I'll cut her fingers off, one by one. He'll cough up his hoard eventually: it's just a matter of time and how much he's prepared to let the old cow suffer."

With pistols in hand, Dominik and Konrad slowly crept to the door, testing every footfall to avoid the slightest noise. They steadied and positioned themselves for action. Dominik was ready to go in first, high and to the right and Konrad prepared to move low and to the left. As more punches rained down and the woman cried out and moaned at the pain of impact, they burst in. Aaron's mother was tied to a chair in the far corner. His father, also tied up by his hands and feet, was lying on his side in the centre of the floor. Both their faces were covered in blood and the woman continued to sob and wail. Four men in their thirties and forties dominated the room. Two stood over the couple: one was brandishing a hunting knife in his left hand and punching out at the woman with his right, the other was holding a large revolver. The third, apparently unarmed, stood guard by the back door and the fourth was sat at a small table counting a pile of notes and coin. A shotgun rested on the table near his right hand.

The initial reaction came from the man with the handgun. He turned towards the sudden noise at the door, but as soon as he tried to raise his weapon Dominik shot him twice in the chest. Before the second report rang out Konrad had squeezed his trigger and the knifeman's throat exploded in a shower of red spray. He was dead before he hit the ground where he bled out. The offender by the door was halfway out into the rear yard when he took a shotgun blast full in the chest from one of the soldiers covering the rear and he collapsed into a heap, blocking the doorway.

Dominik calmly walked across the room and finished him off with a round into the forehead. So quick and decisive was the action that the man at the table was already in shock. He did not move an inch before Konrad, who had him covered the whole time, placed his pistol against the back of his head, picked up the shotgun and called out, "Aaron, come on in. I think this one's yours, but you'd better see to your parents and get them out of here first."

Aaron untied his parents and then led them outside where they were comforted by the girls. Dominik checked the bodies, emptied their pockets for proof of identity and evidence of any other crimes and then called the soldiers at the rear into the house to clear the bodies out. With a gun to his head, the survivor couldn't talk fast enough. The awful sight of his dead friends being tossed out the back like discarded sides of meat and the frightening, ice cold efficiency of the hard-nosed soldiers that had surrounded and intimidated him, was more than enough to secure his full cooperation. They were Polish deserters from the Austrian army who had met inside the prison where they were serving time for offences of theft and violence. They had teamed up when they were suddenly released by the Ukrainians and had then taken advantage of the chaos to attack and rob Jewish businesses. They thought the Polish authorities would be too busy to concern themselves with what happened to a few Jews. At first Aaron was so angry and vengeful for his parents that he wanted to kill him there and then, but the callous, rough handling of the dead thugs and the spreading pools of blood on the floor reminded him of a slaughterhouse and he did not want his home tainted any further.

Konrad assured him, "We'll court martial him and then we'll shoot him for looting. You have my word."

Outside, as the soldiers regrouped and debriefed, Joanna said to the Silbersteins, "It's not safe to stay here and you both need some medical treatment, so you can all come home with me and stay until things get back to normal." Dominik and Aaron agreed with the suggestion and after thanking Joanna for her offer and all the soldiers for their action and support, they cleaned up the old couple's wounds and made their way back out to the city centre with their prisoner. He was shot three days later.

Many believed that the Polish military command in the city condoned, approved or even instigated the attacks on the Jews. The authorities denied such accusations, blaming the criminal elements and deserters. They pointed out that it was they who put a stop to the violence and arrested and imprisoned about 1,500 offenders, for crimes of violence, arson and murder. Amongst those arrested there were over seventy serving Polish soldiers, including twenty officers and independent investigations concluded that about 340 people were killed during the rioting. Of those, between fifty and seventy were Jewish, the rest being a majority of Christian Ukrainians and only a handful of Poles. They also found that the Polish Military had failed to exercise their duty, by firstly not preventing the attacks and then by not stopping them with due diligence.

Similar events in other nearby cities and towns also added evidence pointing towards a pattern of Polish tolerance, connivance and perhaps even the initiation of anti-Semitic and anti-Ukrainian bloodshed. Against this divisive and dangerous backdrop and despite an initial unease, a deep and mutual bond of trust, friendship and respect was forged between Dominik and Konrad and Joanna and the Silbersteins. Their eventful and dangerous experiences during the battle and siege of Lwów was to serve Poland well.

Chapter Four

A Taste of Things to Come

Salisbury – 6th November 2009

I had travelled home late from Stan's and then found it almost impossible to sleep. His story and my mental pictures of the characters and events he had described were swimming around in my head, all competing for attention and proper scrutiny. I tried to imagine what would happen to them next, but I was just too tired to think logically. I was also anxious to examine the contents of the chest that was now waiting in my office downstairs, before I could rush back to Swindon and hear more. I got up very early.

I opened the lid on the box and the first thing I saw – well I could hardly miss it – was a trench gun. The barrel was sticking out of a well-worn, purpose-made, leather gun case. I checked that it was empty and was impressed by how clean and well maintained it was. Although it was probably nearly 100 years old, it was still in good working order. I rummaged through the chest but there were no cartridges. I did find a Smith & Wesson .455 revolver in a leather holster and on the top of the barrel I found the patents from October 1901 to February 1906. There was also a Colt .32 automatic pistol. Both handguns were unloaded, but I did find a full box of ammunition for each. Again the weapons were in immaculate condition, smelt strongly of gun oil and were ready for use. I decided, for the time being at least, to turn a blind eye to the question of the legality of these weapons.

I took out the dagger and the file containing the warrant and placed them safely to one side and then carefully emptied the chest onto my desk. The first thing that caught my eye was the glint of a medal. It was in a small plastic envelope attached to a black and blue ribbon and formed the shape of a golden Maltese cross. I took it out and examined it. In the centre was a gold-coloured circular boss containing a ring of garlands with green studs, enclosing the white Polish eagle. On the arms of the cross were the words 'Virtuti Militari' (to military valour) and although I had never seen one before, the words told me it was the Polish equivalent of our Victoria Cross, awarded for extreme courage in the face of the enemy. Its institution predates the VC by over 60 years. I could find no inscription. I thought it had probably been awarded to Dominik, but I would have to confirm it because surprises were coming thick and fast.

I picked up an old, battered, cardboard box file and opened it to find dozens of black and white photographs and an assortment of typed and manuscript documents, all written in Polish and contained in separate file sleeves. Most of the pictures were of military figures and apart from just a few in Polish, British and Russian Second World War era uniforms, they were all Nazi officers. I didn't recognise any of the most infamous amongst their number. There were also a dozen or so portraits of men and women in civilian clothes and a similar number of small family groups, obviously posing for the camera.

I opened the first file which consisted of several sheets of A4 paper and the contents surprised and shocked me, it was entitled:

Murder of the Jews - A Report of the Ploskirow (Proskurov) Massacre of 15th February, 1919. (An investigation by Professor Adam Berkowicz of Lwów University Press. First Published in The United States of America in February 1920.)

Summary: Following a half-hearted attempt at a local Bolshevik uprising in the town during the morning of Saturday 15th February, 1919 a contingent of Ukrainian People's Army troops, loyal to Petliura, including a regiment of Cossacks, went on the rampage. They were commanded and encouraged by 'General' Semysenko to kill the Jews or the 'enemies of the nationalists' as he called them. In little more than four hours, these 'pogromchiks' had murdered between 1,500 and 3,000 innocent Jewish victims – men, women, children and babies. They rampaged from house to house in the Jewish quarter, abusing, raping and then killing everyone inside, irrespective of age. Most were slaughtered by stabbing and slashing with military shashkas. A priest who appealed to them to stop the killing was murdered in front of his church.

Whilst this report seeks, above all else, to establish evidence as to whether or not Symon Petliura, as leader of the nation, should bear any personal responsibility for this butchery, it cannot be considered outside the context of the broader anti-Semitic pogroms perpetrated right across the Ukraine. In Podolia alone, in just a few months, 150 such massacres took place in over 50 separate locations. According to survivors, more than 100 were committed by the Ukrainians, about 40 by Denikin's White Army and the rest by an assortment of bandits, local mobs, and Poles. The total number of victims has been estimated at about 15,000 but could be many more. Although some Jewish self-defence units had been organised to stand against the pogroms and some managed to fight off the rioters, they could not prevail against regular army units.

I stopped reading and decided to move on. I had no idea that such pre-Holocaust slaughter had taken place in the Ukraine, particularly in an area where half the population were Jewish. They were no small minority here and I simply failed to understand what could possibly drive people to such bigotry and barbaric hatred of their friends and fellow citizens – especially when they were already engaged in a desperate battle against such a potent and overwhelming external threat as Bolshevik Russia.

I then picked up the next item, a handwritten Polish document. Although I could not understand the military location codes and unit terminology at the top of the document the text roughly translated as:

SECRET – Military order – Under Command Seal – to be delivered by hand.
URGENT – To Lieutenant Dabrowski – Blue Army, Lwów.
Message reads: Lt. Dabrowski plus party of four hereby ordered to report all haste to General Haller personally – at Divisional Headquarters: repeat URGENT.

It was dated the 20th May 1919. Well there was no mistake this time. Here was written confirmation of Stan's story. Dominik was a Lieutenant, apparently without going up through the ranks and with very little service and also known personally to a very senior and influential army commander. By any measure, even in wartime, this was highly unusual and he was being summoned by name. Who, I wondered, was the party of four? The questions continued to pile up when I opened the next buff folder. It contained a handwritten and personally signed letter:

From Marshall Pilsudski to Lieutenant Dabrowski Warsaw - 28th July 1919. You have been recommended by General Haller and that is sufficient for me to place my trust in you. I need an English-speaking Intelligence Officer; someone who knows the workings of the Blue Army and an associate of Captain Merian Cooper. You qualify on all three counts. Please report with all haste to my command centre for a full briefing and further instructions. Haller is aware. Bring this note.

Just two months after being summoned by General Haller he is called to an audience with the provisional head of state and commander-in-chief. I wondered why Dominik was having such a meteoric rise in his status and what was his mission? Stan has been telling the truth: he mentioned Dominik meeting Merian Cooper in Lwów so perhaps it has something to do with the Blue Army Air Corps. I moved on and there I found more evil:

Mass Murderer

Stapled at the top of page 1 was a black and white photograph of a bespectacled, middle-aged man in civilian clothes. He was standing alongside a pile of bodies in a snow-covered yard in front of a thatched building. He had black receding hair with a bushy moustache and a goatee beard. His name was typed underneath – Colonel Aleksei Mikhailovich Sokorov, born in St Petersburg on 21.12.1891. The next four pages of antecedent history can be summarised as follows:

He was an enthusiastic Moscow Chekist right from its inception in 1917. The Cheka was a particularly ruthless and powerful organ of state security set up to combat sabotage, counterrevolution and speculation. In November1919 he was transferred to the Protection of Borders Section, where he carried out his duties with vigour but without scruples. He obeyed every order to the letter, relishing the opportunity to murder any and all enemies of the state. In 1926 he joined the Kommandatura branch of the Administrative Executive Department of the NKVD which had been set up under Vasili Mikhailovich Blokhin, Stalin's chief executioner. Sokorov was hand-picked for the position by Beria who was most impressed by his unswerving loyalty and ruthlessness. He joined this select company of killers and assisted in the majority of state murders carried out during Stalin's purges, personally shooting and hanging hundreds. In August 1937 he was sent to Russia's western borders where he organised the 'National Operation' (authorised under secret order No. 00485) to arrest and imprison or liquidate all citizens with Polish connections. Over 100,000 Poles were executed.

He was so successful in his mission that in November 1939, he was the obvious choice to send to Russian-occupied Poland to oversee the interrogation, removal and elimination of anyone suspected of posing a threat to the USSR, or professing support for Polish nationalism. Ruthless and efficient as ever, he set out his own priorities for terror:

> 1. *The aristocracy, military servicemen (commissioned and non-commissioned officers), the police, and other civilians working for the state.*
> 2. *Families of military officers and members of state voluntary organisations (including children and the elderly).*
> 3. *The intelligentsia, artists, teachers, lawyers, engineers, journalists and other professionals, the wealthy (not defined). All property of the executed criminals to be forfeited to the state.*
> 4. *Clergy (no distinction between denominations).*
> 5. *Workers and peasants suspected of not supporting the Soviet government.*

With so much practice he quickly became expert in the quick and efficient dispatch of his victims. Much of the butchery was carried out by his underlings, but he enjoyed killing and boasted of his ability to personally exceed the daily quotas of his staff. In part this was due to the fact that right at the start of his killing career, he had experimented with different methods of shooting his victims in an attempt to avoid the bloody experience of having half-dead victims thrashing about on the ground. By trial and error, he developed what was to become the Cheka's preferred technique for execution, referred to later by the Germans as the 'Nackenschuss' or 'Genickschuss': a shot to the nape of the neck. This caused minimal blood loss and instant death. The victim's head was bent forward and held while he fired slightly downward at point blank range. This also became the standard method used by the NKVD and was employed for the Katyn murders.

The last few handwritten lines in the document sent a chill down my spine: *I hunted the bastard down and exacted my revenge. Finally, after he suffered the cruelty and pain inflicted on his own victims, he was sent to oblivion on behalf of each and every one of them.*

I pinned the names of three to his putrid heart, to claim his black soul and ensure that he always burns in hell. He was a monster and I fear that many more must follow him before we can finally be free of their evil.

I shuddered, moved on and opened the next file and there I found:

The Pabst Plan
Summary of all documents: the New German city of Warsaw (Neue deutsche Stadt Warschau).

On 20th June 1939 Hitler was visiting an architectural office in Wurzburg, the capital of lower Franconia on the River Main in Germany, when he first noticed and became obsessed with a project for a future German town called Warsaw. From that moment on it was included in his Generalplan Ost. It required the complete destruction of the Polish capital (commonly referred to by the Nazis as 'the city of bandits') and the removal of its 1.5 million inhabitants. All this was planned even before the war started. The Nazi 'Chief Architect for Warsaw,' Friedrich Pabst proposed that once the site had been flattened, it would be replaced by a new model Nazi town to be built for some 130,000 German inhabitants of the ruling class who would be moved east to take control of the occupied territories. It was intended to be a provincial transport hub for German rail and road networks which would be improved and/or redeveloped to open up the east for the Reich's exploitation of wealth, resources and labour.

The project documents, incorporating fifteen separate plans, also included a scaled colour schematic created by the small team of German architects in charge of the development, assorted photographs and several pages of pre-build recommendations and specifications. They showed that it would occupy only 5% of the area of the real Warsaw. Revealingly and alarmingly, it also included details of the establishment of a Jewish Ghetto and a chronological, three-stage plan for the 'displacement of the total population of the city – to slave labour battalions, or to concentration and labour camps for extermination.'

I was flabbergasted. Could this really be genuine? The implications were staggering. The complete destruction of a capital city and the enslaving and murder of its entire population was simply unbelievable, even at a time of total war. But this was planned months, perhaps even years, before hostilities had begun. Well it certainly nailed the lie that the Nazis were anything other than totally perverted and evil, and not just the leader and his military ilk either because the cancer had infected all the organs of state. It's one thing for the population to sit back and ignore the blindingly obvious but when peacetime professionals could actually inspire Hitler with their own perverted dreams, then all hope had already been lost. I threw the file down in disgust and moved on, too angry to read any more of this extremist Nazi poison.

The next file was headed:

White Rose – The German Resistance Movement

It consisted of two sheets of paper. Page1 was handwritten in Polish but not by Dominik; the style, size and general appearance was totally different.

These lines I have learnt by heart and share with you because they were written by true German patriots, people I cared about: gifted university students encouraged by the exuberance and idealism of youth, driven by self-discipline and the need for personal freedom and a fervent belief in moral standards and ethics. They risked everything by practising and encouraging passive resistance when to do so was almost impossible in a climate of total control and suppression in Hitler's totalitarian and brutally xenophobic state. I hope that one day they will be recognised as true and selfless heroes. I regret that I was unable to do more to help them.

I quote from leaflet 1:

Nothing is so unworthy of a civilised nation as allowing itself to be 'governed' without opposition by an irresponsible clique that has yielded to base instinct. It is certain that today every honest German is ashamed of his government. Who among us has any conception of the dimensions of shame that will befall us and our children when one day the veil has fallen from our eyes and the most horrible of crimes – crimes that infinitely outdistance every human measure – reach the light of day?

If the German people are already so corrupted and spiritually crushed that they do not raise a hand, frivolously trusting in a questionable faith in lawful order in history; if they surrender man's highest principle, that which raises him above all God's other creatures, his free will; if they abandon the will to take decisive action and turn the wheel of history and thus subject it to their own rational decision; if they are so devoid of all individuality, have already gone so far along the road toward turning into a spiritless and cowardly mass – then, yes, they deserve their downfall.

I quote from leaflet 2:

We do not want to discuss here the question of the Jews, nor do we want in this leaflet to compose a defence or apology. No, only by way of example do we want to cite the fact that since the conquest of Poland 300,000 Jews have been murdered in this country in the most bestial way. Here we see the most frightful crime against human dignity, a crime that is unparalleled in the whole of history. For Jews, too, are human beings – no matter what position we take with respect to the Jewish question – and a crime of this dimension has been perpetrated against human beings.

Someone may say that the Jews deserved their fate. This assertion would be a monstrous impertinence; but let us assume that someone said this – what position has he then taken toward the fact that the entire Polish aristocratic youth is being annihilated? (May God grant that this program [sic] has not fully achieved its aim as yet!) All male offspring of the houses of the nobility between the ages of fifteen and twenty were transported to concentration camps in Germany and sentenced to forced labour, and the girls of this age group were sent to Norway, into the bordellos of the SS!

The second sheet of paper was a yellowing printed flyer that looked and felt like a genuine wartime printed document – and it was in German:

Leaflets of the Resistance Movement in Germany

A Call to All Germans!

The war is approaching its destined end. As in the year 1918, the German government is trying to focus attention exclusively on the growing threat of submarine warfare, while in the East the armies are constantly in retreat and invasion is imminent in the West. Mobilisation in the United States has not yet reached its climax, but already it exceeds anything that the world has ever seen. It has become a mathematical certainty that Hitler is leading the German people into the abyss. Hitler cannot win the war; he can only prolong it. The guilt of Hitler and his minions goes beyond all measure. Retribution comes closer and closer.

But what are the German people doing? They will not see and will not listen. Blindly they follow their seducers into ruin. Victory at any price! is inscribed on their banner. 'I will fight to the last man,' says Hitler – but in the meantime the war has already been lost.

Germans! Do you and your children want to suffer the same fate that befell the Jews? Do you want to be judged by the same standards as your seducers? Are we to be forever a nation which is hated and rejected by all mankind? No. Dissociate yourselves from National Socialist gangsterism. Prove by your deeds that you think otherwise. A new war of liberation is about to begin. The better part of the nation will fight on our side. Cast off the cloak of indifference you have wrapped around you. Make the decision before it is too late.

Do not believe the National Socialist propaganda which has driven the fear of Bolshevism into your bones. Do not believe that Germany's welfare is linked to the victory of National Socialism for good or ill. A criminal regime cannot achieve a German victory. Separate yourselves in time from everything connected with National Socialism. In the aftermath a terrible but just judgement will be meted out to those who stayed in hiding, who were cowardly and hesitant.

What can we learn from the outcome of this war – this war that never was a national war? The imperialist ideology of force, from whatever side it comes, must be shattered for all time. A one-sided Prussian militarism must never again be allowed to assume power. Only in large-scale cooperation among the nations of Europe can the ground be prepared for reconstruction. Centralised hegemony, such as the Prussian state has tried to exercise in Germany and in Europe, must be cut down at its inception. The Germany of the future must be a federal state. At this juncture only a sound federal system can imbue a weakened Europe with a new life. The workers must be liberated from their condition of downtrodden slavery under National Socialism. The illusory structure of autonomous national industry must disappear. Every nation and each man have a right to the goods of the whole world!

Freedom of speech, freedom of religion, the protection of individual citizens from the arbitrary will of criminal regimes of violence – these will be the bases of the New Europe.

Support the resistance, distribute the leaflets!

Once again I was ignorant of the whole topic . It all appeared genuine, just as the subject matter of all the other extraordinary items in the box, but I was completely unaware of any White Rose movement and was at a total loss as to how and why this fitted into Dominik's story. I made a few quick notes to remind me to research the facts later, when I might have more time and a clearer head.

The next sheet of paper was a short Polish memorandum dated 20th October 1944. The sender and intended recipient were only identified alphanumerically. I had no way of knowing whether these were personal initials or acronyms for posts or departments, but the content was highly intriguing:

MOST SECRET Operation Foxley
As per your instructions, three suitable candidates found. All match or exceed the specific minimum operational requirements. Two are fully trained snipers, already proficient with the weapon you suggest. Suitable simulations have now been successfully conducted and all three are to be held in isolation to await further confirmation. I stress that all are most suitable, but their files are attached for your final consideration and selection. Suggest that you arrange urgent joint training for the successful candidate and the British nominee over the next week. All will then be ready. Earlier today I personally returned my sealed and numbered copy of the personnel specification and operation overview to your staff officer and it was destroyed in my presence.

Although Operation Foxley seemed vaguely familiar to me, I just couldn't make the connection, no matter how hard I racked my brains. From the document it seemed to be a proposed joint British/Polish clandestine operation, that was already well past the preparation stage. Bearing in mind the date, the level of secrecy and the probable use of a sniper, the objective had to be a military or political assassination and at a high level. Still flummoxed, I Googled 'Operation Foxley' and there it was: pages and pages of information all about the SOE (Special Operations Executive) plan to kill Hitler. As I read the factual entries, trying to ignore the more fanciful alternative history groups and discussion boards, it became quite clear that such a plan had been devised in minute detail and considered at the highest level. It was even supported by Churchill, but it was never carried out because of controversy over whether it was actually a good idea to kill him. Perhaps we were better served by leaving him in command. Towards the end of 1944 he was already considered to be a poor strategist and his erratic behaviour and deteriorating mental state was having a detrimental effect on the morale and performance of his senior command and their ability to cohesively wage war. It was also thought by many, that if Hitler were assassinated, he might become a martyr to many Germans, making it even more difficult for the Allies to totally eradicate Nazism.

I sat back in my chair and gazed at the ceiling, wondering where all this was going. What did this small group of Poles that had so recently and so completely taken over my life have to do with this extraordinary plot? How did Stan or Dominik obtain these documents? And how many more surprises would I find, waiting in ambush along my long and meandering path and what would I find at the end of it?

As I pondered I automatically, almost subconsciously, reached out for the next file where I found an A4-sized plan and as I picked it up the subject and local connection astounded me. It was headed:

Prisoner of War Camp 23 - Le Marchant Barracks Devizes, Wilts. November 1944.

Attached to the plan was a group photograph of thirty-six soldiers in full khaki uniform bearing the caption, '5th Polish Guard Company'. What possible connection could there be to Dominik? I knew Le Marchant was the old regimental home of The Royal Wiltshire Yeomanry and the Wiltshire Regiment, but I had no idea that it had been a Prisoner of War camp. The plan showed a scaled and detailed layout of thirty Romney Huts (similar to Nissan huts, only much larger) in three rows of ten and a tented area, surrounded by a double barbed wire perimeter fence with watch towers at the corners. The plan also showed the position of nearby workshops, a canteen, storage facilities, pill boxes and machine gun emplacements. The whole complex covered a large area and certainly looked like a high security facility; the type used for the incarceration of hard-line Nazis, definitely not a run-of-the-mill transit or reception centre.

It was bordered to the north by the Horton village side road and a petrol dump; to the west and north-west by the main road; and to the south and east by the Kennet and Avon canal. I wondered if the photograph signified that Polish guards had been employed at the camp. It seemed most unlikely but there again, without the plan I would have doubted the existence of such an important wartime facility in our sleepy old Devizes town.

I compared the sketch plan to a modern street map and discovered that it had been positioned about half a mile north-east of the Le Marchant buildings on the east side of the main Devizes to Swindon road, opposite what had been the Waller and Prince Maurice Barracks. All that remains today is the imposing red-brick, four-storey, twin-towered, south-west facade of Le Marchant Barracks which has been preserved and converted into dwellings. All the rest, the entire military complex, has been redeveloped into a modern mixture of trading estates, offices, residential accommodation and service roads.

I then examined the next file: it contained a deed of title for a farmhouse, outbuildings and land near Luck in Poland dated March, 1922 and issued by a rather bureaucratic sounding Department of the Polish Government that I translated as the National Office for Repatriation and War Reparations. It had been issued to Dominik Dabrowski and contained a plan of the property and a notary seal. This was obviously the farm to which Jan and his family had been evacuated in 1939 and where they first met Dominik. I had finally found something that I fully understood and could put in context!

Pleased with my small but significant flash of clarity and understanding, I didn't want to risk muddying the waters again and so left the last few files for later on, and had a look at the rest of the objects in the box. They turned out to be everyday personal items such as, clothes, boots, shoes, a couple of blankets, two carved wooden walking sticks, a pocket watch, an old wristwatch and right at the bottom, a clean, neatly folded and full-size Polish flag. I found it strange that there were no recent effects or relatively modern personal or official papers, such as birth, marriage or death certificates, driving licences, bank books or statements or normal correspondence, such as letters, bills or receipts. It seemed that the box and its entire contents formed a time capsule for the first four decades of the twentieth century – and in 1944 the story and its epoch abruptly ended. But I sensed that all the answers to my questions could still be found lurking somewhere inside and then, as I wondered what had ultimately happened to Dominik, I realised it was already past the time to leave for Swindon again.

Along with the box and its contents, I took some Danish pastries with me to satisfy Stan's sweet tooth and after we had washed them down with mugs of hot coffee he said, "I take it you've seen Dominik's order from General Haller calling him to the urgent meeting?"

"Yes, I was wondering who the party of four could be and what he wanted them for?

"Well, this was the point when Dominik's greatest adventure really started, during the time that he worked directly for Haller and Pilsudski and I'm not exaggerating when I say it was to change the course of European history." He picked up his thick notebook from the table, rested it on his lap and then over the next two days, he told me exactly what he knew about their association.

Chapter Five

A Marriage of Convenience

Sokal, Polish Ukraine – 25th May 1919

Dominik arrived at Haller's temporary headquarters accompanied by Konrad, a somewhat reticent Aaron and Hannah Silberstein and Joanna Adamska. They were immediately taken to the general's quarters, and after formal introductions he wasted no time in getting down to business.

"Poland is at war. At the moment it's with the Ukraine, but we are already having daily skirmishes with the Red Army and they have invaded our sovereign territory in the north-east. Before too long we will have to stop their plans for spreading pernicious communism through Poland and then into Germany, and beyond. As I see it Soviet ambition is twofold: to attack from within by encouraging the workers to rise up throughout Europe and to use force of arms against what they see as a disorganised Poland and a defeated Germany. So once again Poland stands in the way of the rampaging bear and if we are to have any chance at all of a victory, then we must surprise and confound him."

Aaron immediately responded, "General, with all due respect I don't see what this has got to do with my sister and me. We have no quarrel with the Ukrainians or the Russians for that matter, and even if we did want to help you we've really got nothing to offer. Anyway, we're only here because we owe a personal debt to Dominik."

"Others may judge differently but all I ask is that you hear me out and then decide what you want to do. But you should remember that Russia is no friend to the Jews. Her history is riddled with persecution, banishments and open hostility and now that the heathen Bolsheviks hold sway, it will probably get worse. They murder anyone who is different, even if they are not opposed to their tyrannical dictatorship. They will kill their own supporters just to avenge a petty sense of grievance or an imagined slight or for personal advancement, or even at the merest rumour of weakness. If you want to see what they will do to the Jews tomorrow, then just look at what is happening in the countryside, right across Russia today."

Aaron, never deferential, interrupted, "We've been stuck inside Lwów for the last six months, until your general offensive finally drove the Ukrainians off last week. I have absolutely no idea what's going on down the road, never mind what's happening in Russia."

"I'm sorry for getting ahead of myself, but I'm sure you won't be surprised to hear that we have quite a good intelligence network. It is somewhat ironic that as we prepare for war, we are now reaping the benefits of decades of Polish emigration. When we were occupied the poor and the dissatisfied left in their droves. In consequence, as a nation again, we now have thousands of patriotic brothers and sisters returning to the fold and offering their services. Right across Europe and beyond we are developing a huge network of intelligence sources and Russia is no exception."

Hannah asked, "And what is it they tell you, that makes you think that we Jews are in danger?"

"Even as we sit here, they are burning dozens of villages and killing hundreds of their own people to intimidate them into submission and to discourage the starving from raiding food shipments that they've reserved for the army. Sooner or later they will turn their attention elsewhere and it won't take them long to focus on the eternal scapegoats. They'll find an excuse to purge your people and I think you know that too, because it fits their pattern of behaviour. You are different: you are religious and you are a threat to their perverted ideology. It's already happening in the Ukraine. All four sides involved in the fighting are desperate to gain control and they are all slaughtering your people in the process."

Aaron was not totally convinced, "You may be right but none of us can be certain. What do you really want from us?"

"Very well then, let's get down to it. In a minute I'll introduce you to a very important man whom I have seconded to my staff here in Sokal. His name is Lieutenant Jan Kowalewski and he's the person I hope you will all want to work with. I'll let him explain, but suffice it to say that I'm convinced that victory or defeat against the Soviets will depend on him and his team, far more so than the merits of the opposing forces or any other factor."

Jan wasn't much older than the members of Dominik's group, but at 27 he was a brilliant linguist, mathematician and cryptologist. He explained that he had already cracked General Denikin's White Russian codes and this had proved of immense strategic value because it provided a comprehensive picture of Red Army deployments. This had been particularly relevant across the south of Russia, showing the Poles how the Bolsheviks had been able to block Denikin's volunteer army on its final and ill-fated push to Moscow. Analysis of signal traffic had also revealed that the Ukraine was controlled by over 100 different and often opposing factions, which were incapable of presenting a united front to their enemies.

He also confirmed that he had broken the West Ukrainians' military secrets and ciphers. Encouraged by this early success Haller had authorised the establishment of a select and close-knit team of the most promising mathematics students from the universities of Lwów and Warsaw to work with Jan on the Russian codes. They were also tasked to provide encryption protocols that would ensure the safety and security of all Polish military signals. It was hoped that the science of secure communication –cryptography – would give them the very edge they needed if they were to take on and defeat the huge military resources of Lenin and Stalin's dictatorship. The Polish Radio-Intelligence and Cipher Section was founded, and it was Haller's baby.

Jan told Hannah Silberstein and Joanna Adamska that they had been selected on the basis of their respective university research programmes in advanced number theory, logarithms and probability and on the recommendation of their faculty professor. It was a bonus that Hannah also spoke French and English. Aaron was picked for his considerable analytical, language and literature skills and Dominik and Konrad were required to provide security and ensure full military support and cooperation for the team, both on site and in transit, wherever Haller sent them. This meant close liaison with the PMO and a mutual sharing of resources and intelligence assets.

The general summed up, "The five of you are in a unique position to help Poland and we haven't got much time. The Red Army has already seized Byelorussia (later Belarus) and Lithuania and they want the Ukraine. They have driven a coach and horses through the Treaty of Brest-Litovsk which they signed alongside Germany, Austro-Hungary and the rest, affirming the independence of those very territories. They are now in full breach of international law, but even so you can be absolutely sure that no one else will make a fuss or even condemn them, let alone come to our aid. So will you join us on this critical adventure and perhaps carve your names in history or should I send you all back home where you can simply sit and wait for Poland's fate to be decided by others?"

As soldiers, Dominik and Konrad would do whatever was asked of them and in the end it was Hannah who, in effect, made the decision for the rest. "I can't walk away from such an opportunity. Dominik has already risked his life for us and you, Sir have now shown that you and the Government are willing to put your full trust in us. That is all we Jews have ever wanted. You can count me in." Joanna and Aaron also agreed and early the next day they got down to work in their new unit. Over the next ten weeks they laboured day and night on the Russian codes, making good steady progress. In July, as hostilities escalated and their crucial work and increasingly impressive results were recognised by Pilsudski, they were transferred to his general staff in Warsaw. At the end of July Dominik was summoned to meet his commander-in-chief.

Dominik was in and out in a matter of a minute or two and he was initially impressed by Pilsudski's businesslike, no-nonsense approach. He was every inch the military commander and there were no niceties or preliminaries. It was all business and very much a one way 'listen very carefully but don't speak – I will make myself perfectly clear' exchange. He looked up from a mass of papers and maps and Dominik saw him in the flesh for the first time. The large, dark and drooping moustache with its razor-sharp points and his thick, upturned eyebrows almost sprang out from his pale face and emphasised his broad, furrowed forehead and deep-set, intense eyes. His vertical crew cut hair, greying at the edges and the tight, upturned collar of his grey Legion tunic framed and highlighted his features, adding the final touches of theatre to his impressive appearance. He smiled and said, "Firstly, I want you to fly into the Ukraine and take my personal dispatch to Symon Petliura. You will receive his response and then report back to me and only to me. I also expect an intelligence report from you on everything you see and hear and a full assessment of whether we should do business with him and critically, whether he can deliver on his promises." He paused for a moment and fixed Dominik with a cold, inquisitive stare, looking for any sign of surprise, doubt or discomfort.

Apparently satisfied, he pressed on, "Secondly, on the way back you are to report to Captain Merian Cooper who is preparing to receive more volunteers at Lwów. He is organising things there on behalf of Major Fauntleroy. He will be my Commanding Officer of the Kościuszko Squadron when it is fully established. I have decided to keep them in reserve for six months or so because I want them settled, fresh, eager and hungry for action when the time is right for our offensive. As you know, these volunteers will be a mixture of American, Canadian, French and English pilots. Some are already aces and all are vastly experienced and so I personally want to make sure that we treat them well. They will be needed to help us fight the Russians and in the meantime they can be used to train more of our own pilots. You are to deliver my compliments to the captain and the liaison officer and ensure that we satisfy all their operational needs and expectations. Major Buza will be your pilot and he will instruct you further on the detail and practicalities of the mission. He's waiting outside." He then handed over a leather dispatch case and said, "Thank you and good luck."

He immediately returned his attention to the papers on his desk and that was that. A somewhat surprised and bemused Dominik saluted and left the office reflecting on the marked contrast between his warm reception by General Haller and the curt interview and terse orders issued by Marshall Pilsudski.

As he left the huge building, passing through the seemingly endless 'corridors of power' and suites of offices, all crammed full with bustling staff officers, heads of departments and dozens of senior bureaucrats, he felt an increasing sense of the awesome responsibilities of power. He tried to imagine what the pressures on their leader must be like. Then he wondered if any man had the ability and tenacity to successfully steer this emerging, fragmented and endangered country through such tumultuous times. And in doing so, could he also deliver democracy, freedom and the hope of prosperity to ordinary Poles? He hardly knew the man, but he had been given a brief insight into his confidence, authority, determination and single-mindedness. So as he reached the street, he finally concluded that he was glad it was Pilsudski shouldering the burden. He just might succeed.

Major Buza introduced himself as Adam and explained that he was a member of the Blue Army Air Corps and that they were in the process of setting up an Air Training School for new pilots, now flocking in to join the Polish Air Force. They immediately drove out to the airfield and Adam briefed him on the way. Dominik had never flown before and was surprised by how flimsy and vulnerable the plane looked up close. Adam explained, "This is my personal aircraft and I try to look after her because she always holds my life within her whimsical wings. She's a British Bristol F2B Type 17 fighter or 'Biffs' for short and she's very good at what she does. She's the only one of her type we've got, but the government's trying to buy 100 of them and if we take the Bolsheviks on we're going to need every single one. Having been at the front, you must have seen them in action. They were tried and tested over the trenches against the finest planes and pilots the Germans could muster. They can even hold their own against the very best of the new single-seat fighters."

"I'm glad you have so much confidence in them, but if I'm honest, I would much prefer to keep both my feet firmly on the ground. I know it's every soldier's life just to fight and suffer but going up in that is one duty too far."

"You've no need to worry. You will absolutely love it. Flying is the second best thing a man can do and we're so used to each other that I don't have to do a lot really, just get her into the right place at the right time and she does the rest with her guns and bombs. I hope we won't need them this trip but just in case, I'll give you a full run down on the armaments."

Dominik was even more alarmed when he climbed into the observer's cockpit and saw the fragile-looking, bowl-like wicker seat, suspended by straps in the open turret so that it swivelled round with the guns. His anxiety was not eased when he practised the various firing positions and realised just how vulnerable he would be when using the weapons. His whole body from the waist up was sticking out above the sides of the cockpit. He started to imagine how he would be buffeted by the elements, deafened by the noise of the engine and the sound of the machine guns and stand out like a range marker, attracting fire from every enemy plane within miles. As if that wasn't bad enough, his stomach turned when he saw the dual controls. Unusually, the control column was duplicated inside the observer's cockpit, providing elevator control and there were also two handgrips attached to the rudder cables. Adam eased his apprehension slightly when he told him, "Make sure you keep your hands off the controls. Always leave the flying to me!"

Dominik was only too happy to concur and his confidence started to return when he showed Adam that he was already familiar with both weapons: the forward-firing 303 Vickers machine gun on the upper fuselage and the rear-facing, twin 303 Lewis guns mounted in the observer's cockpit. And so the familiarisation with the weapons, their special mountings and the cockpit drills didn't take long, although he felt rather fraudulent and self-conscious wearing the regulation fur coat, leather helmet and goggles. They were airborne within the hour, heading for their first of two refuelling stops.

As they flew on and Dominik gradually acclimatised to the sensations of flying, he considered what Adam had told him during the briefing. Petliura had, until recently, been in the ascendancy as he rallied national patriotism in the east Ukraine and drove north and west, but things were now deteriorating rapidly. He had simultaneously battled against the Bolsheviks, Denikin's White Russians and incursions by the Romanians. Additionally, following the relief of Lwów, the Poles had already crushed Yevhen Petrushevych's attempt to create a West Ukrainian People's Republic and were currently threatening his western territories. To make matters worse, with Denikin's near defeat, the Red Army had been freed up to concentrate on the subjugation of the Ukraine. They were already gaining the upper hand and Petliura's forces were being driven further south and west. They were now in danger of being overrun. His problems were also exacerbated by the atrocities being perpetrated by the various invaders as well as his own troops, against the large Jewish and peasant populations.

He was in urgent need of an ally and Pilsudski was keen to internationally define and secure Poland's eastern borders by the establishment of a Polish-led federation of autonomous buffer states. Now he saw a golden opportunity to start that whole process in the Ukraine. He was ready to recognise Petliura as the legitimate head of the Ukrainian Peoples' Republic and form an alliance, providing military aid to expel the Bolshevik regime from the Ukraine. He was offering much, but he also wanted a great deal in return. The price of Poland's help would be the full recognition of Poland's right to Galicia and agreement to a border on the River Zbruch, but would Petliura countenance such a deal with his country's old adversary? Dominik wondered if there was anything at all that he could possibly do or say to positively influence the leader and so help to secure his assent: and would he get such an opportunity?

In bright sunshine, Adam started his descent towards the nominated airfield in Eastern Podolia in the Ukraine. The strip was surrounded by forest, but there was more than ample room to land and he could see half a dozen aircraft parked at the eastern end, near a group of timber buildings. His apprehension was first raised when he saw no sign of human activity. There was no one servicing the planes, no sentries, no welcoming party, no movement outside the buildings and no smoke from cooking fires. He decided to do a flypast before committing to a landing. He shouted to Dominik to watch the treeline before he swooped right down causing the 275 horse power, liquid-cooled Rolls-Royce engine to roar and vibrate as he poured on the revs. The parked planes were mostly an assortment of pre-war gunbusses and scouts that looked as if they had been cannibalised for spare parts; two had no engines and all showed considerable signs of recent battle damage. Hundreds of bullet holes had stitched a network of patterns, back and forth across the airframes with chunks of wood and fabric torn clean away. The nearby wreckage and confetti sparkle of shell cases indicated that they had been attacked in situ on the ground.

They saw nothing on the first pass but when they turned, a detachment of cavalry emerged from the trees to the north, galloping towards the centre of the field. As the plane approached to investigate and identify, a machine gun opened fire from the forest edge behind the horsemen, quickly followed by another and then another. Several rounds passed clean through the ends of both left wings but fortunately they missed the four critical struts and their bracing wires. Adam banked to avoid the deadly fire and then dived down, levelling off at about 100 feet before he turned straight towards the machine gun crews. The noise was too loud to make himself heard and so he indicated to Dominik to take on the cavalry who had now stopped and were also firing at them. Adam adjusted the trim so that the nose was in direct line with his target and only then did he fire. Five sustained bursts from the synchronised Vickers machine gun tore up the ground and scythed through the trees. It spewed out 500 rounds per minute, directly through the arc of the propeller. Using this basic 'point and shoot' principle, the pilot could optimise the aircraft's manoeuvrability and increase the accuracy of the weapon.

Dominik also opened fire when he heard the staccato hammer of the Vickers. He had used a Lewis light machine gun on the ground many times, but he was surprised at how well it performed in the air. The Scarff ring mounting took most of the weight and the gun could be swung down on the rail, making the reloading of the circular, self-contained 97-round magazines a fairly easy and quick task. They flashed across the treeline and Adam circled, bringing the plane across the field obliquely to completely change their angle of attack. He accelerated to his top speed of 115 mph, lined the aircraft up and poured fire down on the enemy, whoever they were. Dominik again raked his weapon back and forth across the fifteen or twenty, now dismounted soldiers until none were left standing and the surviving horses bolted into the forest.

He stopped firing and again he could hear the unmistakable and reassuring clatter of the Vickers firing off at the front. When it stopped, the deafening noise was replaced by the distinctive rattle of the machine guns on the ground. He was not too surprised that some of the enemy were still active. When in the trenches he had seen how indiscriminate and unpredictable air attacks on ground troops could be. More often than not they were more frightening than effective. Adam changed tactics, lined up the aircraft again, steadied himself in the forward cockpit and then released the planes bomb load – two 112 pounders. Suddenly a line of holes appeared across the tail and the plane lurched violently to the left. Dominik was thrown down into his seat and lost his grip on the Lewis gun. As he struggled to regain his balance there was a bright flash immediately followed by another and then two loud explosions on the ground and the plane was tossed and buffeted as the shock wave hit them. This was a totally new and frightening experience and he felt sure that after so much punishment the plane was about to plummet earthwards and so he gripped the gun mount as tight as he could and closed his eyes to await his fate.

He felt the plane level off again and then climb and so, more in hope than expectation, he risked opening one eye. He was mightily relieved to see the ground whistling by some 200 feet below and he turned and slapped Adam on the shoulder to congratulate him for saving them both. As he did so, he saw another group of cavalrymen lined up by the trees on the opposite side of the field. Adam had already recognised the light blue and yellow Ukrainian colours on their pennants and their leader was looking up, waving a large white flag from side to side. Adam waggled the plane's wings in acknowledgment and once the bodies had been removed from the centre of the field, they landed safely.

During the introductions they were greeted most enthusiastically, being hugged and kissed on both cheeks by a rotund, jovial and beaming General Olexander Kotzin (Sector Military Commander) who then addressed them through his interpreter.

"Welcome to the Ukrainian National Republic. I'm sorry that the Bolshevik welcoming party got here before us, but I must say that I was most impressed with the efficient way you disposed of them. I think that the aeroplane will prove to be the ultimate weapon of the future."

While making their way to the waiting transport the General introduced his companion, Captain Maxim Munczak, the personal aide and intelligence adviser to Symon Petliura. He gave them a quick and precise situation report.

"I will not try to mislead you. I'm afraid our whole country is in a bit of a mess, similar I suspect to the position Poland found itself in last year. There are no clear or defined front lines between our enemies and the dozens of Ukrainian splinter groups that are now engaged in the battle. Most of our assorted armies, particularly the anarchists, have no mutual or clear objectives other than to carve out their own fiefdoms and to rob and destroy along the way. To make matters worse, the general population in the countryside has little or no interest in any uprising or even the prospect of independence. They're far too occupied slaving away on their precious plots of land, trying to eke out enough sustenance to feed their own families and see the winter out."

Adam replied, "Well, I don't really see much of a comparison. Our people have thought of little else for decades, from peasant to prince – Polish independence is everything."

"Of course, many of us also want our own country and are willing die in the effort, but there is also a great deal of lethargy in the towns and villages where a large proportion of the people don't even think in national terms. Their small neighbourhood is their whole world. Nevertheless, following a few key alliances with other leaders, Symon has some military momentum and he has managed to retain what popular support there is. It's fair to say that we are now the only organisation left with sufficient military strength and political collaboration to deliver on our promises, but you must discover that for yourself."

After a thirty-minute delay they were able to leave, the general explaining that the woods had been thoroughly swept by his men and there was no further sign of the enemy. He suspected that their presence had been purely coincidental, a small Red Army foraging and raiding party looking for food and supplies or targets of opportunity. He posted a substantial guard detail to secure the area and watch over the plane. He also arranged for the bullet holes to be patched up and the plane to be refuelled. He then escorted the Poles to Petliura's Headquarters, some ten miles away.

Whilst he waited to be summoned, Dominik spent a couple of hours being introduced to and chatting informally with a dozen or so of Petliura's senior command and staff officers and then his civilian administrators and advisers. All the while he was gradually building up a comprehensive picture of the man, his country and his organisation, sufficient to make an initial and objective assessment of their strengths and weaknesses. Then Petliura met him alone and his welcome was a great deal cooler than that given by his general: polite and businesslike but lacking any initial interest in his guest's welfare, personal history or current itinerary. He read Pilsudski's letter without comment, sat back in his chair for a moment or two, looked the Pole over and said, "My people ask me, time and time again, how can I possibly contemplate dealing with you Poles when you are still at war with our brother Ukrainians in Galicia and our history with you has all too often been one of hate, confrontation, war and occupation?"

Dominik started to respond but the Ukrainian cut in, "The question to you was rhetorical, but I'll now answer it for you in exactly the same way that I have truly answered it a hundred times before because, being a parable, its veracity is never eroded by repetition – Papa, Papa! Look, a devil is trying to get into our house!' cried a terrified boy. To this his father replied calmly, better a devil than a Muscovite! – So now you see that I have no choice. If I can't find a powerful ally soon we will lose our fight with the Bolsheviks and our fledgling republic will once again be swallowed up and forgotten. I cannot let that happen."

This time Dominik was not interrupted, "You're right, of course, and in some ways we are not so different: both our lands are bordered by powerful and needy neighbours who seek to protect themselves from each other by the control, possession and ultimately the absorption of what they consider to be expendable, satellite and buffer states. So our shared weakness, I would suggest, is mainly geographical, not ideological and we are always more vulnerable and easy prey to the leviathans when we are isolated. As for our war with what I would call the Polish Ukrainians, that is virtually over. They are defeated and can no longer be considered as a barrier to any alliance between our two nations."

"If I deal with Warsaw, many of my people, perhaps even the majority will say I have betrayed them, sacrificed Ukrainian sovereignty on the altar of my own ego. Some will even see it as treason."

"That may or may not turn out to be true, but at the moment it's mere conjecture and future events on the ground may well prove to be of far greater importance in shaping opinion and building support for you. Nevertheless, as I see it the issues are simple, pressing and cannot be avoided by either of us. This malicious revival of Russian power and expansionism which you've seen up close, directly threatens to destroy the whole of the Ukraine and then Poland's turn will come. So, you are left with yet another truism: 'my enemy's enemy is my friend.' Only if we combine our forces, can we hope to avoid occupation or worse. We must collaborate. There is no other choice."

The Ukrainian thought for a moment and then suddenly stood up and offered his hand, "That's one way of looking at it and I thank you for your thoughts. I'll now write my reply to your commander-in-chief and you can take it back with you. Please tell him that before I make my final decision, I wish to look him in the eye and I will come to Poland to do it. You and Captain Munczak can make all the necessary arrangements when the time is right. I hope you have a safe trip back home and by the way, when you stop at Lwów I would like you to call on Adam Berkowicz at the University Press." He then handed Dominik a small locked and sealed dispatch case, "Give him this: it explains my current predicament, my particular interest in you and your government and my authority for him to fully brief you. I am confident that he will provide you with a great deal of useful background information which may even help with your analysis when you come to formulate your assessment report and make the critical recommendations for which you have undoubtedly been tasked."

Dominik shook his hand, "Sir, you are very well informed. I will certainly do as you ask and get back in touch with Captain Munczak as soon as I can. I'm sure you're aware that as a messenger, I personally have no say whatsoever in my country's foreign policy or its international relations, but I do hope we can work together again in the future."

The next morning they took off and headed for Lwów. The weather was fine, but there was a great deal of heavy, towering, dark cloud and although it blew through fairly quickly, it periodically reduced their all-round visibility. They were making good time as they followed the South Bug River westwards back towards home, cruising along at about 7,000 feet with the advantage of a stiff tailwind. They ran into trouble when they approached the major road and rail junction at the centre of the old Polish fortress and garrison town of Ploskirow. Adam spotted the enemy emerging from cloud and closing in from the north-east at a height of about 10,000 feet. They would converge in a matter of minutes and there was no way that the Bristol fighter could now avoid contact. The enemy were too close and they had the considerable advantage of height. Adam identified the aircraft as a German-made Albatross D5, a fighter, escorted by a French Nieuport 17 fighter/scout: both single-seaters and probably old Czarist machines but now in the hands of the Bolsheviks.

Polish and Red Army forces had been involved in numerous skirmishes and a number of significant clashes inside the Ukraine and all along their mutual borders for months, and they were de facto at war. Adam knew that the approaching pilots would be delighted to find a lone Polish aircraft so far east and would not hesitate to attack and destroy such an unexpected trophy. Both enemy planes were lethally armed and the pilots could prove to be Great War veterans and therefore, very worthy opponents. The Albatross had two 7.92 synchronised Spandau light machine guns, each capable of firing 500 rounds per minute. The Nieuport had just a single standard Lewis machine-gun firing from the top wing above the arc of the propeller, but it had still managed to put an end to the 'Fokker scourge' above the trenches in 1916.

Both aircraft were more manoeuvrable than the conventional biplanes because of the lighter sesquiplane design with the wings being fitted closer together and the lower, much smaller wing being reduced to less than half the area of the upper. However, this nimbleness was also the source of its one major weakness as the narrow bottom wing was prone to twist and bend under stress.

Adam knew he would need to exploit this Achilles' heel and so he decided to destroy the heavily armed, more advanced Albatross first and then perhaps the Nieuport would run for home and leave them in peace. He was also concerned about the whereabouts of enemy ground forces because, unlike the Poles, the Russian pilots rarely flew far from ground support and he had heard that Red Army commanders had recently threatened to crucify any Polish fliers taken prisoner and then feed them to the wolves.

He tried to unnerve them, and also limit their considerable advantage of height and so, instead of diving down to rooftop level as they might expect, he started to climb steeply, straight towards them. He checked that Dominik was alert and at his guns and then poured on the power and the distance between the planes closed rapidly. A minute or two later the Albatross broke away first and dived to intercept. Once Adam was sure of the Russian's committed angle of descent, he turned on his right wing and nose-dived, descending almost vertically in an attempt to pass underneath and then inside the Russian. The Nieuport pilot had not yet committed himself to the fight but maintained his altitude and flew on overhead, watching the engagement unfolding below and waiting for the optimum opportunity to strike.

Adam, satisfied that the only direct threat for the moment at least, was from the Albatross, straightened his dive even further, plummeting earthwards like an arrow. Dominik was now as white as sheet and feeling dizzy and faint from the nausea brought on by the plane's sudden and violent acrobatics. He was left hanging on to the gun mounting, screaming in exasperation and anger, frantically trying to clear his head of the debilitating fog and shake off the incapacity of his vomiting and wretchedness. The Albatross pilot turned tightly to follow Adam down and he fired several bursts that passed well wide of the Pole's plane. Adam was encouraged by the Russian pilot's eagerness and pressed on, determined to level off only at the last possible minute. As the ground rushed towards them at an alarming rate and every instinct and all his experience was screaming at him to pull up, he had to use all his considerable willpower to force himself to wait that extra, precious second or two, just long enough to give his plan sufficient time to work. Using all his strength, and soaking wet with sweat from the physical and mental exertion, Adam managed to level off only feet from the chimney stacks and then he started a tight turn, desperately looking up, searching the sky for the Russian he knew must be somewhere above and behind him. He was much lower than Adam had expected, but he was disappointed to see that the Russian was starting to level off and it looked as if he would have just enough altitude left to safely complete the manoeuvre. He would then renew his attack.

In the Albatross cockpit the pilot suddenly found himself panicking. Helpless and ashamed of his own failure, he fought with the now unresponsive controls in a desperate and final attempt to recover the plane into level flight. Too late: he realised that the speed and angle of his dive had exerted such enormous force and pressure on the comparatively fragile lower wing that it had twisted and warped. As he pulled back hard on the stick, being only a matter of a few seconds from safety and another chance to finish off the enemy, the extra strain was just too much for the supporting, and now weakened, 'V' strut. It sheared right off and the wing collapsed. Belatedly he remembered his instructor's oft-repeated words, "If you underestimate your enemy, you will surely die." On impact the plane exploded within its own huge crater and disintegrated in a ball of flame.

Adam breathed a sigh of relief as he watched the crash, but he now had no idea of the Nieuport's whereabouts and so he turned round to see if Dominik could help, only to find him frantically pointing towards it, as it rushed down at them from above and behind. Dominik, having now evacuated his entire stomach contents and seeing the imminent danger, had recovered enough composure to fire the guns, but his first burst was way too high and off to port and as he tried to correct his line, the Nieuport started to return fire. Adam took evasive action, weaving left and right and then climbing, before breaking off into another dive, but the Nieuport stuck with him like a limpet and the turbulent movement caused Dominik to fire even more erratically. A line of machine gun bullets suddenly peppered their right wing and so Adam decided that now, while he still had a fully functioning aircraft, was the time to really test the Russian. His enemy was good, certainly no novice and Adam knew that unless he could turn the tables, it was only a matter of time before the Russian inflicted fatal damage. He pulled up into a very high and tight Immelmann turn and the Russian started to follow. Dominik was abruptly suspended upside down in his safety harness and as the straps dug painfully into his shoulders, he gritted his teeth and screamed obscenities at the Russian, willing him to close up and praying that Adam would not throw the aircraft around the sky again. All he needed was to stop throwing up and have a few seconds of consistent flight and then he would be confident that his Lewis guns could finish the job.

Try as he might, the Russian could not maintain such a tight curve as they both continued to climb rapidly and slowly but inexorably he started to slip away. This brought his rear fuselage and tail into Dominik's view as the Bristol approached stalling point, almost at the zenith of its ascent. Just before Adam applied full rudder to yaw the Bristol around to face down, ready for a high speed dive, Dominik sensed his moment. He slid the machine guns along the Scarff mounting, lined them up on the receding Russian plane and then fired continuously, dipping the weapons to follow his target along the barrels until both drums were completely empty and then the Bristol rolled over for the dive, but he continued to watch the Russian plane. At first nothing seemed to happen but then, seemingly in slow motion, pieces of the tail started to fall off and the left lower wing slowly broke away from the fuselage. For a second or two it appeared to hang by a single thread of over-stretched stay wire, languidly dragging the doomed plane over onto its side and then downwards, breaking up completely and falling back to earth, like pieces of a gigantic jigsaw.

Adam searched the sky for any sign of further aircraft and only when he was satisfied that they were on their own did he bring his plane back down to 5,000 feet and continue on in level flight towards Lwów. Then Dominik noticed the port-side leak in the fuel tank and alarmed at the possibility of sudden engine failure, he immediately pointed it out to Adam. Safety dictated that he should land and try to plug the bullet hole, but he was reluctant to take the risk of dropping in on the enemy and so he reduced air speed and shouted at Dominik. "Climb out on the wing and see if you can staunch the leak. I'll keep her nice and level. It's only about another 20 minutes back to Lwów. You won't be in any danger as long as you always keep a good grip on the struts or stays with one hand. You can sit or kneel on the wing if you like. If you don't manage to put it right I'll look for somewhere to land."

Dominik was speechless. He thought it was bad enough hanging upside down while being shot at. Surely it would now be stupid to heedlessly abandon the safety harness and climb out of the cockpit onto the wings but what else could he do? As he slid out from behind the lee of the pilot onto the lower wing and grasped the first strut, the sudden force of the buffeting wind swung his legs around and off the back of the rear-sloping surface. He had to use all his upper-body strength to hang on, and then slowly pull his legs back up, twisting them underneath his body to adopt a kneeling position. He then tried in vain to plug the hole, firstly with a piece of cloth from his pocket and then, after several other equally futile attempts with his gloves and scarf, he found that the farcical remedy of using his thumbs worked best, reducing the flow to that of a dripping tap. As he periodically changed hands he tried to find a more comfortable position, but his options were severely limited by the engine exhaust which ran along the fuselage between the double wing, in line with his head. If he got too close he would be severely burned and so he had to endure the arm-numbing exertion as he stretched, strained and twisted to maintain pressure on the leak whilst simultaneously trying to keep his distance from the exhaust pipe. He was taking the full torsional weight of his upper body and the pounding force of the slipstream on one arm and shoulder and the pressure and pain increased by the second.

When his arm started to go numb and he could see it trembling with the effort he knew he had to act or he would lose his grip and fall to his death. With desperation came an idea. He removed his thumb from the leak, took his dagger from his pocket and with all the force he could muster in such a cramped position, he stabbed it through the fabric and into the main wing spar. He pulled his knees up further and then wedged one foot in front of it. Sticking up like a giant nail it took much of his weight and he was able to use it to pivot and turn in order to keep a constant pressure on the leak. Although he was now comparatively far more comfortable he was nevertheless, extremely relieved when they finally landed safely. Even then the rutted field, his precarious physical position and the resulting jarring and scorching experience left him covered in bumps, burns and bruises. Adam couldn't help laughing when he saw his discomfort and the strange sight of a foot-long ceremonial dagger sticking up out of the wing. As he put his arm around Dominik's shoulder he said, "I told you she would keep us safe. Even shot up like this she's still a beautiful thing and then you repay her for her protection and service by stabbing her in the back! You'd better get your knife out and apologise or she might take it out on you next time." A joke or not Dominik thought it was wise to do as he was asked, but he was definitely not looking forward to his next flight.

Chapter Six

THE KONARMIA

Swindon – 8th November 2009

Stan checked his notes and then took up the story once more.

"Just as he had been instructed, Dominik saw the Air Force commanders in Lwów. He arranged for the transfer and reception of the new foreign recruits to the Kościuszko Squadron which was to support the Poles in the event of an offensive into the Ukraine against Russia. He also prepared a full political and military written assessment report for Pilsudski on Petliura, covering his international influence, credibility, popular support and leadership potential within the Ukraine. It wasn't very encouraging."

I remembered the Berkowicz file. "Did he have anything to do with the pogroms against the Jews? I never read the whole file from the box but what I saw looked pretty damning. After all, it happened on his watch and it wasn't just an isolated incident or two. It had the feel of a concerted and planned campaign based on the sort of hatred and prejudice that the Nazis later thrived on."

"People are still arguing over it. There's certainly no evidence to show any personal anti-Jewish behaviour on his part or to prove or even suggest that he ordered or sanctioned the killings. He wasn't present at any of the massacres. He also publicly condemned them and had one of the main ringleaders, Semysenko, executed by firing squad. On the other hand some academics and historians claim that Petliura, as head of state, didn't do nearly enough to stop the persecution and massacres and his inaction was then interpreted by the military as tacit approval to carry on. This reinforced the anti-Semitic feeling within the general population, even encouraging further attacks."

"There were certainly dozens of almost identical massacres and the poor victims and their communities must have felt as if they had been totally abandoned by the state and their leaders. As far as I know, no one ever did come to their aid, or did they?"

"No, in fact many of the atrocities were committed by the forces directly under Petliura's command and it's even been suggested that he was afraid to be seen to punish too many officers for fear of losing his military support."

I tried to tie Stan down, "You're originally from that part of the world so what do you think?"

"Well, I don't believe that he can be totally absolved from blame and even his most ardent supporters must have seen that the buck would eventually land on his desk. But there has also been a long-standing Soviet black propaganda campaign to ruin his reputation. When he was assassinated in Paris, the trial that followed brought all these issues right out into the open."

I didn't know he'd been murdered, "What happened?"

Stan explained that on the afternoon of 25th May 1926 Petliura was walking along the Rue Racine when he was approached by Sholom Schwartzbard. He was a thirty-nine-year-old Ukrainian Jew who shot him five times and as his victim lay on the ground, he fired two more rounds into his body. The assassin then calmly waited at the scene of the crime until he was arrested. It emerged that he had lost fifteen members of his family, including his parents, in the pogroms of 1919 and he held Petliura personally responsible. He openly admitted the killing and boasted that he was proud of what he had done. The trial at the court of Assizes in Paris was sensational, attracting enormous press and public interest within France and far beyond. The mass hysteria centred on Schwartzbard's line of defence. His leading lawyer was Henri

Torres, a renowned French defence counsel. He had previously represented high-profile anarchist cases and significantly, as it turned out, also acted for the Soviet consulate in France. Torres cleverly managed to turn the tables on the prosecution and effectively put Petliura and the pogroms on trial instead of his client. He claimed the accused 'was seeking revenge for the victims of the mass slaughter. Such a vile and horrendous crime that his actions were not only understandable but totally justified: a crime-of-passion.'

In turn, the prosecution attempted to show that Petliura was not responsible for the pogroms and that Schwartzbard was a Soviet agent. They alleged that he was acting on their orders to liquidate an enemy of the USSR and they called many witnesses to support their contention. The jury was having none of it and amid tense excitement and an absence of only 35 minutes, the jury acquitted him. In addition to setting the prisoner free, the court ordered Petliura's family to pay the costs of the trial. Then, in the view of his many supporters, it added insult to injury by awarding token damages of one franc each to his widow and his brother. Many of the country's most respected civic leaders, entertainers and intellectuals rallied en masse to the Schwartzbard cause, publicly endorsing the verdict and the apparent justice of his deed. In contrast many others, including conservatives and hard-liners, saw the verdict as a total travesty of justice that mocked constitutional law and ridiculed the integrity and decorum of the French courts.

We stopped for a while and I made us both a cup of tea and when I sat down again Stan immediately returned to the subject of the war with Russia.

"Well, Dominik took the package to Adam Berkowicz in Lwów but somewhat surprisingly, considering Petliura had virtually put him forward as a character reference, he gave a far from resounding endorsement of the Ukrainian leader's abilities."

"Why was that?"

"He liked him as a friend and they regularly met and corresponded as mutual scholars, writers, editors and journalists. Nevertheless, he felt that he just didn't have anywhere near enough popular or political clout to unite a very factious country, particularly one in the throes of an all-out war. But on the positive side, he was sure that he wasn't an anti-Semite, either openly or secretly. Perhaps it's this very point that better explains why Petliura asked Dominik to see the professor in the first place. He must have been desperately keen to have his personal endorsement at a time when others were already accusing him of being complicit in the murder of his Jewish citizens."

"I suppose that Dominik reflected these less than enthusiastic sentiments in the report he gave to Pilsudski."

"Yes, and the C-in-C wasn't surprised to see such a generally negative assessment either, but he was impressed with the mountain of wide-ranging evidence that Dominik had been able to gather together to support his case, especially in such a short time frame. Anyway, the tenor of his arguments validated Pilsudski's own initial reluctance to form an alliance with the man whom he saw above all else as a military failure. In turn he had been deposed by the Germans, defeated by the Ukrainian communists and devastated by Denikin's army. In the civil war he had been defeated and pushed back time and time again and to make matters worse, he then fled his own country seeking the protection of Poland."

"If he was so convinced that he'd always failed to meet these military and political challenges, then why on earth did he do a deal anyway?"

"Because it gave him everything he wanted, just at the time when he needed it the most, and quite frankly there were no other options left. At a stroke of the pen the agreement secured his southern flank, gave him a degree of international legitimacy, put tens of thousands of Ukrainian troops at his disposal and provided a convenient and compliant ally to whom he could hand over a Bolshevik-free Ukraine. He didn't want his troops seen as occupiers but as liberators and he certainly didn't want them tied up or bogged down in the Ukraine. He also had no intention of joining the western powers in their interventions in the Russian civil war or in trying to occupy Russia. His hand was finally forced when the team at the Radio-Intelligence and Cipher Section broke the Russian military codes."

"So Jan Kowalewski and his people achieved exactly what General Haller had set them up for."

"They most certainly did and they discovered that the Bolsheviks were planning an invasion of Poland by striking across the border just north of Minsk. So the alliance provided a golden and timely opportunity to strike first and gain the initiative in the Ukraine, an area where the Red Army was relatively unprepared. They hoped to avoid the Russian troops massing for their own offensive further north and then later, if they did commit themselves to battle, the Poles could strike northwards and outflank them."

"Surely he was taking a huge risk. Did he really believe he could defeat the Red Army?"

"Well, he was convinced that it could only be done by a daring, resolute and limited campaign. He definitely had to avoid a war of attrition which he couldn't possibly win. He hoped to use speed and flexibility to make the initial breakthrough. Then, by organising the various Ukrainian factions to attack their supply lines and disrupt any build-up for a counter-attack, he could keep the Russians on the back foot."

I asked, "Did he have an exit strategy, just in case it all went pear-shaped?"

"Sort of, but I'm sure he wouldn't have described it like that or thought of it in those terms. You see, he had developed a realistic plan to surround and destroy all the enemy forces west of Kiev. He believed that if he could inflict an early, decisive and painful defeat, then the Bolsheviks, who were still in the throes of their own revolution, would have to abandon their own plans to invade Poland and negotiate. Otherwise they would be left facing so many hostile threats and spread so thinly on the ground that they risked being overrun. Poland could then secure her independence and her borders."

"So timing and secrecy were his main priorities."

"Yes, that's it exactly. He was convinced that surprise was the only key that would unlock the Golden Gates of Kiev and that's why he left it right up to the last minute. In fact, he gave the order to prepare for the offensive on the 17th April 1920 but didn't sign the agreement with Petliura until the 21st so that Polish forces were ready to march before the ink was even dry. Command of Ukrainian forces was handed to the Poles on 24th and Pilsudski sprang his assault on the 25th."

Stan explained that the Poles had a real stroke of luck on the eve of battle when mutiny broke out in the three Red Army Galician Brigades. Rather than fight their fellow countrymen who now faced them in the Polish lines, they turned on their Russian comrades. One whole brigade went over to the Poles en masse and the others managed to disrupt the local Bolshevik army to such an extent that it stood little or no chance of conducting a successful defence. The unrest also sparked off a series of major partisan attacks on the Russians' supply and communication lines and these irregulars were not just a band or two of thugs and deserters operating independently but whole armies of battle-hardened radicals and anarchists. Some estimates suggest that they numbered some 65,000 in total and had more manpower deployed on the front than the Poles and the Russians put together.

The Poles rushed across 50 miles of the Ukraine in the first day and they achieved total surprise, leaving the forward, mutiny-weakened Russian defensive formations badly mauled, scattered and demoralised. Paradoxically, the Bolsheviks' unpreparedness worked to their own advantage because it triggered an immediate general retreat and with the help of a few desperate rearguard actions, the main force managed to escape before the Poles could encircle them. Had they been ready and like a few of their forward units, stayed and fought then they too would have been overrun by the force and momentum of the numerically superior and battle-ready Polish motorised columns. The Russian high command, although surprised and embarrassed at the sudden collapse and chaos, felt that they had conceded little other than territory. They decided to deliberately extend their retreat in order to conserve their assets, regroup and draw the Poles in, whilst they prepared for a decisive counter-attack. They evacuated Kiev on May 6th and the Polish forces marched in the following day.

I said, "I remember my father telling me that as a young schoolboy he was shown photographs of Polish troops marching in victory inside Kiev. The teacher talked of the incredible wave of national pride and euphoria that swept across the young Poland when Pilsudski stood there on parade as a hero and liberator and then handed the capital city back to Petliura and his people."

"That's true, but the celebrations didn't last long though because the Russians soon got the upper hand and there was some bitter hand-to-hand fighting as the Poles were forced on to the defensive." He settled back in his chair, studied his notebook for a couple of minutes and then over the next hour or so, he told me exactly what had happened...

On 24th May 1920, Polish forces were engaged for the first time by Semyon Budionny's famous Konarmia, the 1st Cavalry Army, consisting mostly of Cossacks. During the next two weeks they mounted continuous attacks until they eventually broke through. The Soviet commander then exploited the breach by pushing additional resources forward and deploying mobile cavalry units to disrupt the Polish rearguard. By 10th June the Poles were in full retreat along the entire front, and on 13th June, Petliura's Ukrainian troops abandoned Kiev to the Red Army. With momentum now on their side and their left flank secure, the Russians then prepared for their invasion and launched a massive attack along their whole front. Over the next two months four Soviet armies pushed towards Warsaw on their northern and western fronts, and two more across the Ukraine towards Lublin and Lwów, driving the Poles back at an alarming rate.

It became clear that the Bolsheviks intended to conquer their neighbour and thereafter, as their propaganda described, 'onward to Berlin, over the corpse of Poland!' They were very serious about regime change across the whole of Western Europe. They hoped to provoke a communist revolution in Germany and beyond, and they were not without popular working-class support. In July Lloyd George, pressured by Winston Churchill and others, had announced that he would send huge quantities of surplus military supplies to Poland, but the Trade Unions objected to any support for capitalist Poland and in protest threatened a general strike.

The Prime Minister (who had always only been lukewarm to the idea of supporting Poland because such a stance threatened his planned trade deals with Russia) backed down and similar actions and blockades by workers in Austria, Germany and other European countries caused severe delays in the shipment of their munitions and aid and prevented supplies leaving their ports or crossing their frontiers. Poland's allies were very few but France sent a 400-strong advisory group of military personnel including the future president, Charles de Gaulle. Britain sent a much smaller delegation and Hungary did eventually manage to deliver arms and ammunition.

On 6th August, with Warsaw in grave danger of falling and Poland facing defeat, Pilsudski risked everything by ordering the wholesale regrouping of all Polish assets in order to simultaneously defend the capital and also prepare for a massive double counter-strike. He was not interested in just driving the enemy back from the capital and then looking for ceasefire terms as advocated by a jittery international community; he was intent on complete victory. His codebreakers had identified a weakly defended enemy corridor between Deblin and Lublin. This gap was to some extent inevitable, as two advancing fronts of the Russian offensive were driven apart by having to respectively negotiate north and south of the geographical wedge formed by the vast Pripet (Pripyat) marshlands. Although the Soviets had recognised this potential problem, the force they sent to plug the gap (the Mozyr Group) proved to be too small and too thinly spread.

Pilsudski intended to launch an assault group (comprising the most experienced and battle-hardened units drawn from across the country but primarily from the southern front) through this gap and then drive north, right through the left flank of the Russian forces that were attacking Warsaw. This, he believed, would cut off their supplies and reserves and trap them within a pocket formed right in front of the Polish armies massing to defend their capital. At the same time he intended that the Polish 5th Army, deployed to the north of Warsaw, should counter-attack north to cut off and isolate the Russian forces of their north-western front. This included their elite 3rd Cavalry Corps, under the command of General Gay, who was rushing towards Pomerania to encircle Warsaw and attack the Poles from the rear.

Pilsudski first ordered forces to withdraw across the Vistula/Wieprz river line and then radically redeploy to defend Warsaw (from prepared trenched and fortified lines) and the many bridgeheads, and also to assemble for the counter-attacks. In just one week he wanted them to secretly disengage, change their commands and positions, with many units travelling between one and 200 miles and then reform at their concentration points. It was an immensely risky, complex and detailed operation: a logistical and administrative nightmare which could have so easily ended in total chaos and disaster. One determined push by the enemy during this critical phase and the whole operation would have been fatally compromised. A failure that would have cost Poland her independence, Pilsudski his career and perhaps his life and the Red Army would have found themselves well along the road to Berlin and Paris. It was a huge gamble made on the last throw of the dice and it was considered too unorthodox, hazardous and desperate by many senior officers: so much so that the French advisors strongly opposed it. Similarly, when a copy of the plan was found by the Russians on a captured Polish officer they immediately dismissed it as impracticable, implausible and an obvious deception.

Even Pilsudski became racked with doubt when he visited the 4th Army on a confidence-boosting tour only two days before the attacks were to be launched. He found them exhausted, downhearted and ill equipped. In one division he was alarmed to see that 40% of the men on parade to greet him were barefoot and wearing a motley assortment of tattered uniforms and defective equipment. The fact that his complex and perilous plan to disengage and reorganise did not fail was a marvel in itself and testament to his ability to organise on a grand scale, lift morale and inspire his troops.

∞∞∞∞∞∞∞

On 8th August Dominik and Konrad were summoned to see General Haller who had been given the critical command of the 1st, 2nd and 5th Armies, tasked to defend the capital at all costs. The whole offensive hinged on his troops' ability to absorb the massive Russian frontal attack. The general carried this most awesome responsibility with both pride and trepidation because he knew with absolute certainty that if Warsaw was to fall then all would be lost and Poland could disappear from the map for another 200 years. When they arrived at his command post they found Aaron Silberstein waiting for them. Haller greeted them warmly and outlined the plan that had been authorised by Pilsudski. Then he added, "It's difficult, audacious and very risky, but if it works the Russians will be finished."

He still had much of his own planning to complete and his uncharacteristic nervousness and impatience showed in his voice and he allowed no time for comment before moving on to explain why they were there.

"I need the three of you to go back to Lwów straight away. Most of the units selected for the assault group have been extracted from the southern front and to be perfectly frank, other than a few divisions and the Ukrainians, precious little remains down there and now they've got to fend for themselves. So I want the three of you to use all your influence and contacts in the city to help the commander mobilise the civilian population to replace the units that are now going to take part in the central offensive."

Konrad asked, "How long have we got?"

Haller knew he was asking for the impossible, "Not long. You've got to plug the gaps left in the line somehow and prepare the city for a siege. Use all the resources you can muster from right across Galicia, that's regulars, militia and civilians. You must protect the right flank of the offensive by engaging all the Russian units currently deployed down there. Their 12th Army and the Konarmia mustn't be allowed to disengage and rush up to attack us in the rear. When the assault group turns north to cut through and isolate the Russian advance, they'll be at their most vulnerable. Your job is to protect them at all costs and I reckon you've only got a week, ten days at the most, to get it right and even then you'll have to tie them down for another week or more."

Aaron could see where this was going, "I suppose you want me down there to bring my people on board?"

"Yes, but it's not only your people we want. You've got to involve the Ukrainian population as well, but if our recent history is anything to go by, that won't be easy either. We've got Petliura's Ukrainian army already fighting down there and they're doing a really good job. You'd think that having them would really help us to rally their countrymen but it's a double edged sword, since most of the local Ukrainians still think that he abandoned them last year when they tried to seize Galicia from us. Now they're very reluctant to throw their hand in with him. Between the three of you, you've got to change all that and muster every man and woman that you can."

Haller then became fidgety, appearing preoccupied and all too ready to move on. He invited no further questions or comment and ended the audience by shaking them all by the hand and wishing them luck. As they left, his thoughts immediately refocused on the three men they would soon be up against: the commander of the Russian 12th Army, Alexander Ilyich Yegorov – the ambitious and influential member of the Soviet Revolutionary Council of War attached to their southern front; Joseph Vissarionovich Stalin; and the leader of the Konarmia, Semyon Mikhailovich Budionny. The Pole had no idea that the outcome of the whole campaign would turn on the combined actions of these three Russians, but he did wonder how his people would measure up against them.

They were flown back to Lwów by Adam Buza and other members of the Kościuszko Squadron who, along with a Polish Squadron, had been given the task of supporting the defence of Lwów. From the air looking to the east they could see mile after mile of triple entrenchments and barbed wire defences arching around the capital, and the considerable build-up of Polish troops and supplies. These included hundreds of artillery pieces, dozens of tanks, three armoured trains and numerous machine gun positions, many manned by teams of women. When they swooped down for a closer look, they were cheered by a large contingent of Jewish volunteers labouring to prepare an additional defence line. On the road leading south they flew over several battalions of workers and peasants marching in formation towards the capital. They were all shouldering six-foot-long scythes with honed, razor-sharp and slightly curved blades glinting in the morning light. More troop concentrations were seen gathering to the south of Lublin at the jump-off point, from where the assault group would make their move.

From height looking down, these military units were spread out below like children's tin soldiers and appeared to Aaron as chess pieces lined up on a gigantic board, awaiting the first move at the start of a game when all results are still possible. When they came in to land in the south-west of the city they spotted Petliura's 7th Ukrainian Army to the west of Ternopol, straddling the railway line in the triangle formed by the River Dniester and its tributary, the Strypa. Once on the ground they soon discovered that the military presence within the city was not heavy and that the militia and civilian defenders (including the Eaglets) were the ones digging trenches, erecting defences, issuing weapons, manufacturing grenades and Molotov cocktails and generally preparing for battle.

They arrived on the 10th August and that very afternoon attended a conference arranged and chaired by the Southern Front and Garrison Commander, General Iwaszkiewicz and all the civic and military leaders attended. It took six long and at times, fractious hours of hard negotiation and compromise, but a comprehensive plan of defence was thrashed out and in the end agreed by all. Critical posts were established and suitable appointments made and a small defence committee approved to oversee all the preparations. The plan covered everything, including the evacuation of the very young and most vulnerable; inventory of provisions; emergency rationing; the transport, security and maintenance of vital supplies; emergency medical and field hospital plans and conscription categories and targets. They set up joint fire-fighting and rescue teams; drew up policing and riot-control response plans; identified prisoner-handling units and communications systems. They established clear chains of command and appointed inter-service liaison officers and sector and area commanders for the militia and civilian fighters.

Finally they set out their objectives and tactics; authorised the issue, storage and resupply of all arms and ammunition and signed off on final deployments and intelligence-gathering teams and systems. In the end, age-old animosities were overcome and irrespective of race, religion or background, everyone agreed to fight to save their city. Dominik and his team spent the next two days rushing from town to town and village to village rounding up more volunteers and going from command post to command post, rallying, organising and encouraging the defenders. Several times they ran into General Iwaszkiewicz doing his own rounds, armed only with his trademark cane and a bottle of Vodka: the only two things he considered absolutely essential to the tasks of maintaining discipline and boosting the morale of his men and women. He used the stick to chivvy and the alcohol to reward. Their plans were constantly reviewed, amended and improved and all the time the defenders continued to train, dig in and prepare for the inevitable battle.

Early the next morning Dominik was called to the communications centre where a coded message had been received by the Intelligence cell at Warsaw and passed on to all Army Commanders.

Soviet Flash Intercept dated 120820 reads:

The Konarmia is to cross the Bug immediately and destroy the enemy on the right bank with all due haste. It will chase the retreating 3rd and 6th Polish Armies and take the city of Lwów. Flash Intercept of 120820 ends.

Haller had sent the message on to Dominik adding:– *Investigate and report. Immediate reply required – treat as most urgent. This order is from Soviet south-west command, signed personally by Stalin (not from Yegorov {X11 Army} at his headquarters in Kiev). This may be significant! Inter-command rivalry? It was sent to Budionny on 120820 and directly contradicts an original signal of 050820 and also a second Top Priority order of 120820 from Soviet Supreme Command to Commander of X11 Army. Both of which instructed him to pull back in preparation to join up with their western front, specifically ordering the Konarmia to set off north-west for Lublin and await orders from Tukhachevsky (Commander Western Front). This must not happen – keep them engaged on the Bug or at Lwów at all costs. I will send help as soon as I can.*

Repeat: This is critical. They must not move north. Report on all aspects without delay including your intelligence assessment of significance of contradiction.

Signed – General Haller – OIC – Northern Front – Warsaw –130820

Dominik immediately consulted the map and discovered that according to the previous day's aerial surveillance report, Budionny's headquarters was just outside of Werba, about 50 miles east of the Bug where the Konarmia had been 'resting'. He ran out of the building to find Adam, Konrad and Aaron. It was time to take a look at the Russian lines.

Dominik discovered that Konrad had been ordered south to liaise with Petliura and make a joint assessment of the intentions and capability of the Soviet XIV Army which was facing him across the river Dniester. If the situation allowed, he hoped to divert a contingent of Ukrainians to Lwów to act as a rapid mobile reserve unit, ready to rush to any breach point in the city defences. Aaron had been tasked to obtain situation reports from all battle commanders in the field and organise reconnaissance patrols targeted at the capture of prisoners for interrogation. If the Poles were to stand any chance of complying with Haller's orders then they needed immediate and accurate intelligence on enemy strengths, deployment, battle readiness and morale and so Dominik took off with Adam and headed east for Werba.

They could clearly see the Polish lines dug in on the west bank of the Bug and hundreds of soldiers looked up and waved as they flew over, heading for the Konarmia. They saw a few Polish patrols east of the river and several larger concentrations of Polish troops south of Radziechow and around Lopatyn and Brody but no early signs of Russian aircraft or ground troops. A few minutes later Adam turned in his seat and gave him the 'thumbs up', momentarily throttled back and shouted, "I'm going up. We'll get a better view and be out of ground fire range."

As they climbed, Dominik took the chance to review what he had learnt about his enemy and he started with the one he believed to be the most dangerous, Budionny the commander of the Konarmia. He was a strong, tall man from peasant stock, an ideal Bolshevik and a natural leader. He had the commanding presence and physique of a heroic regimental sergeant major, an appearance reinforced by his flamboyant handlebar moustache and his effortless bravado and bravura. Although an exceptionally courageous, decisive and inspiring commander, his self-confidence which bordered on arrogance occasionally led to rash actions. Nevertheless, his exhilarating charisma meant that he was always held in loyal respect and admiration by his men. He was also a born survivor, ruthless and without compassion or pity. Many likened him to a pirate.

He had been appointed to command Stalin's First Cavalry when it was created in November 1919 to take on the Czarist Cossacks and Denikin's cavalry. Since then, by success after success on the battlefield it had built up such an elite reputation as a brutal strike force that it was considered by many, including its own officers and men, to be all-conquering and invincible. Although collectively brave and determined, this unit of four divisions, some 18,000 men, owed its triumph not to charges against well-prepared positions with machine gun cover but to always exploiting the weakest defensive points. They would attack on a very narrow front with overwhelming numbers and rapidly punch a hole clean through and well beyond the line. Then they would spread out to left and right, viciously falling upon the enemy from the rear. The speed, ferocity and shock of the assault would invariably create so much chaos and panic that it would trigger wholesale retreat. They would then embark on an orgy of wanton slaughter, pillage and looting, constantly and deliberately adding to their wished-for reputation as a bloodthirsty and unstoppable marauding horde.

When Adam dropped the right wing and started to bank he pointed out, "There they are!" and Dominik got his first view of the Konarmia. They were spread out below in exactly the same position as they were the day before but now they were breaking camp. The site was massive and he was daunted by the vast numbers of horses and men scurrying around, preparing to set out for battle. There was a huge dust cloud building up off to the left where regiments were already forming for the advance and although his visibility was restricted, he still thought it an impressive but disheartening sight from the air. He could see row after row and column after column moving off, lines of battle-hardened Cossacks with their almost legendary long sabres hanging from their belts and their Mosin-Nagant model 1907 carbines aslant across their backs.

Suddenly, there was a stampede outwards from the centre of the camp as hundreds of men reacted to the sight and threat of the aircraft. Seconds later several machine guns opened up from positions in front of the encampment, but Adam felt safe as he had too much altitude to be within their range. Then he saw three aircraft in the process of being refuelled on the flat ground about half a mile to the rear of the camp and so he took a wide descending sweep to the left to attack them from the flank. He could not ignore such a threat to his own pilots who simply had to retain command of the skies in order to deny the enemy the ability to strike at will. As he turned and dived down, one of the planes started to take off, moving away into the wind. He lined up, gave chase and opened fire from 500 feet, perforating the other two unmanned and stationary Nieuports from nose to tail. Both planes exploded when dozens of heavy-calibre rounds pummelled the fuel tanks with the explosive force of hand grenades.

Adam broke off when they started to receive small arms and machine gun fire from the ground and the change of course allowed Dominik to line up on the third machine just as it reached take off speed. He aimed at a point a few yards in front of the plane and simply let the enemy pilot fly into the continuous stream of bullets. As round after round smashed into the propeller, the engine cowling and then the head and body of the pilot the plane suddenly nose-dived back down into the grass. The force of the impact and the weight of the engine combined to drive the plane into the ground, burying and wedging the nose into the black earth as far back as the cockpit so that it remained firmly stuck there with the tail pointing grotesquely skywards.

Dominik changed magazines and when he looked to their right he saw a team of four horses tearing towards them, pulling an open cart, chariot-style. It was bouncing across the uneven ground and the weight of the Maxim M1910 heavy machine gun mounted in the back (with its crew of a driver and a two-man gun team) was kicking up a long, high dust trail. It was followed wide on its flanks and slightly slower, by two more similarly equipped wagons but each of these was pulled by just a pair of galloping horses. These 'tachankas' (named after the Ukrainian diminutive 'tachka' meaning cart or wheelbarrow) were the cavalry's most effective weapon against aircraft attack. Dominik knew of the fearsome reputation of their Polish equivalents and so he tapped Adam's shoulder and pointed them out. The pilot immediately turned away, because having already lost two of the squadron to these primitive but effective contraptions, he was also aware of their capabilities. He had no intention of taking unnecessary risks on what was primarily a reconnaissance mission.

They turned and headed for home, but as they went they started to strafe the cavalry, from both front and rear. The two airmen swathed lines through the mighty Konarmia as they scattered across the plain, dashing for cover. The devastating firepower produced by their machine guns hammered into the columns that had been caught out in the open, killing and wounding dozens of men and horses. Then they dropped their two bombs right into the very heart of the huge cloud of dust being kicked up by hundreds of hooves. At least a third of the Soviet 1st Cavalry had been caught off guard at their most vulnerable time and with their supposed air cover still on the ground. It had cost them almost 100 dead and wounded. Adam flew on, over the last of the enemy and when Dominik looked back at the carnage below he took no personal satisfaction from adding yet more bodies to the countless corpses eaten up by this rich, fertile and coveted soil: the scene of so many bloody and gruesome battles across the centuries. Nevertheless, as a professional soldier he was heartened by the fact that the Konarmia, the elite cutting edge of the Soviet military, could be so vulnerable to air attack.

Chapter Seven

THE MIRACLE ON THE VISTULA

Lwów – 13th August 1920

Once back in Lwów, Dominik reported that the Konarmia was on the move and so the Kościuszko squadron set off to intercept and report on their direction of travel. Nearly all of their original planes (Italian Ansaldo A1 Balilla's) had been lost on the retreat from Kiev, but they had now been re-equipped –mostly with 200 horsepower Albatross D.III's (with reinforced wings and struts) but also with the odd Bristol F2 B, plus they kept the sole-surviving Italian fighter. During the early part of the 1920 campaign, pilots from this one squadron had flown over 200 combat missions and they had developed very effective high-speed, low-level tactics and manoeuvres for attacking cavalry formations and infantry positions.

In the air they were rarely challenged by any significant numbers of enemy aircraft and so they enjoyed and exploited their air superiority. They gained a fearsome reputation amongst the commanders on both sides. The Russians were so concerned about the way they were driving down the morale of their forces that they offered a huge bounty on the head of every member of the squadron. On the Polish side they were a massive boost to confidence. As one commander said, "Just like us they must be exhausted but they fight on, relentlessly raining machine gun bullets and bombs down on the heads of the Cossacks. Without them we would have been done for long ago. We cheer them and we salute them every time they fly over."

Somehow they also found the time to pass on their skills to the eager and equally brave but inexperienced young Polish pilots. These were the hard and dangerous combat lessons they had learnt in the costly aerial battles in the crowded air space above the trenches of the Great War. They had been further refined and developed above the vast expanses of the Ukraine. When the squadron had returned safely to refuel and rearm, then the Polish squadron took off to continue to support their ground troops by strafing and harassing the enemy wherever they could find them exposed. Over the next few days the two squadrons would fly over 100 combat missions.

Within a few hours the news had spread across the city and to all the defenders and they knew that the Konarmia was indeed marching on the city and their own desperate fight was about to begin. Dominik remained puzzled by the fact that the Konarmia seemed intent on seizing Lwów when they had already been ordered to break off and head north. He thought he had just enough time to seek Aaron's view of the contradictory Russian signals. He was anxious to obtain another perspective on the strange, almost dysfunctional relationship that Budionny, Stalin and Yegorov in the south had, with their commander in the field, Tukhachevsky, and their supreme commander in Moscow. Afterwards, having also obtained the latest surveillance and intercept reports he was ready to draft his reply to Haller. Aaron encoded it for transmission. He also sent a hard copy encryption by armed courier:

To General Haller OIC – Northern Front – Warsaw. From DD Lwów. 13.8.20.

Konarmia moving on Lwów today. Current position approaching Radziechow, Brody and Lopatyn. All defended but cannot hold. We will attack and fragment enemy on approach to city. First major stand will be on the upper Bug, but he will force a crossing by sheer

weight of numbers. It will cost him dearly. The longer we last, the weaker their resolve. The closer they get, the harder we fight. Full defence plan for Lwów agreed with OIC Southern Front and now implemented. Lwów will not fall! At least not within ten days.
I believe Budionny and Stalin are deliberately ignoring orders to move north so that they can attack Lwów. I suspect his motive is based on a military or political tactical preference rather than a personal disagreement. Yegorov is covering for them by delaying responses and exploiting the failings of their unreliable and slow comms systems. The timescales, their close relationship and their history of previous clashes with their superiors over strategy, preclude any other explanation. Therefore the attack on Lwów will continue until their High Command force the issue and Yegorov backs down. Budionny is being manipulated by Stalin who is the driving force, but all of them will be compelled to comply before long. I estimate a maximum of one week. Suggest cavalry raids into his flank from north when you are able and prepare a welcome for him when he does turn north.
DD Lwów 13.8.20.

The Defence Committee met and General Iwaszkiewicz listened to the various progress reports, made a few changes to the deployment of the Ukrainian troops and the militia contingents that had been drawn in since they last met and issued his final orders. When the meeting broke up he called Dominik aside.

"We're in a strange situation here – stuck right out on a limb and unlikely to get any help, and this committee thing is also rather unique, you know. I bet that I'll be the butt of many a derogatory jibe from my brother generals for setting it up in the first place, but I think it was necessary to get everyone on board and bring them around to my way of thinking. The almost tribal murder and bloodshed that happened here last year when we were in charge proved to me that where the law and compassion ends then the road to hell begins. I don't want any civil unrest or attacks on the Jews this time."

Dominik agreed, "Well it's worked so far because they all seem to be pulling together now and concentrating their efforts on the common enemy."

"To be fair, I also saw it as a means to an end because shouting and hollering or just sitting here and issuing commands to a bunch of frightened civilians, a lot of them little more than children, certainly wouldn't have worked. I decided to be a bit more adventurous and involve them right from the beginning but once the fighting arrives here, there won't be any more committees or meetings. It'll just be my orders and I will demand instant obedience from everybody."

Dominik thought that the general had indeed got the best out of the civilian population and because of that they were about as ready as they possibly could be. They had managed to raise and fully equip two extra regiments of cavalry and three of infantry, and as a result the city was now defended by a total of four makeshift divisions including the extra Ukrainian infantry reserve that Konrad had brought back from the south. With the defence plans finalised he asked, "What are your orders for me and my two friends?"

"The Konarmia are preparing for a three-pronged attack and we've a pretty good idea of where they're going to try to cross the Bug. I've already got that covered and we'll blow the bridges when they approach, but we also need to be ready for them when they force a crossing. I'm sure that they will keep probing until they do"

"Yes, they're bound to break through and probably sooner rather than later. We're spread too thin to hold them for long. What have you got in mind?"

"I want to take the fight right out to them wherever they are, to slow them down and break them up as they approach, but to be successful we need to deprive the Konarmia of its obvious advantage. They love to fight out in the open in large numbers where they can manoeuvre at speed so we'll make a stand and draw them in at every bridge and road or rail junction inside the main towns and villages, all along their approach. We'll have to use relatively small groups – anything from two or three hundred up to a couple of thousand fighters – and if they pass us by, we'll attack them from the rear. And all the while we'll use the air force to keep whittling away their numbers. Our infantry can use their machine guns and small arms fire to good effect in the built-up areas and in order to winkle us out, the Cossacks will have to do the one thing they hate the most: dismount and fight on foot."

"That sounds good to me and they can't afford to leave their rear too vulnerable, especially to a large force so I don't think they'll risk just bypassing us all."

"I'd like to make best use of your combat and command experience so I'll allocate you and your sergeant to lead one of my young volunteer groups, but I do need to keep Aaron here in our communications centre. He's proved invaluable and they don't want to lose him."

He then sent Dominik to the Command Centre to be tasked and briefed for action. Dominik thanked the general and saluted. He thought the plan was sound overall but knew its success or otherwise largely depended on the fortitude, skill and fighting spirit of these relatively small, almost independent combat units. He realised that each of them would need to destroy very significant numbers of the enemy if overall, they were going to deplete them to such a low level that it would become impossible for them to breach the last lines at the city. Even with significant air cover it seemed likely that for many, these would turn out to be suicide missions. By and large he thought that it would be a race against time on two fronts. Firstly, could they hold out in the south until the Konarmia finally obeyed the order to move north? Secondly, when they did so would Haller have had enough time and resources to organise a big enough block operation to finally neutralise their reduced threat?

They left at dawn the next morning, just as Budionny was awoken by the sound of battle in the street right outside his temporary billet in Lopatyn, a small town just under 40 miles north-east of Lwów. During the night, under cover of darkness and fog, a force of over 2,000 Poles had slipped by the pickets and infiltrated the town. As the Poles closed in on his position, for just a few minutes he was in real danger of being shot or captured but with the help of his Mauser side arm, his command post guards and a few personal staff he was able to shoot his way out. The fighting lasted all day and the delay frustrated Budionny who realised that he was racing against time because the pressure from Moscow to break off would only increase. He pushed on towards the Bug, but every time he made progress the Poles would counterattack to take back another town or village.

Dominik found himself in charge of nearly 180 fighters, mostly civilians but with a core of 25 experienced infantry soldiers who had already fought their way to Kiev and back. The civilians included Poles and Ukrainians, a mixture of Catholics, Jews and Ruthenians (Greek Catholics) who ranged in age from 14 to 55, but three quarters of them were under 18. Thirty were eaglets who had fought with distinction in Lwów in the Ukrainian uprising of the previous year. All had received a modicum of basic training and were firearms proficient. Counting Konrad he had a total of six NCOs and so his squad was divided up into six platoons, each armed with a light machine gun, an assortment of rifles and hand guns, bayonets and hand grenades.

They set off in a north-easterly direction along the Lwów to Krystynopol railway line heading towards the Bug to the south-east of the Bialowieska Forest. Their destination was Kamionka Strumilowa, a town on the river just under 25 miles away and where their latest intelligence suggested that the spearhead of one of Budionny's three attack columns was attempting to cross. Polish forces were already deployed in an effort to stop them, but their own mission was to assume they would be successful at some stage, as more Konarmia arrived, and so set up an ambush point about a mile west of the river and kill as many of the enemy as possible.

They made good time and were delighted to see that both their squadrons were up and taking the battle to the enemy. It seemed that there were twenty planes in the air virtually all the time and their presence overhead particularly comforted the younger fighters. They crossed paths with eight other groups of Polish soldiers along the way, some regulars from the 6th Army, others a mixture of militia and civilian personnel, all making for different points on the River Bug to await the enemy. As they marched along the side of the track, everyone sensed that they were entering into a critical battle, one that could well decide the fate of their city and many were terrified. Others were deeply absorbed in their own thoughts of family, home, and how they would perform in action. This apprehension increased dramatically when mid-morning they heard the distinct initial sounds of battle ahead. First the whine, screech and explosion of artillery shells, then the scream and roar of aircraft engines followed by the chatter of numerous machine guns and rifle fire. Then as they closed right in, the crump of hand grenades and the high-pitched and desperate neighing of horses, accompanied by the clash of bayonets and sabres and the shouting and screaming of men fighting for their lives.

Dominik didn't know that this was the third such attack of the day and yet the defenders were still hanging on and managing to dominate the crossing. The bridge had been blown at the last minute to allow retreating Poles to cross and join the defenders. The fairly steep banks had now become extremely muddy, slippery and unstable by the clawing and trampling passage of thousands of heavy and twisting hooves as one wing of the Konarmia had unsuccessfully tried to ford the river. The approach and the river banks were littered with the dead and wounded from both sides, lying under and alongside dozens of horse carcasses. Scores more had floated downstream, lodging and snagging on the riverside vegetation and piling up on the bends. In the shallows and eddies the water was red with blood and the artillery shells from both sides were peppering the surrounding land and dismembering and eviscerating the victims, showering those still clinging on to life with gore and body parts. It was a scene of carnage as thousands of men fought to the death over a few hundred yards of waterside. There would be no surrender here.

Dominik set up his ambush point on the Lwów road a few hundred yards south of the main crossroads in the centre of the town. He was going to fight from the streets and buildings and he wanted the freedom to move in any direction, without risking being driven out into the fields. Most of the population had already left, but the stubborn few that remained were ordered to save themselves by fleeing westwards. Where necessary his men forced the doors and he placed his teams in the street-side ground-floor and first-floor rooms but deliberately left about half of the adjacent properties empty. If the Konarmia opted for close quarters' house-to-house clearance, then he wanted to keep them guessing as to his numbers and locations. The longer he could tie them down, the heavier the losses he could inflict.

He also staggered his positions along the street to reduce the risk of his men shooting each other and he took great care in setting up his machine gunners' positions, ensuring that they covered every approach. His NCOs made sure that all rear exits were clear and that guards were posted in suitable positions to prevent infiltration. Exit routes and a fallback position were established so that any withdrawal could be orderly and coordinated and he stationed a team armed with hand grenades and two machine gunners on the roofs of the buildings to give the signal to retire and buy the rest time to get clear. His best marksmen were identified and scattered throughout the deployment with orders to take out the officers first and then concentrate on anyone else shouting orders, rallying their colleagues or posing a particular threat. Once everyone was briefed and in position, Konrad and three of the most experienced soldiers were sent out on reconnaissance.

They discovered that the attackers had withdrawn to regroup but more Konarmia were arriving all the time and the Polish CO at the river thought they would launch another larger attack in the morning. He was sure that they would succeed before too long, but he was determined to fight to the last man. He was not going to withdraw. The decision had been made and his men were aware of it. An hour later Konrad reported to Dominik and added, "I even offered to recommend to you that we all move forward and help him defend the bridge, but he refused point blank. He thought our numbers wouldn't make a lot of difference for him now and he would prefer us to stick to our plan. He thinks we've a great chance of springing the trap and catching them cold when they come charging through here, high on their success and looking to plunder and loot. He said we should avenge all the men he has already lost and those that he will lose in the morning. He's a brave man that colonel."

Dominik agreed, "Yes he is and that's a real soldier's life for you: fight and suffer, suffer and fight and I'm sure he'll hold them off for as long as he can, but realistically I think we should expect them here early in the morning. Let's make sure we're ready and that we don't let the good colonel down."

So they worked out the night sentries' rota and then went over their plans once again with the other NCOs. Dominik did his rounds alone, encouraging his troops to get some sleep and making sure that they all knew what was expected of them. He didn't sleep as he considered the coming action and what more he could do to improve the chances of survival for even just a few of his small force. He was distressed to think that most, if not all, would not see the day out and he was saddened even further by a sudden and unexpected thought, that for every life lost tomorrow whole generations of future lives were also being sacrificed. Hosts of marriages, families, babies, school children, lovers, perhaps even great scientists, doctors, musicians and philosophers: all would be lost to the world and he knew it applied equally to the enemy. He thought the list endless and the responsibility and burden weighed him down, but he was a soldier and killing had become second nature. Only in the loneliness of command and the darkness of night did such thoughts assail him. He prayed, not for himself but for his boys, young men and the twenty women and girls scattered throughout his makeshift force. The next day, the 15th August, fighting would intensify further on the approaches to Lwów and Dominik's unit would join the battle.

At dawn the fighting started again at the river and this time Russian planes escorted the Konarmia. Four Soviet Nieuports attacked the already weakened Polish positions along the west bank causing dozens of extra casualties in the trenches and amongst those hiding in the shell holes and behind the barriers and palisades. Intermittently, above the sound of the aircraft engines they could hear the cheering and jeering of the Russian cavalry as they watched and prepared to attack. Nevertheless, having already survived so much punishment and stoically denied the enemy for so long, the 100 or so survivors were not easily intimidated by either the aircraft or the Konarmia, whose reputation and mystique had drained away by the hour. The defenders readied themselves for yet one more attack and it was their turn to cheer a few minutes later when six Polish planes arrived and the Russian aircraft were chased off.

Their relief was short-lived because the Russians then resumed shelling and machine gunning the Polish positions, softening them up for their next attempt to cross over, but the struggle waged on through most of the morning. Finally, the defence was shattered when the 6th Cavalry Division managed to swim the river and climb out over the steep bank. They did so under fire from the few Poles that remained in a fit enough condition to fight on and although their own casualty rate was high, they quickly cut through to the rear of the fragmented line and at that point the battle was won. They took no prisoners when they turned and charged with sabres drawn, screaming out their frustration and hacking and slashing into the rear of the men who had held them up for too long. One of the last men to die was the colonel, proudly and bravely standing amongst his fallen men, repeatedly firing his sidearm at the charging Russians until he too was cut down and trampled by the tidal wave of the Konarmia at full gallop.

The Russians quickly formed up and immediately pressed on towards their target and prize, the city of Lwów. The previous evening Budionny had received his new instructions from the Supreme Commander: he was to place his Konarmia under the orders of the Western Front Commander by 1200 hours that day.

He knew the time was now fast approaching when he would have to obey the directive, but he decided to ignore it for the time being, hoping that he could take the city first and then move north.

Dominik had been waiting all morning, listening to the noise of battle and constantly receiving reports from his forward observation post, which he had set up at first light. By mid-morning he knew that the Konarmia would soon cross the river and he made his final preparations. Thinking of their planned withdrawal, Konrad asked him whether they should set booby traps throughout the buildings to slow the Russians down when they tried to follow. They had learnt a great deal about this facet of warfare in the trenches where explosives such as perdite, mines, hand grenades and shells had all been used to kill and maim the unwary. Items of clothing, weapons, cap badges, even pieces of shrapnel and bullets, anything that was likely to be picked up as a souvenir had been attached to charges and left in the trenches and dug-outs, primed to explode when picked up. Doors, stairs, stoves, chimneys, trench boards, cooking utensils, even whole buildings and churches had been rigged to explode using a variety of percussion detonators, electrical contacts, delayed-action fuses or even clockwork devices, all triggered by simple pressure or movement or by using string, cables or tripwires. Dominik quickly decided against the idea, partly because he wanted to be sure that all his munitions were made to count and not defused and wasted, but most of all because he didn't want to kill and injure his own people when they eventually returned to their homes.

When everyone was in position Konrad reminded the NCOs of Dominik's final instructions, "Hold your fire until the street is full, right from end to end. The boss will throw a hand grenade when the time is right and the detonation's your signal to open up and give them everything you've got. Pay them back with interest for what's happened at the river and remember – every man we kill here is a man less at the city walls. The signal to break off and run for our secondary position will be a coordinated volley of hand grenades. Good luck."

Less than half an hour later they arrived, first the few forward scouts who rode through unmolested and unaware of the Poles hiding in the buildings.

Ten minutes later they heard the approaching noise of massed horses trotting on the cobbles and the rattling and clanking of weapons and equipment before the vanguard of a full cavalry regiment turned the corner, four abreast in close formation. The noise grew ever louder as more and more Russians filled the street and many of the young Poles were surprised at what they saw as they peered out at their enemy. In their imagination they had expected an army dressed in uniform: regimented, disciplined and orderly, similar to the units of Polish cavalry in service with the Austrian Empire that had been a common sight as they grew up. What they now witnessed was something entirely different. The Konarmia were dressed in a variety and mixture of military and civilian clothes of all colours and shades. Some wore fur hats, others the leather-pointed Tartar cap bearing a five pointed star and the rest a curious mixture of military and civilian headgear. Their outer garments were just as varied: there were raincoats, capes, leather tunics and short jackets scattered throughout the column and a few even wore blankets like ponchos. At the fore they carried several large dark banners and standards, each escorted by its colour party. They looked like a large band of marauding brigands, which is exactly what they were but they were also skilled horsemen and well-trained, fearless fighters.

When the street was jam-packed and more were still turning the corner at the top end, Dominik threw his grenade into the middle of the column and the Poles let loose. They suddenly appeared in the windows and doors as one, along the whole length of the road catching the enemy completely by surprise. The snipers did their work well in those first few moments of shock and incomprehension, and they managed to bring down several officers and a dozen or so of the colour parties as the fusillade of rifle fire from their comrades ripped into the heart of the column. When the unscathed horseman started to react, the column was already disintegrating into chaos and those at the front attempted to gallop forward and those at the top end of the street tried to turn to escape. Two machine guns concentrated on these troops at either end and within seconds the cobbles were covered in more writhing horses, many mortally wounded and their dead and injured riders.

A few dozen managed to trample or leap over this obstruction and escape but even more were brought down as they did so, until the street was virtually blocked at either end by a bank of dead and injured animals and men. The area looked and sounded like a slaughterhouse. The sight of the butchery and the screams of the injured men were horrendous. The unnaturally high-pitched, pain-induced cries of the horrifically injured horses, struggling to move or stand on the blood-drenched and slippery cobbles were ghastly and nauseating. This was all happening only a few feet from the Poles and it was just too much for one of the boys. He broke down, weeping and sobbing uncontrollably.

Those still alive along the road, and there were still several hundred, started to dismount and return fire wildly into the nearest buildings before running to get inside, out of the deadly shooting gallery. Their actions, driven by self-preservation, fear and anger, were uncoordinated and lacked military purpose, but every time someone tried to give orders or rally the survivors they were shot by a sniper. On several occasions by more than one. Before many had reached safety by entering an unoccupied building, many others had perished receiving a bullet from a Pole waiting inside. Such was the randomness of battle. Then the fragmentation grenades rained down from the roofs. Fifty or more fell amongst them in one salvo with the combined effect of several artillery rounds, adding more deaths and mutilation to the carnage.

Dominik's men started to withdraw to their fall-back positions as soon as the grenades were thrown and on his way out Konrad grabbed the collapsed boy and half-carried and half-dragged him away. Once out of the back of the houses they made good progress and quickly reached their rendezvous, a school just a few hundred yards away. Konrad looked at his watch and was surprised to see that the whole engagement had lasted less than five minutes, and it had taken them nearly as long to reach the school.

Konrad reported on their status, "We've lost four dead and eight wounded but only two seriously and one of the machine gunners on the roof hasn't made it back so his weapon's gone as well but what a success!"

Dominik agreed, "We certainly performed better than I could have hoped for. We cut them to pieces. Anyway, none of them were on our heels as we fell back but we'd better post lookouts and get ourselves ready. There's no time to waste. They'll find us soon enough."

Ten minutes later, Dominik gave Konrad and the NCOs his orders for the defence of the empty school and then said, "They can't afford to leave us here to threaten their rear so they've probably already sent out patrols to look for us. Although we're in a reasonably good position with good views all around and a solid stone building to defend, I'm worried about our ammunition so we've got to conserve as much as possible. Anyhow, let the men know what I want and then share out what we've got." There was nothing left to do but wait.

Late that afternoon the Konarmia surrounded the school, but they seemed to have learnt little from the earlier fight and Dominik was surprised when about fifty charged straight in. He had thought that they would occupy the nearby buildings on the edge of the school courtyard and spray them with bullets or bring up artillery to pound them, but they had decided to do what came naturally and put the Poles to the sword. This time all the defenders picked their targets very carefully, determined not to waste their precious ammunition and only twenty Cossacks made it right up to the school. A group of about six burst through the front door, holding their sabres high and screaming obscenities.

They were met by a stream of machine gun bullets that literally ripped right through their bodies as they tried to squeeze through the doorway into the entrance hall. The weapon was a Bergmann MG -15nA, light machine gun, one of some 6,000 that had been manufactured for the German Army in the Great War. It could be ground fired using a tripod or carried into action. It weighed 28lbs, was 44 inches long and would discharge all 200 7.92 mm rounds from its metal-linked ammunition belt in less than twenty-five seconds. It was fired from the school floor only ten yards from the door, directly into the upper bodies of the Russians. With a muzzle velocity of 3,000 feet per second, the simultaneous impact of multi rounds was explosive and dreadfully destructive: ripping out large chunks of flesh and bone and turning internal organs into pulverised pulp. They never stood a chance and were reduced to a pitiful pile of bloody gore in just a matter of seconds. The remaining Russians were picked off by rifle fire as they tried to smash their way through the windows but not before four more Poles were killed when one managed to throw a grenade in.

The Konarmia attacked five more times throughout the late afternoon and into the early evening but were beaten back on every occasion. However, more and more Poles were dying and being injured in every assault and with only 100 battle-fit men left, Dominik felt they were reaching the stage where he would have insufficient numbers to defend the whole building. They were also receiving a great deal of incoming rifle fire and his men were very tired. Morale was slipping as their casualties rapidly mounted and their injured friends perished from lack of medical treatment. To make matters worse and despite their reduced fire power, their ammunition started to run out and many realised that their position was becoming hopeless. Konrad rushed around the building checking on his men, keeping them alert and encouraging them to hang on until darkness came when they could try to extract themselves.

At about 7pm the end seemed to arrive when the ground shook to the detonation of several artillery shells. The first landed in the courtyard, the second in a nearby house but the third hit the centre of the school, bringing the chimney crashing through the roof. The explosion ripped through the larger of the two classrooms which immediately filled up with choking dust and piles of fallen masonry and debris. A side wall was completely blown out and the Poles in the rest of the building were deafened and disorientated, looking around desperately for orders, not fully comprehending what had happened. Dominik ran into the shattered classroom where he discovered that only three of the fifty men had survived and they were barely alive. Many of the bodies had been blown apart, some had been decapitated or lost their limbs and others were buried under tons of rubble.

Dominik made his decision: he was not going to wait for the next shell and so he ordered everyone out. Carrying their wounded, Dominik, Konrad, three surviving NCOs and 52 fighters poured out of the back of the school and ran straight for the nearest buildings about 100 yards away. The Konarmia, sensing victory at last, charged. The Poles fired as they sprinted straight towards the Russians. One of the NCOs fired a machine gun from the hip as he ran and then another joined in. Half a dozen horses fell, tripping and bringing down others galloping behind but within seconds the Poles were hit by the full force of the charge. Many were shot by the Cossacks who could fire their carbines from the saddle while their mounts darted forward: others were knocked down and trampled over or cut down by sabres.

Only ten Poles were left on their feet as the Cossacks passed through and slowed down to turn. Dominik looked round and saw one of his 'boys' get to his feet about ten yards behind and then just stand there in total shock and horror, with blood pouring from a sabre slash on his shoulder and arm. Bullets were hitting the ground near his feet and singing through the air as several Russians fired from their horses, deliberately targeting the petrified lad. Without thinking Dominik ran back and picked him up and as he began to spin round, two horsemen charged at them. He put the boy down and drew his sidearm, a Smith & Wesson .455 given to him by Adam. He took careful aim and fired. The bullet hit the first rider in the chest and he slumped sideways, dead in the saddle and his mount swerved off course. The second Russian was almost on top of him when he fired again, but the bullet hit the rider in the shoulder and the horse kept coming.

Konrad suddenly appeared alongside him with one of the machine guns and he fired a burst into the horse and rider and they crashed to the ground only feet from the terrified boy. The other Poles had now formed a line in front of a row of houses 30 yards ahead and provided covering fire as Dominik picked up the boy and ran back with Konrad. Firing at any sign of a horseman they scampered from house to house and garden to garden, heading deeper and deeper into the tightly packed homes and narrow streets, trying to evade their pursuers in the maze-like warren of the Old Town area. Once there was no sign of pursuit they sheltered in a cellar, tended their wounds and when darkness finally hid them away they collapsed into sleep; their bodies and minds totally exhausted.

Konrad woke at dawn to the sound of battle and raised the others. There was only one logical explanation – the Poles had counter-attacked. One of the NCOs volunteered to investigate and he was back within the hour. The Russians had been pushed right back to the river where they were making a stand on the bridgehead, occupying the very positions that they had taken less than 24 hours ago. Eleven fighters, including the wounded boy slowly made their way back to the Polish lines near the school where Dominik gave his report to the sector commander, a colonel from a reserve brigade attached to the 6th Army. He just could not believe that any of Dominik's men could have possibly survived after being so outnumbered or that they had inflicted such massive losses on the Konarmia. He told Dominik that nearly 400 had been killed in the street ambush and another 120 at the school. Dominik was more concerned for his own losses: 167 of his fighters – men, women, girls and boys, who were his responsibility – were gone forever and he regretted every single death, but he was also proud of their bravery and endurance. The survivors were immediately evacuated from the line and returned to Lwów.

Pilsudski's main Polish counter-attack further north was also a complete success. Warsaw was saved by the miracle on the Vistula and Budionny never did manage to capture Lwów. When he finally turned north on the 19th August he was far too late to be of any help as his comrades in central and northern Poland were already in full retreat. His Konarmia was then harassed by Polish cavalry units and driven into a trap at Komarow where the largest cavalry battle for over 100 years took place. It was also the last great battle of any significance in which cavalry was used as intended and not as mounted infantry. He was almost surrounded but managed to escape. The engagement, although not decisive in itself, marked the beginning of the end for the Konarmia and the whole, chaotic and disintegrating Red Army was rapidly and relentlessly driven back until a ceasefire was finally agreed on 16th October. Of the five armies which invaded Poland, one was totally destroyed and the others badly mauled and Russian losses of dead, injured, captured or interned in Germany, reached over 200,000. There were also 40,000 Polish casualties, but their country had survived and the war was finally over for Dominik and his friends.

Dominik was awarded the Virtuti Militari for his bravery and outstanding leadership throughout the battle and specifically for saving the injured boy when under fire near the school. Konrad and two other survivors received the Cross of Valour. The medals were presented the following year in Warsaw by General Haller who paid tribute to their courage and military skill. He stated that he was proud to have been the one who had first spotted Dominik's exemplary leadership qualities when he was in the trenches on the Western Front, fighting with the French. The rest of the survivors from the action at the school also attended the presentation ceremony and later, at the Church of the Holy Cross they held a memorial service for all those from their unit who had sacrificed their lives. General Iwaszkiewicz from Lwów, still proudly carrying his stick in his hand and his vodka in his pocket, read the tribute.

Chapter Eight

THE SINS OF SOKOROV

Swindon – 9th November 2009

We settled down in Stan's lounge and he took up where we had left off very late the day before. He explained that once the fighting had ended, the government, looking to cut the military budget, had no further use for a large proportion of the army and so along with thousands of others, Dominik was discharged. He found himself in fierce competition with his former comrades as they desperately but unsuccessfully looked for work. Initially he had considered going back to America, but the adventurer in him was attracted to the idea of returning to the very cradle of the Polish nation and so he took up a government offer. They provided financial incentives and started a massive programme of resettlement, handing out land to people who would move east.

Life was far more basic there, with few home comforts and at first he really struggled with the ferocious winters and the unrelenting labour. When he arrived at the farm near Luck, he had found that the land was scarred and pitted with the aftermath of countless battles. There were shell holes everywhere, several deep and extensive bunkers and trenches and dozens of shallow graves scattered across the higher ground. The flotsam and jetsam of advancing and retreating armies were strewn across his land and it all had to be cleared and the ground made safe before it could be levelled and planted. Gradually he worked his way through it and as the years went by he learnt how to get the most out of the land. He met Bogdana in Luck and together they built their lives around the farm and had two children. Then Stan told me how their hopes and dreams were shattered by the German and Russian invasions.

"You'll probably remember some of what I'm going to tell you next because it concerns what happened in 1939 after the two Nowaski boys had been taken prisoner by the Russians and their mother and brothers had left to try to get back home to Pelpin."

Indeed, Jan Nowaski had told me the amazing story of his family's fight for survival during World War II, including their short but fateful time as evacuees on Dominik's farm at the end of 1939. I said, "I know that two of the boys were captured by the Russians and accused of stealing food. Tomek was sent to the Gulag, but Jan managed to escape and came to England. After I had helped to arrange their reunion last year he told me about the tragic deaths of his brave parents and his sister, Maria and brother, Jozef at the hands of the Nazis and how Tomek and his other brother Jacek had managed to survive."

"Have you any idea at all about what happened at the farm after they had gone?"

I remembered that Jan had told me that he had never seen or heard from Dominik or his family after they left and suspected that they had all been killed by the Russians. "I was led to believe that, like millions of their countrymen at that time, they had been murdered at the farm or shipped off to the Gulag to be worked to death, but from what I've found out over these last few days, that's by no means certain."

Stan opened his notebook, took out a family photograph and passed it across to me. "That's Dominik, his wife Bogdana and their six-year-old son, Michal and their daughter, Karolina, who was eight. Some would say that they weren't as lucky as their father, but I wouldn't describe what happened to him as in any sense fortunate either."

I turned it over and saw an inscription, '10th June 1939 – Bogdana's birthday!'

Stan said, "That's the only photograph he had of his family and I would like you to bear that image in mind while I tell you what happened."

The Dabrowski Farm – 12th February 1940

When the Russians had first arrived in September, 1939 they immediately launched an occupation of terror. They encouraged the Ukrainians, Jews and other minorities to rise up and seek revenge on their Polish neighbours. This lawlessness and bloodshed was exacerbated when the Russians released all the criminals from the gaols and used many of them to form militias to hunt down Polish administrators, police officers and military personnel. All the institutions and organs of government were closed down and then renamed and reopened under Russian control and direction. The zloty was abolished and the rouble (with only 10% of the purchase value) was introduced on a par, which meant that any savings became almost worthless overnight. In addition any balances over 300 zloty were confiscated along with all valuables. The banks were nationalised and all safety-deposit boxes were also seized. Heavy taxes were introduced alongside rigid state controls in all walks of life.

The Polish language, literature, culture and all visible signs and representation of the Polish state were abolished. The media was controlled and became an outlet for Soviet propaganda, which was also broadcast on speakers erected in the towns and cities. Religion and the clergy were persecuted, many churches were shut and children were told to worship Stalin and were even given a picture of him as an icon. Almost miraculously and in no time at all, thousands of murals, posters and statues of him appeared everywhere, in every conceivable size and shape. Schools were closed down and the official languages became Russian and Ukrainian. The occupiers stole everything: first they looted all the shops and businesses and then their attention turned to the general population. They intimidated, threatened and stole at will, taking money, food, livestock, produce, clothing, furniture, coal, even farm implements and everyday household items: anything they could turn into cash.

Then the roundups, the killings and the real horror started.

Bogdana was woken up at 2am, surprised and frightened by the heavy and constant banging on the door. In the firelight she could see the door and frame vibrating with every impact and the wooden slats started to splinter and split. She sat bolt upright, on top of the huge bread oven that they used as the family bed and pulled her waking children, her beloved Michal and Karolina into a protective hug. Dominik was away on the orders of the occupying power, working three days a week at the rail yards in Luck, the nearby town. He was not due back until the following evening. Suddenly the banging stopped, but she was still unable to move, terrified that their turn had come. She had heard rumours from neighbouring districts that the Russians were rounding up the Polish families and transporting them east to work in their fields and factories. Every week Dominik had become increasingly reluctant to leave them and return to work, but the Russians had made it clear that any conscripted absentees would be shot and their families arrested or worse. They had good reason to believe that this was no idle threat.

Despite the cloak of secrecy that shrouded Stalin's murderous repression, they had discovered from Bogdana's Ukrainian relatives what had happened to the Poles living just a few miles away inside Russia only two years previously. During just one episode of what was to become known as the 'Great Terror' 140,000 people were arrested and over 110,000 were executed, just for being Polish. When Stalin heard that there had been nearly 25,000 citizens of Polish origin arrested in just one four-week period, he was quoted as saying, 'This is excellent news! Continue to dig, cleanse, and eradicate all this Polish filth! Liquidate them all in the interests of our USSR.'

Bogdana was even more terrified when the silence was broken by harsh commands in her native Ukrainian. "Dabrowski, I am Sokorov of State Security. You are an enemy of the revolution and your fate is now in my hands. This is the only chance you'll get so open the door immediately or you will all be executed! I'll count to five and then we'll shoot our way in."

She knew from his heavy accent that he was Russian and from his menacing and assured tone she had no doubt that he was used to wielding power. Yes she thought: here is a man who expects immediate obedience and means exactly what he says. So she did as she was told and when she removed the wooden bar from the door, three men barged past, knocking her off her feet. "Get up you stupid bitch and shut those whimpering brats up or I'll do it for you," said the same voice, reinforcing his threat and frightening her even further by slowly and deliberately moving his right hand to the butt of his automatic pistol. She grabbed her sobbing children and tried to comfort and reassure them.

Sokorov was in civilian clothes, but he was obviously the leader and an NKVD officer. He was accompanied by a uniformed Red Army soldier from the nearby garrison and a member of the 'red militia', a local communist from Luck who wore a red arm band and a cap with a red star on the front. The latter two were armed with rifles and torches and they immediately started to ransack the house, scattering clothing, crockery and kitchen utensils all across the floor as they searched for 'the evidence of her subversion'. Sokorov stood just inside the door and waited silently, but he never took his eyes off of Bogdana who was sat at the table holding her children close. The militiaman scattered the contents of a small wooden box on the floor, then bent down and picked up a piece of card and an official-looking document, looked across at Sokorov and said, "Here they are sir, just as you suspected. It's his discharge papers and he fought against us in 1920."

Sokorov then examined them and proclaimed, "Excellent! Now we've got him for sure and he won't wriggle out of this. They clearly show that he was a lieutenant and that makes him a number one on my list," and then he looked at Bogdana. "That means that you and both your children fall squarely into category two and you are now under arrest. All three of you will be taken away for interrogation. I'll give you five minutes to gather some belongings together before we leave." Bogdana sensed that it would be pointless to argue and so she remained silent, content not to do anything that would put their lives in immediate danger. They were taken to the prison at Luck and pushed into a cell that normally held three people but a total of twenty-two prisoners had been crammed and wedged inside. Everyone had to stand upright, pressed tight into each other. Bogdana could see that four or five men in the corner close to her had been beaten about the face and she wondered if she would also be attacked. As they waited the air became fetid, they found it more difficult to breathe and an old man fainted, but he was held upright by those next to him. Her children started to cry and gasp for air and she wept with relief and gratitude when two men picked them up and sat them on their shoulders, soothing them with kind words and softly-spoken folk stories.

Three hours later they were taken to the nearby court building where they were searched, stripped of all personal possessions and put up in front of Sokorov and a female member of the newly formed Revolutionary Committee. Two NKVD guards stood at the door. The woman entered their details into a formal register and then asked Sokorov, "What shall I put down as their crimes?"

He replied, "They're the family of a Polish military officer. He's a nationalist who fought against us and he's ideologically opposed to the honourable principals of Soviet Socialism. Even as we speak he's plotting against us. That's more than enough to categorise them as 'dangerous and subversive elements'. Fill that in and I'll countersign it."

"I take it that you want me to include the children as well then?"

"Of course! That's what the directive demands: otherwise they'll grow up to threaten us and our glorious revolution with their nationalist, capitalist and subversive ways, just like their treacherous father."

They were taken back to the prison block but this time to an empty cell, and as she was pushed in through the door her children were snatched from her and dragged away down the corridor, shouting and crying out for their mother. She tried to push her way past the guard to go after them, but he pulled her back and threw her to the floor, before slamming the heavy metal door as he left.

An hour later Sokorov returned carrying a sheaf of papers. "I have brought your confession along for you to sign." He then indicated where she should put her signature and added, "There's no need for you to read any of it. Every crime you've committed is fully listed and it confirms and corroborates your husband's anti-state and dissident activities."

She refused to sign, "I won't give the slightest bit of credibility to such a pack of malicious lies. We've done nothing wrong at all. Your behaviour towards us is outrageous and that guard had no right to remove my children. Where are they? I want them brought back to me immediately and I want to report him for taking them from me in the first place and for assaulting me. He deliberately threw me onto the floor."

Sokorov put the papers down and called in the guard. "This stupid woman just doesn't get it, and now she wants to complain about your brutal behaviour and she won't sign her confession either, so I think it's time to move on! You hold her down while I convince her to see things our way." She braced herself, expecting to be grabbed, but the guard surprised her by punching her hard in the face, a vicious right arm jab that split her lip, broke her nose and knocked her down. In reflex, her hands flew to her face and she tried to stem the gush of blood. The guard bent over her and pulled her left hand away. Sokorov grabbed her little finger and bent it back against the joints and she screamed in pain. He increased the pressure until wave after wave of agony ran up her arm and through her whole body and then, with a clearly audible crack, it snapped and dislocated sideways. She had never known such pain and was barely conscious, but she still felt him grab her index finger and start again. This time he jerked it back quickly as he held his own thumb behind her middle knuckle and the bottom two joints shattered. As she moaned and whimpered Sokorov said, "We can do this to every one of your fingers and then we'll crush your toes, but I'm already beginning to lose interest. I think we'll move on to your children and see how strong their tiny young bones are. Come on comrade, let's go see the little ones and break their arms and legs."

She could hardly speak, but she knew that he would do it and the dreadful fear gave her strength. She sobbed and pleaded, "No please, no! For God's sake leave my children alone. Don't hurt them. I'll sign it. Bring it here. I'll do whatever you say." Sokorov left a minute later with his 'evidence'.

As darkness fell the children were brought back to her, but as soon as they arrived all three were forcibly and cruelly gagged and blindfolded by three NKVD gaolers. Their hands were tied behind their backs, they were repeatedly slapped around the head and then they were made to sit on the floor with their heads almost touching their raised knees. It was a very uncomfortable and numbing position but every time they stretched or tried to move their heads they were beaten with whippy hazel sticks. Bogdana felt as if she was swimming in a sea of pain. She could still just about stand the mounting hurt from her own mental and physical injuries but to hear her vulnerable children so abused and to be completely unable to protect or comfort them, that really broke her heart and spirit. Self-recrimination and guilt intensified the emotional turmoil and she was overwhelmed by despair.

Half an hour later Sokorov entered. With no preamble or even a word to the guards, he bent down and whispered in Bogdana's ear, "I want you to know that it's me and that I'm going to shoot the kids first." Her muffled shrieks and the noise from her stamping feet and her frantic thrashing about as she desperately but unsuccessfully tried to free herself were drowned out by the deafening discharge of two gunshots. He listened to her maniacal screams for a moment and then he viciously twisted her ear until she stopped.

The last words she ever heard were Sokorov's, "Well my Polish whore, that's two less spoiled brats to bother us in the future and now it's your turn because we don't want you turning out any replacements, do we? Do you know that once you've been dispatched that'll be yet another quota filled? Uncle Joe will be pleased and then that's me done for the day!" He smiled to himself, pulled the trigger and then took a lingering and admiring look at his latest handiwork before leaving the guards to clean up the mess. He rushed off because he didn't want to be late for dinner.

∞∞∞∞∞∞∞

Even though I had read the file on Sokorov, knew about the secret order to murder Poles in Russia in 1937 and seen his grotesque and chilling terror list for 1939, I was still profoundly shocked, sickened and incensed by the cruel reality of what had been meted out to ordinary people, even women and children. Like the term 'Nackenschuss' with its frightening implications, the cruelty and vindictiveness of it all was completely beyond my comprehension, and it chilled me to the bone. I asked Stan, "You were closer to all this than me. So can you tell me how on earth anyone could do such things to small innocent children?"

He sighed deeply and scratched at his scar, "The answer's in the file. He was a killer, a monster devoid of all humanity who demonised his victims until he no longer saw them as people or children or babies but simply as obstacles to be removed. He totally detached himself from their suffering. His mission in life became the destruction of anyone who had been labelled as a threat to or an enemy of the only thing he cared about – the glorious revolution."

Neither of us wanted to delve any deeper into his warped personality or explore his motivation. The hard cold facts of his crimes were more than enough to deal with and so we took a break and had a cup of coffee. Then Stan told me what happened next.

Dominik arrived home to find the house ransacked, his family gone and a typed notice nailed to the inside of the door:

Luck District Military Commissariat
1)   Notice of Arrest
2)   Order to Surrender
Notice is hereby given that the occupants of this dwelling have been arrested for committing serious offences against the state and have been removed to Luck prison, where they will be interrogated. This property (and all its contents) has been confiscated and along with its lands, outbuildings, stock and stores, it awaits reallocation to suitable workers. Nothing here can be used, consumed or removed without the express permission of the senior Soviet authority for this district.
Furthermore, Dominik Dabrowski is ordered to immediately surrender himself to the authorities at Luck. If this does not occur within 24 hours of this notice he will be added to the list of fugitive enemies of the state and liable to be shot on sight.
Issued and signed at 0600 hours by
Colonel A M Sokorov – For General B. Petrov
Dated: 12th February 1940 – District Commander, Luck.

Dominik was frantic with shock and worry. He was unable to think clearly and slumped down into a chair, angry, despondent and desperately frightened for his wife and children. He let the terrifying and pessimistic pictures of his imagination slowly burn themselves out. As he regained some composure he started to examine the Russians' actions and motivation and the practicalities of his own new and desolate situation. He was aware that for the last week or so local people had been disappearing from their homes and whole families had been spirited away by the NKVD. The rumours suggested that they were being sent to Russia on cattle trains to be used as slaves on the land. However, he had never heard of the Russians leaving notices saying people had been arrested. On the contrary, they always tried to operate in secrecy, in the dead of night so why the change and why did they want him?

He had always kept a low profile and had not been involved in the resistance movement and so there could be no possible excuse for them to arrest his family. In any case, they already knew where and when he worked because he had been required to register with them before he could even start the job. They had also issued him with a travel pass and yet it seemed that they had expected to find him at home. He thought that they must have taken his family away because it turned out that he wasn't there and they hoped to use them as hostages to force him to give himself up. But why go to all that trouble when they could have simply arrested him at work in Luck? After all, that's where they would take him anyway. None of it made any sense, unless it was just another example of military incompetence: the old 'left hand – right hand' problem.

Why did they want him? Why was he an enemy of the state? The idea was ridiculous! He had done nothing wrong and neither had his wife and children so why had they seized his house and farm? The more he thought about it, the more sinister the situation became. Although he was sorely tempted to obey the order and give himself up to save his family, his intuition and training convinced him to find out what was really going on first, before he committed himself to a firm and irreversible course of action that he would probably quickly regret. In any case his 24 hours were long gone, and so he had to be careful.

He lifted the stone slab in front of the oven and removed the old ammunition box containing his emergency kit from the well-concealed hiding place. For nearly 20 years he had maintained, updated and augmented the contents so that he would never be totally defenceless. He was a soldier after all, and history showed he lived in a dangerous place. He removed his trench gun, the Smith and Wesson revolver and a handful of ammunition for both. He loaded the weapons and then pouched them in the inside poacher pockets of his greatcoat. He ripped the fur lining on the outer side of his right boot and slipped the dagger and sheath snugly inside. He also removed a photograph of his family, a false identity card, a blank railway warrant, the parchment scroll, a fistful of Russian Roubles and his Virtuti Militari before carefully replacing the box. He then shaved off his beard and moustache, re-nailed the notice to the door, took a last look around to check that everything was just as he found it and left. The familiar feel of the weapons and the fact that he was now taking some positive action boosted his confidence and he continued planning as he walked.

His first stop was his neighbour, another farmer who had a son fighting with the ZWZ (Union for Armed Struggle) underground, a forerunner to the Home Army and he asked for an urgent interview with the local commander. In order to bolster his chances of success he gave a brief rundown of his military history and his association with General Haller and Marshal Pilsudski, and then he hid in the barn and waited. The following morning he was collected by a man driving a cart loaded with timber and heading for the sawmill on the outskirts of Luck. His request had been granted, but first he was to be interviewed and vetted by the organisation's local security officer.

As they travelled along Dominik told him about the circumstances of his family's arrest and in response the driver asked him a series of questions about their family history and his military career. Once satisfied he said, "In the last week hundreds of people have been rounded up in this one area alone and I understand the same thing is happening right across the Russian-controlled region. It's not just military personnel either; they're taking anybody and everybody. It seems to be totally random and we can't just sit back and let it go on."

"I've heard all sorts of rumours and gossip but do you actually know what they're doing with them all?"

"Some of them are being taken deep into the Soviet Union, to prison camps or labour gangs but worse still, others are being shot."

Dominik suspected as much. He had already seen what they were capable of, but he had hoped for the sake of his family that his troubled thoughts would prove to be overly pessimistic. He dreaded the answers but the questions had to be asked.

"How certain are you and have you any idea of the numbers involved?"

The security officer chose his words carefully, "At least half of them are being murdered. I know it for a fact because we've got someone on the inside. Even with your experience and impeccable credentials I can't tell you any more than that, at least not until the commander authorises it."

Dominik was stunned. He never expected such a bleak outlook and a knot formed in his stomach. He broke out in a cold sweat as the real possibility of the loss of his wife hit home for the first time. He would never give up hope, but he was unable to shake off his growing apprehension and he sat in silence, immersed in his thoughts for the rest of the journey.

Colonel Turek spent a few minutes in private conversation with his security officer before introducing himself to Dominik who ran through his story once more before asking, "Can you find out where they are and what's happened to them?"

The colonel promised to help, "I don't know where they are at the moment; things are difficult for us too and we all have families and friends to worry about, but as you know we've got a source inside the prison. He's a member of the Jewish Red Militia and although most of them hereabouts have been collaborating with the enemy, turning in their neighbours and betraying their countrymen, he is completely loyal and a true comrade and patriot. I suppose there are good and bad everywhere and I know some of our own people are just as treacherous, but he risks his life for us every single day. I'll have him find out for you, and meanwhile you can't possibly go back home so I'll arrange lodgings for you. Stay there tonight and come back and see me again at the same time tomorrow."

Dominik spent a sleepless night worrying about his family and thinking about his future. He decided that whatever the outcome he would join the underground. He could not stand by while the Russians were in occupation once again, killing and making slaves of his people. A potent mixture of duty, military discipline and personal honour ran through his veins, and unlike many of his fellow citizens he knew how to fight and wage war and perhaps even more importantly, he knew others who were just as committed. It was time to call in some favours and find his old friends. With the arrival of daylight he lay on his bed, stared at the ceiling and for the next two hours he thought about his options and made his plans.

Later that afternoon Colonel Turek sat Dominik down and gave him the dreadful news.

"Sadly, our contact has confirmed just what I was afraid of. Your wife and both your children were murdered in the prison here yesterday, along with nearly 100 other poor souls."

Dominik had tried to prepare himself for the possibility of losing his wife, but when he heard that his dear children had been killed too and his last vestige of hope was shattered, he could not contain his emotions any longer. He broke down, disconsolate and sobbing and he cried out their names in disbelief and mental agony. The pain of loss was physical and overwhelming and he held his head in his hands and wept uncontrollably.

The colonel said, "I'm so sorry Dominik. I'll leave you alone for a while and then we'll talk." He left the room, doubtful as to whether he had even been heard.

Dominik's immediate and piercing sorrow slowly ebbed away with his tears and was replaced by a burning, vengeful anger that called for immediate and massive retribution. As soon as the colonel returned he asked, "Who is responsible for these murders?" He then learnt about Sokorov and his manoeuvrings to rid the area of Polish nationalists and their supporters. He demanded to know precisely how his family had died and he was told the truth, exactly as the informant had reported it. Nothing was kept from him. The colonel also told him of Sokorov's penchant for quotas and his boastful pride of how he personally always exceeded those of the other executioners.

Dominik asked, "Why on earth haven't you already assassinated him? Surely he's your top target?"

"We've tried twice and failed both times. He's well guarded, clever and very security minded. He's been doing Stalin's killing for a very long time and he's learnt the art of survival. There's not many of us either. I've lost six men going after him already and I can't really afford to lose any more. Most of our military officers and troops were either captured when they invaded or have since been arrested. We're still recruiting but it's difficult, what with so many non-Polish residents and the constant sweeps and raids. We've also got an endless list of other logistical and organisational tasks that means we can only take on a fraction of the approved operations. Our priority has got to be to build up our numbers and develop the organisation into an effective and formidable underground army. Only then, once we've got sufficient arms and equipment can we can carry out a full-scale uprising."

Dominik was only half-listening but he didn't hesitate, "Don't you worry, I'll do it myself. I'll kill the bastard and I'll enjoy doing it."

"Look Dominik, I know how you must feel and I'd like to help you, but I can't possibly allow that. You're overwrought and not thinking straight and I've already told you it's far too difficult for one man. You wouldn't get anywhere near him and even if you did, you'd probably be killed or captured and then you'd endanger all of us. I absolutely forbid it!"

Dominik took out the dagger and sheath from his boot and the scroll and his medal from his pocket and slammed them down on the desk and shouted, "Take a bloody good look at these and then tell me again, exactly what you think! You can't forbid it. I've got the royal warrant. For Christ's sake listen to me!"

The colonel did as he was asked and as Dominik began to calm down, he explained the story behind the articles and how he had come by them and then he asked quietly, "Now, have you changed your mind or not? I've never asked for anything for myself before, but I'm begging you now."

"This is incredible! If I hadn't seen it with my own eyes I would never have believed it. What a story. You'd better tell me what you want from us and I'll see what I can do."

Dominik breathed a sigh of relief, "Nothing much, certainly no manpower. I'll put my own team together and we'll use our own weaponry so we won't deplete your resources, but I'll need accurate and up-to-date intelligence. I'd be really grateful for the help and cooperation of your intelligence officer and the use of your informant inside the prison. There's no need for us to know his identity and he needn't know of our existence. I'll also put the plan together but let you see it before we act so that we don't compromise each other's efforts. Is that acceptable to you?"

Colonel Turek thought for a moment before replying, "Okay, but on condition that I alone decide whether or not you get the green light to go ahead and that if any difficulties occur during the run-up to the operation they are resolved directly between us. I don't want my staff involved in any disputes or sidetracked from their own duties."

Dominik agreed, they shook hands and he quickly filled in his rail warrant and left for Lwów to find his friends. The city had been besieged yet again in September the previous year, only this time by two powerful armies.

The Germans had arrived first and within days they were joined by the Russians but the defenders, although massively outnumbered, fought on. German and Russian Artillery and the Luftwaffe pounded the city, targeting not only the defenders, their fortifications and barricades but also the water and power plants, churches, schools and hospitals. Over a week later both enemy commanders, competing for the honour of victory, simultaneously called upon the Poles to surrender to save the city, its citizens and its culture from total destruction. Then Hitler, in accordance with his agreement with Stalin to divide up Poland between them, ordered his army to withdraw west to the Vistula-San River line and leave the city for the Russians to deal with.

The Russian commander then proposed that if the Poles surrendered, all privates and NCOs would be allowed to leave the city, register themselves with the Soviet authorities and then go home. Furthermore, the officers would be allowed to leave

Poland for any country that would accept them. The formal act of surrender was duly signed in the morning and by the afternoon it had already been broken by the Russians. The NKVD started to arrest the Polish officers and NCOs and most of them were later murdered at Katyn.

Chapter Nine

THE ABDUCTION

Lwów – 30th January 1940

Konrad had lived in western Poland before he emigrated and was forced to learn German as a child, but in 1923, after the Polish wars, he had married and settled down in the Zboiska suburb of Lwów. It had developed into a beautiful and vibrant cosmopolitan city and a beacon of academic, literary and theatrical life but everything changed when the Germans invaded. Old interfaith tensions that had been dormant for a decade or more rose back to the surface and were then exploited by the invaders.

He joined the volunteers inside his own district to fight the enemy and his knowledge of their language proved very useful to the defenders. Unlike many of his friends and neighbours he survived the short but ferocious battle and after the surrender he went back home to his wife, Joanna Adamska, and his son, Stanislaw – back to a life of occupation and hardship.

Imagine his delight then, when he saw his old commander and friend turn up unannounced on his doorstep some four months later. They had last met at Stanislaw's christening in 1924. They were devastated to hear Dominik's news but confirmed that 'disappearances' and transportations to the east were also a regular feature of life in the countryside all around Lwów.

Later that evening when Dominik was alone with Konrad, he told him what he was planning and asked if he would help. He was careful to explain that they were no longer military personnel and not even members of the underground movement and although that organisation would give some limited help, they were really freelance and would be operating on their own, without any backup. After further discussion Konrad decided to sleep on it and give his answer the following day.

Joanna and Konrad lay awake most of the night trying to decide what he should do. They both felt that his responsibility to his own family was more important than his acknowledged duty to his comrade, but he also had an obligation to his country. Dominik was grieving, angry and seeking personal revenge, that was clear enough. They agreed that his emotional state could so easily have a detrimental effect on his military judgement and effectiveness. But they also knew that Konrad was the best equipped to ensure that Dominik kept his focus and that should he refuse to help, then his friend would carry on alone, regardless of the consequences. They also accepted that Sokorov was a sadistic mass murderer and a racist and he deserved to be in the cross hairs of every Polish patriot and both of them had proved themselves, time and time again, on that particular point. They also faced up to the possibility that Konrad might well be killed on the mission. It could even be the probable outcome, given the circumstances, but on the other hand what lay ahead in Lwów? How long before it was their turn to appear on a list or receive a visit from the NKVD? They carefully weighed all these factors and many others, but still it was the hardest decision of his life. In the end they both agreed. He should go.

The following day Konrad went to find Adam Buza the pilot who had, until the invasions, been an instructor at the civilian flying school and also resided in the city, while Dominik saw Hannah and Aaron Silberstein who still lived in their parents' old house in the Jewish quarter. He discovered that they were now both lecturers at the university but were becoming increasingly alarmed at the way things were going. The Russian guards at their college had been heard talking about plans to send half the Poles in Lwów into the German-occupied zone and that all the rest were to be sent off to Siberia. Eastern Poland was to be cleared of its people to make room for Russians. Some of their most senior colleagues, including the chairman of their own faculty, the Department of Mathematics, had already been arrested by the NKVD and there was a growing atmosphere of hostility between the occupiers and the population.

The ZWZ was actively recruiting at the university and hundreds were taking the military oath every day. They were also ashamed of the way many Jews had gleefully collaborated with the Russians, particularly in the first months of the occupation. They had formed Red Militias (Workers' Guards in the towns and Peasants' Guards in the country) and hunted down Polish officers and then handed them over to the NKVD. Gangs of Jewish youths had viciously ridiculed, spat on and stoned Polish prisoners of war as they were led away by the Russians. Occasionally, even Soviet troops were surprised at the levels of hostility and hate shown by some ethnic minority Polish citizens towards their own soldiers and felt the need to step in to protect them from their tormentors. Most Poles and the majority of Jews were astonished and indignant at the high levels of anti-Polish sentiment, betrayal and treachery they witnessed. To a lesser degree some Ukrainians also collaborated and informed on their Polish neighbours and members of most minority groups right across eastern Poland seized on the opportunity to settle their real or imagined grievances. With Russian collusion and encouragement it became a time of suspicion, betrayal and tribalism. The Bolsheviks were past masters at the policy of divide and conquer.

Hannah explained that their parents were now dead and being single, with both their jobs and their lives under threat, they were eager to escape the city and would gladly accept Dominik's offer, despite the obvious dangers. They both needed to feel that they were fighting back. Later that day Konrad and Adam also turned up. Adam, who was on the verge of joining the ZWZ, agreed to help on the condition that if successful in Dominik's personal war, they would all join the underground together and fight to help free their country. They immediately agreed and then Dominik allocated their specific roles and tasks within the unit and together they started planning the logistics of the operation.

Konrad would arrange for false documents to be provided for them all, including local refugee and employment certificates to show that they were originally from the Nazi Occupation Zone. These papers would, to some degree, lessen the level of Soviet harassment they were likely to receive because it showed that they were 'the property' of the Nazis. Their limited protection might not last long though because the NKVD and Gestapo officers were already cooperating. They had held week-long meetings in Zakopane, Krakow and Lwów, and as a result they were now drawing up plans to tighten their grip on the entire Polish population. If they were caught up in one of the random NKVD sweeps they could easily find themselves handed over to the Nazis before they could complete their mission, but it was a risk worth taking to give them some freedom of movement in and around Luck.

Dominik made it perfectly clear that a sniper or explosives option was not on the table, "I'm going to be the one to kill Sokorov and I'm going to do it up close so that I can look him right in the eye. I would also prefer to take him alive first so that we can interrogate him and get any information out of him that would be useful to the underground. Either way we'll still have to deal with his guards first."

Hannah was not so keen, "That will make the job much more difficult. It means we need reliable and up-to-date intelligence and an assortment of weapons. Not just to outgun the guards, but if things go wrong at the snatch point we'll be terribly exposed and may even have to fight our way out. Managing a dangerous prisoner and trying to keep him alive at the same time really complicates things for us."

Dominik explained how he had the intelligence angle covered and then handed a piece of paper over to Aaron and said, "I've got a couple of weapons already and that's a list of the other guns, ammunition and extra kit that we still need. I'm appointing you as quartermaster and I suggest that you get what you can from within the Jewish community. Can you do that?

Aaron scanned the list, "I think so. There certainly doesn't seem to be any dearth of weaponry within the various Jewish groups across the city. But I'll have to spread it between several sources to avoid suspicion. If they find out that I'm helping you it wouldn't take long before someone betrays us all."

Next Dominik turned to accommodation and transport and said, "I'll go on ahead, back to Luck and arrange for a couple of suitable addresses where we can base ourselves during the surveillance and rehearsal phase. I'll also find somewhere safe and out of the way where we can take our prisoner." He then gave them a rendezvous point near the market square and said, "I'll be there at 0900 hours and 1400 hours for three days starting the day after tomorrow. You should all travel separately and please be careful because I can't afford to lose even one of you." Then he said to Adam, "When you get to Luck I want you to get us a vehicle – a trade van would be best. Find something old, rusty and beat-up but with a good engine, something that will fit in and would be seen delivering or moving around the centre on daily basis. Then you'll have to steal it just before we mount the operation and we'll use it to get away. You'll be the nominated driver and Konrad and Aaron will deal with the guards while Hannah and I snatch Sokorov. Well, that's about as far as we can go for now, but has anybody got any more questions at this stage?

They all shook their heads and Aaron replied, "No I don't think so but I'm sure there will be plenty once we've got a firm date, time and location. That's when all the difficult decisions will have to be made."

Just before the meeting broke up Adam said, "Just a minute Dominik, I think you should know that you've now achieved in just a few seconds what neither the Germans nor the Bolsheviks managed to do to me in six long years. Some might say I was once a man chosen from the elite to fly for his country. Yes, a gentleman who became used to having great power and a thing of beauty under his control and the latest in-flight technology of war at his fingertips. Now you've literally brought me down to earth, grounded me in fact and transformed me from a high-flyer of high birth and high principles into a common car thief. No, I'll rephrase that, I'm not even that far up the status league table of criminals. Now I'm merely a scrap-metal merchant, a rag-and-bone man dealing in old bangers. Woe is me – I'm a vagrant!"

All his friends laughed and despite his mournful mood and his troubled soul, Dominik could not resist a broad smile and a chuckle at Adam's levity. It was just what he needed at that point and with it came the realisation that the team was definitely back together and that they really had a fighting chance of seeing the operation through to success.

Swindon – 10th November 2009

I arrived back in Swindon rather later than usual and as it was approaching lunch time, I called in for a take-away and decided to take Stan his favourite – pizza and chips. He had told me that he was too old to worry about healthy eating and in a weak moment, despite my burgeoning waistline, I had decided that it would have been rude not to enjoy the same meal. As I waited in the queue, looking back out through the window onto the busy and bustling street scene, I was suddenly struck by the incredible gulf between the lifestyles of my generation and that of Dominik's.

I had never known hunger, but he had lived through rationing, famine and starvation. In his early life he was never full and replete. I lived in a civilised western democracy where, despite the recession and credit crunch, there was peace and tranquillity, but he was constantly fighting for his life and his country. I could walk in the sunshine, free, happy and protected, whereas he had been hunted, always wary and surrounded by murder and oppression. The stark contrasts that ran through my mind seemed endless. Yet millions – not hundreds or thousands, but millions – of his countrymen and women had endured those impossible hardships and tragedy, such that we cannot even begin to imagine, yet they

An Abiding Legacy

survived. Many were damaged in the process and there was no counselling or support services or compensation for them, or for the relatives of more than six million who died.

These thoughts made me impatient to hear more of Dominik's story and for a while I found myself in total sympathy with the man and his cause, eagerly willing him on towards his revenge. I assumed that the chilling note at the end of the Sokorov document was written by him. As I walked back to the car I tried to imagine myself in Dominik's shoes. What would I have done? Of course, I had no real idea, but with every pace I started to feel less sure about the legitimacy of his revenge, particularly if, as the note suggested, it included torture and making Sokorov pay in kind. This sudden ambivalence and rectitude worried me because just a few short moments before I had felt so sure that anything was justifiable and Sokorov deserved a dreadful death. Then it clicked and I realised what was really bothering me. It wasn't the deed itself, for Sokorov was the author of his own misfortune and surely deserved to die. No, it was the long time-lapse between the event and the retribution, the cold and calculated planning and most of all, the fact that Dominik compromised and demeaned his friends by bending them to his will. It was no longer a hot-blooded act of revenge but a bitter and calculated ritualised execution, a disdainful replica of Sokorov's own mortal sin, but I was equally convinced that that was exactly what Dominik wanted. Nothing less could slay his demons.

After lunch Stan surprised me yet again, "Before we carry on I think it's time to tell you one of the reasons why Jan and I decided to involve you in the first place."

"Stan, you really do amaze me. When I was desperate to know what this was all about you kept digressing and putting me off, teasing me with tempting morsels of information and hints of breathtaking derring-do. But now, when I'm totally wrapped up in the whole adventure and hooked just for the story's sake, you offer to answer an old and tired question that has almost become irrelevant. So forgive me if I don't expect the epitome of openness and clarity from you. You're an old rogue and a clever one at that."

He laughed, "I'm not so sure about the clever bit, I'm a simple country boy really. But I know I can be a bit of a rascal sometimes so I suppose that's a cross you've got to bear if you want to see this through to the end." He then smiled broadly, opened up his notebook on one of the numerous pages sprouting a yellow post-it and said, "Back in November 2008 you gave Jan and his family a comprehensive written report covering your successful investigation to trace him and return the missing letters etc."

I had no idea of where this was leading but humoured him anyway. "Yes, I told them what I'd done, listed the various lines of enquiry that I'd taken together with the people, organisations and agencies that had provided useful information. I also attached copies of all the critical documentation just in case any of the family wanted to follow up on a specific area or personally thank one of the contacts."

Stan, as if by magic and with a theatrical flourish, produced a copy of the ten-page document from the back of his notebook and waved it in the air, "And here it is and Jan was very impressed with it. He liked your style of writing, the fact that you were always analytical, incisive and concise and never wandered from the evidence. But as he said himself, these are all qualities that you would expect from any good detective, but what he appreciated even more was the way you made it so readable. You crafted an interesting and absorbing story out of what was basically a technical report."

"Come on, Stan, you're either taking the mickey or talking about something else altogether. For goodness sake! It was just a regular report not a Shakespearean play."

"Well, perhaps I am but just a tad. I've got to admit that I thought he was way over the top too when he went on to suggest that even your timelines were 'interesting and informative'. That's just too much to accept! Anyway, the point is that he was impressed and I agreed with him." He then chuckled and added, "Mind you, our choice might also have had just as much to do with the fact that you can speak and write Polish – and you come relatively cheap. But seriously now, we want you to take Dominik's diary, my notebook and any other materials that I can provide and write his biography. It's got to be done or at least put in train before I'm gone. It's too important to be lost in the mists of time. I'm sure you'll agree with that and believe you me, the best is yet to come. That's why I'm telling you his story in so much detail. So come on, what do you say?"

I thought for a minute or two, wondering if I even had the time, let alone the ability to take on such an important commitment. Surely it could best be done by an experienced and published author. I voiced my concerns, "I appreciate being asked, but I'm sure that you could easily find a professional biographer who would bite your hand off at the chance to take on such a project and any one of their number would achieve everything you want."

He was not put off easily, "We want you to do it. Anyway, all the professionals are probably far too busy knocking out the next 'gripping and amazing' life story of the latest X-Factor winner or a wannabe from 'I'm not a celebrity get me into here' or a fifth-rate screen idol, or some WAG or another that I've never even heard of. Whoever it is, they're bound to be doing the obligatory round of talk shows promoting their talent and their wonderful book. The sort of hardback that hundreds queue up to have signed but are then left, forgotten and unread to gather dust amongst all the other 'must-have' designer publications."

I laughed at his cynical but heartfelt rant, but it did strike a chord with me. "That's a bit too strong Stan, but I know what you mean about the self-promotion. I've always thought that the chat shows are just a barely disguised but never-ending publicity carousel for the needy and less talented. They're constantly spinning around to a tune of self-congratulation and mutual appreciation. Even so, I'm not in their league and I wouldn't know where to start."

"You undersell yourself. Not only do you definitely have the ability, but you've also got a strong emotional and ethnic bond with Dominik and the other characters and a relationship with me, which no professional could ever have. I've listened to you and I know you have the words and the imagination to bring the dead back to life so that the reader can feel, hear, see, smell and taste what life was like – whether down in the trenches or up in a plane or standing firm against the galloping Konarmia."

"I'm still not sure that I can do it justice. I've no experience to fall back on and it's certainly not as easy as you make out."

Stan was not going to be deterred. "When you read his diary I bet you fully experienced the action for yourself. You understood their motivation and you felt the red-hot and shredded emotions of those involved. If Dominik can do it, so can you. Your job is simply to ensure that the reader feels the same, by your use of language and description. Just paint the mental pictures for them; their imagination will do the rest. I want today's generation to come to fully understand what drove Dominik and his friends and why they did such incredible things. That's why Jan chose you and now, with the story nearly half-told, you can make an informed judgement. If I'd asked you before I think you would have dismissed me out of hand. I can also positively guarantee that you will in turn marvel and despair at what I'm going to reveal to you over the next few days. There's no rush either. It doesn't have to be published until the middle of 2014, ready for the 75th anniversary of the start of WWII so you've got plenty of time."

He was probably right because, by now, I was most definitely intrigued and ensnared by Dominik's life and his constant battle with adversity and hardship and I was just beginning to understand what really made him tick. I had also come to admire the qualities of fortitude and loyalty so admirably displayed by his friends and the way in which they all refused to yield to the tyranny of hate that infested their country and contaminated so many. It was an incredible and valiant story that simply cried out to be put down on paper and so I decided to do it but prayed that I wouldn't let them down, because I was still daunted by the prospect. Then as I thought about it, another penny dropped. "Just now you said, 'one of the reasons why you asked me to become involved'. What are the other reasons then? What else haven't you told me about? I'm beginning to think that you're up to your old tricks again."

He smiled mischievously and shook his head. "No, I'm really not being difficult. There's only one other thing that we want you to do, but we haven't yet reached the relevant part of the tale, so please just be patient for a little longer. You'll know soon enough."

I was not too disappointed or surprised by his answer as I had more than enough to think about as it was and I knew that he would tell me in his own good time and not a second sooner. He relished such moments; a time when he was in total control and he could slowly lead me by the nose down the snaking path that Jan and he had mapped out months ago. Then he rubbed his hands together, cleared his throat and told me what happened to Sokorov...

Back at Luck in the Old Town district, Dominik was met by a resistance courier and taken deep underneath the buildings in Daniel Halicki Street (aptly named after a thirteenth-century prince who was only too familiar with the problems of war and occupation). They descended into a labyrinth of sixteenth-century vaults and passageways. He was led blindfolded through the tunnels into the disused and largely forgotten dungeons under the Church of Saint Peter and Saint Paul. There in an isolation cell he was again seen by Colonel Turek of the ZWZ.

"I'm sorry about the cloak and dagger stuff, but one of our operational units was located and destroyed yesterday by the NKVD and it won't take long to break the two men they captured alive. So we've all had to move and now we really do live up to our name because we've regrouped down here and it's amazing."

Dominik looked at the creamy brown, coral-like rock walls and the high-vaulted ceiling and asked, "What is it?"

The insurgent replied, "I've lived in the city all my life and we were brought up on stories and legends of salt mines right underneath us. As kids we were beguiled by tales of heroes being chased by monsters through the huge caverns and the maze of escape tunnels going under the city walls and out into the surrounding villages. Until recently I didn't know they actually existed. Then a sewage engineer found a way in for us and now we're opening them up across half a dozen streets or more and fortifying them as we go."

Dominik was impressed, but he was also impatient to move his plan forward. "My team are all here now and we've got our weapons and kit safely hidden so we're ready to go. What have you got for me?"

"Your man will be going to visit the hospital on Shepel Street at 1100 hours tomorrow to visit one of his officers who was wounded in the shoot-out with our people. Apparently he's a cousin of Sokorov and a particular favourite of his, so you can now add nepotism to his catalogue of crimes. He'll arrive in his staff car with a driver and two guards and go straight to the ward on the second floor. One of the porters there works for us so if you need any further information about the hospital itself, he'll supply it. I've arranged for him to see you here when he comes off shift in about an hour's time. In the meantime, my intelligence officer will be along to brief you regarding Sokorov's escorts, their transport, strengths and weaknesses, routines and weapons. If he can, he will answer any other questions you might have."

Dominik thanked him and said, "I appreciate you didn't have to do any of this so I'm in your debt and I won't forget. I'll make sure I get something out of Sokorov that will be of real value to you and your organisation."

The colonel shook his hand, wished him well and as he left said, "Whatever happens I hope that one day you find the peace that you deserve and the freedom that we all fight for."

After his meetings Dominik went back to his team, armed with a sketch plan drawn by the porter showing the streets and buildings around the hospital. While they studied it he did a 'walk-through' to thoroughly familiarise himself with the location, confirm the accuracy of the drawing and check that there were no unforeseen problems that could disrupt the operation. When he returned they finalised their plan, then cleaned and readied their weapons and equipment before repeatedly rehearsing their individual roles and timings. Finally, they rotated the various tasks and responsibilities until each of them knew the operation inside out and could step in to cover the extra assignment if one of them was hit. They slept a little, but it was soon time to set off. At the end of curfew at 0600 hours, while it was still pitch dark, Konrad and Aaron left to keep the hospital under observation to make sure there had been no leaks. The last thing they wanted was to find an unexpected reception committee waiting for them. Twenty minutes later Adam stole the van he had already identified. He quickly returned to the shelter and anonymity of their temporary base inside the disused slaughterhouse. It was at the rear of a very rundown and neglected commercial area which backed onto the Styr River. The three of them loaded up and waited for the agreed start time.

Sokorov's staff car left on time for the ten-minute trip to the hospital. They took the most direct route and one of his guards sat alongside him behind the driver and the other occupied the front passenger seat. He had been told that his cousin was already sat up in bed talking to the doctor and nurses, bragging about how he had destroyed a nest of terrorists and now had the wounds to prove it. He had been shot in the upper arm, but Sokorov had discovered that the offending bullet was a ricochet, fired by one of his own men during the shoot-out. He had wanted all four men taken alive and felt that the whole operation had been badly handled. He had his own reputation in Moscow to think about and so he was determined to show that it was neither his own fault nor that of his cousin. Self-preservation meant that somebody's head would have to roll and it only remained for him to pick a suitable scapegoat. As the vehicle pulled up right outside the front entrance to the hospital, he decided that person should be the idiot who shot his cousin. Nevertheless, he was determined to give the patient a good dressing down over the incident and tell him to stop his ridiculous boasting and to keep his mouth shut in the future.

Konrad was standing in a recessed doorway about 20 yards from the hospital watching and waiting. There was little motorised traffic on the streets but plenty of horses pulling carts loaded with peat, coal, firewood and furniture, anything to keep a fire burning in the grate and the cold out. A few pedestrians hurried along the wide pavements with their heads down against the drizzle, looking for a shop or bakery. Anywhere that might have some bread or a few scraps of food left, hoping against hope that the morning rush had not cleared the shelves yet again. Perhaps today they just might be able to put something on the table for the family to eat. Konrad saw Sokorov's car slow down as it passed him and then it came to a standstill at the edge of the pavement, ten yards short of the hospital steps. He was relieved to see that it was a 1938 black Mercedes-Benz four-door 170 V sedan, a recent goodwill present from the Gestapo, just as the intelligence officer had said it would be. He hoped that all his information would be just as reliable and they could implement the plan exactly as originally intended. Aaron was just inside the hospital doors waiting for the signal from Dominik who was standing on the opposite pavement with Hannah – for all intents and purposes a couple waiting for the tram.

When the car pulled up, the staff driver didn't move but as expected, the guards did. They got out together and the one from the front immediately started to visually check the road ahead of the car and then across the street, turning slowly, scanning for any obvious sign of a threat. The other did the same but firstly to the rear and only then turning towards the hospital and completing his own initial arc of responsibility. Their protection training dictated that each of them was accountable for a full 360-degree first sweep, starting at opposite points of the compass. As they both then turned their attention towards the hospital the team made their move, immediately responding to Dominik's signal of stepping into the roadway. They all knew that these two guards were good at their job. They had foiled two attempts to kill their boss already and they were taking no chances. Both of them took up a position on the footpath on the inside of the car, ready to cover Sokorov to the front and rear when he emerged onto the pavement. They were both fully alert and ready to draw their weapons at the first sign of danger.

Aaron came through the hospital doors and as planned he started the action by screaming out "Freedom" at the top of his voice. At the briefing Dominik had made it perfectly clear that he was not to shoot at the guards from the steps; the risk of killing Sokorov was just too great. And so he kept his weapon in his pocket. His first task was to draw the attention of the guards away from Konrad who would then approach from their rear. Both guards reacted instinctively and turned towards the shout, drawing their weapons as they moved and then backing into Sokorov's door, preventing him from getting out and exposing himself to the danger. So far they were responding exactly as expected – exactly as they had been trained. Success or failure would now depend on how the driver reacted. If he drove off as he had probably been taught to do, then Dominik would be forced to use grenades to destroy the car and all chance of taking Sokorov alive would be gone.

Konrad's approach had been silent and swift and he was quickly down on one knee on the pavement, into a stable and practised firing position that also reduced him as a target. He was only ten yards from the rear of the vehicle with his gun in both hands and his left elbow firmly braced on his knee when he shot both the guards in the back. The second guard hadn't even reacted to the first shot before he too was cut down. They had been concentrating on Aaron, drawing their own weapons to deal with the sudden threat from the front. When they hit the pavement he fired another round into both their bodies and then he was up and running, looking for his secondary target the driver, but he couldn't see him in the vehicle – his seat was empty.

Aaron, the decoy for the operation had dropped flat as soon as he had shouted, just in case the guards managed to get off any rounds but as soon as they were down he went for his primary target, the driver. However, he had already reacted to the first shots, either panicking and ignoring his training or more likely, reacting to an order from Sokorov to get out and help the guards. As he exited the driver's door into the roadway he saw Dominik and Hannah striding out towards him with their weapons drawn and he quickly took in the rest of the grisly scene. He threw down his pistol, dodged round to the front of the car and immediately dived underneath to save himself. He didn't like the odds and unlike the guards, he didn't think Sokorov was worth dying for.

The angle of fire was all wrong for Aaron. He was too high up on the steps to shoot beneath the car and the driver's head and torso were already disappearing behind the front wheel. He fired four shots in rapid succession at the driver's legs and then ran down the steps arriving at the front of the car at the same time as Konrad. They took one leg each and dragged him out. His legs were a bloody mess as three 9mm parabellum rounds from Aaron's powerful and accurate Luger P-08 had smashed into him. He was screaming in pain as Aaron shot him in the head and their attention finally refocused onto what else was happening around them. Their job now was to protect Dominik and Hannah as they dealt with Sokorov.

From inside the car the Russian heard Aaron's scream and immediately realised something was going on at the hospital entrance and so he started to open his door to get out on the pavement side, but the door was pushed back and blocked by his own guards. He slid across the back seat and tried the other door but he saw a man carrying a shotgun and a woman holding an automatic pistol striding across the road straight towards him. He knew he was the target and he was terrified of being trapped in the car, at the mercy of his would-be assassins. He briefly considered ordering the driver to pull away, but he sensed that he was outgunned and perhaps surrounded and if they had hand grenades the move would be suicidal. No, he decided to fight not run and at least take some of them with him. He drew his own weapon and shouted at the driver, "There's at least two of them in the road, get out and shoot the bastards. Get out!!"

He then turned his attention back towards the man and woman, but they had disappeared from sight. In a matter of a few seconds he heard the first shots, saw his guards fall and then heard two more blasts followed by a very loud volley of fire from the front of the car. At no stage had he seen Konrad. He opened the door onto the road, trying to move away from the gunfire and as he stepped out he was hit across the shin of his leading left leg with an iron bar. He heard his own fibula and tibia snap before he lost consciousness as the back of his head hit the road when he was fiercely yanked from the seat by his shattered leg.

Dominik had seen Sokorov in the car as he approached and when the Russian had unsuccessfully tried to get out on the pavement side, he motioned Hannah to hide behind the boot and then he bent down just behind the rear wheel. He carefully put the shotgun down and took out the crow bar from his coat. He watched the door as it swung open towards the front of the car and as Sokorov put his leading leg down onto the cobbles he stood up and hit it with all the force he could muster from a full-blooded, backhanded swing. They now had their man and just on cue Adam screeched to a halt in the van.

The street had cleared at the sound of the first shots. Everyone either ran inside and kept well clear of their windows or made off towards the nearest junctions to escape the violence and the inevitable aftermath of searches, roundups, arrests and executions. There would be no witnesses as the residents and workers rushed to become as invisible as possible. The whole incident had taken less than two minutes, but there would soon be a major reaction from the Russians and their paramilitary collaborators, so the team positioned themselves defensively covering Dominik as he bundled the unconscious Russian into the back of the van.

The first to respond to the sound of gunfire were the two Russian soldiers who permanently monitored hospital admissions, checking for wanted Poles and possible insurgents. One telephoned the local police office and reported in, the other ran down two flights of stairs from their office to the front entrance to investigate. At the same time another Russian soldier stationed at the bank on the opposite side of the road about 100 yards down from the hospital, also came out into the street to investigate the shots. His rifle was at the ready.

The team knew that their time was running out and the enemy would soon respond in force and pour into the area. In their planning phase they had estimated that they would be lucky if they were to have three to four minutes to capture their target before they could expect significant enemy interference. Hannah and Aaron sprinted for the van, but before Konrad followed them he pulled the pin on a Russian F1 grenade and threw it into the staff car. He then dived for the back of the van where Aaron and Dominik were sat on top of the still unconscious Sokorov and holding the rear doors wide open. The van was already moving and so he grabbed the side racking and with Aaron's help he was able to pull himself in. He slammed the rear doors shut just in time and the vehicle sped away. The F1 grenade, nicknamed the limonka (lemon grenade) was a recently developed type, with a 60-gram TNT charge ignited by a UZRGM fuse with delay variants of anything from 3 to 13 seconds. Konrad's was fitted with an 8-second fuse. It carried a real punch, throwing out both large and small, heavy fragments of metal, with a range of 100 yards and an effective lethal radius of 25 yards.

The noise of the explosion, exaggerated by the close proximity of the street-side row of stone-built, three-storey buildings, was deafening. The windows and doors of the staff car blew out and then the petrol tank exploded spewing more debris across the road surface and filling the street with smoke and flame. Several pieces of metal pinged and hissed against the rear doors of the van, but at that extreme range they were virtually spent, and they did not penetrate through the double-metal skin.

The Russian soldier had arrived on the front steps of the hospital just in time to see Konrad being pulled into the van and as he raised his rifle to fire, the grenade exploded. Despite a great deal of the force being dampened within the vehicle, he was so close that he stood little chance of remaining unscathed. A piece of shrapnel, no bigger than a pea and travelling at the speed of a bullet, struck him in the side of the head, killing him instantly. He was blown off his feet by the force of the blast and his body was left pockmarked and smouldering by the peppering it had received from dozens of white hot pieces of shrapnel from the grenade and car fittings. Some were as small as a pin head.

Hannah braced her legs under the footwell and pointed her secondary weapon, which she had originally concealed in the van, out of the side window. Being just over four feet long and weighing some 10lbs it was certainly not the ideal weapon to deploy from a vehicle, but it was all Adam could get in the line of heavy firepower when they were in Lwów. It was a Tokarev SVT-38 semi-automatic rifle, fitted with a detachable magazine of powerful, high penetration .762 rounds. It was also a high-maintenance beast of a weapon with vicious recoil that could, over time, damage its working parts, but this was a brand new one and Hannah knew how to use it. She had also practised handling it and dry firing it from inside the confines of the van but despite her battle experience, she was still reflexively startled by the loud reports of the shots as they boomed and echoed around inside the metal panels. She fought to control the kick and lift of the weapon and winced at the pain in her shoulder as she sprayed a full magazine into and all around the Russian soldier outside the bank. She had been relieved to see that he was armed with a bolt-action rifle and he only managed to get off one round before he fell: his shot passing harmlessly behind the now rapidly accelerating van.

More shots chased after them as the other soldier at the hospital reached the steps and vented his rage, firing wildly after seeing his fallen comrade, the burning wreck and the bleeding and blast-bloated bodies of the dead guards. The van turned left into the corner at the first crossroads with the engine screeching under the strain of very high revolutions as Adam changed down into second gear. He was trying to squeeze every ounce of traction and speed out of the van and escape the scene before they were hit. He nearly overdid it and the rear wheels slid across the wet cobbles. The vehicle canted over dangerously, throwing the three in the back into a tangled heap as they slipped across the floor and collided with the metal side. Adam resisted the temptation to brake and turned the steering wheel into the drift as he struggled to regain control of the vehicle and prevent it from turning over onto its side.

The rear of the van sideswiped a telegraph pole, giving the two in the back with the Russian another fright, and sending them sprawling again as the metal panelling collapsed inwards, forming a two-foot-long dent with a split right down the middle. The force of the impact prevented the van from toppling over and bounced it back onto the road. This allowed Adam to regain control and he continued on in a more reasonable manner, trying not to attract any further attention. Hannah pulled her weapon inside and with their ears still ringing from the impact, Dominik and Aaron sorted themselves out in the back. Five uneventful minutes later they were safely back at the slaughterhouse with their prisoner.

Chapter Ten

RETRIBUTION AND THE ARMIA KRAJOWA

Luck – 25th February 1940

Dominik tied Sokorov's hands behind his back and anchored him with a three-foot length of rope to a heavy metal ring. It had been screwed into the concrete floor and had probably been used hundreds, perhaps even thousands, of times over the years to tether terrified animals, waiting to be slaughtered. The Pole smiled to himself at the irony and poetic justice of the current role reversal. The hunter had been captured by his prey and was seriously injured in the process. He had now become the victim and his situation was going to get a whole lot worse, because all the power and control had shifted and was now in the hands of a new torturer. A reluctant one, perhaps, but a determined one because he was being driven by the most powerful of motivations – the all-consuming but blinding need for justice. Not state justice, not divine justice but the justice of revenge; the only justice that would quench the fire in his soul and the hate in his heart. He sat down, waiting for his prisoner to regain consciousness and stared at the photograph of his wife and children, remembering their happy times before the war and regretting leaving them at the mercy of the animal staked out in front of him.

He was on his own because he had sent the others back to the safe houses to prepare for departure. He didn't want them to see or hear what he was about to do and he feared that if they remained, then one or more of them would try to stop him. Before they left they had decided that as soon as he had finished with Sokorov they were going to cross over into the Nazi-controlled area and make for Warsaw. They hoped that their various military skills, some of which were almost unique, could be used by the High Command of the newly established National Resistance Movement called Armia Krajowa (The Home Army or AK).

He was brought back to the present by Sokorov's groans as he started to come round. He walked across and looked down at him. His left leg was swollen to twice its normal size and the blood-soaked material of his trouser leg was stretched so tight and was under such tension that the stitching was beginning to fray away and was being pulled through the edges of the fabric by the relentless pressure. Dominik easily pulled the seams apart and at the very first touch Sokorov screamed out in agony. Instinctively but unsuccessfully he fought against his bonds and raised his uninjured right leg up in an attempt to kick Dominik away. But the unbelievable pain overcame him and he collapsed onto his back, sweating profusely, breathing heavily and muttering incoherently. Dominik slowly walked around him and examined the back of his head, where he found a lump the size of an egg, but there was no blood.

The Pole felt calm and ice-cold in his resolve to follow through on his promise, but he was also aware of his own limitations. His greatest concern was that by his own clumsiness or inexperience of inflicting deliberate and gratuitous pain, he would kill Sokorov prematurely. He needed to control his smouldering lust for revenge and try to progress slowly, keeping his enemy conscious right to the end. He lined up his tools on the floor and got down to work. He threw a bucket of cold water over the motionless but groaning Russian's head and he immediately started to cough and spit. Dominik picked up the hammer from his line of tools, stood to Sokorov's right-hand side and spoke for the first time.

"My name's Dabrowski and I'm going to kill you, but not quite yet." He then waited for a response, but the Russian said nothing at first, as he fought the excruciating pains in his leg and head.

After a few seconds, knowing that there was going to be no way out for him, he screwed up his eyes in pain and effort and through clenched teeth he hissed and wheezed, "You took me, so you must know who I am. You'll be hunted down for this; you're as good as dead already. Do your worst and get on with it, you Polack shit."

Dominik did not reply but grabbed the Russian's right leg and pulled off his shoe. Sokorov screamed and went rigid; even the movement of his good leg sent fresh waves of agony rippling through his body. Dominik forced his right foot flat against the concrete and swung the hammer down hard, just above his big toe. The crunch and squelch of the impact, as flesh and bone were crushed and pulped, was accompanied by another high-pitched scream which petered out into a series of moans and gasps. The whole foot started to swell immediately and Dominik spoke quietly and asked his first question, "What are your orders?"

At first Sokorov could not speak, the pain was just too great but eventually, a few words at a time he managed to groan and rasp out, "Kill you bastards... every single Pole... who's a threat to us... and from what... I've seen... that's the whole... stinking country."

"That's just not good enough. The next time I ask a question I want chapter and verse. What exactly you were told? Who told you? Who do you report to? What your priorities are. Where the killing takes place, and who carries it out? What do you do with the bodies? What's the purpose of it all? I could go on, but let me just put it like this. You will start talking and you will keep talking until I tell you to stop."

Sokorov felt like both his legs were on fire and he bit down hard on his lip and shook his head against the stabbing and throbbing agony. His lip split and his mouth filled with blood, and at the first movement of his head his vision exploded into a flash of bright lights. It felt as if the back of his head would explode from the unbearable pounding pressure. He spat out the blood and waited for the waves of misery to subside before he could speak. But he never got the chance because Dominik picked up the next item in his makeshift line of torture instruments – a three-foot length of one-inch diameter metal bar. He smashed it down from above head height onto Sokorov's right knee, a nine-foot arc of accelerating energy that almost severed the lower leg, shattering the joint and totally displacing the kneecap. This time the Russian passed out, but Dominik thought he was feigning, so he left him to stew in his pain and thoughts for a few minutes longer.

When the Russian opened his eyes, Dominik approached him carrying his third and fourth items from his line on the concrete: a half-inch chisel and a knife with a four-inch, razor-sharp blade. He slowly waved them to and fro in front of his prisoner's face, like a hypnotist drawing his victim in, and in a quiet and controlled voice he said, "I've been told that before you shot my wife in the head you broke her fingers and then threatened to do the same to our children so that she would sign a false confession. Well, now that I've reduced your legs to two useless lumps of raw meat, I'm going to untie your hands. I'll drag you to that wooden bench over there in the corner. I should think the pain from just moving you will be unbearable, but I'm in no hurry. I can wait until you recover, and you can scream as much as you like. No one can hear from outside, I've tested it. Then I'm going to drive this chisel through your hands, first the left then the right, and as each one is pinned to the bench I'll take this knife and cut your fingers off, one at a time."

Sokorov whimpered but said nothing as Dominik untied his bonds, fully prepared for the Russian to make a grab at him despite his crippling injuries. But nothing happened until he had been dragged halfway across the rough concrete and he could stand the unremitting pain no longer. He knew that his captor was working to a methodical plan and, like himself in the recent past, he would steadily increase the torture, the intimidation and the threats, always intensifying the dreadful anticipation and fear. Although he could no longer bear the present pain, he knew there were no limits or thresholds to such agony and that Dominik would continue to inflict injury upon injury, continually ramping up the suffering until he only wanted the release of death. Eventually, he would crave it. He was not there yet, but he knew that Dominik was good at it and again just like he himself always had, he would get the information he wanted in the end. This inside knowledge and his own history of merciless and perverted success was the real reason that he broke at that precise moment and he gasped out, "Please stop, no more please! I'll tell you everything."

Over the next two hours he gave Dominik a full account of his units' activities and suspecting that Dominik already had a fair idea of what was happening, he did not play down his own role. All he wanted was to be spared any more torture. He knew that the Pole would kill him in the end. He could tell it from his voice, see it on his face and read it in his eyes. He hoped it would be quick, and as he was wracked with yet another series of sharp and blinding waves of agony from his shattered limbs, he hoped that it would be soon. He knew he was already dying and between the spasms of pain and moments of semi-consciousness, he answered every question he was asked and as he spoke, Dominik wrote it all down.

When the Pole was satisfied that he had everything recorded on paper he pulled the dagger from his boot, wrote the names of his wife and children on a piece of paper and then knelt down beside the barely responsive Sokorov. He looked the Russian in the eyes and said, "If I just left you here I don't think you'd last very long because you've been bleeding internally and you're getting weaker and weaker, but I can't let that happen. I will see you die for your crimes."

The now feeble and failing Russian mustered his defiance, contempt and authority for one final warning. He coughed, spluttered and dribbled throughout his mutterings and Dominik had to lean over him to hear, "Just get on with it… if you've got the balls… I've had my fun… and done my duty to Uncle Joe. You're the one… who's already lost everything… if you survive long enough… for your anger and hate to ebb away… you won't be able to live with… what you've done today."

Dominik put the piece of paper on the floor beside Sokorov and then thrust the dagger into his heart, driving it up and under his ribs with all the strength he could muster. Sokorov convulsed as blood spurted from the wound and red foam bubbled from his mouth, but Dominik twisted the dagger and worked it from side to side until all movement ceased and he was left kneeling in a pool of blood and urine. He carefully withdrew the weapon and wiped it clean on Sokorov's shirt tail. He picked up the piece of paper and put it on Sokorov's chest and then located the final item in his line of torture tools: a six-inch nail. He hammered it into the chest of the corpse, pinning the paper to his evil and macerated heart.

Dominik stood up to leave but took a final look at his enemy. He was saddened to see that the names of his loved ones were already being obliterated as the blood soaked into the paper and ink. He walked away, secure in the knowledge that the deed was done and unlike his words on the note, the memories of his family would never fade away. He felt no guilt for his actions, only regret that Sokorov had made it necessary: for he was the evil psychopathic killer of thousands. He was Stalin's executioner and he deserved to die in agony and alone, just like his victims. He hoped that some good would come out of it, but he feared that in the long run, it would make little difference as long as the Georgian Bolshevik and Hitler were in control.

An hour later he reported back to Colonel Turek and wrote up his report, which he immediately handed over, together with Sokorov's confession. The colonel read the papers and then decided that they were so shockingly detailed and politically explosive for the Russians that he would need to consult with his own commander and intelligence officer. They would decide between them exactly how they could make best use of the disturbing and detailed information. Dominik then left to return to his friends, suspecting that like them, the papers too would eventually be bound for the headquarters of the Home Army in Warsaw.

Swindon – 11th November 2009

Although the comments on the Sokorov file had prepared me for Dominik's revenge, I found the realism profoundly difficult to process and accept. The vivid imagery and my moral ambivalence towards the dreadful act had kept me awake for most of the night. The calculated, barbaric cruelty seemed so out of character for the man that I imagined him to be. Everything I had read and been told about him painted a picture of an honourable and decent man, capable of great humanity and sacrifice. Certainly, I also knew him as a professional soldier who killed the enemy but never as a violent, revengeful sadist. His remorseless and brutal actions and the minutely detailed and methodical planning reminded me of the behaviour of some of the most infamous, modern-day serial killers. The way in which his tools were placed out and lined up and the ritualistic coup de grâce reinforced that feeling. I voiced my concerns to Stan, "That's horrific and sickening. How could he ever deal with the enormity of what he had done?"

Stan sighed deeply, leant forward in his chair and speaking quietly and thoughtfully said, "I think it was a mental aberration caused by the torture and murder of his wife and children. Whatever label we put on it or however the psychiatrists would categorise or diagnose it, it seemed to disappear or at least dissipate, with the death of Sokorov. He very quickly returned to his normal self and becoming involved with the Home Army helped him recover. He never spoke about it again and his friends never mentioned it either. I don't know if he ever regretted what he'd done, but I think he spent the rest of his life trying to make up for it and by the end of our story I think that you'll agree that he most certainly did."

I still found it hard to accept, "How could he stoop so low, right down to their level, crawling about with the filth in the gutter? He was fighting to rid the world of the tide of hate and prejudice that had swept that behaviour to the surface in the first place. I just can't see how he could have made such a monumental jump: from doing what he intrinsically knew was so obviously right one minute, to ruthlessly and clinically breaking every moral and religious principle he had ever held dear the next."

Stan defended his godfather and old friend, "I think you're judging him far too harshly. What's more you're doing it 70 years later, from your own cocooned and comfortable world, far removed from his fears and troubled emotions. Unlike you, he didn't see it in such simple terms and you also have the benefit of hindsight. He was in a turmoil of passion and he didn't know how it was all going to end. When a country is fighting for its very survival, its soldiers will do desperate and deplorable things. And if you don't mind me saying so, you've also given very scant regard to the effects of the repeated massacre of civilians, for that's what it surely was, being unleashed on his people, with his own family being the latest victims. Look, I don't know exactly what the precise trigger point was for him, there were so many but given his circumstances I do know one thing: I might have done exactly the same."

I wasn't so sure, "No I don't think so. It was just so wrong and brutal, and unforgiveable."

He came back at me with a verbal barrage, "Why is it that those who take the moral and ethical high ground and shout their condemnation and outrage at us, are always the ones not being murdered, tortured and abused? Go on, tell me why they're the ones sat in the most comfort, feeling smug and cosseted within their own bubble of pious self-satisfaction? It's so bloody easy to spout off about human rights and international law when you don't have to fight or die for them. And let's face it – it's even easier if you're middle class, privately educated and a liberal lawyer, judge or politician, living in another world. A world so far removed and insulated from the struggles and aspirations of ordinary working folk that we've now become an alien concept to all of them." Having really warmed to his subject he stopped for breath, and slightly red in the face he stared at me, willing me to challenge him.

I admired his passion and his loyalty, and I didn't want to get into an argument with him. I also had some sympathy with the main thrust of his tirade: after all we should never judge history by our modern norms and attitudes. But I thought he couldn't excuse such a blatant case of torture and murder simply by clouding the issue with sweeping generalisations. So I moved on and quietly asked another question that had been bothering me, "Did the Russians take any reprisals after the attack?"

He tutted and grinned, "You're obviously not up for an argument then. Okay, we'll carry on regardless. But just be warned, at the end of my story I'll be giving you an example of the potentially horrendous consequences of a world being far too eager to move on and in the process ignoring a community's burning sense of gross injustice, betrayal and victimisation."

"What do you mean?

"Not now, I promise you'll find out in due course, so let's get back to the question of reprisals. The very next day they publically shot fifteen prisoners they were already holding as suspected military officers. They would have probably been killed in the end anyway but they made a big event of it and alleged that they were involved in planning the assault at the hospital. They didn't find Sokorov's body until two weeks later and by then his replacement was already in post, but the killing continued. The deportations to Siberia also carried on, right up until the time when the Germans drove the Russians out, but sadly for Poland, things didn't improve then either."

I was struck by the thought that in the early 1940s, Poland must have been the most terrible and dangerous place to live in the whole of Europe, perhaps even the world. This realisation reminded me that it was against such a dark, brutal and sinister backdrop that Stan was telling me the illuminating and incredible story of ordinary people living in extraordinary times. I was humbled by the notion and charged myself to be far less judgemental in the future. So now I was ready to go on, and I asked Stan, "What happened next?"

"Before we move away from Luck and go into the Nazi-controlled area of 'General Government', as it was called, there's one more thing you should remember. Over the last 20 years, as the secret Russian files have been made available for examination, dozens, perhaps even hundreds, of NKVD murderers have been identified. However, unlike many of the Nazi war criminals who survived, they have never had to face trial and what's more, most of them continued to enjoy very good pensions and a comfortable life for decades after the war. At least Sokorov was denied that opportunity." Then he opened his notebook, refreshed his memory and continued with his story...

∞∞∞∞∞∞∞

On returning from the slaughterhouse Dominik called the team together and they made plans for the immediate future. It was agreed that as Konrad had to return to Lwów anyway to collect Joanna and young Stan, they would cross over the San River at the Przemysl Bridge, just over 50 miles due west of his home. The border between the two occupied zones in that area followed the river and it ran right through the middle of the ancient city, which was a major communications and trading centre. The population was growing by the day as more and more Jewish people fled from the German-controlled area, and as it was the major crossing point in the far south, it was very busy and chaotic, providing the best opportunity of avoiding detection.

They decided once again to travel separately and rendezvous at the city in four days' time. They arranged to meet at midday outside the seventeenth-century Carmelite church of St Therese, which was just a few hundred yards from the railway station on the Russian side but not too far from the bridge. Konrad, who knew the area well, told them of its outstanding and obvious identification features. It was crowned by an unusual dome, a beautiful, nineteenth-century addition, modelled on St Peter's

Basilica in Rome. The main building was of a striking baroque design and inside could be found a unique and finely carved wooden pulpit built in the shape of a ship!

When Dominik suggested that it would be more sensible to meet inside, Konrad explained that it had become a Ukrainian church during Poland's partition and it still remained so. Therefore, the Russians were unlikely to be on the lookout for Poles at that location, but on the other hand, if they were seen or heard inside, then the Ukrainians would certainly become very suspicious. He urged them to arrive outside, just before the appointed time. He also agreed to contact the local Home Army commander and seek his guidance regarding documentation and also obtain the latest appraisal of the general military situation within the German sector.

The crossing turned out to be far less problematic than they feared. The Home Army contact assigned to Dominik by the local commander explained that the German and Soviet Cooperation Commission had just finalised their preparations to return to Germany all those Poles who had fled to the east in September the previous year when Germany invaded. The underground movement was going to use the opportunity to move a small number of key staff across to Warsaw during the first few days of the implementation – hopefully, before either the Russians or Germans could perfect their security systems. Dominik's team joined them two days later, in possession of a small quantity of Deutschmarks and false papers and identities, courtesy of the Home Army. They all successfully crossed over, interspersed amongst the throng of returnees. They knew they were going to be searched on both sides of the bridge and so they had to leave their weapons behind with their contact, who assured them that they would be put to good use. Dominik regretted the loss of his trench gun and would certainly try to get another if he could, but he managed to keep his dagger, scroll, photograph and medal all safely hidden inside the lining of his boots.

They were met by another Home Army contact on the other side and in the course of the next two days they were escorted to Warsaw, where they were interviewed separately by members of the Home Army Intelligence Service. The action against Sokorov was covered in some detail, but as Dominik had been the only one present and was responsible for his death, they accepted his somewhat sanitised version. In the course of the debrief Dominik and Konrad both made mention of their years with General Haller and were pleased when they were told that he was alive, having escaped through Romania and joined Sikorski's government-in-exile in France.

Once their accounts had been checked out they were put to work training new recruits in the art of urban warfare, something they all, bar one, had considerable experience of. Sixteen-year-old Stan found himself in the strange position of being taught close combat skills and weapons training by his own parents, who made sure that he worked twice as hard as everyone else. Nevertheless, his fellow trainees found the situation highly amusing and as Stan put it himself, "even though I worked harder and received no favours at all, they still ribbed me mercilessly for being the teacher's pet and potential officer material. It was mostly good natured but I soon got fed up with it, and that's a fact."

On the 6th May 1940, just before the Phoney War in the west came to an end with the German invasion of the Low Countries, secret orders finally came through for Dominik and his team. They came directly from General Haller who was now a Minister in the Polish Administration in France. They were to be smuggled out of Poland in two teams via Gdansk and then by cargo boat to neutral Sweden, where they would be met by a foreign liaison officer for the government-in-exile. A plane would be provided at a secluded airstrip and Adam would fly them all out at night. Their destination was France and if all went well it would be a trip of about three days. They were to report to the Chateau de Vignolles in Gretz-Armainvilliers, 25 miles north-east of Paris where Aaron, Hannah and Joanna were to join the staff at Command Post Bruno, a Polish and French joint intelligence station where German and Italian ciphers were being decrypted. Hannah was the most delighted because at long last, she would be able to practise her French in the very heart of France. From there Adam, Dominik, Konrad and Stan would fly on to London to meet General Haller for a personal briefing and further orders. The general was currently on a recruitment drive for the Free Polish Forces and was visiting old colleagues and friends, now settled within the Polish communities in England.

On their arrival at Bruno they were met by the Director, French Army Radio Intelligence Officer Gustave Bertrand and Lt. Colonel Gwido Langer, the Head of The Polish Cipher Bureau. They were to learn later on that most of the Polish cryptologists had managed to escape from Poland and had been assigned to Bruno. The staff included some fifty French personnel, fifteen Poles and seven Spaniards. The latter worked on Italian and Spanish fascist ciphers. Although the administration, logistics, radio interception and security was provided by the French, most of the German message decryption was carried out by the Poles. As early as December 1932 Langer's team in Poland had broken the German Enigma cipher and from then on managed to continuously read it and were still doing so when Aaron and the two girls joined them in France.

Poland's cooperation with France and Britain on Enigma had leapt forward on 25th July 1939, five weeks before the war started, when they hosted a conference at the small Polish decoding centre in Kabaty Woods at Pyry, just south of Warsaw. Senior representatives from the various military intelligence services of all three countries attended. Wishing to help the Allies and hoping to secure action on their promises of military alliance, the Poles handed over everything they had on Enigma, including diagrams, a model of a captured machine, their decryption techniques, their electromechanical bombe machine and code books. In fact, they shared all that was needed for their allies to carry on reading the German encoded military transmissions. Alan Turing's later work and ultimate success at Bletchley Park was based on the development and refinement of the Polish Bombe. Alastair Denniston, the first director of Bletchley Park, was at the meeting and was inspired and impressed at what he saw. Rightly so, because the intelligence later gleaned from this source, code named "Ultra" by the British, was a massive boost to the Allied war effort. The influence of Ultra on the course of the war may be open to debate but an often quoted assessment is that the decryption of German ciphers hastened the end of the European war by two years. Winston Churchill told King George VI, "It was thanks to Ultra that we won the war."

The Polish Enigma story was a classic 'cat and mouse' struggle. Every time the machines were improved or new features, such as extra rotors (which turned plain text into incoherent cipher messages) were added, the decryption became much more difficult and took far longer. However, by using a bigger and more complex bombe, the team eventually managed, once again, to determine the daily settings of the Enigma rotors. However, they were never in a position to decipher all the intercepted messages and at times the success rate was as low as 10%. Nevertheless, they had managed to read the so-called 'unbreakable' Enigma traffic and gave advance notice of the invasions of Denmark, Norway, Belgium and Holland. They were regularly decoding messages sent from the German high command, police and German agents operating in occupied territory, and local Nazi commanders in France and North Africa.

In contrast, at least to start with, the British were years behind. They had only seriously and earnestly turned their attention to the Enigma problem in1936, during the Spanish Civil War, when the Axis powers started to threaten their interests in the Mediterranean. However, in the late 1930s, when they drastically built up their Enigma resources and widened the scope of their research and experimentation, they rapidly caught up with and then overtook the Poles.

When Bletchley Park (sometimes known by the name of its Radio room, Station X) opened in 1939, it employed thousands of staff. At that point the Enigma enterprise, despite a few continuing rivalries, became much more of a team and shared effort amongst the Allies. The work at Station X culminated in the design and success of the mainframe valve-driven computer Colossus. It was able to perform thousands of calculations every minute, automatically testing all the possible permutations of the code. Despite this British success and a spirit of mutual aid, the Poles were never allowed to work at Bletchley Park. The reason given was 'overriding security concerns' but surprisingly the Americans were fully integrated into the programme, once they entered the war.

The credit for the breaking of the Enigma code, and the jingoistic language that has driven many public debates since, was obviously a 'bee in the bonnet' for Stan. As he told me the story he let his national pride and growing frustration at the perceived injustice boil right over.

"Do you know, even today after all these years, it makes me angry that we did all this for Britain and France, the very countries that had signed a written pact to come to our aid if the Germans attacked us. Yet, when we were invaded, our so-called friends were nowhere to be seen. They didn't lift a finger to help but sat on their hands while our country was carved up again, and looking back I suppose they never did intend to fight with us. What makes it ten times worse is that despite all the evidence that's come to light since, Poland still gets precious little credit for its amazing achievements. They either show the British receiving all the plaudits or as is often the case, the Americans stand the truth on its head to cover themselves in glory. Then to add insult to injury, in the modern films like *Enigma* they totally ignore the fact that we showed them how to do it. They even have the effrontery to show the Pole as the traitor, when we gave them the damn thing in the first place. It's a bloody travesty! That's what it is, and it makes me sick to my stomach!"

I decided to remain silent, as I had the feeling that nothing I could say would mollify him on this subject. His view was fully fixed, having been reinforced by his experiences and those of his comrades, over and over again down through the years. I suppose it's only natural that people will tend to play up their own country's contribution and play down the efforts of the others but nevertheless, he probably had good reason to feel aggrieved. After he had calmed down he carried on with the background.

At the beginning of May 1940 the Poles at Bruno asked Warsaw to assign extra experienced staff to the unit and in response, Aaron, Joanna and Hannah were sent immediately. Recent Nazi alterations and modifications to a number of Enigma machines now meant that greater resources were needed to crack them. Much of the Polish unit's success up to that point, had been grounded in their exploitation of a weakness in the German 'indicators' (the starting positions for sending the Enigma messages) but when the Germans suddenly changed these as well, the Polish bombe became redundant and they had to start again. The three new arrivals got straight down to work and a week later the others took off for England.

On the 15th May, 1940 General Haller greeted his visitors in person when they arrived at the rather grand and opulent Rubens Hotel in Buckingham Palace Road, London. He hugged them all in turn then stood back and looked them over.

"My, goodness, haven't we all aged! But it's great to see you again. These are desperate times once more and I have need of you, but I really have been looking forward to this. I feel so much more confident when I'm dealing with people I know and trust, and apart from young Stanislaw here, we've been through a great deal together. Welcome to you all. Please come on up and we'll have a drink and talk."

The general explained that he was staying at the hotel for just a few days and admitted that things were not looking too good in Holland. Rotterdam had fallen, the Dutch government had fled to England just before their military surrendered and a French counter-attack had failed. He summed up his feelings, "Our allies have gravely underestimated the enemy and I think their armour will roll across France, just as it did back home and it will all be over in a month or two. I predict that France will fall and we'll all be moving over here to London very soon, and that's why I sent for you."

Adam asked, "If France falls, do you think England can hold out on its own?

The general didn't hesitate, "I think they will. The appeaser Chamberlain has resigned and gone, and Mr Churchill is now the Prime Minister and he's a soldier at heart and a fighter. I've met him several times and I've been impressed. He's so calm and determined and he's a born leader and a great orator. I listened to his acceptance speech in Parliament just a couple of days ago and at long last I've heard a voice of reality in England. He knows exactly how bad it's going to get and he's preparing his people for the dreadful Nazi assault that will reach here soon. If anybody can stiffen up the English resolve, then he can."

Dominik knew exactly what he meant, "We heard that speech on the radio in France just before we left and when he said 'I have nothing to offer but blood, toil, tears and sweat' we knew that there was hope. He's not going to surrender."

Konrad was keen to point out, "The English won't be on their own anyway, they'll have us and every other Pole who manages to escape. We certainly know how to fight – we've been doing it long enough."

Haller smiled and said, "Yes, and most of the time we have been isolated too. And that reminds me, when we move across the English Channel, I'm going to recommend to Sikorski that we set up our headquarters here. At this very fine hotel, right next door to the Royal Buckingham Palace! It will be quite fitting that the leaders of two such great countries, facing the might of Hitler's war machine together, should reside within walking distance."

He then called them over to a paper and plan strewn table where he briefed them. He explained that he had met with an army captain who had proposed the setting up of a unit of Polish Special Forces to operate covertly across occupied Europe and that the commander-in-chief was considering this idea alongside the training of paratroops and the air delivery of arms and supplies. Contingency plans were being drawn up, but he was optimistic that it would receive the go-ahead and he wanted Dominik's team to 'volunteer' for the first intake and undergo the secret training. He wanted them as highly skilled as possible for the task he had in mind. He also pointed out the distinctive advantage that both Dominik and Konrad spoke fluent German and he was adamant that the others would have to learn the basics as quickly as possible. They all agreed, but only after Haller had assured them that their respective ages were not a disadvantage (Stan being only just 17 and the others in their early 40s), because they would all find it easier to blend in, whereas men in their 20s and 30s, being of normal military age, always drew the attention of the enemy security forces.

They had to wait nearly eighteen frustrating months in London before their orders finally came through. During this time Stan and Adam learnt to speak German to a reasonable standard and they all trained hard to maintain their fitness and combat skills. Also, following a chance meeting at the Rubens Hotel with a United States liaison officer from Chicago, Dominik struck up a friendship based on their shared memories of the windy city and the American's interest in Dominik's military career. When the visitor left a few weeks later he presented Dominik with a replacement for his favourite weapon, the trench gun which he had been forced to leave behind in Poland. Fourteen days later they were summoned for duty at the Polish Parachute Brigade training school at Largo House in Fife. This establishment became known to them as the 'Monkey Grove' because the trainees were hoisted up in a trapeze, into the trees and various towers (75 feet in the case of the highest) and then required to swing and jump down. In this way they learnt the correct postures for all the stages of a parachute jump. Following this initial course they went to the Ringway Central Landing School (now Manchester Airport) where they first jumped, with a great deal of trepidation, through the hole in the floor of a rickety basket, suspended from a tethered air balloon.

Next they progressed to the real thing, and made three daylight and two night-time practice jumps from an aircraft, before they were considered 'qualified' as parachutists. These two courses took about five weeks in total and then in the summer of 1942, together with another thirty Poles, they moved on to Station 43 at Audley End House in Essex. This was one of the two secret training stations used almost exclusively by the Polish Section of the SOE. A memorial to the 108 Poles who died whilst serving in this select branch of the service still stands in the main driveway today. It bears the inscription, 'Dulce et decorum est pro patria mori' (sweet and beautiful it is to die for one's own country). The other establishment was at Pollards Park House at Chalfont St Giles in Buckinghamshire, where the facilities were split into three sites STS 20, 20a and 20b. A third establishment, STS 63 at Erlestoke Park (now the site of a prison complex) near Devizes in Wiltshire was later used for Operation Bardsea, the dropping of Polish agents and saboteurs into occupied France to operate just behind the bridgeheads on D-Day.

Chapter Eleven

SECRET AGENTS

Audley End House, Essex – 10th August 1942

The successful volunteers for the SOE's Underground Warfare Course had been drawn from right across the Polish Forces. Many applications had been rejected at an early stage, either following psychological testing or during the preliminary training courses. Those finally selected had quietly slipped away from their units during the night and this 'nocturnal disappearance' first gave rise to their name, 'Cichociemni' ('the silent and unseen' or by alternate translation, 'the dark and silent ones'). The candidates included men and women from all ranks, from general to private and also a number of civilians. The gruelling, comprehensive and rigorous course was prepared jointly by Section III of the staff office to the Polish commander-in-chief and the British SOE. It demanded a very high level of skill and competence throughout. Those who fell short in any discipline or who were considered unsuitable for any other reason were sincerely thanked for their efforts and then returned to their original unit.

The course concentrated on achieving outstanding physical fitness, total self-reliance and combat versatility. The first requirement was achieved by cross-country runs, a demanding assault course, regular physical exercise, wrestling, boxing and unarmed combat: a combination of which brought the students to the peak of condition. The second was accomplished by using the best, most experienced, credible and highly motivated instructors and by undertaking continuous and demanding practical exercises. These included map reading, target identification, photography, fieldcraft, interrogation and counter-interrogation techniques and survival skills, enabling the trainees to gradually assume the persona of a secret agent. The third objective was reached by undertaking every conceivable form of weapons instruction, explosives and demolition practice and commando training where they learned to kill in a dozen different ways. However, they did not really see themselves as spies, not in any strict espionage sense. When one considers the background of the brutal occupation of Poland and the attempt to eradicate their country, its culture and its people, then it is easy to understand why they saw themselves as freedom fighters: Special Forces soldiers, inspired to destroy their enemy and liberate their nation. It is no exaggeration to say that their patriotism was such that their spirit was never crushed and their country was more important than their own lives. But first they had to become criminals!

They would learn how to pick locks, break into buildings, steal, rob, set booby traps and blow things up, all aimed at destroying their enemy and his ability to wage war. Furthermore, they had to do all these things deep in occupied territory with minimal support and without leaving evidence behind. Such a wide skills base and high level of expertise was attained and sustained by the immense diversity of the curriculum and constant practice. They learnt how to forge documents, how to carry out acts of insurrection with or without explosives and how to use micro-photography, invisible inks and weapons of every kind, including those of their enemies. They were constantly blowing things up, using small charges inside the buildings, experimenting with fuses and detonators, and within the extensive grounds even destroying cars, vans and a tank! They learnt to drive vehicles of all descriptions and practised evasion and escape techniques whether on foot, in a vehicle or on a bicycle or motorcycle. By the time they completed the course they were proficient at armed and unarmed combat. Day or night, they could kill quickly and quietly with or without weapons.

A highlight of the course was the visit of General Sikorski, their commander-in-chief, who met all the trainees and the instructors at the end of August and commended them for their zeal and dedication. Less than a year later he was killed in a plane crash at Gibraltar and because of the way he had challenged and ridiculed Stalin (over the disappearance of the Polish officers murdered at Katyn and elsewhere) many Poles believed that the tragedy was no accident. They suspected Soviet sabotage and were convinced that, as was the case at Katyn, the dictator himself had a major hand in his death. The controversy still rages today.

Additional specialist or sandwich courses were also held for those most suited, such as radio operator, languages, sniper skills, camouflage and disguise, underwater demolition, forgery and deception and rock climbing. The main course was also interspersed with practical initiative tests and evasion and infiltration exercises, culminating in the final test.

Swindon – 12th November 2009

As soon as we had settled down with a coffee and a Danish pastry, Stan told me about his own final test at Audley End House.

"I was always allocated to a different group to my father in all the practical tests and exercises, but when it came to the ultimate assessment, the make or break test as we called it, I found myself in Adam's group. Dominik and my dad had already successfully completed theirs and so the pressure was really on us two not to let them down. There were four of us in our group and by then we were so used to our code names that we never used our real ones, not even with the few people we knew. I was Marshdog and Adam was Hawk. The other two were Birch and Cloud. I remember them both as if it was yesterday, I—"

"What did you have to do?" I interrupted, trying to discourage Stan from embarking on one of his long monologues or digressions. I was keen to hear exactly how they were tested.

"We were briefed at midnight in the stables, where all the vehicles were garaged and our explosives were stored. We were kitted out for a night operation with dark clothing, black gloves, black balaclavas and commando boots but with pickaxe handles which were also painted black, instead of our usual weapons. We had to capture an officer or NCO from the local Home Guard and take him to a rendezvous point at Littlebury Church, where we were to hand him over to another team of agents once we had received the correct password. We had to take back the 'physical evidence' of his identity card and uniform and deliver them to the instructor before daylight. We also had to break into a post office and copy its official stamp without the postmaster or anyone else finding out. We were not allowed to take any personal possessions at all and we were denied any maps, plans or sketches. We were not even allowed a pen or pencil and they searched us to make sure."

I wondered how realistic it had been and whether or not the Poles took it very seriously, "Did you think it was worthwhile?"

"Most definitely! It was our one chance to prove we were ready for action behind the lines but it wasn't easy. Nobody on the outside had been told anything so it was as authentic as possible, and without any firearms we felt very vulnerable so we needed to be even more careful. It wasn't that unusual you know, to get shot at on those tests and a number of trainees were quite badly injured.

"How could that happen?"

"SOE would quite often deploy the local British soldiers and the Home Guard as the 'enemy' and they would try to prevent us from getting to or from our objectives. They would organise road blocks, ambush positions and cross-country searches. I don't know what they were told, but they took it pretty seriously and did all they could to catch us. There were quite a few serious scraps, I can tell you. You've got to remember that if we failed or got caught or even if we were hurt and incapacitated, then we were finished and sent back as failures. So it's no wonder that on the occasions where we did carry out armed exercises – and there were quite a few – it didn't take too much for us to start shooting back at them."

I was surprised at such a dangerous level of reality, "Are you really saying that you fired on the British during simple training exercises?"

"Yes of course, and I'm sure that any of us Poles would have done and there was nothing simple about it. The pressure after all we had been through was immense and we were all desperate to prove ourselves. When we were being assessed the adrenaline was really pumping and we couldn't let ourselves fail. We had been building up to this for months and we would have done anything to get back into the fight with the Nazis."

He then explained that they had to sneak past the British army sentries who guarded the gates and their armed patrols within and outside the grounds. But they had over 100 acres to cover and all the students had already worked out the weak spots during their training periods in the gardens and parkland. This was not the first time they had slipped out at night and they were familiar with the layout of the local area and the approach roads. They decided to avoid the quickest and most direct route, alongside the River Cam on the London Road which led directly to the church, just in case a hostile reception committee had been arranged. Once outside they headed north-east until they reached Windmill Hill and then turned left following parallel to the road but just inside the treeline of Spring Wood. As they approached the junction with Walden Road they heard voices off to their right on Windmill Hill and so Adam crept forward to investigate, wriggling very carefully through the carpet of ivy, dead leaves and twigs. Five minutes later he reported that a six-man team of British regulars were lying in wait in the ditch on the far side of the road. The Poles cut back through the wood to avoid contact and then struck out north-westwards straight across to the mill. Here they crossed the River Cam, avoiding another likely ambush point at the road junction just before the bridge at the entrance to the village.

They came out onto Mill Lane, just south of the junction with Church Walk, and carefully crossed the road straight into the graveyard to the east of the church at the centre of the southern margin of the built-up area. There they sat down behind the boundary wall in the shadows of a small copse and made their plans. Although they knew where the post office was, they had no idea of where any of the Home Guard personnel lived. They split up and Adam went with Birch and headed for the post office while Stan and Cloud went in search of the Home Guard. They agreed to meet back at the copse, fully aware that both objectives would have to be achieved or they would all fail.

Adam and his partner waited in the rear garden of their target premises until 3am when they hoped the occupants would be in a deep sleep. By this time their night vision was good, aided by a half moon and a clear starlit sky. They picked the twin locks on the rear door in a matter of minutes with the three slivers of metal that had been shaped and perfected by Birch. He had carefully secreted them under the hollowed-out heel of his boot, along with a length of string and a few matches. The alteration was so cleanly fashioned and well disguised that it had not been discovered during the instructor's thorough search. Aided by specialist SOE staff, all the agents had developed inventive hiding places for their most valuable pieces of kit.

They quietly entered the living quarters where they found the internal door leading to the post office section at the front of the building. They had to be very careful at this stage because the door was situated at the foot of the stairs below the postmaster's bedroom. They covered the metal locks with Adam's balaclava to suppress the noise as the large iron bolts were slowly inched back through their triple brackets. Adam stood guard at the bottom of the stairs and Birch went in. He searched the counter and shelves, but the stamp was nowhere to be seen. As he turned to give Adam the bad news he saw a small safe tucked away behind a half-drawn curtain in the corner. It took him almost ten minutes to open it, but inside he found two ink stamps along with a pile of bank notes, official forms and postal orders. He only took out the stamps and because he couldn't distinguish between their patterns in the dim light, he made an impression of both into the remains of a bar of soap found in the kitchen. He then cleaned off the stamps as best he could and returned them to the safe and locked it before leaving.

They were back in the copse by 3.45am and felt very lucky and relieved that the postmaster was not a dog lover, although they were prepared for that eventuality. They had been trained in how to swiftly dispatch canine guards but it was always a risky enterprise and sometimes the animal managed to bark first. Once the alarm had been raised, then achieving their objective and subsequently making their escape undetected became far more difficult, if not impossible. In any case, neither of them wanted to kill a pet dog. They relaxed and waited for their colleagues.

Stan took up his own side of the story.

"We crept around the village for nearly an hour looking for a Home Guard sentry or a patrol but drew a blank. After another hour of waiting in a shrubbery near the triangle right in the centre of the village and still seeing no sign of any activity, Cloud came up with his idea."

"What did you do?"

"We found the village police station and banged up the constable. When he opened the door in his pyjamas, we rushed in and laid him out before he could make a sound."

Naturally I felt some sympathy for the policeman and I thought that the Poles' heavy-handedness was way over the top. "I hope you didn't hurt much more than his pride. After all, you were supposed to be on the same side!"

"No, he soon came round, but even though he was gagged he still tried to kick up a fuss, so we had to punch him a couple more times, just to show him who was boss. Then he calmed down a bit. Anyway, we found his handcuffs hanging on a hook in the hall and tethered him to the radiator. I spoke to him and Cloud searched the house. We discovered that he was alone. Apparently his wife was a nurse working nights in the local hospital in Saffron Walden."

"I suppose you went to the police house because you thought he would know who the local Home Guard people were."

"Yes, and he did, but he wouldn't tell us. Although all our training was done in Polish, I had been in England long enough to have learnt the language pretty well. We threatened him, slapped him about a bit more and prodded him with the pickaxe handles, but he wouldn't give in. Give him his due – he was a tough old bugger. I think he knew who we were from our accents and felt bolder because his wife was safely out of the house."

Stan went on to explain that the Polish trainees were unsure of exactly how much the locals knew about their existence or the purpose of the training school. It was top secret and everything was done to make it look as if it was a normal British Army facility. But with so many of the students taking part in exercises around the place, the Polish instructors often visiting outside the camp and what with the explosions and everything, they felt sure that the locals must have had some suspicions. Stan also believed that the police commanders and the senior military figures, including the Home Guard, must have been given some sort of Official Secrets Act briefing or a suitable cover story. He was surprised to learn after the war that most of the locals had no idea of what was really going on right under their noses. The few that did know the truth carefully guarded the secret.

I asked, "So what happened with the policeman?"

Stan laughed, "It was so easy in the end. When Cloud searched the place he discovered a list of local addresses and telephone numbers on the wall in his little office and about halfway down were the names and addresses of the two Home Guard people who lived in the village. I suppose he sometimes had to call them out. Fortunately for us one was a sergeant. We left the copper chained up to the plumbing and walked the 200 yards to the address and just banged him up."

"Did you have any trouble with him?"

"Well, he came to the door with a pistol in his hand, but he was well into his fifties and we had no trouble disarming him and then we found it wasn't even loaded. It was about 3am by then and once we had tied his hands, collected his uniform and identity card and frog-marched him back to the copse, we could see the first traces of light away to the east. We handed him over at the church, met up with Adam and Birch and headed for home by the same route, avoiding the so-called enemy forces. We got back just in time – and we passed the test."

"I bet that was a relief for both of you but tell me, how was it all smoothed over after the exercise, with the police and the Home Guard?"

Stan scratched at his scar and said, "Their bosses were given a broad cover story about commandos and reminded of the national requirement that all their staff should assist in vital and realistic behind-the-lines training: covert combat preparation that couldn't be replicated in any other way. The individuals concerned were seen personally by an anonymous man from the ministry who firstly apologised for their rough treatment, then thanked them on behalf of the government and finally swore them to secrecy. They had it off to a fine art."

He then explained that less than 25% of the trainees successfully finished the course but even then their preparation was not over. They had to stay for another month to complete the final briefing course which would prepare them for daily life under Nazi occupation. Once deployed, their mission could turn on a slip of the tongue, an inconsistency in their background information or documentation or simply a lack of local knowledge. Capture, torture and death could be triggered by their body language or attitude at a checkpoint or when being searched or questioned in the street. Therefore, when this consolidation course was finished each one of the students could create a credible cover story, encrypt and decrypt messages, use a radio, lie with a consistency and conviction that appeared confident, natural and convincing and also resist interrogation and torture.

They were also familiarised and updated with the ever-evolving but strict rules, procedures and regulations imposed by the Germans in the occupied countries, especially France and Poland. This included an examination of the various types of identity cards, work permits, travel documents and food coupons. Despite the fact that most students were experienced soldiers and many had already fought the Germans in Poland and France, they also had to learn to distinguish between the plethora of German political, security and military organisations and ranks: their dress, equipment and insignia, their differing responsibilities, their bureaucracies and their internal relationships. In short, they came to know their enemy well and were equipped to wage a guerrilla war in the most effective of ways. The successful few were then officially sworn in as members of the Home Army (Armia Krajowa) and were ready for clandestine operations anywhere inside the occupied countries.

During the training courses Stan had been recognised by various instructors as an extraordinarily good shot, across the whole range of weapons they had used. This talent was highlighted in his final assessment report and so he was sent on an intensive, three-week snipers course. The others were due to take some well-earned leave, but before they all left they were entertained by the Polish Forces Theatre. The troupe, originally known as the Happy Lwów Air Wave toured the whole of Britain entertaining Polish servicemen. They would perform their mixture of music, satire and comedy anywhere: often in the open air on a parade ground or from the back of an army lorry or on a makeshift stage. They had even entertained on board a Polish submarine. One of the players, Wlada Majewska, had become very popular throughout Poland before the war with her delightful singing voice, a razor-sharp wit and an amazing talent as a mimic. They also performed in theatres to British audiences and service personnel, and donated their takings to war charities. As passing-out celebrations went, it was a roaring success, but there were many sore heads the following morning when they all went their separate ways.

In mid-December 1942 Dominik and his friends were called back to the Rubens Hotel, where they were met by Captain Robak, an Intelligence Officer (French Section) attached to the commander-in-chief's personal staff. The hotel had indeed become Sikorski's headquarters and it was now alive with activity. Dozens of Polish Army personnel and civilian support staff rushed to and fro, maintaining and feeding the numerous communications and administrative systems required for managing a government and controlling its regular and underground armed forces. A business-like air of excitement, commitment and urgency was clearly evident as they were led along the corridors and up the stairs to a newly converted office.

Captain Robak sat them down and addressed them rather formally. "I'm going to brief you for your mission, but first of all I've been authorised to provide you with some background information. I don't exaggerate when I say that the survival of Poland is still set finely in the balance. The Nazis have marched into Vichy France and now the whole country is under the jackboot. On the other hand it finally looks like they will be defeated at Stalingrad, but that's not necessarily a good thing for us either, because the Reds will march into Poland again as soon as they can. Our pilots are fighting around the clock with the RAF to take the bombing war back to Germany, but the Nazis have tightened their grip right across Western Europe. I think things could get far worse for us yet and so we've got to do everything we can to tie them down in France and at home."

Dominik thought he was being overly pessimistic, "The Germans may still feel very powerful but as you say, they haven't had it all their own way in Russia. Now that winter has really set in again, Stalin will counter-attack hard and try to cut their supply lines. Then the Nazis will find themselves fighting three enemies simultaneously. Firstly, sub-zero arctic conditions; secondly, starvation; and thirdly, a rejuvenated and resurgent Red Army. They may defeat one, perhaps even two but never all three. The cold will surely kill them in their thousands, and then a combination of famine and the Russians will annihilate them. The Bolsheviks will remember Stalingrad and so they will show no quarter and once the Nazis start running, they won't stop until they reach Warsaw. Yes, I think they will pay dearly for going too far too quickly, just like Napoleon did."

The captain nodded, "Perhaps that's true, perhaps not, but we still need to take the war to them rather than sit here and wait.

We've now been ordered to tie down their troops right across the occupied countries by waging our own secret war: a war of insurgency, sabotage and assassination."

Konrad was beginning to get impatient, "That's exactly what we've been trained for and we're very anxious to get on with it. The time for talking is now long past. For goodness sake, what do you want us to do?"

The officer ignored the exasperated interruption, "I know you're the most committed and loyal of soldiers but some of you, perhaps all of you, might not come back. So it's important that you're told the full extent of what we are facing, just so that you know exactly what you are dying for." He then gave them a briefing sheet outlining the Pabst Plan and waited.

Adam was the first to react, "Raze Warsaw to the ground! Kill all its people! Good God! Surely, this can't be real. Even the Nazis wouldn't do something like this. It's just not possible." The others started to join in, adding their incredulity and scepticism.

The captain was quick to squash any disbelief, "It's all there – carefully written down, to be done in stages and with typical German efficiency and ruthlessness. The complete project plans have already been presented to Hitler, along with the fully documented proposals for the elimination of the citizens of Warsaw."

Dominik still found it difficult to accept, "Are we absolutely sure about this? Where did this information come from in the first place?"

"The source is secret, but I can tell you that it's an agent of ours who's managed to penetrate the German High Command. That's all I'm prepared to tell you and you must never talk of it or even mention it again. Rest assured, every word in that document, including the references to slave labour, concentration camps and death camps, reflects their exact intentions. They're determined to wipe Poland from the face of the earth and they mean to start with our capital city."

Much later in his life, Stan was to learn that a Polish agent code-named Knopf (Button), who was in fact a German, had operated alongside a number of informants within the Nazi's top military echelons. He had provided the highest-grade intelligence, including details of German intentions on the Eastern Front, the battle order for Operation Barbarossa and the location of the Wolf's Lair.

Captain Robak went on to explain that there was a population of about half a million Poles living in France (over 100,000 had fled from Russian rule in the early nineteenth century and they were followed by other mass migrations after the uprisings later that century, with a further exodus between the two world wars). These Poles, who all had friends and relatives in their homeland, had every good reason to resent the Germans and they had quickly organised themselves to defy the occupation. Almost as soon as the Germans arrived in France they fought back. However, such levels of anger and determined resistance were not initially shared by the general population. Following their surrender and the setting up of the Vichy Regime, life for the majority of the population of France had continued more or less normally, with the civilian population neither collaborating nor resisting the German military or Vichy authorities. The population had been stunned by the speed of the German victory and the collapse of their own forces. In contrast, the Poles had been fighting occupation and oppression for generations and passive and armed resistance at all levels was etched into their national psyche. Back home, organised groups of fighters sprang up from the very moment their country was carved up by the Nazi and Soviet regimes.

The French movement towards an underground war was much slower to emerge. Momentum only built up as the Germans' oppressive and harsh regulations and collective punishments really took hold. These included curfews, censorship, constant propaganda and a never-ending demand for labour, compensation and resources. At first the fight back took the form of an underground press network with only a limited intelligence gathering and sabotage capability. This initial discontent, involving only a small minority was accelerated even further by the German over-evaluation of the Deutschmark against the Franc. Consequently inflation soared and prices rocketed, eventually leading to food shortages and malnutrition. This was particularly evident amongst the young, the elderly and the vulnerable. Only then, after the true brutality and tyranny of the occupation spread right across the nation, did the French resistance movement reach the numbers, organisation and efficiency that it would later become famous for. Nevertheless, even when French resistance was at its height in 1944, Poles still made up 25% of their partisan organisations.

Many of the expatriate Poles, some third or fourth generation, were employed within the coal-mining basin around Lille, Lens and Denain in the Pas-de-Calais but others were scattered throughout the country, working in heavy industry, forestry and agriculture. They tended to live in their own neighbourhoods and a fair proportion was fluent in French as well as German and Polish. Many of these migrants immediately formed their own resistance movement known as PON (The Polish Independence Organisation) with the stated intention of 'causing havoc to the enemy through all forms of subversive activities'. Within weeks of occupation they were feeding very useful intelligence directly to the Polish Government, carrying out acts of sabotage and establishing safe routes for escaping allied pilots.

Dominik's mission was to parachute into northern France and rescue a resistance fighter who had been captured by the Gestapo. He was in possession of information that could lead to the identification of several other cells and also a valuable radio operator. The locals had reported that they lacked both the military expertise and the equipment and explosives deemed necessary for the operation. In turn the SOE were hoping that by mounting a successful action to directly assist PON on the ground, they would encourage this large and potentially very potent Polish underground force to move towards overall British control. An aim that Churchill himself viewed as absolutely essential. He had conceded that the Poles could have their own radio network, their own wireless stations and their own codes. All transmissions were in Morse and they had their own dedicated frequencies which were regularly and randomly changed. He was also happy for them to employ additional layers of security within their networks but he certainly wanted British oversight.

The moon was right and they left the following night. They had their false documents and had learnt their cover stories. They were each fully kitted out with jump suits over French civilian clothing, well-filled money belts, weapons, ammunition, explosives, detonators, a fighting knife and a suicide pill. First they endured a road journey in the back of an army truck. Despite the fact that the canvas sides were tightly lashed down, it was cold, draughty and uncomfortable. A few miles from RAF Tempsford in rural Bedfordshire, the most secret and secure RAF base in the country, they encountered another security measure when they had to swap over to another identical vehicle but with a different driver.

They were then driven down a country lane straight to the eastern corner of the airfield, passing the guards and signs stating 'Road Closed to Civilians' and 'No Entry'. A few minutes later they arrived at the reception building known as Gibraltar Farm Barn (of solid brick construction but disguised by wooden cladding to look just like a normal farm building). Here they were carefully searched to ensure that nothing incriminating had been missed. Labels on clothing had to be authentic, buttons, styles, fasteners and footwear all had to be French. Cigarettes, matches, lighters, keys and any other personal items had to be checked thoroughly. Nothing was left to chance. It was even possible to provide the agents with vital last-minute updates because secure live communications had been set up directly to SOE and SIS intelligence sections in Baker Street, London.

They were then fitted out with leather gauntlets, rubber helmets and their parachutes. They each carried a Thompson submachine gun and spare 30-round box magazines. This weapon was preferred by the agents because of its compactness and the substantial stopping power of its .45 large calibre ACP cartridges and because its high-volume automatic fire made it most effective and reliable during close combat. They also carried a Colt .32 automatic pistol inside a special pocket in their jump suits so that it could also be used immediately on landing, a hand torch, first-aid kit and another smaller knife that could be used to cut away any snared or tangled parachute lines.

Their explosives and equipment, including Dominik's trench gun, was checked by a Polish Equipment Officer and packed into a large C-type cylindrical parachute canister which also contained 18 Sten guns with 5,000 rounds of ammunition, 18 pistols with1,000 rounds of ammunition and 50 hand grenades, all for the local underground unit. Next they received their final briefing from a Polish Intelligence Officer: this included the latest developments on the ground, the reception party passwords, the name and address of a 'last option' contact and a map reference for an emergency rendezvous point. Only Polish was spoken throughout, as security was paramount. Even the pilot of their aircraft, a Handley Page Halifax B Mk II Series1, was Polish, from 138 Squadron, Special Duties Flight.

They were driven to the plane where the crew of seven were all in place with the engines warmed up and running. They boarded immediately, sat on the floor at the back and were strapped in, safely secured to the air frame and although they had all jumped before, they were briefed yet again on flight and exit procedures. Final clearance was then given and with the engines roaring they took off. They flew low across the Channel to confuse enemy radar and thereby avoid the coastal defences and the dangerous flak.

The noise and vibrations from the four 1,400-horsepower Merlin XX engines was deafening inside the fuselage and any attempt at conversation was immediately drowned out. So they sat quietly, all absorbed in their own thoughts and apprehensions but eager to land and start the mission. Their biggest fear was failure. So many people had placed their faith in them and they desperately wanted that confidence to be rewarded. Many lives, including their own were at stake and despite their training, their weapons and their experience they all knew that the randomness of war and the vagaries of circumstance would probably be the true arbiters of success or catastrophe. The odds were very much against them.

When they approached the drop zone the dispatcher warned them to stand by and as they rose he started their final equipment and safety checks. The radio operator helped him open the exit hatch in the floor and they lined up waiting anxiously for the green light. A few months later in the war these Halifax aircraft used by the SOE were adapted to improve overall performance and a parachute door was inserted. Other alterations included the removal of the forward armament and dorsal turret to allow the fitting of a 'Tempsford' or 'Z' smooth fairing that streamlined the nose section and increased the aircraft's speed. Additional fuel tanks were also installed to facilitate the 2,000-mile round trip to Poland.

Dominik, being the first to go, was sat at the hatch in the floor with his feet and legs dangling through when the green 'jump' light came on. Eerily, it illuminated his clenched teeth framed by features set rigid with concentration and resolve. Then he dropped through the hatch, immediately followed by Stan and Adam with Konrad bringing up the rear. Floating down towards the twin-fire beacons marking out their landing ground, Adam suddenly realised that he was dropping into complete uncertainty and for a moment or two as he anxiously searched the ground below, he vividly pictured betrayal and a German ambush. The only sound they could hear was the noise of the aircraft's engines as it circled around to head home after dropping the equipment pod as near to their landing site as possible.

Stan was only just 19 years old and he felt cold with fear as he floated down through the cool night air. He took a last lingering look at the disappearing Halifax as its silhouette was swallowed up by the dark shadow of the northern sky. He thought that his final link with the relative security, familiarity and comradeship of Audley End House and everything noble that it represented had just been suddenly and irrevocably broken. It had been a welcome and hope-filled refuge that had nurtured his need for companionship, his fervent nationalism and his burning desire to fight. But as the ground rushed up to meet him, offering little but danger and hostility, he felt a profound sadness overwhelm him, suddenly convinced that he would never again see the comforting and stately Jacobean mansion with its warm and inspiring 'Capability' Brown gardens.

Chapter Twelve

THE BETRAYAL

Valenciennes, France – 19th December 1942

Leon Mulak also watched the plane disappear beyond the North Wood as he waited in the treeline on the opposite side of the landing site. He was a forty-nine-year-old veteran of the Polish-Soviet war of 1919-1921 and a collier by occupation. He had moved to France in 1925 looking for work and a better life. He found both within the expatriate Polish mining community at the French town of Denouvry, near Valenciennes in the Pas-de-Calais, and had stayed. However, once Poland had been invaded again he became determined to fight the Nazis, and his opportunity arrived when France was also overrun. He helped to set up PON and had been a district commander ever since, responsible for overseeing all operations of sabotage. His military experience and familiarity with the use of explosives in the pits made him a natural choice and he was very good. In fact, so successful had he been that the SS and Gestapo had made the elimination of his operation their number one priority in northern France. With the recent capture of one of his key operatives they believed they were on the brink of a major breakthrough.

He was relieved to see all five parachutes touchdown, well within the confines of the twenty-acre riverside meadow and together with his four-man reception team, he sprinted out of cover to meet the new arrivals and extinguish the fires. This was his first drop for over six months and being desperate for help and resupply he was taking no chances with security. He had chosen the isolated drop zone with great care. The reflected silver thread of the river was the best possible navigation aid for the pilot and the agents. The large empty meadow stood out in the dappled light cast by the winter moon and the stars, which frequently broke through the patchy cloud, in stark contrast to the shadowy woodland of its surroundings. The only approach road was full of potholes and frequently narrowed into a single carriageway, and was more gravelled farm track than a normal metalled country lane. More importantly, it was relatively easy to defend and he had kept the site under observation for three days to protect against any German infiltration. He now had a four-man fighting team set in position in both directions, some 400 yards out along the track – his best and most experienced soldiers, heavily armed and lying in wait: the perfect ambush.

Although confident that he could not be surprised by the enemy, he was anxious to secure the men and supplies and get them to safety, because any movement during curfew was extremely risky. Collaborators and informers, rather than the secret police, posed the greatest threat because there were so many and they lived within the community. Your neighbour, your friend, a relative, even a member of your own underground cell could be about to turn you in at any time. The incentives to inform were many and varied. Money, power and influence, jealousy, self-preservation or the need to protect a loved one, blackmail, personal rivalry, fear and politics; all had lit the fire of treachery, very often with fatal consequences. Leon hoped that his man's capture had been brought about by his own carelessness, perhaps a chance remark or an unlucky break, but he suspected and feared that one of his own men or women was a traitor.

Leon reached Dominik first and they quickly exchanged passwords, before running on to check the others. They had all landed safely and quickly formed up ready for action whilst Leon's reception party collected the heavy supply container and the parachutes. The men were well aware of the heightened danger when out in the open. They worked together efficiently in well-drilled silence, reaching the road and the waiting truck within ten minutes of the drop. They drove for two miles along the lane and then turned onto a logging track to their temporary safe house, a semi-derelict and isolated farm in the centre of the forest, just north of the town. Once they had arrived and whilst the others settled in, Leon immediately left to check on the sentries. Next, he arranged for his radio operator (always referred to as 'the pianist') to send a 'package arrived safely' signal back to the SOE, Polish Émigré Section (EU/P). On his return he told Dominik, in whispered conversation, only what he felt it was safe to divulge. Then they formulated their rescue plans which also included a final, fall-back option. If all else failed they would kill the prisoner to prevent him suffering further and talking under torture. They both hoped that it was not already too late.

It was only 7.30 am when Gestapo Kriminalkommissar Dieter Hoffmann walked into his office on the second floor of the Stapostellen in the centre of Denouvry, but the telephone was already ringing. It was his boss in Paris, the head of the French Section of Department D1 (charged with the suppression of all enemies of the state outside the Reich) and he was not happy.

"Now listen to me Hoffmann, and don't you dare interrupt – you make him talk today or you're finished. It's been almost a week now and you've given me very little to act on. These terrorists have done enough damage already and I'm coming under all sorts of pressure from Berlin to round them up and make an example of them all." He paused and Hoffmann could hear him shouting at someone else in his office, "Get out! I'll deal with it later. Can't you see I'm busy, you incompetent idiot!" He came back on the line and his exasperation was clear. "Get me results by tonight or I'll give your job to someone who can, and then you'll clear off back to Berlin and explain your failure. I'm not going to take the blame for you. Now get on with it!"

He slammed the phone down before Hoffmann had said a word. Although the Gestapo officer was irritated by the needless call, it made no difference to his intentions. Knowing that success would soon come, he was not going to be intimidated by his superior's threats. This prisoner was proving to be particularly resistant to torture, but he was progressively and effectively being worn down by the process. The German knew that his approach could not be rushed if he was going to keep him alive long enough to obtain a full and truthful confession. He was confident that he would talk in the end and that it would be well worth waiting for.

Before the Nazis rose to power Hoffmann had been a police detective in Bavaria, but in the early thirties he had been passed over for promotion several times and had become very disillusioned with the clique of old men that ran the department. He resented their nepotism, favouritism and the contempt, bordering on open hostility, shown towards the young officers and their fresh ideas and aspirations. He wanted them out. He wanted change. So, when the Nazis offered just that, he became an avid supporter and now he loved his job in their new instrument of state control, the Gestapo. The old order had been ruthlessly swept aside and together with his SS colleagues, he could now operate without the previous hindrance of civil restraints. He had the blanket authority of 'preventative arrest' and his actions were not subject to any form of judicial appeal. He had been liberated from personal accountability and so the absolute power of life and death was in his hands. He was free to inflict pain, extract information and terrorise the civilian population, whatever the cost. He had learnt quickly and he had learnt well and he revelled in his hard-earned status. He would not be rushed in his duty. He firmly believed that his allegiance was to the great Führer and to him alone. He, by the awe-inspiring force of his personality and patriotic vision, had saved the nation and Hoffmann would bow down to no other man.

Twelve hours later Marcin Malecki was barely conscious, but still he refused to talk. Literally, he never said a word. Since he had been seized at his rented room, he had been asked hundreds of questions and he had ignored them all. He was a sergeant in the 4th Polish Infantry Division, left behind after Dunkirk and he had hidden amongst the Polish settlers. He had a Polish father and a French mother and they had both been killed in a bombing raid in Warsaw on the second day of the war. He had joined the resistance to carry on the fight and to take revenge. Initially when he was captured, he was determined not to betray his friends and thought the best way he could buy time for them to reorganise and relocate, was to act dumb: not giving his interrogators an easy way in. But now, after so much pain, he knew he was reaching the limits of his resilience. He had been given no food and only a few sips of water since his capture. His strength was fading.

He had been stripped naked, punched, kicked and humiliated. He had been strung up and left for hours on end, suspended from a ceiling beam with each end of the rope tied to one of his wrists, until it felt as if his arms were being ripped from their sockets. Then he had been returned to his cell to dwell on the pain and the fearful anticipation of what was still to come. He sweated and groaned all night and each second seemed like an hour. Every time he moved to seek relief from the pain of one injury he discovered another, lying in wait to surprise and stab at him, adding to his misery. All the while he knew that there would be no respite, because the sadistic routine returned with the first light of the new day.

Since 8am he had been repeatedly hoisted back up on the beam and slowly spun around on the rope, which screwed tight and shortened considerably as it twisted, squeezing against his wrists and cutting into the tender flesh, until they were lacerated and bled freely. As he was spun back the other way, with the rope unwinding, he was beaten with sticks and whipped. Every half hour or so he would be lowered down and questioned. He would not answer – and so the process was repeated. Hoffmann repeatedly threatened him with the 'Nacht und Nabel,' a pointed reference to the Tarnhelm (magic helmet) spell of invisibility from Wagner's Rheingold, suggesting that unless he fully cooperated he would simply vanish into the German 'night and fog'.

"If we two don't get along well together, then I'll send you off to Natzweiler where you can spend an hour or two in the company of Commandant Herr Josef Kramer, the magical ringmaster himself. I'm sure you've heard of him. He's gradually working his way through your organisation, dismantling it piece by pathetic piece. Now he really is a most unpleasant man, and you'll soon wish you were back here answering my questions."

But still Marcin would not speak, not a word, just moans of pain and the spitting of blood, and so once more he was hauled back up and the punishment started again. As darkness fell and Hoffmann grew tired he barked out his last order of the day.

"That's enough of the softening up. I think he's about ready to move on and I've just got enough time left this evening to make a start. Lower him down and bring him over to the tank."

A guard and Hoffmann's deputy, Kriminaloberassistent Meyer, dragged him across the floor to the stone water trough and with his arms pinned behind his back his head was immediately forced down into the ice-cold water. He tried to take a deep breath before he was engulfed, but he was too slow and almost immediately he started to swallow water. The panic and terror was instinctive and he shook his head from side to side and tried to kick and jerk his legs and torso backwards, desperate to break free of the hands holding him under. But the experienced, burly Germans held firm and more water poured up his nose. He started to drown. They knew from years of practice, exactly when to pull him up. Not too soon, before he could feel the full horror and helplessness of water in his lungs but not too late to save him. Just long enough to ensure that he would do anything to stop it from happening again. They threw him down on the hard flagstones and he rolled over onto his side, frantically and noisily gasping for air and simultaneously coughing up water and choking on bile and vomit.

Hoffmann gave him a few minutes to recover and then dragged him, now shivering from the cold and still coughing up water, into a chair that had been bolted to the floor. The German was pleased to see that the Pole now had even more cuts, grazes and bruises on his battered body and he added more pressure.

213

"If I say so, these two can keep on doing this all night and then all day tomorrow, and we haven't even started to cut you up yet. You won't die. It will just feel like it because we'll leave you under for just a few seconds longer every time. You don't have to suffer like this. You can stop it just by talking to me. You've proved you're a brave man, but now it's time to give up." He bent down over his prisoner and shouted in his ear, "If you don't, it's back to the tank." Then he waited.

Marcin's mind was racing. His small combat group had discussed what was likely to happen to them if they were taken alive. They had heard stories of the various punishments: the beatings, hangings and firing squads, and they had a fair idea of the probable torture methods, but nothing in his imagination had prepared him for this brutish, painful reality. He had tried to hold out by fiercely concentrating on his friends, his unit and his country. Locking these things into his mind to the exclusion of all else. Always looking back – back into the light of freedom, comradeship, warmth and happiness. He could countenance no thoughts of the dark present or his ominous future. This had worked for several days but as his body weakened, so too did his spirit and resolve. They had been ebbing away with every beating and each passing hour and now suddenly, as Hoffmann's words finally broke through his defences, he realised that he had no more to give. He was ready to give up.

He felt defeated, consumed by the explicit knowledge and fear of what was still to come. With that recognition came guilt and relief in equal measure. Guilt that he was about to betray his friends and relief that his suffering would soon end. Surely, once he started talking he would receive some basic care and respite. He was just about to try and speak for the first time when Hoffmann leaned in close again and interrupted his thoughts.

"You've had just a little taster of the tank and you don't like it one little bit. Tomorrow we'll start bright and early and we'll be dunking you all day. You think about it overnight, dwell on the pain and the panic and the risk. When we speak in the morning you can spare yourself further suffering and tell me what I want to know. You will in the end and we both know it."

Hoffmann then strutted away towards the gate, telling Meyer to leave him until the morning. Marcin was thrown back into his cell where he would continue to be tormented by his own thoughts.

The resistance fighters had been fully briefed and individually tasked throughout the day and they moved out of the woods as soon as it was dark. Leon was in charge of the diversion party with six of his men, two women and Konrad. Dominik led the rescue team, consisting of Stan, Adam, a guide and three of the most experienced partisans, all ex-military. Through his municipal contacts Leon had obtained plans of the Gestapo building and before the war, when it was the Mayor's office, he had also visited it several times. Over the last four days he had been back, making two nocturnal reconnaissance visits. He found it was now so well guarded, front and back, that without the use of heavy weapons it was pretty much impregnable to a conventional assault. Nevertheless, the plans had helped him find what he believed was the only really weak point in their defences. So the rescue team was to go in through the sewers, while the diversion team kept the guards busy. They moved into the town just after midnight and the two teams split up, each taking their separate but predetermined routes to the target. Leon, Konrad and his fighters had a job to do en route.

They were after any clearly marked German vehicle, but the first to turn left out of the garrison gates was ideal: a Type 82 Volkswagen Kubelwagen (bucket seat car) based on the 'Beetle' and designed by Porsche. The first production models had been 'road tested' during the invasion of Poland and it proved to be a versatile, reliable and durable general-purpose military vehicle, both on and off-road. It was the German equivalent of the American four-wheel-drive jeep. It was fitted with an air-cooled 985cc flat-4 engine and was some 600 lbs lighter than the jeep. Although it was only a two-wheel-drive design, the 12 inches of ground clearance and the smooth, flat underbody combined to act

215

as a powered sled when its wheels sank into sand, snow or mud. This enabled it to follow on behind armoured columns, even in the most difficult terrain. Although there is still debate over the comparative performance of the two vehicles, there can be no doubt whatsoever that they both performed well in all theatres of the war. The Kubelwagen approaching the bend was of the standard four-seater design, rather than one of the many specialist variants, but it only had two occupants: the driver and a Feldwebel (staff sergeant) in the front passenger seat.

The underground spotter, 50 yards from the entrance, raised his torch above the ditch in which he was hiding and flashed his 'go' signal along the road towards his colleague, waiting on the apex of the sharp bend 300 yards away. He relayed the signal to Leon and the others waiting about 60 yards beyond the corner. They dragged the bicycle, with its badly buckled rear wheel, out into the centre of the road and the young woman took up her position alongside it, face down on the road. She hooked her dress right up over her waist to make sure that her long pale legs and white underclothes would stand out like a beacon. It would be quite a shock for the driver when the vehicle cleared the bend and its headlights veered back round, to once again illuminate the road ahead. When she was settled, Leon poured the chicken blood over her legs. He stayed with her until he heard the vehicle approaching the bend and then he raced back to his position in the ditch.

It was travelling at less than 20 miles per hour as it rounded the corner. The driver reacted instinctively to the sudden and alarming sight, pulling up ten yards short of the bike. The passenger leapt out immediately and ran towards the girl calling back to the driver, "Quick, bring a field dressing pack over. She looks pretty bad."

He bent down over her and she moaned as he tried to slowly roll her onto her back, "What's happened to you?" he asked in his best French as he eased her over. She didn't answer but moaned again and then slowly opened her eyes. Too late, he saw the flash of the blade, reflected in the vehicles headlights, just before she drove it up into his throat, severing his jugular vein and his windpipe. He was dead within seconds. She was only 25 years old, but she had been in the resistance since the German invasion. She was Polish and she was Jewish and she killed German soldiers. This was not the first. The young driver died at the same time, stabbed in the side by Konrad, as he leant into the back seat of the vehicle, anxiously rummaging around, looking for dressings or bandages. They stripped the bodies of their uniforms and weapons and then dumped them in the ditch before driving off to their rendezvous.

They synchronised their watches at 0200 hours before Dominik and his team entered the sewers through an inspection hatch at a pumping station, 400 yards and three streets away from the Gestapo building. Two men were left behind to guard their escape route. Their guide, a water engineer, slowly led the way underground through the foot-deep, stinking effluent. They walked in a crocodile, each person holding on to the clothing of the man in front with one hand and steadying themselves with the other braced against the side wall. The stench made them nauseous and it became increasingly difficult to keep their balance on the ice-like, slime-encrusted bricks of the floor. They were bent over to avoid banging their heads on the roof of the tunnel. The only light was a quick flash of the guide's dimmed torch, when he took his bearings before changing direction into one of the many, even smaller branch tunnels. Here they were forced to their hands and knees before dropping down into another main line.

Fifteen minutes later they arrived in the basement of the building next to the Stapostellen. Within months of taking up occupation and following a full security review, the Germans had sealed the inspection hatch covers on the streets outside their building and concreted over the access point to the storm drains within their own basement. The Poles, however, were going to blow a hole in the party wall to gain access directly into the guard office, situated within the basement cell block. Dominik had already prepared the shaped demolition charges and now he positioned them so that most of the explosive force would be concentrated in the middle of the wall. He wanted to punch a hole, roughly six feet by four feet, clean through what he believed to be a double-skin brick wall, without bringing about a major collapse, which could entomb them all. There was no guarantee of success because there were too many variables. These included: the actual thickness of the wall (the plans were not that detailed), the construction methods used, the types of bricks and mortar and whether wall ties had been incorporated. He also had no idea of the amount of reinforcing or concrete filler within the wall, or whether there were any additional piers or buttressing on the other side. He could only rely on his training and his regular practice at Audley End House. Once all was prepared they waited for the diversion to start at 0320 hours.

The Poles drove the Kubelwagen towards the front of the Gestapo building. They were stopped at the checkpoint on the approach road, but their prisoner transfer documents and their vehicle and general appearance were accepted as genuine. The front passenger seat was empty and Leon was sat in the backseat alongside Konrad. Leon was in civilian clothes but Konrad and the driver were dressed in the captured German uniforms and carried the dead soldiers' weapons. Right on time, the vehicle pulled up outside the main entrance in the dim pool of light cast by the twin lamps set either side of the massive oak doors. Konrad, having been promoted to a Feldwebel, was out first and immediately and forcefully grabbed Leon by the collar and dragged him from his seat, throwing him onto the pavement. He kicked him in the side for good measure and then bent down and checked the bindings on his wrists. Apparently satisfied, he shouted out in perfect German, "Get up you murdering terrorist bastard." Leon did not move from his position, lying face down with his legs spread-eagled across the footpath and his hands tied behind his back. Konrad called to the driver, "Come and give me a hand, he's too heavy for me. The fat pig has probably been stealing food left, right and centre. From his own people too. That's what they're like. They're treacherous and absolutely bloody useless."

The two German sentries standing either side of the front doors watched with amusement as Leon was dragged to his feet by the two escorts. As all three finally stood up straight Konrad reached into his top pocket saying, "I've got his transfer papers here and you're welcome to him. He's been nothing but trouble. If it was up to me I'd shoot the pig and be done with it, but apparently he has to be interrogated here first." When they reached the doors, one sentry held out his hand for the papers and the other, apparently already satisfied and well used to the arrival of suspects at all times of the day and night, started to turn. He gave the password through the speak-hole to the guard inside, authorising him to unlock the door for the new arrival. Konrad held out the papers when he heard the noise of the sliding bolts and the guard reached out for them, just as the key was turned in the massive mortise lock. Instead of being given the papers the guard's wrist was grabbed and he was jerked violently forwards onto Konrad's blade which opened up his stomach. Konrad covered the guard's mouth and stifled his scream as he slowly lowered him to the ground.

At the same moment the driver shoulder charged the other sentry, knocking him right through the already opening door which then smashed into the unsuspecting and unprepared guard inside. The leading edge of the thick and heavy panel caught him full in the face, knocking him to the floor and leaving him unconscious. The other sentry was also carried through the portal by the force of the impact and went sprawling across the parquet flooring. The team were in – and the time for silence had passed. Konrad finished off the guard outside and rushed in as the driver shot both the Germans on the floor. Konrad cut Leon's wrists free and then all three started throwing hand grenades through every door they could find leading off the main hall. They had no intention of sacrificing their lives by progressing any further into the building and becoming trapped. They ran back towards the front door.

When they heard the gunfire, the rest of Leon's force attacked the road blocks at both ends of the approach road, using automatic weapons and hand grenades. Their objective, in addition to killing the soldiers, was to make as much noise and cause as much confusion as possible. When they left the scene, running towards their rendezvous point, they sprayed the upper floors of the building with concentrated fire, to cause as much visible damage as possible. They wanted the general population, as well as the occupiers, to know that no German was beyond the reach of the resistance.

One of the defenders had the presence of mind to activate the 'general alarm' and the loud, urgent and deep-pitched 'ah-oo-gah' of the klaxon horn echoed throughout the building. Several dozen SS soldiers and Gestapo officers jumped from their beds, immediately reaching for their clothes and their weapons, making ready to rush to their stations. When they heard the distinctive crump of hand grenades within the building they all realised that it was not a drill. The SS Oberscharführer (sergeant) in charge of the three-man guard team in the cell block was quick to act in accordance with his standing orders. He had no need to waste time by referring to his written instructions as they had been regularly rehearsed and tested, and he knew them off by heart. Whenever the alarm sounded he was to ensure that both of the metal barred gates at the entrance to the cell area were secured and double locked. He was to personally retain the keys and ensure that all prisoners were moved into the central cell, where they could be most easily monitored and 'protected'. He was then to refuse all entry until he received new instructions, either on the telephone or in person, from the duty officer and he could only act on those orders if he was given the code word of the day.

In the cellar next door Dominik was checking his watch, counting down from the first sound of the grenades. Along with his rescue party he had retreated 20 yards back into the sewer, just behind Adam who was unravelling the detonation cable as he went, so that they would still have an escape route if the worst should happen and the cellar collapse. They all held handkerchiefs to their faces to provide some protection from the inevitable dust cloud and waited. When the agreed four minutes had passed, Dominik pressed the plunger and detonated the charges – or to be precise, the green plasticine-like Nobel 808 – or as shown on the SOE packaging: 'Explosif Plastique'. The noise, being confined within the underground rooms, was much louder than they expected, but as Dominik emerged through the hatch he could see light piercing through the dust from beyond the party wall, and as he approached, a hole emerged from the gloom.

It was larger than he had hoped, approximately ten feet square. It was still unstable, particularly around the very loose and ragged edges from where loose masonry was still falling, but the ceiling was intact. Most of the demolished wall had been blown into the guard room where it had almost buried two of the guards and Dominik had to scrabble over the pile of rubble and their bodies to gain entry. He was quickly followed by the others. The door into the guard room from the cell passage had been blown off its hinges and when they entered the cell block proper they found that all the occupants were either collapsed on the floor or staggering around in a daze. The only immediate danger came from a German sergeant standing in the passageway between the double rows of cells. Blood was pouring into his eyes from a head wound and he was holding himself upright by desperately clinging onto the vertical bars on either side. Although he was unarmed, as were the other guards within the cell block, Dominik shot him twice in the chest and then jumped over his body to run and check the entry doors.

Relieved that all was secure and there was no sign of any approach, he returned to find his colleagues. They had agreed during the briefing that they would not spare any of the hated SS guards, the men that tortured and killed their friends and murdered dozens of innocent civilians in reprisals. The keys were quickly recovered from the sergeant's body and Marcin Malecki located. He was barely conscious and so they carried him out. There were four other prisoners, all showing the signs of beatings and torture, but two appeared relatively unharmed by the explosion itself. They were also released and they helped to support the other two. Adam made a final check of the cells and was the last to leave.

Hoffmann was woken by the loud, penetrating and wailing alarm accompanied by the sound of gunfire and explosions in the street. As he pulled on his trousers he heard and felt an explosion within the building. He knew they were under attack and his first thoughts raced to the prisoners. He ran down three flights of stairs demanding a situation report from everyone he saw. It was chaos. No one had the full picture, but before he reached the ground floor he had pieced together the various accounts and established that there had been a frontal assault on the building and the two road blocks had been destroyed. He was horrified by the extent of the damage caused by gunfire and grenades at the front of the building. He was even more outraged when, in answer to his repeated demands, he discovered that the cell block in the basement had not been checked and the response to the attack had been disorganised and ineffective. Heads would roll and he would start with the duty officer who had merely mustered the first fifteen or so personnel to respond to the alarm and immediately led them out to chase after the attackers. Many others then followed haphazardly, acting without orders and adding to the general confusion. Hoffmann thought he would have the duty officer shot for any and all of his incompetent actions: he had not stayed at his post; he had not properly secured the building; he had not ensured that the pursuers were suitably directed and controlled; he had not checked on the prisoners; he had not briefed his commanding officer; and he had certainly not waited for his orders.

He tried to regain some control, ordered two SS soldiers to follow him and ran towards the basement. When he saw the thick layer of dust on the concrete steps he slowed down, drew his Luger P08 sidearm and quietly approached the double gates at the entrance to the cell block. The first thing he noticed was the sergeant's dead body, surrounded by rubble and an even thicker layer of brick dust, criss-crossed and scuffed by boot prints. Then, as he sensed movement, his gaze shifted towards the far end of the cell passage and he was quick to react, firing four shots in rapid succession at the person disappearing into the guard room. His target went down and only then did he notice the huge hole in the wall at the back of the guard room. He shouted at the nearest soldier, "Go and get the emergency cell keys from the duty officer's safe so we can get in there and bring some reinforcements down here." The soldier waited, expecting something more specific as to where the reinforcements were to come from. As far as he could tell virtually everyone had already gone after the attackers in the street. But he would have to work it out for himself because Hoffmann was impatient.

"Don't just stand there like an idiot, go on run! Schnell, schnell! And get that building next door surrounded as well. That's how they're getting out."

Dominik heard the shots and scrabbled back through the hole to find Adam lying on the floor, head first in the doorway of the guard room. He crawled towards him, keeping out of sight below the window level, and grabbed his shoulders. More shots rang out when he started to pull him in and at least two bullets hit Adam's legs. He never made a sound as the rounds impacted and Dominik feared the worst. Another fighter came back to help and between them they managed to pull him back over the heap of rubble and through the wall, where they were able to examine him. He was dead. Two rounds had hit him centrally in the back, one of which had exited just to the left of his sternum, above his heart. It was a kill shot and he never stood a chance of survival.

Far more than usual, Dominik felt the heavy burden of command and loss and he was devastated by his friend's death. He blamed himself. They had been through so much together and the pilot's skill and bravery had saved him from disaster so many times. In the air Adam had always protected his charge but now, on the ground with roles reversed, the soldier judged that he had failed to match up to Adam's high levels of responsibility, care and diligence. Yet he was supposed to be their leader: the one they should all be able to rely on. Then he remembered the sergeant's words in the trench and realised that he couldn't afford a second of self-pity or a moment to mourn. They had been discovered and time was running out for them all. So they left Adam where he lay and retreated into the sewers.

Dominik knew the Germans would probably follow them underground and so when they were halfway through and still within a main section of the tunnel system, he sent the others on ahead and then set the explosives. This time he used the No. 10 delay switch – also known as a timing pencil, which was a brass tube with a copper section at one end containing a glass vial of cupric chloride. The timer was started by crushing the copper section of the tube to break the vial, releasing the corrosive chemical which slowly ate through a wire holding back the striker. The spring-loaded striker then shot along the detonator onto a percussion cap at the other end to initiate the charge. He selected two ten-minute delay (the minimum possible) timing pencils, bit down on the copper ends of both, removed the brass safety strip which held back the striker and then inserted them into the explosives. He used just enough to ensure that the tunnel would collapse and he always used two timing pencils, just in case one failed.

He caught up with the others at the first junction and then the guide led them out as quickly as he could. They were above ground, back with their own guards at the pumping station when the plastique exploded and they were safely into the woods long before daybreak, on the shortest day of the year. Although the mission had been a success, they all felt a deep sense of sadness and disappointment at the deaths of their comrades. Leon had also lost one of his men when they attacked the roadblocks and another as they made their escape. He had abandoned the Kubelwagen a few streets away from the Stapostellen and destroyed it with hand grenades.

Leon thanked his partisans and told them to disperse back to their normal lives until they were contacted again. He had spoken to Marcin and then taken the decision to abandon all operations and training for a week or two to allow the inevitable German hue and cry to die down. He knew there would also be reprisals and so he wanted his people back at their homes where they could help their families and friends, and avoid suspicion. More reprisals would in turn heighten the already considerable pressure on the whole resistance movement. Both the local population and certain factions of the leaderships in exile constantly urged them to cease, or at least curb, their military activities. They wanted them to concentrate on intelligence gathering and anti-German propaganda, whilst building up their forces and planning for a major uprising, aimed to coincide with future Allied landings on mainland Europe. Leon and many other underground leaders were not persuaded by these views but fervently believed that the enemy should be attacked at every opportunity. Furthermore, he advocated that all occupiers who deliberately murdered civilians as a form of collective punishment should always be hunted down, whatever the cost.

Leon helped Dominik and his two friends take Marcin to a gamekeeper's shack about three miles from their original hideout, where they could rest up for the day. They were also accompanied by a female fighter, who being a nurse by training, doubled up as the unit's medical orderly. The nurse, Camille, immediately started cleaning and dressing Marcin's wounds and gave him some painkillers. Within a few hours he felt and looked more like a human being. The swelling and bruising on his face and the lacerations and violet weals on his body were the same but most of the dried blood had been sponged away and his wrists had been neatly dressed. He had managed to swallow some soup, a cup of wine and a few mouthfuls of soggy bread. He then told them all exactly what had happened.

"They came for me at five in the morning when I was still in bed. They just kicked the door in and that was it. There were two Gestapo and two SS men and Meyer, Hoffmann's deputy. There was nothing I could do, but I swear to God I never gave them a thing."

Dominik asked, "How did they get on to you?"

"Well it wasn't the landlady. They dragged her out the door into the road, right in front of me and Meyer shot her. He didn't even say anything, just waited until I was outside. He already had the gun pointing at her head and as soon as I looked up at her, he pulled the trigger."

Leon said, "I know you've been over it with me several times but tell them the rest."

"It must have been two or three days after I was caught when I had just taken another beating and they thought I was unconscious. Anyway, as they walked away I heard Meyer say that it was taking too long and they needed more leverage and he asked Hoffmann if he should find out from 'o m' if I had any family. He suggested that my relatives would be much more amenable than me and even if they knew nothing, they could make me talk by torturing them."

Dominik asked, "What or who is o m?"

"Well that's the point. At the time I automatically assumed that o m must have been an acronym O.M. for a records system or a local Gestapo or police office, or perhaps the initials of someone who worked there, but Hoffmann's reply has made me think otherwise. He snapped right back at Meyer, called him an idiot and told him to shut up and concentrate on the job in hand. I could hardly bear the treatment I was getting at the time and it got a lot worse, so I had more than I could cope with and the significance never really registered. It's only since you got me out that I've had time to think more clearly about it."

Konrad said, "Well, what do you think now then?"

Marcin replied, "What if it wasn't an acronym at all but a code name for the traitor? That would explain why Hoffmann shut him up so quickly."

Konrad was not convinced, "What sort of code name is o m? It sounds rather improbable, even plain stupid to me."

"That's exactly what I thought at first but then it clicked. He didn't say o m at all: he actually said Ohm. I just misheard it. It's all about Georg Ohm, the famous German physicist who wrote the complete theory of electricity, and the ohm is named after him."

Leon added, "We think Meyer made a major slip-up by using the sobriquet in front of Marcin, and that's why Hoffmann cut his legs right out from under him. So you see – it could mean the traitor's an electrician by trade. Then it all makes perfect sense and the less than subtle linkage smacks of German arrogance. We've only got the one under my command and he wasn't on the raid because he's supposed to be with his firm working in Lille for a week. Anyway, we'll soon see because I've sent two men to pick him up."

Marcin took it further, "The selection of Ohm for a code name would have seemed very fitting and secure to Hoffmann. I'm sure he would have been delighted with the clever choice and very smug and disdainful of us. You see, it's a Nazi supremacy thing and he's very big on that. He was making fun of us and it also allowed him to show off his dominant Aryan intellect to his subordinates – and all because the ohm is the unit of electrical resistance – and he was certain we were too thick to make the connection."

Nobody laughed at the German pun but it gave Dominik an idea, "I've been taught that a soldier's role in life is merely to fight and suffer, suffer and fight, but I think it's about time Hoffmann realised that fact too. We should use our traitor to get to him. We've all got a score to settle with the bastard now and with a bit of luck we might get Meyer as well."

Leon thought for a moment then said, "Let's see what the electrician has got to say for himself first. I've already arranged for you to be picked up tonight and taken through the forest to another farm near Beauforet. It's only about ten miles away so I'll get him taken there as well and we can both ask him our questions." He then left to make the arrangements.

Chapter Thirteen

THE SNIPER

Pas-de-Calais – 22nd December 1942

Their guide arrived early in the evening and he confirmed their fears. Nine men had been rounded up in the town centre and publicly shot and then hung up on lamp posts, each holding a sign saying 'blame the terrorists'. On the walk along the forest tracks their thoughts were with the innocent French victims and their families. They also remembered Adam and all they had been through together. Konrad thought he would always be known as the courageous and flamboyant fighter pilot – the scourge of the Konarmia. Dominik had loved his humour and warmth and as he trudged, he had the time to grieve. He pictured him as the archetypal enthusiast of speed: whether it was in the air, commanding the sky and denying it to the enemy, or fearlessly driving the getaway van. He was always the daring pathfinder, born to hit-and-run and striving to cause maximum damage for minimal effort and invariably being chased by Ukrainian, Russian or German bullets.

Dominik missed his charismatic friend already and in the refuge of darkness, his eyes filled with tears. He remembered how he had died and the fact that he had left him behind – abandoned him, half-buried in a filthy basement. He imagined Bogdana looking down on him. Her flashing eyes suddenly stopping to fix him with an accusatory stare. She tearfully demanded an explanation for his desertion of those he should have held most dear. He felt wretched and unworthy, but he accepted the painful guilt he carried and he prayed for the strength to persevere.

Stan also shed a tear for his friend. He had been a father figure and mentor throughout their comprehensive and gruelling training programme. He knew that he would not have qualified without his constant advice, support and encouragement. He smiled as he recalled how they had reduced their German language teacher to hysterical laughter. In friendly competition, they had both strutted about the classroom, goose-stepping up and down the aisles. They imitated Hitler in their mock German accents and gave Nazi salutes to the imaginary hordes of cheering fanatics. Only now he felt cheated: resentful that he had lost such a loyal friend on their very first mission together. Although they had rescued Marcin and saved his life and also inflicted considerable damage on the enemy, he doubted whether it had really been worth it, especially after the deaths of nine innocent Frenchmen.

They had been fed and watered in the farmhouse as soon as they arrived and then taken out through the quagmire of farmyard mud and dung to the largest of the three barns, where they were to spend the night. Shortly after, Leon arrived with two of his men and their prisoner. His hands were tied in front of him and he was pretty badly beaten up.

Leon explained, "He tried to get away and so they roughed him up a bit. He's admitted it. He sold you out Marcin, and he did it to save his own skin."

Despite Marcin's own injuries he ran straight at the traitor and shoulder charged him, knocking the escort out of the way at the same time as his target crashed to the floor. He looked down at the man, who curled up into the foetal position to protect himself as best he could. Marcin kicked him twice in the rib cage. They were fierce, bone-cracking blows that drove the air from his lungs and left him gasping and terrified of what would come next. Marcin stopped. He recognised the hopelessness and the suffering of his victim and suddenly he didn't want to inflict any more pain. He had had his fill of torture. Just like he had been, the traitor was now defeated and vulnerable, unable to defend himself, either physically or morally.

He sank to his knees beside him and rolled him over. "Why did you do it? I've only seen you a couple of times and I didn't even know who you were or what you did. Why me?

He didn't answer. Leon told the escorts to take him to one of the other barns, tie him down, and guard him overnight. When they had left he filled in the blanks. "He had a black market deal going, with a German soldier who was stealing electric cable and fittings from their stores. He was using it in the course of his business and they were splitting the profits. The German was caught and arrested, so he implicated the electrician to avoid being court-martialled or shot. He preferred to take his chances on the Eastern Front, rather than face the prospect of a firing squad in France."

Konrad asked, "But surely he couldn't have known that his partner in crime was in the resistance?"

Leon said, "No, that was Hoffmann's doing. He would have received a copy of the arrest report as a matter of routine because it involved a serving soldier who had made himself vulnerable to blackmail. He decided to interview the electrician, probably to see who else was involved and whether there were any security implications. When he saw him, he literally smelt a rat and a few threats and a beating were enough to make him admit a connection to us."

Stan asked, "Then why did they let him go so quickly?"

Leon said, "He didn't look much of anything just now, lying on his belly in the grime, but he's a crafty bastard. He probably told them that he just ran the odd errand or two and that he didn't know any of the fighters or leaders and most of the little he did know was based on rumour and guesswork."

Marcin added, "Like all good liars he rooted his answers in the truth. In our position it doesn't pay to know too much. We try to keep tight security by using 'a need to know' principle and

Hoffmann would know that. So he might have accepted that he was small fry."

Leon told them of the arrangement, "Anyway, the traitor agreed to work for Hoffmann. He offered to spy on us and report back. As he put it, to worm his way in and find out as much as he could about the whole organisation. But I reckon that over the next few days his over-willingness to cooperate, his familiarity with secrecy and security procedures and his general eagerness to please made Hoffmann suspicious. I think he guessed that he knew far more about us than he was suggesting and so he decided to test him out straight away."

Marcin asked, "This must be where I fitted in?"

Leon brought them up to date, "He threatened to send his wife off to a concentration camp unless he agreed to turn one of us fighters in. Well, at least he says that's why he collaborated, but we obviously can't verify it. In any case Hoffmann had nothing to lose. If the electrician failed he could simply pull him back in at any time and put him right under the microscope. On the other hand, if he was successful then he knew he had a golden source – the ideal double agent."

Marcin said, "If Meyer hadn't made that verbal slip in the cellblock, then who knows what damage he could have caused. It doesn't bear thinking about. Anyway, he wouldn't tell me why I was picked. Can you?"

Dominik thought he had worked it out and suggested, "He couldn't give up anybody close to himself because he would have come under immediate suspicion. He knew he would have to be careful and so he picked a relative stranger."

Marcin also caught on and answered his own question, "He simply picked me out when we were training or at a briefing or on a joint operation, and then followed me home."

Stan asked, "What happens now?"

Leon said, "We try him tomorrow. He's already confessed, but we've got to do it properly. He'll be charged with treason, in accordance with military discipline. Then, once he's been convicted, he'll be shot."

Dominik thought there was a better option, "Can't you put it off for a few days? Like I suggested before, we can use him to set Hoffmann up. They've both got a lot to answer for and I think it would work." He then explained what he had in mind and two hours later they had all agreed on a plan.

Stan needed a suitable weapon –preferably something he was reasonably familiar with and had the necessary range, reliability and accuracy. The best that the underground could offer was a French MAS 36, bolt-action rifle. It had a 22½-inch barrel, weighed 8lbs and had an accurate range of up to 400 yards. It took a 7.5 mm French cartridge from a clip-fed, five-round box magazine. He had fired one on his snipers course and felt reasonably comfortable with it, but his weapon of choice during training had been a British Lee-Enfield No. 4 Mk 1. It had been selected for its accuracy during factory tests and then modified by adding a cheek-piece and telescopic sights. However, he had to manage with what he had and the MAS had no telescopic sight but was both reliable and effective. He recalled his instructor describing it as a classic weapon of war. It had a spike-shaped bayonet stored in a tube below the barrel and unusually, it had no safety features at all. Once a round was chambered it was ready to fire. It certainly wasn't childproof or even idiot-proof, as a few unfortunate French infantrymen had discovered when they forgot that it was supposed to be carried unloaded or at least, with a loaded magazine but an empty chamber. He set off into the forest to test it and zero in the dioptre rear sight, which was marked from 100 to 1,200 yards in 100-yard increments.

Leon went into town to search out a suitable location for the coming action and Dominik put their proposal to Ohm. He agreed to do what he was asked on the condition that his family were moved away to safety. He knew that if they stayed in the locality, once the news that he had been accused of treason was out, their safety and even their very lives would hang in the balance. The locals would take their revenge. If they moved away, towards the urban sprawl of Paris perhaps, at least they would have a chance of starting again. Leon even agreed to provide them with new identities and papers to match.

The following day Leon took Dominik, Stan and Konrad to see the site he had chosen. It was a small elementary school on the edge of the town centre, surrounded by terraced housing and a few shops and small businesses. There would be little activity in the streets on a Sunday morning and the nearest church was over 200 yards away. At the back and sides, the school building was surrounded by a six-foot-high wall which prevented any direct access from the rear and enclosed a concrete playing area. A four-foot-wide path down either side permitted all round pedestrian access. The frontage consisted of another concrete playground bordered by a four-foot-high wooden fence and ten-foot-wide wooden double gates. Judging from the weeds, dirt and leaves trapped underneath, it must have been wedged wide open for months.

The single-storey building was of brick construction with a tile roof, containing two classrooms, a cloakroom and a small kitchen. It catered for about fifty children. They agreed it was ideal for their purposes. There was only the one approach road, but it provided rapid frontal access from the east and west. There was plenty of parking space in the road and also in the front playground. Stan did a 360-degree visual sweep and as soon as he looked due south, he saw exactly what he was looking for. When they were all satisfied, the operation was set for 1000 hours on the coming Sunday (27th December) and that left just the three days over Christmas to prepare. They also wanted to take full advantage of the fact that many of the troops and security personnel would still be away on festive leave.

The following night Dominik dictated a note and the electrician wrote it down. He finished by signing his code name and appending his agreed authentication number. The risks of using a traitor were self-evident to all, but they hoped that he was sufficiently concerned about his family to be truthful regarding his security details, the location of the emergency letter drop and the collection arrangements. They also had to time the delivery just right so that the Germans couldn't get to the school before they were ready but had just sufficient opportunity to respond, without the advantage of proper planning and with little time to muster their forces.

At 0750 hours on the Sunday morning Leon placed the note behind the loose stone in the churchyard wall. As he walked through the entrance gate some 20 yards further on he drew a small circle in chalk at the top of the right-hand stone pillar before entering the building for early morning Mass, just as the traitor would have done. He left via the vestry door a few minutes later, circled round and kept watch on the drop site from a window on the third floor landing of a corner apartment building. He couldn't actually see the dead letter box because of the angle of the wall on the bend but he could see enough. At 0830 hours precisely a man strolled by the gate and then stopped at exactly the right spot, looked all around, lifted one foot onto the top of the wall and retied his bootlace – evidently removing the note at the same time. What really surprised Leon was that he was a gendarme. "Surely not another traitor," he thought, before he considered the possibility that it was a disguised Gestapo agent. He quickly dismissed that notion; it was just too preposterous to believe. As soon as the policeman had disappeared round the corner he left and rushed to meet up with Konrad for their next task.

At 0845 Hoffmann answered the telephone in his room, to be greeted by a very excited and agitated Meyer.

"I'm in the office, in the process of calling everyone in for an immediate briefing. We know where the terrorists are going to meet in about an hour's time."

"I'll be straight down. You make sure nobody, and I mean absolutely nobody, goes anywhere near that location. I don't want them spooked. And don't you dare organise anything else till I get there. I'm taking personal charge of this."

As soon as he walked in the door Meyer gave him the note from Ohm. It was obviously considered vitally urgent by the spy as it was in plain text, but he still questioned Meyer on the 'letterbox' location, the time frame, the checking schedules and the agreed indictor signal just to make sure there were no anomalies or suspicious circumstances. Satisfied, he read it carefully, checking the handwriting, the security code and the use of the check word 'specific' which Ohm had been instructed to use in every communication, whether encoded or not. Then he read it again:

RZ2147 Ohm – Full command meeting at St Joseph's elementary school Rue de Charlemagne – 0930 hours today – Sunday. No knowledge of any specific or current hostile action but much activity across area. I suspect build-up for major operation. I will not be there – RZ2147 Ohm.

He took it across to the briefing table and called for the street map off the wall and a list of all available resources, both military and police, and after a few minutes study and further discussions with Meyer, he had formulated his initial response.

He whispered his intentions to Meyer, "We will kill or capture everyone inside that school and show the bastards in the Paris office exactly how to run a counter-insurgency operation. Kowtowing to Berlin or setting impossible knee-jerk deadlines for those of us in the provinces isn't the key to defeating the resistance. No, it's positive leadership, careful planning and ruthless persistence – that's what it takes and they need to be told."

At 0850 hours Stan and Dominik walked across the back of the town park towards its main entrance. There they climbed the wooden steps up the square-shaped clock tower, past the four clock dials and the impressive mechanism and into the room above. It was a rather grand, neoclassical, light grey-coloured stone building with a tiled domed roof, but it had seen better days and was now falling into disrepair. A window was set centrally within the dome above each clock face and they were framed by columns set below a dark, contrasting pediment. The building had been damaged by shell fire during the invasion and the clock had been out of order ever since. The town council had neither the money nor the spare parts to carry out the repairs. All precision engineering work had since been diverted away from civilian activity and was now dedicated to servicing the Nazi war machine. It was not the highest point by any means. Several surrounding churches and apartment blocks were higher, but from the north window it had an unobstructed view of the school front and the approach road, right back to the junction at either end – a frontage of about 100 yards.

According to Stan's measurements the school was 225 yards from his position. He checked his watch at 0850 and began his preparations. He was right-handed and wanted to keep as much of his body as possible behind cover. So, he very carefully used the glass cutter and a suction pad to remove a six-inch-wide by twelve-inch-high rectangle of glass at the bottom left-hand corner of the window. He was already dressed in all grey clothing and now he smeared his face and hands with a grey-blue mixture of mud and oil that he had prepared to hide his white skin and he also donned a grey balaclava. He intended to fire just two shots before he withdrew. The muzzle flash was not a real problem in daylight, but there was nothing he could do about the noise. His enemy would soon realise that the shots were coming from the south and there were only a limited number of likely sniper positions in that direction. The camouflage was intended to ensure that he blended into the grey background of the window and the darker backdrop inside. His exact position would not be easy to spot and it would certainly buy him a few more vital seconds. Dominik, having helped Stan carry up his kit, withdrew through the hatch and down the steps to the entrance at street level. He was armed with a Sten gun, his trench gun, a Colt .32 automatic pistol and hundreds of rounds of ammunition. He also carried ten hand grenades. His task was to protect the sniper at all costs until the shot had been taken and then support his escape.

At 0855 hours Konrad picked the lock on the front door of the school and together with Leon he took in their equipment, which bizarrely included a tailor's mannequin. It took them ten minutes to make their preparations and then they closed all the blinds, shut three of the internal doors, leaving the fourth slightly ajar and left the front entry unlocked as they left. They both paused for a few seconds outside the front door and again in the street outside, just long enough to give Stan an advance and realistic sight picture. Then they drove off in their baker's delivery van. It was time to get a more suitable vehicle for the escape.

Stan was going through his drills. First he concentrated on posture. He preferred to shoot from the prone position but that was impossible in the clock tower. The bottom of the window was four feet off the floor, so he would have to shoot from a standing position. He took out three very small sandbags from his haversack. Each measured one foot long by four inches thick and was made from a grey-black fabric. He had used strips of the same cloth to camouflage his rifle. He found that he only needed two sandbags placed along the window sill to create exactly the right support platform for the weapon. He practised by dry firing until he was happy that he had a good stable stance, where most of the weight of the MAS 36 was being borne by the compacted sand. He relaxed and repeated the process several times until he was perfectly balanced and comfortable. He was then able to hold the weapon, without any muscular tension or movement whatsoever, so that at every pause in his breathing it naturally returned to his point of aim, directly at the very centre of the road right in front of the school.

Breath control was vital for a clean shot. If he breathed during the shot, then the rifle would move and he would miss. So he had to use the natural, two-second pause between inhalation and exhalation. Unfortunately two seconds is nowhere near enough. By practice and breathing exercises he had learnt to extend it to between eight and ten seconds, providing the time window he needed. He knew just how to keep his muscles relaxed whilst breathing steadily and evenly, before and after the shot. He had also worked on his vision. Most people normally blink once every three to ten seconds but when you concentrate by reading, writing or working with your hands this will increase up to three minutes or so, but Stan, by repetitive optical exercises, could go ten minutes or more without blinking. He loaded the weapon and waited.

By 0930 hours Hoffmann had managed to assemble fifty staff, a mixture of Gestapo officers, SS troops and Wehrmacht soldiers. He spent ten minutes briefing them all on their group and individual roles and allocating the transport. He concluded the meeting with a summary of the plan.

"We will go in fast and take them by surprise. We will enter the front and give them the option of surrender, but I suspect they will run out through the back door. Either way, their poisonous terrorist cell will be wiped out for good. Take no chances at all, and if they resist, then we will destroy the school with them inside."

He dismissed the men and they left in convoy for the five-minute journey. He was convinced that the resistance would have lookouts posted and that the leaders inside would scatter at the first sign of trouble, rather than make a stand or surrender. So speed and overwhelming force was the answer.

There was no time for reconnaissance or stealth and so the convoy split into two on the approach. The first four vehicles raced for the front of the school whilst the last two, under the command of Meyer, screamed to a halt alongside the wall at the rear. The front convoy had a 4.5 ton model 222, four-wheeled, light-armoured car at the front and another behind, and they were used to seal off the street at both ends. The two in the middle of the sandwich, Hoffmann's staff car and a 3 ton Opel Blitz truck (identical to the two at the back of the building) stopped at the school gates. Soldiers poured out of the three trucks, and those at the rear used the ladders they had brought for the purpose and climbed over the wall. Once in the playground they paused, weapons trained on the rear door, awaiting Meyer's orders. The armoured vehicles, each equipped with a 20mm armour-piercing cannon and a 7.92mm machine gun, were facing outwards protecting Hoffmann's perimeter with their considerable fire power.

Stan saw the commotion at the school, but he was calm and he waited, concentrating on his breathing and his sight picture.

Then he saw Hoffmann get out of the staff car: he looked exactly as Marcin had described and there was no mistaking his swagger of self-importance. He acquired his target immediately. He carefully engaged the trigger with the centre of the pad on the end digit of his forefinger. He made sure he could see daylight between the inside of his trigger finger and the stock, so he could be sure that no finger movement whatsoever could be transferred to the body of the rifle. To gain maximum mechanical advantage he automatically placed his finger as near the bottom of the trigger as possible without it touching the trigger guard. He breathed normally and waited as the troops formed a solid line across the front of the school. He exhaled and paused his breathing. The target's chest was squarely in the centre of his sights. In his mind he heard his instructor's words, which had been repeated hundreds of times during his training: 'Watch and shoot. Watch and shoot.'

He was totally relaxed, free of strain and tension, his mind closed to everything except the discipline of the shot. He kept his head firmly in contact with the stock and put tension on the trigger, very gradually increasing the pressure, slowly squeezing in a dead straight line back towards the stock, not allowing the merest of sideways movement. He continued to squeeze even after the shot broke, allowing the rifle to recoil before he released the trigger. It felt so right and he felt so good. It was the perfect shot and he knew Hoffmann was dead. He breathed normally, worked the action and readied himself for the next shot. Only then did he allow himself a second or two to think of Adam and he desperately hoped that he had at least started to pay the huge debt he owed to his friend.

As Hoffmann's body hit the ground the first soldiers he had ordered in had already entered the front door of the school, but Meyer held his position at the rear, exactly as he had been instructed to do. The SS Rottenführer (team leader) crept carefully along the front hallway and paused. The only noise he could hear was the strident shouting of orders outside, the metallic rattle of equipment and the distinctive sound of army boots on the road as men ran for cover. None of which was his main concern and so he refocused on the rooms ahead and saw that the door to his right was shut and so too were the two further down the corridor, but the one on his left was slightly ajar. He dropped to his knees and crawled across the floor towards it, intending to peer through the crack at the bottom. He wanted to clear that room first to protect his exit if he had to get out quickly.

He couldn't hear any gunfire or commotion in the rear playground and so he was fearful that at any moment the underground fighters would burst forward into the corridor from behind the other doors. So he stayed flat on his stomach, presenting a smaller target and giving himself a precious second or two when the enemy would have to adjust to his unexpected position. He looked through the gap but with the blinds down the light was not good. In the far corner he could see the legs of a man lying prone on the floor and he could just make out two hand grenades and a Sten gun by the side of his right knee.

He knew what he had to do and he had to move quickly. He signalled to the three men moving in behind him to back out of the building and then he slowly stood up. He unscrewed the cap on the bottom of a stick grenade and made ready to pull the cord. This would drag a roughened steel rod through the igniter causing it to flare up and start the five-second fuse burning. He pulled the cord and then pushed the door open another few inches to create enough room. The last thing he wanted was for it to snag on the door or frame as he lobbed it in through such a narrow gap. But the weapon was still held firmly in his hand when the explosives inside the room detonated and blew him apart. The door had been rigged with a pulley switch connected to the safety pin on a hand grenade. The fuse had been removed to make the detonation instantaneous, which in turn then set off the main charge, a small amount of plastic explosive moulded around the outside.

Stan didn't flinch or react to the explosion; he was expecting it. Then he took his second shot and he had prioritised the target. He knew from his training that the armoured car had a crew of two. The commander doubled up as the gunner and the radio operator could act as the loader. He selected the commander of the vehicle on the west side of the school as soon as the distinctive gull-wing, mesh cover was thrown open and he appeared in the hatch. The German, wearing the familiar Panzertruppe black uniform, started searching to the south with his binoculars, looking for the source of the shot. But he was found first. The bullet struck him in the base of the throat and with that one shot Stan had ensured that the vehicle's considerable fire power was effectively eliminated.

Meyer was bowled over by the force of the explosion inside, but he escaped serious injury, unlike several of his men. He was very aware that he was achieving absolutely nothing at the back and he had no clear picture of what was happening at the front. He felt impotent and decided to move, despite Hoffmann's orders. He led a group of ten men down the side of the building, leaving the rest behind for containment. He had to scrabble over glass and debris because the windows had been blown out. He could see nothing inside, his view being blocked by the dense fog of dust billowing out through the blackened brickwork.

Stan was making ready to leave when he saw Meyer and once again Marcin's description was bang on. Despite the excitement of the identification he hesitated, thinking through this new dilemma. His instructor had repeatedly impressed upon him the importance of the 'two shots and move' rule. He had stressed that a sniper should never be on a suicide mission and that the longer he remained in one position, the greater the risk that he would be found, targeted and outgunned. But this was Meyer, the number two target and one of the men responsible for torturing Marcin and as he saw it, killing Adam. He stayed – because the exuberance of youth and his sense of duty overrode his professional judgement.

He relaxed back into his breathing cycle and took aim, tracking Meyer as he ran towards Hoffmann's body. Meyer stopped and looked around for any obvious explanation as to why all the men were in cover, not looking towards the school but staring in the opposite direction towards the south. He never heard the shot or the desperate screams of 'Sniper!' shouted by half a dozen collective voices as they first noticed him standing by his dead boss. The shot took him high in the centre of the forehead with an explosive force. Still on its downward trajectory it burst through the saw-tooth joints at the top of his cranium, flattening out on impact. It then tore a tunnel right through his brain before – just like opening a coconut with a hammer – it shattered the back of his skull, leaving a massive exit wound. His brain matter and ragged discs of ivory-white skull were splattered across the school playground. Stan was just satisfied that the shot was accurate and so relieved that Meyer would never torture again.

The commander of the second armoured car heard the shot and then spotted the merest movement in the window of the clock tower. Instinctively he knew it was the deadly marksman and he immediately opened up with the cannon. He was too eager and tense and his aim was far too low, but the stream of small shells gradually crept up the building until the clock face disintegrated. Each round had a muzzle velocity of 900 yards per second and reached the target in .25 of a second and at that distance would pass clean through two inches of armour plate. He gradually increased the elevation until the window was peppered with small explosions. Bits of masonry, glass, mortar and white-hot shrapnel were blasted across the room at incredible speed. Many of the shells entered through the destroyed window and then punched clean through the back wall and domed roof.

Stan knew that sudden movement was his biggest enemy. The human eye is always drawn towards it and so when a sniper moves, he always moves slowly to give himself the best chance of remaining unobserved. When he saw Meyer go down he slowly started to move across the room, walking backwards away from the window, holding his rifle and dragging his rucksack towards the hatch. He heard and felt the first rounds hitting the tower just as he reached for the hatch cover. He managed to pull it open and started his descent. As his shoulders dropped below floor level, the room seemed to explode all around him. He started to fall. He was still conscious when he hit the top landing some twelve steps below but his head felt as if it was on fire and he was covered in blood. He could feel it pouring from his head and as he floundered around his hands became wet and slippery from it. His vision blurred and his hearing became distorted and muffled. He could just about make out Dominik's familiar features looking down at him, but he couldn't understand a single word he was saying. He tasted the blood filling his mouth and he was slowly being blinded as it swamped his eyes. He knew he was in a bad way.

Dominik had rushed up the steps at the first sound of the cannon and had almost reached the top landing when Stan fell. He could see blood spraying through the air as he slid down the first few steps on his right side and then, as his bottom foot caught the wall, he tumbled head over heels onto the landing where Dominik managed to stop him from falling further. The whole left side of his face had been opened up, from the temple to halfway down his neck. There was so much blood that it was difficult to see the depth of the wound along its entirety but it was very ragged, with large folds of skin and flesh flapping free at the sides. Dominik used both hands to lower his head, clear the blood from his throat and push the two edges together. He saw shards of glass and grit inside the gushing wound. He also discovered that for two inches or so, the cheek had been sliced right through to the gums and several teeth had been shattered in his upper jaw. He cleaned it as best he could and then applied two field dressings, maintaining the pressure while he waited for their escape vehicle to arrive.

Konrad and Leon arrived in a builder's truck, accompanied by Camille. Konrad was visibly shaken when he saw the dazed and bloody condition of his son, but Camille took a look at the wound and reassured him, "It's not as bad as it looks. Although head injuries like this always bleed so badly, I don't think there's a great deal of underlying damage. But we need to get him somewhere safe, so I can clean it properly and sew him up."

As they carried Stan out, Leon told Dominik, "We attacked their headquarters again, just as you suggested: hit and run with hand grenades and rifle fire. There wasn't much obvious opposition, probably because it's a Sunday and most of the ones on duty were already attacking our fictitious meeting. Anyway, we didn't hang about to find out, just stayed long enough to make a lot of noise and smoke to draw them back from here."

Dominik said, "They won't be so gung-ho now that they've had a real taste of what we are capable of but even so, some of them are bound to come after us and pretty quick too. So we had better get a move on."

When they were boarding the vehicle they heard the sound of a small explosion about 100 yards away, towards the school and Leon said, "That must be one of our hand grenades. We blocked both approach roads with a couple of lorries and booby trapped the doors. That'll definitely slow them down a bit more, and now they'll have to come after us on foot."

They drove off across the town park, and had already cut across the recreation fields towards the urban outskirts just as the first German arrived at the clock tower. Too late to do anything other than watch the vehicle disappear from sight. Once into the countryside they travelled on the tracks and lanes towards the forest and relative safety.

Camille tended Stan and administered an intramuscular injection of morphine from her emergency pack. After a few minutes she picked out the remaining fragments of glass, grit and teeth and then sterilised the wound with iodine. Then came the delicate and slow task of suturing the wound with catgut. Because it was so jagged and irregular in depth it was impossible to join the two sides in a neat thin line and she knew that even her best endeavours would leave him terribly scarred. She was also worried about the possibility of infection and she told Konrad that he should be taken to hospital in England as soon as possible.

Two days later at 1am on 29th December, in a field on the outskirts of the forest, a light plane landed to take them home. The Westland Lysander had proved to be a total failure in its primary role. It was commissioned as a liaison or army cooperation aircraft, employed for artillery observation, battlefield reconnaissance or transporting commanders. Four Lysander squadrons had been moved to France during the Phoney War. When the Germans attacked in May 1940, they were supported by scores of Me109 aircraft and the Allied fighters were overwhelmed. Of the 170

Lysanders sent to France, 90 were lost in aerial combat and 30 were destroyed on the ground. 120 crewmen were lost. Only 50 aircraft survived to return to Britain.

It did, however, prove ideal for covert work because it flew at low altitude below the enemy radar, allowing it to 'disappear' at night. At a time when planes were flying faster and faster the Lysander bucked the trend. It was a slow-moving plane, designed for hard work and able to take off and land in the most difficult of terrain, on very rough and improvised landing strips, often no more than a field. Powered by a 905-horsepower Bristol Perseus XII, sleeve-valve engine, it had a maximum speed of 205 mph, a range of 700 miles and a crew of two. It needed just 250 metres to take off and 320 metres for a landing and was armed with two 303 Browning machine guns fitted into the wheel spats, and some also had a Lewis machine gun in the rear cockpit. Along with its three passengers it could also carry two supply canisters. To the SOE, the Lysander came to be known as the 'Scarlet Pimpernel of the air' and it flew over 400 sorties into occupied France. The resistance movement called it 'l'avion de Londres' and at one time or another right across France, their operatives had stood in the moonlight waiting to light the fires or flares to guide it in. After one of them had flashed out the Morse code recognition letter, clearing it for landing, the reception team would breathe a collective sigh of relief and rush out of cover. They were eager to unload the valuable cargo, delivered by the lifeline from England.

They said their farewells to Leon and his comrades. Stan spent a few private moments thanking Camille for her care, tenderness and company. The others unloaded the two canisters which were crammed full with medical supplies, ammunition, weapons and more explosives. With a lighter plane and the blessing of SOE, the pilot agreed to squeeze in another passenger and so Marcin Malecki joined Stan, Dominik and Konrad on the flight back home to RAF Tempsford. Forced into inactivity inside the plane Dominik inevitably dwelt on his dead friend, Adam, and the injured Stan, the dear son of a man whom he looked on as his brother and he considered how he might have done things differently. Although they were all now battle-hardened soldiers who understood the great personal risks of war and accepting that the mission had been successful, he still felt a deep sadness and a great sense of personal and professional loss.

Swindon – 13th November 2009

The telling of this section of Stan's military adventure had been particularly difficult for him and the lines and shadows of exhaustion and burden were clearly visible on his leathery, disfigured face. I made him a cup of tea and cooked his dish of choice for the day – a microwave meal of shepherd's pie. As I prepared his table he said, "I probably wouldn't survive now without these frozen meals. They're delivered every fortnight and there's quite a wide menu, but I couldn't stand them at first. I thought they tasted like cardboard but beggars can't be choosers and I found that if you're really selective, a few of them are quite palatable. The puddings are great, so it's not so bad, especially as I now know exactly which ones to avoid."

I sat down quietly while he ate and I drank my tea. Then as I prepared to leave for home he said, "My life changed dramatically after the injury, you know and quite literally, I was never looked at in the same way again. Tomorrow I'll tell you how my wounds were treated and how I became a spy, a real undercover agent working as a German, right in amongst the Nazis."

My immediate reaction was one of surprise and after another long day I was not as tactful as I should have been, "But surely with your scar that would have been impossible. You'd have been rumbled in no time at all."

He chuckled and rubbed his hand across the puckered and grey skin several times as if confirming the size and extent of the injury. "When I was in my twenties I was very self-conscious of this and ashamed of the way I looked. So I tried to hide most of it by growing a beard but the hair wouldn't grow on the scar tissue and so it looked ridiculous and even more unsightly than when I was clean-shaven. Nevertheless, I didn't learn because about ten years later vanity got the better of me once more and I tried to grow it again but much longer this time. I thought that once it was really established and bushy, like you often see in the Middle East, I could do a grand comb-over. You know, like that famous 1960's football player did. He was convinced that he could cover his large bald spot with a few four-foot-long wisps of hair so perhaps I could cover my scar but as with him it didn't work, so I never bothered again."

I tried to make up for my insensitivity by changing the subject, "Then tell me Stan, exactly where did you do your spying?"

"Sometimes it's strange how things work out and my existence as a Nazi soldier came to quite a climax, only 20 miles down the road at Devizes. Anyway, I think I've said enough for today. I'm tired and just about ready for my pit. So I'll see you in the morning and try not to be late again!"

I smiled to myself as I got in the car. I was 60 years of age and yet even now I was not fully in control of my own life. I was always dancing to Stan's tune and being playfully teased and chastised for the privilege. But as I drove off I thought of how extraordinary and courageous these men and women had been and I realised that there was no shame in being bent to their will. I was still just as eager for the next chapter to unfold and I had no idea where it was all leading.

Chapter Fourteen

BACK TO POLAND

London – 24th March 1943

Dominik and Konrad were met at the Rubens Hotel by Captain Robak who escorted them to the fifth floor. When he had debriefed them on their return from France at Christmas he had told them that their next mission was already being planned by a colleague. He now introduced them to that man who was waiting for them in his office. Captain Ludwik Wolak (German Section) greeted them warmly. As he invited them to sit down at the small conference table, he handed them three sheets of A4 paper, typed up on one side only.

Captain Robak took his leave, "Thank you once again for what you did in France and I'm so sorry that Adam didn't make it home. He was a true patriot and a brave fighter and I'm sure you will both treasure his memory." He paused respectfully for a moment or two before continuing, "I'm bound to have need of your team again before too long, but at the moment Wolak's requirements are much greater and I'm not exaggerating when I say that the whole course of the war could hinge on your success. So good luck and please stay safe."

They all read the briefing document:

<u>*Top Secret*</u>
Special Bureau, Intelligence Group Lombard
Assessment Report and Operational Brief – Peenemünde
Prepared by 'Rafal'

<u>*Background*</u>
Intelligence Group Lombard is responsible for all espionage inside the Third Reich and all areas of the Motherland which Germany has illegally annexed. During the summer of 1941 we first started to receive reports from our field agents within Germany and from our sources within the Labour Camps that the enemy were conducting unspecified secret arms testing on the island of Uznam (Usedom) in the Baltic Sea. A special bureau within Lombard was set up to investigate the facilities on the island and coordinate all information and future intelligence.

<u>*Source Information*</u>
We have cultivated an agent inside the facility. For the purposes of this paper he is known only as T-AS2. The following information has been provided by him and wherever possible confirmed by other sources.

Peenemünde is a small remote village on the Baltic island (peninsula) of Uznam at the mouth of the Peene River (about 100 miles from the pre-war German-Polish border in Pomerania). The peninsula is just 50 miles long, with an average width of six miles (being 15 miles wide at its broadest and only 300 yards across at its narrowest). The prohibited military area starts at this pinch point and incorporates the whole north-western quarter of the island. The Germans located their Heeresversuchsanstalt (military research and laboratory facility) there in 1937. It is an ideal site for secrecy, high security and weapons testing, allowing the enemy to easily control access and establish a military no-go area. It consists of a complex of laboratories, massive industrial plants for the generation of electricity and liquid oxygen for rocket fuel, labour camps and test and launch sites.

The project is headed by Wernher von Braun and Walter Dornberger who first worked on the 'Vergeltungswaffe' (vengeance

249

weapons) at Kummersdorf, south of Berlin. However, that site proved inadequate due to a lack of suitable testing facilities, but they consider Peenemünde to be perfect as the weapons can be launched out over the Baltic in relative secrecy. They are currently working on two main weapon systems that we know about: the V1 sub-sonic flying bomb and the V2 ballistic missile rocket. The latter is fitted with a massive amatol explosive warhead (also known as the A4 project).

T-AS2 has recently made contact confirming that records show that test firing of the V1 project began late 1941 or early last year and the V2 on the 3rd October last. The V1 has a gasoline-powered, pulse-jet engine that can produce a thrust of about 1,100 pounds. It was originally called the Fieseler Fi-103. The V2 is much larger and bears no resemblance to the V1. He has now sent out sketches of the V2, which he describes as a 'flying torpedo', each capable of causing hundreds, perhaps even thousands of deaths and major structural damage. It has an estimated range of 200 miles in comparison to the 140 miles of the V1.

In recent months the British have also shown a great interest in the site, following several successful surveillance flights and the subsequent analysis of their aerial photography. Despite this development and the comprehensive and compelling intelligence picture, there are still those amongst our allies who believe that the development of such weapons is impractical and technically beyond the enemy's capability. They maintain that the whole base is nothing more than an elaborate hoax, designed to divert our time, resources, manpower and weapons away from far more important sites.

Mission objectives

1 Prove beyond doubt that super-weapons are being constructed and successfully tested.
2 Provide a full assessment of the current and likely future threat posed to the Allies.
3 Present your preferred options for the destruction of the plant and its weapon systems.

Method

Despite the efforts of the SS, quite a large Polish population remain in the German-annexed areas of Poland, particularly in the Kaszuby area of Pomerania, extending across the old border into Germany proper. You must exploit this security weakness to infiltrate the local forced labour gangs (some 3,000 strong) that are employed within the facility. Once established inside, you must provide detailed intelligence on the operational readiness of the complex. Then you should examine the relative strengths and weaknesses of the construction of the various components of the plant, the associated structures and launch sites and provide a priority list, identifying all optimum targets.

On consideration of your findings we will then decide how the facility can best be destroyed or at least put out of production and then present a wide-ranging plan to our allies.

You will not make contact with T-AS2.

All further briefings and mission preparation will be conducted by Captain Wolak personally.

As soon as they had finished reading Captain Wolak collected the briefing notes and destroyed them in a hand-cranked paper-shredder, a machine that his visitors had never seen before. He saw their inquisitive looks of surprise and explained, "It's a present from the British. I'm told it was patented in '36 by a German but a good German, an anti-Nazi, and he got the idea from a simple pasta-maker machine that cut sheets of dough up into strips."

Konrad said, "All very interesting I'm sure, but if we don't do something about these V1's and V2's pretty damn quick, then they'll be cutting us to shreds and we can then say goodbye to any invasion of France."

"Of course, you're dead right and that's why it's a top priority and why SOE is working with us again on the planning, but for obvious reasons it will be a Polish operation."

Dominik asked, "How many of us will be going in?"

"You can take a small backup team into Poland with you but only you two will go into the plant. Arrangements are already being made at the other end. The AK will provide all identities, cover stories and the right documentation, but I'm afraid you'll have no help once you've entered the restricted area. I don't need to remind you that you can't trust anyone and there's one more thing. A further complication has cropped up since the mission brief was prepared."

He went on to explain that despite their use of Polish labour gangs there was still a shortage of manpower within the complex and this was holding up production. The Germans were desperate to create an industrial-scale production line for their 'Wunderwaffen' (wonder weapons) so that they could be deployed to turn the tide on the Eastern Front back to their favour. They now believed they had the answer. In April, Arthur Rudolph, the chief production engineer at the Peenemünde V2 assembly plant and a pre-war colleague of von Braun, had toured the Heinkel aircraft plant near Berlin. He was so impressed by their ruthless and extensive use of French, Polish and Russian concentration camp labour that he had pushed for a similar and immediate deployment at Peenemünde for the production of the V2. His preliminary target was the delivery of ten concentration camp workers for each individual German worker already employed there. Wolak added, "The SS are now running the selection, delivery and detention procedures and since the decision was made over 1,000 men have already been moved in and at least another 10,000 are due to follow. A new assembly line has been set up on the lower floor of Building F1 and the first batch of prisoners is being kept in the basement. So you see, in order to limit civilian deaths, you've also got to identify the exact locations where they intend to lock up the rest."

Dominik only had the one question left. "Why can't you use surveillance aircraft and the intelligence you've already got to make your decisions?"

"We do send in reconnaissance flights and will continue to do so, but the German's have good radar coverage there and it gives them 20 minutes or so of warning, sufficient time to camouflage their most sensitive sites and fully activate their pre-prepared deception plans. We would do the same in their position. Anyway, the photographic results are not always very clear and we can't guarantee the weather either. There really is no substitute for eyes and ears on the ground and we certainly don't want to over expose our inside man. He could prove to be one of our most vital assets in the months to come and we don't want him blown."

Konrad asked, "When do we leave?"

"You've got a maximum of eight weeks to train and organise. In that time we've got to liaise with our people on the ground and prepare all the documentation and support that you'll need. It all takes time and we want to get this just right, but we can't extend our Polish flying season much beyond the middle of May. The nights become too short and even then it's making it almost impossible for the crew to get back."

Konrad said, "Where do we train for the mission?"

"From here today you'll be taken back directly to Audley End House. I'll meet you there in about four weeks' time with the latest intelligence, aerial photographs, maps, plans, sketches and technical details. We can then thrash out a full and final operational plan with two or three solid options. When you arrive I want you to select your support team and let the staff there know straight away so that they can arrange to have them join you as soon as possible. We've got some unusual but very useful equipment for you that's been specially prepared by the SOE. They'll meet you at Station 43 later on to brief you about it. Good luck."

They were delighted to be back 'home' at Audley End House and wasted no time before selecting the rest of their team. Hannah, Aaron and Joanna had only just managed to return to England in the middle of February. They had continued to work at Bruno until, in the face of the German invasion, they were evacuated on the 10th June, 1940. Along with all the key members of staff, they were flown out to Algeria, but in the following September they secretly returned to Vichy, France. A new intelligence station code named 'Cadix' was established at Uzès, a small medieval market town near the Mediterranean coast. They successfully worked there decoding German and Russian ciphers until they were again evacuated on 9th November 1942, just two days before the Nazis occupied Vichy France.

They were moved along a newly established MI 9 'escape line' that stretched hundreds of miles. In 1939 this section had been established at Room 424 of the Metropole Hotel, Northumberland Avenue, London. It was charged with aiding resistance fighters in enemy-occupied territory and recovering Allied troops who found themselves behind enemy lines. It consisted of a string of individuals and safe houses, where for security purposes each person in the chain only had one or two contacts at most. He or she would receive an innocent sounding telephone call or a letter giving warning that a number of escapees or evaders needed collection from a prearranged rendezvous point. The subjects would then be concealed and fed for several days before being sent on down the line to the next contact. All forms of transport were used, both private and public, and where the conditions required it they walked, sometimes in the most arduous and challenging of conditions for tens of miles.

One such route had been successfully used by Dominik's friends and it had taken them over three months to travel across France, over the Pyrenees into Spain and then into Portugal and home by boat. Five of their colleagues, following on two weeks behind them, were not so fortunate and were captured by the Germans as they tried to cross the border into Spain. Despite prolonged interrogation and torture, they never revealed any information about the Allies' success with the Enigma codes or details of their underground contacts.

On his return to the UK in December, Stan had been admitted to the Polish Military Hospital at Taymouth Castle near the village of Kenmore in the Highlands of Scotland. Following dental work, a forward-thinking Polish doctor identified his need and suitability for the relatively new technique of skin grafting and he was transferred to Park Prewett Hospital near Basingstoke in Hampshire. It had been a Canadian military hospital in the Great War and then a mental hospital from 1921. However, at the onset of WWII it reverted to military use. In February 1940 the old private patient facility, known as Rooksdown House, was taken into use as a plastic surgery unit by Sir Harold Gillies, the pioneering and renowned plastic surgeon. He had volunteered his services as a consultant to the Ministry of Health and the Armed Services and had also organised additional plastic surgery units in various parts of Britain. He was pre-eminent in his field and between the wars he had built up a thriving private practice and had also travelled widely, promoting his most advanced techniques worldwide.

Stan arrived at Rooksdown House on the 3rd January and then received two separate grafts over a ten-week period. During his stay one of the nurses told him that a Polish pilot, who had been shot down the previous May, was also being treated for severe burns on an adjacent ward. Not unnaturally, Stan started to visit him and they soon became friends. They talked for hours about everything, everything that is except the details of the crash that had left him blind in one eye and terribly scarred by major 28%, second-degree burns to his face, neck, chest and hands. Eventually, on his fourth daily visit, Stan had told him exactly how he had received his own wounds. He concluded by blaming himself. "I should never have taken that third shot. Why I didn't follow my training and instinct, instead of allowing the temptation of another target to get the better of me, I'll never know."

"Don't be so hard on yourself. You got him and you survived. You did well."

"But the point is that I know I could have done better. If only I'd used the third shot to take out the commander of the second armoured car, then I probably would have had the time to get Meyer as well and not have lost half my face in the process."

"You don't know that. Anything can happen in combat. Anyway, you did what you had to do and it's no good looking back all the time and asking what if."

Stan doubted that the airman ever listened to his own advice, but he let the issue go and plucked up the courage to ask, "Do you remember what happened to you?"

Flight Sergeant Bernard Slawinski eased his body into a more comfortable, upright position in the bed and answered, "It's all literally burnt into my mind, and in graphic slow motion too and I don't think I'll ever forget it. It cost my best friend his life and left me like this but bear with me for a minute or two and tell me what you know about the Baedeker Raids?"

Stan told him what he had heard through the grapevine at Audley End House.

After the RAF's attack on Lübeck (an industrial city and port on the Baltic coast) the Germans retaliated by bombing some of England's most beautiful and treasured but strategically insignificant towns. Hitler had been incensed by the British attack and promised revenge and so they apparently used the Baedeker tourist guide to Britain to select the most picturesque and architecturally sensitive targets (those that had been awarded three stars for their historic significance) and Exeter was the first to be hit.

"You're very well informed. Not too much of that has been made public. Anyway, I was stationed at RAF Exeter with 307 (the city of Lwów) Night Fighter Squadron and was flying a Bristol Beaufighter MarkV1F on the night of the 3rd-4th May, and it turned out to be the most severe of the Baedeker raids on the city—"

Stan interrupted, "Well what a coincidence that is! Here we both are: two of the finest examples of baby-frightening ogres you wouldn't wish to see. We're over 1,200 miles from home and our lives have been shattered because we were both trying to protect foreign cities. And all the time, our own are being reduced to ruins and occupied by the Krauts and to cap it all, we've both come all the way from Lwów, our jewel of the south."

"Life is full of coincidences. I bet you don't know that Lwów and Exeter also share the same motto – *Semper Fidelis*, 'always loyal', and a three-turreted castle appears on both their coats of arms."

Stan was surprised, "I had no idea but I knew the American Marines have the same motto as us. I reckon it's going to be bloody hard for either of us two to live up to it from now on. We've come such a long way, just to end up right here, festering in the same hospital. I wonder if we'll ever be anything other than just a couple of homeless shrivelled-up and worn-out red prunes."

Bernard thought for a moment and then said, "You don't pull your punches, do you? And I thought I was the one that needed cheering up. I think some people would still consider us to be the lucky ones. After all, it's just a question of perspective and relative suffering. For instance, on that one raid when I was shot down, over 150 people were killed on the ground, over 500 seriously injured and nearly forty acres of the city were totally destroyed, mostly by incendiary bombs. St James' chapel was lost when the cathedral was hit and a number of other historic buildings were completely burnt out and a million books were lost when the library was reduced to rubble. Four hundred shops, 150 offices, nearly 40 clubs and pubs and 50 Warehouses were also destroyed but perhaps worst of all 1,500 private homes were lost and nearly 3,000 badly damaged. Many of the dead were buried in a mass grave."

Stan was surprised by the scale of the damage, "I didn't realise it was that bad. I suppose the British authorities try to play these things down so that public morale doesn't suffer but if you add it up, right across the country, it must be quite a head count. Anyway, how do you know these figures in so much detail?"

"I've made it my business to dig around and find out because I had grown to love the place. When our squadron moved in the locals gave us the warmest of welcomes. We were treated as heroes and at first, when we went into the centre for a night out, they wouldn't let us pay for anything. They were the most generous people. The cinema, the pub or even a meal, it was always offered free, but after a while we insisted on paying. We didn't want to appear ungrateful but after all, we probably had more money than most of the population.

Stan knew what he meant. He thought a soldier should always know exactly what he is fighting for and not just in a general sense but locally too, on a mission-by-mission basis. He brought the conversation back on track, "What actually happened to you that night?"

"It was about 0130 hours when we engaged twenty enemy bombers as they flew up the Exe Estuary towards their target. I hit one amidships as I dived through their formation, but on my second pass, as I came up behind another one, we were riddled with machine gun fire from the dorsal turret of another Heinkel HE111. I knew it was bad straight away but we were too low to hit the silk and so I made straight for the deck."

He paused and shifted position again and when he leaned forward, Stan fluffed up his pillows and asked, "Was the plane already on fire?"

"No, but as I tried to land in some open fields the controls didn't respond properly. They must have been shredded and then the starboard wing clipped the ground and we flipped right over. As soon as we came to a stop, smoke started to fill the cockpit and I found I was trapped by the legs. I panicked big time and shouted hysterically for Ludwik my observer/radar operator, but it was all to no avail. He didn't answer. Then the fire started creeping towards me from the waist of the aircraft. I was terrified. Being trapped in a burning cockpit is every airman's worst nightmare. I could feel an incredible, unbearable heat surrounding me and I actually saw my gloves and flight jacket ignite, but I couldn't move and within seconds my whole body was covered in flames. I felt my face melting and at that moment I knew for certain that I was going to die."

"But you didn't. You're here to tell me about it."

"I'll be honest with you. There have been many times since when I've wished and prayed for the grim reaper to take me and spare me any more pain. But he wasn't ready for me and as it turned out, I was saved by a brave farmer who smashed his way in with an axe and managed to free me. He dragged me out and pulled me clear."

"Do you remember what happened after that?"

"I was just about conscious but by then everything was darkness. No flames, no moon, no light. I was blind. Apparently the farmer had burnt his hands badly, but he ignored his own injury and smothered my burning clothes with his own coat. And believe it or not, he then went back in and somehow, miraculously I should think, he got Ludwik out, just before the old crate blew up. That farmer deserves a medal and I don't even know his name. But it was already too late for Ludwik. When they got him to the ambulance he was deeply unconscious and he had been burnt even worse than me. He never came round and died just two days later."

"I'm sorry you lost your friend. It's a lot to cope with, I know, but I suppose we've got no choice now. We just carry on and fight back in any way we can."

Bernard thought for a moment before answering, "Look Stan, I can't fly again, I'm still blind in one eye and as you said, I frighten the ladies something terrible. So, you tell me – what am I good for?"

Stan knew from his own experience that sympathy, platitudes or the offer of false hope would not help. "I honestly don't know. Well, not yet anyway. But let me think about it and I'll talk to some people I know. Before that, the first thing we both need to do is to recover enough to get ourselves discharged and then we can move on."

Bernard was not convinced.

Although the plastic surgery had helped to keep Stan's wound infection-free and speeded up the healing process, his face was still badly disfigured by the thick, raised and discoloured scar tissue. When he was discharged a week later, Sir Harold Gillies assured him that the angry colouring of the scar and surrounding skin would fade a little over time. But he also warned him that considerable blotching and ridging would always remain around the wound because it had been so wide, deep and irregular. He told him quite bluntly that he would never regain his rugged good looks and because of his conspicuous abnormality, his days of operating behind enemy lines were well and truly over. Konrad, on the other hand, had made it perfectly clear to his son that as far as he was concerned nothing had changed. His love and friendship was unswerving and he would do everything within his power to find him a suitable post within the AK if that was what he wanted.

Stan was definite in his response, "I know you mean well, but I'm bound to be treated differently now and I'll just have to learn to deal with it but I've had enough of rest, hospitals and inactivity. I need to be needed and I desperately want to feel useful again and get back into action. You tell Dominik I'm ready for anything he's got on offer."

At 10am on Saturday 22nd April, 1943 they were all reunited in the briefing room on the second floor of Station 43, along with the new recruit, Marcin and Captain Wolak. Marcin had agreed to Dominik's request to replace Adam on the team, primarily through a sense of honour, duty and gratitude, but he was also looking for adventure and the chance to fight in Poland. He was mightily impressed when he entered the driveway into the West Park and saw the large imposing mansion and extensive grounds sweeping into view. His delight was heightened further when he walked through the grand arch of the mellow stone porch and entered the hall, to be greeted by the Polish Eagle on a plinth and the Polish flag on the wall. He suddenly felt close to home and was filled with hope and pride. He also seemed to hit it off with the girls straight away and after he had been introduced and had explained how he had arrived in England, there were no objections to his continued presence.

Although Stan was becoming accustomed to the shocked stares of adults and the finger-pointing of children in the street, he had still endured another sleepless night, dreading that his appearance would destroy his relationship with his colleagues. He remembered his mother's first apprehensive looks when she had visited him, a mixture of surprise, shock and concern. Until she returned to England in February she had been totally unaware that he had been wounded. When Konrad broke the bad news she immediately rushed down to Basingstoke and had spent many hours with him since and had slowly come to terms with the new and ugly face of her son. He was worried that his friends would not be able to do the same. To his great relief he was hugged and welcomed exactly as the friend he was and they treated him as if nothing had changed. Feeling completely at ease for the first time in months, he was able to explain to Hannah, Aaron and Marcin in a matter-of-fact and unemotional way, exactly what had happened in the clock tower and outline his subsequent medical treatment and prognosis. Unburdened, he felt revitalised and told them that he was ready and willing to take on any role that they felt would be most useful.

Konrad answered straight away, "I've already had a chance to discuss this with Dominik and the staff here and we think that between us we've come up with the ideal solution."

Dominik was eager to make the situation clear. "You must understand that this proposal hasn't been manufactured or designed just to find you a job. It's genuine, it's important and it's dangerous so please feel free to turn it down, if that's what you want. We will all understand if you do."

Konrad continued, "The SOE and the AK are already looking ahead to when the invasion of France takes place. The Allies will certainly be taking German prisoners and if all goes well it will be thousands, perhaps even tens of thousands and that provides us with a massive intelligence-gathering opportunity. So we are looking for volunteers that can be trained to impersonate German soldiers and go undercover in the POW camps that will be set up in England."

Aaron said, "I think you'd be ideal because you now speak and write German like a native. You're also the right age: young enough to ensure that your cover wouldn't involve a long military history that could catch up with you and lead to your downfall. No, even with your scar, you're far less susceptible to suspicion and exposure by enemy prisoners who might have served in the same units as in your cover story."

Stan had listened with growing interest, "Do you really think I could do it? Could I confidently pass as a fully paid-up Nazi and win their trust? It's bound to be difficult, what with my background and recent events, so what training will I get?

Dominik tried to answer, "You'll be one of just a very select few and the training will be intense, detailed and technical. I'm told that the instructors, and some of them are German, will turn you into the very model of a loyal Kraut. The AK are also working on a way to give you support within the camps, but I'm afraid that

I can't say any more about that yet. I know it's a massive challenge, but I wouldn't be recommending you for it unless I was absolutely sure that you're the right man."

Stan made his decision, "I'll do it. I think my scar might even help you know, a sort of badge of honour. Jerry likes that sort of thing."

Konrad said, "You're right there, son but I'm glad you were the one to say it. Anyway, now you've decided, you need to go and see the boss. He's waiting in his office with the paperwork and I think he'll be sending you off for an initial briefing and a full suitability assessment. If that works out, and I'm sure it will, then you'll be off for the first round of your training. I'm told it's going to take place at one of our sister establishments and it's not far to go. Less than 50 miles from door to door; in fact and you'll be pleased to know that it's another Polish training centre. It's Station 20 at Pollards Park House in Chalfont St Giles near Amersham."

When Stan was interviewed and accepted for assessment and training by the commanding officer he took the opportunity to talk about the possibility of also recruiting Bernard. He spoke German fluently and, in Stan's view, his severe injuries could also help him as a POW plant. Stan was satisfied once the C O agreed to look into the possibility but as expected, he made no promises. The team all agreed to check in on Stan before leaving for Poland and once he had left the meeting they talked through their own operation. They also worked on their individual 'what if' lists so that all the wrinkles could be ironed out later. Just before they broke up for the evening meal, Dominik informed them that he and Konrad would be undertaking a three-day refresher course, but the rest would have to successfully complete two weeks of intensive and demanding familiarisation training, to prepare them for working with the AK in occupied Poland and Germany proper. In addition Hannah and Joanna, although already experts in radio communication, ciphers and decryption, were to undertake a personally tailored and practically based wireless operators course so that they could both take a radio on the mission and ensure that the team could be fully self-reliant. He saved the best news for last.

"All training starts tomorrow at 0500 hours sharp, so get to bed early."

Ten days later they were brought together for one day's joint training and they were met by staff from Station IX, based at The Frythe, an exclusive but requisitioned hotel near Welwyn in Hertfordshire. They were responsible for the research and development of special items of equipment for the use of SOE agents. They demonstrated several objects to the whole team. First was the 'little Joe' a tubular, aluminium-alloy crossbow with a collapsible stock (for ease of concealment) powered by multiple rubber bands. It could shoot wooden and metal darts at a speed of 180 feet per second and was very accurate up to 50 yards, with a total range of 250 yards. It was also capable of firing an incendiary bolt. It had been designed for quietly eliminating sentries and guard dogs or causing diversionary fires. They took it in turns to assemble and fire it in the grounds and after an hour or two they were all reasonably competent.

Next came the Welrod Mk II A, a single shot 7.62mm (.32 ACP) bolt-action, eight-round magazine fed and silenced gun, also known as 'the assassin's pistol.' It took the form of a one-foot-long, 1.25-inch-diameter cylinder, containing the bolt, the barrel and the expansion chamber of the 'silencer' with the detachable magazine also acting as the grip. The suppressor was very effective indeed and despite a range of 70 feet, the weapon was designed for up-close, direct-contact discharge. It was loaded by the use of a pull-push bolt action, controlled by twisting a round knob at the end of the weapon. It was fired by a single-action trigger with a simple on-off safety. Although it was basic, reliable and quiet, an agent needed considerable practice to feel really comfortable with it and so two were left behind with Dominik for the whole team to use in their 'down time'. As it was intended for covert use behind enemy lines it was a fully sanitised weapon, bearing no markings whatsoever.

Interestingly, most of the names given to the inventions at station IX began with Wel (short for Welwyn) such as the Welbike, a small folding motorcycle for use by parachutists and the Welman submarine, a miniature submersible. Many of the items were in production long after the war. For example the Welrod gun was a real success and more powerful versions were introduced later and it was still being used in the Falklands War, during The Troubles in Northern Ireland and by British Special Forces in Operation Desert Storm.

Finally, they were shown an assortment of disguised explosive devices incorporating plastique. They all laughed and acted the fool when they picked up and examined the realistic, life-size exploding rat: the land mine that looked like a pile of cow dung and lumps of coal designed to destroy the boilers of train locomotives. They were also given an exploding pen and a can of oil that had been laced with carborundum powder (silicon carbide) and other abrasive and grinding materials to sabotage industrial machinery.

The rats were later to become immortalised in SOE legend. They had been gutted, filled with plastic explosive and then sewn up, and were designed to destroy enemy boilers by being left on a heap of coal. The fuse ignited when the rat was shovelled into the fire and it was hoped that the resultant explosion would also damage any other plant and personnel that were nearby. However, the very first consignment was seized by the Germans and the secret was blown. The rats were then exhibited at the top military training schools in Germany and the high command became almost paranoid, undertaking systematic and extensive searches to find the scores of 'rogue rodents' which they believed had been planted by agents. SOE records show that this action proved to be far more disruptive than if they had remained undiscovered and been successfully used as intended. The source of the dead rats was a London supplier who was under the mistaken belief that they were to be used for research by students at London University.

Two days later Captain Wolak arrived with the latest intelligence, including more plans and sketches, aerial photographs, weather forecasts, flight information and AK reports on their reception procedures and liaison arrangements. It then took them another eight hours to deal with all their 'what ifs' and allocate the numerous tasks and back-up roles. Finally, the detailed plan was formally agreed and signed off by Dominik (for the AK) and the captain on behalf of SOE (Polish Section).

On the night of the 17th May they were back at RAF Tempsford. Final flight and operational briefings, equipment checks and personal security searches were all conducted in the newly converted Gibraltar Farm House. It was now a well-organised and highly efficient agent-reception and pre-flight preparation area. They boarded one of the three huge, specially modified American B-24 D Mk III Liberator bombers that were attached to 138 (SD) Squadron. Because of its workhorse reputation and unique slab-sided appearance it had quickly been given the nickname of the 'flying boxcar' but many crews came to know it as the 'flying coffin'. Surprisingly, the only way in and out of the aircraft was at the rear and it proved very difficult, if not impossible, for the flight crews and nose gunner to reach the tail when they were wearing a parachute and under attack. They would have to walk through a possibly damaged plane and over the extremely narrow traverse through the bomb bay. When the bomb bay doors were open, one slip when crossing this very constricted lattice catwalk could mean falling thousands of feet to the ground beneath, probably damaging or destroying the parachute as it snagged on the way through the narrow gap.

The four 1200hp Pratt & Whitney fourteen-cylinder radial engines were already warmed up and as soon as they were aboard, they taxied rather erratically towards the runway. They had been forewarned about the jerky and disconcerting start to their extremely low-level, 800-mile trip out across the North Sea and over Denmark and southern Sweden into the Baltic. On the ground the plane was steered by alternately applying and releasing pressure on the brakes, almost 'crabbing' its way to the runway. There the huge aircraft vibrated dramatically as it throttled up to full power. It was slow to accelerate as it rolled down the runway, using every last available yard before it rose rather languidly and reluctantly into the night sky. They were to be flown to their drop zone just inside Poland by an all-Polish crew of ten. The pilot, already an expert in low-level flying, had received additional specialist training on his transfer to Special Duty Operations and the navigator had been expressly selected for his pinpoint accuracy during night operations. Five of the crew had seen action in Poland, France and North Africa. They were now on their fifteenth mission together, back over their home.

The aircraft had a top speed of 300 mph but would skim across the wave-tops much nearer to 170 as it tried to conserve fuel, fight a stiff headwind and avoid enemy radar. The feared German night fighters would quickly respond should they be spotted. The Liberator was defended by ten .303 calibre M2 Browning machine guns strategically positioned in the hydraulically powered nose, tail and dorsal turrets and also in the two-waist gun ports. It had also been painted with a special black anti-searchlight paint to reduce its visibility from both ground and air. A cold wind constantly whistled through the uncomfortable and incredibly noisy, juddering cabin and it was extremely difficult to move about during the four to five-hour flight. Equipment of every conceivable size and shape, cables, wires and ducting, all lined the walls floor and roof, with sharp obstructions and awkward protrusions everywhere, waiting to snag the unwary and unfamiliar passenger.

Just before 2am, nearly four hours into the flight, Dominik felt the plane climbing as it headed further out into the Baltic to start its wide loop towards landfall and its final approach to the drop zone. No sooner had it levelled out again than he heard and felt the four machine guns in the Boulton Paul tail turret open up, followed very quickly by the two in the starboard open gun port. The deafening hammering of the weapons was accompanied by the hollow metallic ringing of hundreds of ejected bullet casings hitting the collection chutes. Jacenty Sitarski, the tail-end-Charlie had spotted the Heinkel He-219A-Owl glinting in the moonlight as it attacked from below and behind. It was still too far below for his guns to cause any damage, but his prompt action alerted the whole crew and also caused the enemy pilot to reduce his angle of climb to avoid the deadly stream of shells. Jacenty immediately informed the captain and crew over the intercom, "Tail gunner –engaging lone bandit – Heinkel Owl – closing – six o'clock low," which was almost immediately followed by his colleague in the starboard beam position reporting, "Engaging four o'clock low. Corkscrew – Starboard – Go!"

The captain of the Liberator was well aware of the Owl's capabilities and knew exactly what he had to do to survive. The beam gunner had made the decisive call. The Owl was a relatively new design of warplane, a fearsome night fighter with a top speed of 400 mph. It was armed with two 30mm and two 20mm cannon and most worrying of all, two 30mm 'Schräge Musik' (slanted or jazz music) configured guns. The latter fired upwards at an angle of between 60 and 80 degrees, allowing the pilot to attack from below and riddle the underside of his target, right from the very tip of the tail to the nose, as he swept on past. The hundreds of explosive cannon rounds would smash effortlessly through the thin aluminium skin destroying wiring, control systems, engines, weapons and the crew, and ripping huge chunks from the body of the aircraft. Although the Liberator was fitted with self-sealing fuel tanks and partly armoured, it was still extremely vulnerable to such attacks because of its size and relatively slow speed. By carrying thousands of gallons of fuel and oil and tons of ammunition, any single enemy round was quite capable of causing a catastrophic explosion or fire. So quite often the German pilots' biggest problem was avoiding the falling debris from the target as it broke up, or dodging the crippled plane as it plunged earthward.

The Liberator pilot also knew that the fighter could not fly blind at night and so he now had to achieve two objectives to ensure the survival of his own aircraft. First, he had to escape the immediacy of the enemy's lethal guns and then he had to lose him entirely by escaping the reach of his onboard radar. Germany had developed a radar shield called 'Freya' which, in effect, set up an effective early warning system for occupied Europe, detecting incoming aircraft up to a maximum range of 100 miles, but it was unable to accurately establish altitude. So when the target closed to within 20 or 30 miles it was then picked up by, and handed over to, the more accurate, shorter-range (20 to 50 miles) 'Würzburg' radar, which also tracked its own night fighters. The operator could then guide his fighters towards the enemy aircraft. This was how the Owl had homed in on the Liberator. It had first appeared on the Würzburg screen when it climbed into its sweep and then the Owl pilot, having been talked in towards it, had used his own onboard 'Lichtenstein' radar, with its 60° cone of coverage, to pinpoint it exactly and then make visual contact and attack.

As soon as the captain heard the words "Corkscrew – Starboard – Go!" from his gunner he reacted instinctively, turning the aircraft sharply right, diving into the start of the life-saving 'Corkscrew Manoeuvre' and calling out, "down starboard!" something that the crew dreaded. They knew what was coming. Just as the name suggested, it was a desperate attempt to escape the reach of the enemy's guns by diving, rolling, climbing, turning and pitching the massive, ungainly and heavy plane around the sky. After losing nearly 1,000 feet in altitude he called, "changing – up starboard!" as he climbed steeply to the right. He rose 600 feet and then called, "Rolling!" as he started to climb to port and when he reached his original height he reversed the manoeuvre, calling out the opposite track so that the gunners could change their aim and deflection at every single stage. Then he did it all again and again.

The whole manoeuvre was extreme, with his air speed fluctuating from the original 160 mph to 285 mph at the bottom of the first dive and then back to about 150 mph at the end. At first, when the plane turned down sharply, Dominik and his team had absolutely no idea of what was happening and they were thrown about, only held down by their safety harnesses. When the plane continued plunging and accelerating in the first steep dive, they all feared that it had been mortally hit and was crashing, their mission over before it even started. But by the end of the mother of all big dipper rides they were left totally befuddled, unable to focus or function, drained of all colour and covered in their own and their neighbour's vomit.

The gunners had fared little better, struggling to realign their weapons while straining their eyes to quarter and scour the night sky, constantly searching for the deadly hunter, in the unlikely event that he had managed to track them through the corkscrew. If he was there and they failed to spot him early enough, particularly when they were at their most vulnerable in level flight at the top and bottom of each climb, then they knew they would be dead – because he would have shown himself to be one of the enemy's best pilots.

The Polish crew had regularly taken part in fighter affiliation exercises with Spitfires and Hurricanes, practising this very manoeuvre and only once had a fighter pilot been able to line them up for a simulated burst – yet once was enough to illustrate the lethal risk. But the corkscrew was not designed purely for evasion; it also had an offensive element, in that the gunners were given the advantage over the fighter pilot of always knowing their own course, speed and aspect in advance. In theory, this gave them the opportunity to fire first. In practice, however, after the first two or three dives and turns, they found it increasingly difficult to keep their focus.

They were anxiously and constantly searching for the now elusive enemy, whilst fighting their own personal disorientation and discomfort and their levels of vigilance and coordination inevitably suffered. But the pilot had performed the corkscrew many times and he instinctively knew when it was time to change and so he extended his seventh dive to level out below the enemy radar and then they changed course to bring them in to the drop zone from the east, flying over northern Poland. He calculated that it was the safest option to avoid the coastal night fighters and despite the extra miles, he would still have sufficient fuel to return home.

The pilot climbed once again, leaving it to the last minute as he headed down the compass-bearing guiding him in to the drop. He started to search below, slowly sweeping his eyes from extreme left to right, looking for the fires that would be lit by the Home Army fighters on the ground as soon as they heard the distinctive sound of the four engines. But it was not friendly beacons they found. Suddenly, the plane was lit up in a cone of bright light and almost immediately it was rocked by the thunderous impact of a shell from an 88 mm Flak 36 anti-aircraft gun. It had taken a direct hit at the back of the fuselage, but fortunately the shell had passed clean through and exploded, not inside the Liberator but about 50 feet above. Nevertheless, at the entry and exit points it had ripped ragged holes some two feet square out of the fuselage and a spray of white hot shrapnel from the shell peppered the roof of the plane. Larger pieces exploded through the tail section and dorsal turret instantly killing Jacenty and his colleague above. As the pilot took evasive action, turning to port and diving to increase speed, they were surrounded by more exploding shells as the long-distance eighty-eight was joined by a shorter range 40 mm Bofors and the 240 rounds per minute, 20 mm Flak 38.

Time and again the searchlight zigzagged around them, temporarily thrown off target by their erratic and increasingly frantic flight. But it was rapidly, almost inevitably, drawn back towards the roar of the engines. It would briefly flash across and then pass beyond the seemingly magnetic silhouette and then slowly return, to pin them to the sky once more, allowing the ground weapons to catch up: homing in for the kill. Every time the searchlight caught and harried them, their aircraft was filled with dozens of shafts of blinding light. They burst through the colander holes in the damaged fuselage; bright dancing rays, exposing every pinhead puncture at the front and mockingly illuminating the gaping and potentially fatal breaches at the rear.

As Dominik turned away from the glare, another shell exploded alongside the aircraft and the fuselage was again riddled with shrapnel, starting a fire amidships and another in the remains of the rear turret. The beam gunners were the first to react, ignoring the smoke, flames and exploding ammunition from the turrets and doggedly tackling the burning oil and equipment at the seat of the fire with extinguishers. Dominik and Konrad joined in, throwing water from their drinking bottles, beating the flames with their blankets and throwing and kicking burning equipment and material out of the plane. The dispatcher was also busy risking his life, using another extinguisher to kill the fire in the rear turret and an axe to hack away the ammunition belts to stop more rounds going off.

Meanwhile the pilot had managed to lose sufficient height and gain enough speed to finally leave the searchlight and the gun battery behind. He then pulled up to just under 1,000 feet to gain the minimum altitude necessary for his passengers to be able to bail out safely. The dispatcher, having finally succeeded in dragging out the live ammunition and cutting both hands on the shattered metal clips in the process, gave a damage report to the captain via the intercom. In response, the co-pilot came back and spoke directly to Dominik.

"The Boss says that he's back on the drop zone course, but he's not sure whether or not we've already over-flown it. He's not going to risk turning back after what has just happened and with the aircraft in this state it could prove suicidal. Anyway, we think that your reception team might well have been compromised by now as well and we've not come this far to throw your lives away. We'll give it another five minutes on this course and then we're turning for home." He made his way back to the cockpit.

Just a moment or two later, much to the pilot's surprise, he spotted ground beacons and immediately changed course a few degrees to starboard to correctly line up an approach. The red lights came on and the bomb aimer/dispatcher then prepared the passengers for the jump and checked the two equipment chutes. Dominik and his team waited by the hatch for the order to go. Then the co-pilot came back again.

"We think we're at least ten miles further west from the authorised drop point so we can't be sure that they're our people down there. They've given the correct recognition signal, but they also keep repeatedly flashing the Morse code for the letters AK and that's never happened before, so it could well be a trap. The Boss says it's your decision and you've got to make an immediate choice: either bail out and take your chances on the ground or abort the mission. The decision is yours and we're not putting any pressure on you either way. But we can't hang about."

Dominik never even thought about it, nor did he consult with his team. As the commanding officer he alone took the responsibility, "Tell the Captain that we're going. The sooner we get off your plane the quicker you can try to get back to base. I'm really sorry about the gunners, we all are and I hope the rest of you make it back safely. I'm really grateful for all you've done and thank the captain for me too. Godspeed. Who knows, perhaps we'll meet again back in England one day or maybe even in Poland when the war's over."

They shook hands and following right behind their equipment canisters the team lined up. The lights changed to green and then in quick succession, they dropped through the hatch. They fell out into the night, where they were buffeted by the slipstream and thoughts of a most uncertain future. Each, in turn, felt the reassuring and forceful yank of the static line, just before their parachutes opened and they floated through the pale moonlight towards the fires below.

Chapter Fifteen

BREAKING IN

Occupied Poland – 18th May 1943

Konrad was the first out of the aircraft and he immediately gazed down, searching from east to west looking for landmarks, anything that would hint at their exact location. The lake off to his left was shimmering and sparkling in the reflected moonlight. It was quite a contrast to the dark shadow of the juxtaposed forest, the western edge of which was almost directly underneath him. It struck him that the outline bore a remarkable resemblance to a galloping horse and rider. For a second as he relaxed into his harness, he imagined it tearing across the open fields of northern Kaszuby – flying like Pegasus, winging its way towards its next invigorating draught. It would alight only to savour the crystal clear waters from another glittering jewel: one of the thousand lakes that sprinkled this fairy-tale land. Then he saw the fires off to the west in the centre of the fields that nestled between the forest and another dark but U-shaped area of woodland about a mile away.

He could clearly hear the sound of the light wind singing through his suspension lines as the noise of the Liberator's engines began to fade into the distance and he pulled on the risers to make the most of the limited manoeuvrability that was available to him.

As he rushed towards the ground at about 20 feet per second, he watched the flames die away and he guessed that the reception committee had spotted them in the sky, doused the beacons and were now moving towards them. The breeze was blowing from the south-east, just strong enough to combine with his own limited steering to ease him out into the fields. Within a minute of leaving the aircraft he hit the ground hard. He let his braced legs collapse underneath him to absorb the sudden impact and he used his momentum to complete the now well-practised and familiar forward roll, taking the weight on his right shoulder. He gathered in his parachute as the others were landing further out into the fields but all nicely grouped within 200 yards of each other. When they mustered, Dominik wasted no time urging them forward, weapons at the ready.

"We've got to get back to the treeline just in case this is a trap. We can then disappear into the forest if we have to. We just can't afford to get caught out here in the open."

They found the canisters which had only just cleared the trees and between them they managed to drag them, one at a time, the 50 yards or so to the forest edge where they waited. Within five minutes four men, in single file and wearing dark civilian clothing, approached rather slowly and cautiously and the one in front announced his arrival by rather self-consciously and nervously calling out the agreed contact phrase, "School is the place to study." Dominik immediately responded correctly, "And church is the place to pray." Mightily relieved, they all shook hands and introduced themselves, using only their code names of course. Dominik insisted that before they move out, the leader, Moz should explain exactly how they had managed to set up at the new location because, as far as he knew, they were at least ten miles from the proper drop zone. He was genuinely mystified at the surprising achievement.

Moz was secretly pleased with himself, but he modestly put their success down to luck – bad and good.

"The Germans suddenly moved the mobile anti-aircraft guns and the searchlight into the village yesterday morning. We're not sure whether they had been tipped off or not, as they do move them about quite a bit and they have been in the village before. But it was only a couple of miles from the drop site and so we knew we had to cancel in any case."

Marcin asked, "But it wasn't cancelled, was it? Nobody told us what was going on. It was nearly a disaster as it was, two crewmen dead and for all I know the plane might have been lost on the way back."

"I'm sorry, but unfortunately our pianist couldn't get through to London. She's tried several times today, but it looks like her radio's gone defective and the spare is shot as well. It's not surprising really. For relatively fragile pieces of kit they take an awful lot of punishment being carted about from site to site and being hidden away on an almost daily basis. I really hope you've brought some replacements with you."

Hannah replied, "Yes we've got three spare sets for you and some new valves, but first of all tell me how you managed to get your team here? It just doesn't seem possible in such a short time."

"We knew the Germans were almost certain to hear you and attack the plane. Then you were bound to abort the drop. We figured that if you survived you'd head off west, back to England and stay very low to avoid their radar. So we picked another site to the west and within ten miles – one that we've successfully used before. We thought we stood a better-than-even chance of being close enough to your likely course to hear your engines. If we could do that, then with a bit of good fortune you would see the beacons. We've been here since early this afternoon, hiding out in the other woods and waiting to see what would happen."

Moz told them that moving about during curfew was extremely dangerous and so they had to wait for daybreak before they could travel the five miles to the safe house. Then they would have to lie low for a few days so that they could be issued with alternative identities, work permits and cover stories. They were also to be briefed on 'all matters of local significance' in order that they could better blend in with the local population. He went on to explain that early in 1940 the Nazis had started to move all the Polish citizens out of Kaszuby and the rest of the western part of Poland. They had immediately and unilaterally absorbed these lands into the Third Reich and wanted to replace the Poles with German citizens. However, their plans had been thrown into disarray when they invaded Russia and they found that they no longer had sufficient manpower to conduct the Germanisation program and to fight a burgeoning resistance movement.

They now needed all the Poles they could get in their factories and fields and increasingly to service their armaments programmes and maintain and repair their infrastructure. The Red Army mincing machine was remorselessly sucking in more German fathers, brothers and sons. Hitler's conscription parameters were being forced ever wider, relentlessly ensnaring the erstwhile exempt: the young, the old and the less fit, leaving a massive hole in their skilled labour pool. Civilians from all over occupied Europe were being rounded up, formed into labour battalions and deployed within Germany. Skilled labour was also being siphoned off from their concentration and labour camps.

As they settled down and shared their rations Joanna asked Moz, "Exactly where are we?"

He said, "I'll show you all on the map when it gets light, but we're right on the edge of the Debina Forest, about a mile south-east of a village called Zwortowo. That's about ten miles from the original drop site at Gniewino and ten miles north-east of Lauenburg (Lebork). Now, my job's to get you to the safe house today and then once you're all up to speed, to take you on to Koszalin (Köslin). That's about 80 miles further west and the whole trip will be inside Germany proper. We're right up against the old border here and from now on our friends will be few and far between. I'll hand you over to another guide once we get there."

Dominik asked, "What have you been told about us?"

Moz answered straight away, "My commander told me that you're on an important mission but then again, we're always told that. I didn't even know how many of you to expect so I was very surprised to see six of you because I've never heard of more than two or three being dropped before. To be honest, I have absolutely no idea of why you're here and I don't even want to know. It's safer for us all that way."

Ten days later they arrived at their next stop, a forester's hut on the outskirts of the village of Policko (Politzig) six miles east of Koszalin. They had travelled by train and truck in two separate groups, each with a well-rehearsed history and the correct documents (Bescheinigungen) showing them to be 'essential workers', employed by a Wehrmacht-related company. Once Moz had handed them over to their new contact he left almost immediately, anxious to return to his own unit. After they had been briefed by their new man, Hannah wandered into the woods to use her radio to send a situation report to London. She was more flustered and anxious than she realised and nearly made a basic, novice-like transmission error.

The Germans were now using the radios of captured agents to mimic the real operators. They would send false messages to gain vital intelligence and ascertain the whereabouts of other agents so that they could infiltrate additional cells. They were becoming very proficient at this deception and it had led to the rounding up of dozens of resistance fighters. They made it a top priority and had christened the process, 'Funkspiel' (the radio game). The SOE operators were most susceptible to this ruse early on in their deployment, before their colleagues in London had received enough calls from them to reliably recognise each individual operator's 'signature'. To enable the London staff to identify such false transmissions and thereby nullify that aspect of the security threat, Hannah and her colleagues had to take extra precautions.

They had been taught to always include one special word and to spell another incorrectly in every message they sent. In her haste and stressed state she had almost forgotten to do the latter, but she remembered just in time and keyed in the mistake before she signed off. She had learnt a valuable lesson. Irrespective of previous combat experience, there was a world of difference between training for war deep behind the enemy lines and actually being there. The tension, danger and fear of capture were constant, all-consuming and corrosive. From then on, she spent even longer formatting the messages, condensing them down to the fewest words possible and where necessary spreading the content over two or more transmissions, changing location every time. Her personal mantra became 'shorter message and no mistake'.

When she returned she found that they had been joined by a woman. She was introduced only as Danuta and she had vital information.

"My being here with the full authority of the AK should be sufficient proof of my worth and reliability. This is high-grade intelligence, but I cannot reveal my sources or even discuss my own involvement. You must understand at the outset that I will answer no questions that even touch upon such matters." She paused and looked at them in turn. They all waited in silence, so she continued, "You need to tell London that the Nazis have started training their V2 crews at the Freiherr von Fritsch Barracks in Koszalin."

Konrad asked, "Can you tell us all about these crews? For instance, how are they formed and what do they do exactly?"

She had the information at her fingertips. "There are about ninety on each course and they are the army technicians who will be directly responsible for fuelling, arming and firing the rockets when they are operational. They will make up about a quarter of the total personnel in each launch section."

Dominik asked, "What do the rest do?"

"Well each section or Abteilung is virtually a battalion. It's a large and independent unit consisting of about 400 men, including eight officers. They incorporate support personnel, such as mechanics, drivers, guards and a recovery unit for the launch failures. They also have their own field kitchen, medical unit, supply and communications personnel, and about 100 assorted vehicles. But only the firing battery is trained at the barracks. They predicted that about 40 to 50% of the rockets will never even get off the launch pad or crash immediately after launch, but I've been told that when they started testing the prototypes last autumn the launch pad failure rate was over 80%."

Dominik asked, "They're bound to improve on that. So how many rockets have been launch tested so far?"

Danuta said, "I don't know exactly but my information suggests somewhere between twenty and thirty."

Hannah asked, "Why does it need ninety people in a firing battery?"

"It's intended that when the tests finish and they go operational, each Abteilung will be responsible for several firing sites within a mile or two of each other, perhaps as many as six or more. Every man has his own area of responsibility and specific tasks. But with such a technical program, using highly combustible fuels, it's obviously vital that they all work closely together and perform as a well-practised and efficient team. That's another reason why the firing battery is going to be trained all together in one place."

Marcin asked, "Do you know when they'll be in a position to launch them at us in Britain?"

She replied, "I can't be certain, but the engineers have been told by the SS that they've got six months to iron out all the problems. They think it will be closer to a year but who really knows what could happen if they should have a real technical breakthrough or if they just become desperate for a devastating strike at the very heart of their enemy."

Dominik agreed that there was little time to waste and he thanked her for the information but she hadn't finished.

"There are one or two other very worrying things you should know about. A total of fifty of the best fighter pilots from across the whole of the Luftwaffe have recently been recalled from operational duty and sent on a special training course. I don't know exactly where it's being held or how long it's for, but from what I have heard, they're living at a country house not far away from here."

She went on to explain that there had been some drunken boasting amongst a few of her guests who had met a couple of the pilots in town and gone drinking with them. Apparently, they had been told that the Luftwaffe had developed a new wonder plane that was light years ahead of anything currently in service. Finally, she told him the latest piece of information and although she had no idea of the significance of the development herself, she felt that it would probably mean something to the aircraft experts in London. "Just a handful of the pilots have since been singled out to undergo a special oath-taking ceremony and the two in the bar were overheard referring to them as 'Leonidas' and collectively as Spartans."

Dominik started to ask another question, "Guests? Leonidas? What are—" but she firmly interrupted.

"I'm very sorry but there really is no point in probing away, looking for further snippets. There is nothing else I can add."

Then she left and Dominik sat for a while and reflected on what he had heard. He also pondered on what the reference to guests could mean. Was it an inadvertent slip? He thought not. So what was she trying to tell him? He came to no firm conclusion but the intelligence she had supplied had helped him to focus in on exactly what his priorities would be inside Peenemünde. He then prepared a short radio message to update London on their progress and gave it to Hannah for her next scheduled transmission. When he tried to sleep later that night his thoughts kept returning to Danuta.

His initial assessment was that she was about 30 years of age, a professional, well-educated and independent woman. Considering the shortages and increasing poverty, she had been well dressed and carefully groomed. He thought she had a confident, almost aristocratic demeanour and her tone, vocabulary and mannerisms illustrated someone well used to having authority over others. She spoke with a slight German accent and her poise and assertiveness somehow seemed natural, without being domineering or dismissive. As he pictured her again she appeared stylish, almost elegant, certainly overdressed and far too neat and tidy for a rendezvous with the Home Army after a stroll through the woods.

The more he thought about her visit and replayed the tapes of his memory, the more he became convinced that she was a high-born city girl. He felt that even in such dangerous times she would not be without power and influence and perhaps it reached deep into German military circles. After all, even sat in a drab and draughty log cabin, miles from the clean comfort of the mansion home he had imagined for her, she had been a strikingly beautiful woman. He wondered if he would ever see her again and immediately felt a pang of guilt because he had hoped he would. He silently apologised to his dear wife, Bogdana and asked her forgiveness, before he forced his thoughts back onto the operation and the dangers that would surely lie ahead.

Two days later they left, heading for their next staging post: the tiny village of Lubin (Lüben) on the Baltic island of Wolin. Once there they would only be 35 miles from Peenemünde and twenty-five away from the start of the intensive security cordon, known as the 'prohibited area'. Here they would find a proliferation of electrified fences, listening devices, guard dogs, coastal patrols and much more. However, their first major problem was to cross the Dziwna River from the mainland onto the island. Although their documentation was in order, the two bridges and the ferry were rigorously controlled by the military and so they each crossed over separately, using all three crossings. The women were documented as nurses, heading for the famous Spa Hospital at the major sea port and resort of Świnoujście (Swinemünde). The town was also well known because it was built on a number of islands with long sweeping sandy beaches and was home to a most impressive and historic seafront windmill which, at 220 feet high, was the largest in the world when it was built in 1859. It was still the largest on the entire Baltic coast.

Lubin had been selected as their next laying-up position because of its relatively isolated location and its proximity to the railway line that was vital to their plan to gain access to the prohibited area. The village was surrounded by hilly forest, consisting of ancient deciduous woodland mixed with thick swathes of conifer plantation. The beech, oak and birch stands stretched right across the glaciated landscape to the very edge of the steep cliffs of the north shore. Here, their sometimes massive trunks were surrounded by scented orchids and eye-catching red helleborine. These colours contrasted stunningly with the seemingly endless yellow, willow green and silver swathes of the sea holly running along the beach and over the dunes, some 100 feet below. But even the most ancient oaks and beech trees were being felled, along with the pine, to supply the Reich's insatiable demand for timber. Recent and urgent building development at Peenemünde had also added to the local need and lumber processing had been dramatically increased. So the men were posing as drafted-in woodsmen and they all managed to cross over without drawing attention to themselves. Their guide, a bargeman, also managed to smuggle all their equipment across, crated and concealed in a consignment of pots, pans and assorted kitchen utensils, heading for the barracks at Trassenheide, just to the south-east of Peenemünde. Late in the afternoon, after a short bus ride and a long hike, they arrived at their hideout deep in the woods, just over a mile north-west of Lubin.

Dominik and Konrad kitted up and left on a reconnaissance patrol at first light, leaving Marcin and the girls to organise and further camouflage their campsite. They were back within eight hours, having confirmed the intelligence provided by their contact and in mutual agreement on both their method and point of attack. After Dominik had explained to the rest exactly why the train provided their best opportunity to penetrate the tight Nazi security ring, they spent the whole evening planning the fine detail of the operation. They soon realised that they would have to make it work, no matter what the cost, because they would only get the one chance. Furthermore, they feared that getting out again would prove to be even more difficult, and as there could be no communication between the two elements of the team once they had separated, they were forced to work to a fixed timetable. They arranged that the extraction team would be in position on the Sunday, four weeks hence and hoped that this would give them all enough time to complete their allocated tasks. If, following the agreed diversions, Dominik and Konrad failed to show at the designated rendezvous point on the beach by 0300 hours, the others would assume that the mission had failed and withdraw. The survivors would then radio London for new orders.

As the sun came up they struck out through the woods in a northerly direction, making for the railway line about three miles away. Within a few minutes they came across the first of many glades and they paused briefly to watch a group of deer quietly grazing on the far side. There were also signs of wild boar activity everywhere they looked. They passed over dry, shallow scrapes in the ground which had been lined with twigs and leaves and then used as day nests. They also saw trees and saplings where the bark had been worn away around the base and the underlying wood was covered in dry mud, showing that they had been used as regular rubbing posts. Others had been badly scraped and scarred by tusk marks where the boars had used them as territorial markers. But these nocturnal and usually shy creatures remained well hidden. Perhaps just as well, because they were often ferociously protective of their young and all the Poles had heard stories of people being gored by a startled boar's tusks or badly bitten by a charging, open-mouthed female intent on driving an intruder away from her litter.

They did, however, catch sight of a white-tailed sea eagle as it was mobbed and harassed overhead by two buzzards. Despite their exposed position on the edge of the clearing, they stood and watched, just for a minute remembering normality and peace. They stared skywards, fascinated by the soaring and diving acrobatics of the birds of prey and their high-pitched calls of alarm. The buzzards continuously and aggressively flew into the much larger eagle in their determined efforts to drive it off and all three tumbled through the air and then recovered many times. Even when the group of fighters reluctantly walked on, called forward towards their target by Dominik, the birds' aerial struggle for dominance and control over such a rich and beautiful hunting ground continued.

Half an hour later they safely crossed over the main east-west road and about a mile further on they arrived at the railway track and immediately set to work. Dominik and Marcin set the charges with great care. The others carefully chose their positions, hiding

in the undergrowth on both sides of the line. They all waited for the train. Hannah heard it first and gave the signal – just a minute or so before it rounded the bend, some 400 yards away. Dominik immediately detonated the two charges and the trunk of a massive beech tree cracked and split and a large bough, still attached to a triangular flap of trunk and a slab of thick bark, broke away. At first, almost as if in slow motion, it arced through the air and then, with a loud crack of splitting timber and the salvo of breaking and splintering branches, it crashed across the track.

The train came into view, travelling at about 30 miles an hour, belching clouds of grey smoke as it struggled up the long incline. Aaron and Joanna left the others in position and headed off to set their own trap. They walked just inside the trees on either side of the line and headed west, towards the German army checkpoint five miles away. It was situated on the outskirts of the seaside resort town of Międzyzdroje (Misdroy). Before the war this had been a health resort, famous for its recuperative saline and mud baths and was known to the Poles as the 'Pearl of the Baltic'.

The train stopped just short of the felled tree and the engine driver and fireman jumped down onto the track to examine it. A German soldier soon joined them and unslung his rifle, warily looking all around. Being the only guard on the train, he was well aware of his own responsibility and potential vulnerability. He was not even entrusted with the keys to the locked railcars. He was there solely to watch over the driver and his mate, to ensure that there were no unauthorised stops and that the cargo arrived on time. Sensing his discomfort, the driver was the first to speak.

"There's really nothing to worry about, bits are always falling off these old trees. They've been here for decades. Many for hundreds of years and a few of the real giants have witnessed over 1,000 years of history. And now some of the larger branches have just become too heavy or rotten and so they eventually break off at their weakest point. The engine will push it off all right. But to get enough power I'll have to disconnect the trucks first."

The driver and soldier climbed back on the engine as the fireman unhitched the wagons. There were eight in all. Large, timber cattle trucks, uniformly painted brown with a reinforcing steel frame and a sliding door in the centre on each side. The only ventilation was through a letterbox-like window vent, placed high up at opposing ends, both covered inside and out with a web of barbed wire. The doors were pulled into the closed position from the outside using a 'D' handle which was then engaged by a heavy, pivoting metal bar that was secured in place with a strong, purpose-made steel padlock. Each one was proudly stamped above the keyhole guard with the letters DR (Deutsche Reichsbahn). It measured nearly five inches high and four inches across, with a half-inch diameter shackle that could only be locked and released by use of its own key.

When the engine crept forward and started to push the bough from the track Dominik, Marcin and Konrad broke cover and sprinted towards the last truck. Marcin used his pick to carefully work away at the tumblers within the padlock's integrated locking mechanism and within thirty seconds, and much to his relief, the hasp was released.

They opened the door a couple of feet and Konrad whispered in Polish to those inside, "We're friends and we've got to join you for a while. Don't worry, we won't put you in any danger and anyway, it's not much further to go."

Someone replied from the shadows in the middle of the wagon, "Get a move on then. We're sick of this bloody war and we're sick of working our bollocks off for the Krauts. We're knackered and we need our rest, you know. So shut that bastard door before somebody spots you and we're all back in the shit again."

No sooner had many willing hands pulled them in through the small gap than Marcin was relocking the padlock back in place. A minute later, as the engine struggled to clear the track, he sprinted back into the woods to join Hannah who was watching from the treeline. Konrad and Dominik picked their way through the thirty or so men sat around on the floor of the railcar and then settled down in the far corner to wait for the train to resume its journey. It was a relatively short trip of 30 miles to the Prison and Labour camp at Karlshagen, some seven miles inside the secure area and just two miles south of the Peenemünde complex.

Aaron and Joanna had taken up their positions about two miles ahead of the train. They lay in wait about 30 yards from the rails on either side of the track, just within the treeline and had covered themselves with bracken and small branches. They had blackened their faces with a mixture of mud and boot polish and were wearing green balaclavas. They blended right into the dark background and were virtually invisible from the trackbed. They knew they were far too close to the German outpost to use firearms and so they had each assembled and loaded two of the team's 'little Joe' crossbows, using the razor-sharp metal bolts. They also loaded a Welrod each and made sure their knives were to hand.

The approaching Germans were given away by a startled pheasant's alarm call as it took flight from the trackside undergrowth when they were still 200 yards away. Joanna wondered if they were just on a routine patrol or whether they had heard the muffled explosion or the bough falling or had simply been sent out to see why the train had been delayed. Anyway, they had to be dealt with and she was there to do just that. There were two of them and Aaron was disappointed that they were not chatting together or strolling side by side along the trackbed with their minds elsewhere. He had been hoping that they would be a couple of bored soldiers patrolling along a familiar route, confident of their own safety because they were still reasonably close to their base. No such luck: these soldiers were all business, fully alert, weapons at the ready and constantly looking around, checking for movement or anything unusual.

They were SS guards and they both carried an MP40 (Maschinenpistole) submachine gun: a superb 9mm weapon with a muzzle velocity of nearly 1,300 feet per second, fitted with a folding metal stock and a thirty-two round stick magazine. The Allies mistakenly referred to this weapon as a Schmeisser, named after the WWI designer of the MP18, the first mass-produced submachine gun, even though he had no connection with the design of the MP40. Also, contrary to the impression given in many war films, computer games and some contemporary accounts, this weapon was only carried by platoon leaders, paratroopers and some police and SS units. In comparison to assault rifles they were very expensive to produce and always being in short supply, they were only issued on a very selective basis. To make matters worse, one of the approaching SS men had a large Alsatian dog on a ten-yard leash and it was quartering back and forth across the track in front of them, searching for scent.

As the Poles watched they both realised that they were now up against a formidable enemy and with every closing step, the presence of the dog threatened to reveal them. If the element of surprise was now seized from them and the soldiers started shooting, then all could be lost. Not only would both of them be quickly cut down by the SS patrol, but the whole operation could be uncovered because the enemy would then thoroughly and ruthlessly investigate the reasons for their presence. Their focus would very quickly shift to the train. In the planning stage Aaron had not been embarrassed or regretful to acknowledge that Joanna was clearly the better shot. The question of guard dogs had also been raised several times during the 'what ifs' and so now, clearly remembering the agreed sequence, he took careful aim.

They both waited until the dog was 40 yards away and just as the animal froze and barked in alarm, indicating that it had caught their distinctive scent, Aaron fired. He had aimed at the guard who had both his hands free and the bolt was slightly off target, hitting him in the right shoulder. As he cried out in pain and shock, he dropped to his knees and Aaron immediately grabbed his second crossbow. The dog handler reacted quickly to the attack, dropped the leash and brought up his weapon, searching unsuccessfully for a target but preparing to fire blindly into the trees. Before he could squeeze the trigger Joanna's first bolt sliced through his throat, severing his carotid artery and spinal cord and leaving the shaft firmly wedged between two vertebrae with the tip protruding three inches on the other side of his neck. Blood sprayed through the air from the entry wound, and already dead, he fell sideways to the ground, turning the grey ballast red. Aaron fired again at his own target who was trying to stand back up and this time the bolt hit him in the chest. He toppled over backwards onto the rails.

At the distinctive sound of the first bolt being released the dog leapt from the tracks and ran full pelt, straight towards Aaron's position. The Pole saw it coming as he fired his second shot and stood up pulling his knife and bracing himself, ready to thrust his left forearm firmly into the animal's jaws, forcing the animal upwards so that he could then stab it in its exposed heart. He knew that he would probably be severely mauled because he was wearing a loose fitting jacket and the thin sleeves would offer no protection against the powerful dog's teeth. It was only a couple of yards short of him when it was poleaxed. He heard the twang of the crossbow and the almost simultaneous hiss of the bolt through the air, accompanied by the thudding, squelchy impact of the missile. The speed of the bolt made the noise irrelevant, because before even the most skittish of animals could react to the sound, it was already too late: it would have been hit.

The dog lay dead at his feet with its eyes half closed into slits, its jaws still open and its lips retracted in a fearsome snarl. It had been an impressive shot. The whole length of the bolt had been driven through its rib cage. Aaron waved an appreciative acknowledgement to Joanna as she emerged from her position in the trees almost opposite, but some ten yards further away from the Germans. He gathered up his gear and she walked on ahead of him, reaching them first. Surprisingly, the one Aaron had shot twice was still alive. Foaming blood was running from his mouth and he was barely conscious, wheezing and gurgling every time he struggled for a breath. The second bolt had missed his heart but punctured his right lung. Joanna calmly looked down at him with neither hatred nor pity, placed her Welrod on the centre of his forehead and pulled the trigger.

They stripped the soldiers of their weapons, uniforms and equipment and buried the three bodies in a badger set about 200 yards inside the forest. Joanna had chosen the site with care. She thought it was far enough outside of the obvious search area alongside the tracks to remain undetected by any initial search and that the profusion of badger scent would be sufficient to mask the smell of decomposition from a searching dog, at least for a few days. With this in mind, they stuffed each corpse into a separate and apparently old, redundant entrance. They rammed the men in head first, pushing hard and twisting their legs together to gain more rigidity, forcing them down inside, as deep as they could. When their shoulders were firmly wedged in place they forced their knees up until they were also stuck fast, jammed right into the roots and stony earth that formed the roof of the tunnel. They did all they could to prevent the bodies being easily dragged free or dug out by the badgers or other predators. Afterwards, while they were plugging up the entrance holes, they heard the train pass by and Aaron said, "Well, so far so good, it looks as if they're in, but we had better get a move on just in case they're missing these two already."

Joanna said, "Yes, but give me a hand to camouflage this exposed earth first. It's a certain giveaway as it is."

So they spent a few more minutes scattering dry twigs, leaf litter and fallen branches across their work, before heading back towards their rendezvous with Hannah and Marcin.

Chapter Sixteen

SLAVERY AT PEENEMÜNDE

Uznam Island – 27th May 1943

The train pulled into the station on the southern edge of the village of Trassenheide, just over a mile south of Karlshagen. Here the track deviated from its northern route and took a long sweeping curve to the southwest. It then traversed the narrow island (on average only three miles wide) to terminate at the ferry port, which gave direct access to the mainland and the route on to Berlin. The Poles were ordered off, one car at a time and then all lined up in the roadway under the guns and scornful gaze of their enemy. There were a total of some 300 prisoners being guarded by a detachment of 30 heavily armed SS guards who were commanded by an Untersturmführer (second lieutenant). He led the column, sat in an armoured car as the prisoners marched through the small built-up area and out onto the road to Karlshagen.

There were German troops everywhere and Dominik thought that he must have arrived during an exercise or security alert. Roving foot and mobile patrols could be seen on the tracks and across the open ground and every half mile or so along the road they encountered static checkpoints manned by military police with field telephones and dogs. Motorcycle and sidecar crews armed with machine guns and speeding despatch riders were also constantly moving back and forth across the island. The column had to move off the road several times to allow military convoys and staff cars to pass by. When they marched through Karlshagen the tops of vast buildings and cooling towers and the barrack and factory chimneys of the military complex that was Peenemünde, gradually came into view through the gaps in the buildings. In less than an hour they arrived at their labour camp, just to the west of Karlshagen and within sight of two large German army bases.

They were housed in long, narrow, wooden huts, set out in rows of five. Each hut contained sixty wooden, double-bunk-bed units, fitted with straw mattresses and lined up in three files of twenty. There was very little room left around these beds but that was deliberate because most of the time the prisoners would be working. Whenever they returned to their quarters, the little time they had would be spent sleeping. A primitive washroom and toilet facility was attached to the back of each hut, but for security reasons the only access was from the outside. From the last parade at night to morning appel they had to use buckets. The camp was surrounded by barbed-wire fences and machine-gun watchtowers and the shifts of armed guards were rotated from the two adjacent military camps. The capacity at this particular facility was 3,000, but there were other similar camps on the island and even a concentration camp for the Jewish skilled workers. In total over 30,000 such slaves toiled there and many were starved, beaten or worked to death.

Upon arrival each new prisoner had a number tattooed on their left forearm and to the Nazi regime they immediately became that number. As far as they were concerned the prisoner had no life before and would have none after. Whether as individuals, shifts, entire camps or even a whole nation they were seen only as a source of labour and nothing else. These people were an expendable and unworthy resource, to be harvested and then consumed so that another arbitrary production target could be met. Once branded, they were allocated to a work detail and Dominik and Konrad lined up separately to ensure that they were given different duties so that they could optimise their chances of obtaining the information they needed. Konrad was sent to the oxygen plant and Dominik to the pre-production works.

Over the next three weeks they were worked from dawn to dusk in their respective labour gangs and they discovered that the island's terrain was mostly flat with a mixture of heath, moorland and forest. Dominik strained, sweated and pushed himself to the point of exhaustion every day to lift and transport huge loads of metal and industrial materials from the massive outdoor stockpiles into the works. Konrad was employed digging trenches from the coal-fired power station to the oxygen plant so that dozens of high-voltage electric cables could be hidden from view. As they worked in the hot summer sun they investigated, listened, watched and learnt.

They made mental lists of the quantities and nature of all the raw materials and equipment they saw and handled. They tested all the site rumours, soaked up the camp gossip and eavesdropped on the guards' conversations whenever they could. But they only ever asked questions of the other prisoners when it was safe do so and always in a roundabout and conversational manner. They never made too many enquiries of any one individual and deliberately avoided making any friendships, but gradually and incrementally they built up a comprehensive intelligence picture. All that mattered to them was the mission and so they kept as low a profile as they could. They strove to be invisible and unmemorable: lost in a dirty tide of nondescript, sub-human slaves, always keeping their eyes averted from their guards – working vigorously whenever one was present and immediately and blindly reacting to any order or direction. Not to be noticed was to survive and succeed.

Each night they shared what they had learnt that day and planned how they could then take matters further, seek corroboration and reduce the risk of arousing suspicion by switching the outstanding tasks between themselves. Sharing their knowledge, they also built up a mind map of the facility. This included the position of the labour camps, the location of the various army barracks, the scientists' and staff quarters, the layout of the various production, factory and experimental buildings (including a supersonic wind tunnel) and, as far as they could, the suspected purpose of each one. They confirmed that several hundred Jews continued to be housed in the basement of building/workshop F1 and that a satellite concentration camp was also under construction, to cater for the large numbers still arriving every week. In whispered discussions they considered which buildings and facilities should be considered as high-priority targets and which were the most vulnerable to high-explosive or incendiary bombing.

They were convinced that sabotage on any major scale was impossible. The place was just too big, too well dispersed over three separate facilities and all aggressively patrolled and secured with mines and electric fences. A major commando raid was out of the question, the distances involved were prohibitive and the sea and air defences formidable. The AK did not have the technical or military capability either and so aerial bombing was the only solution. Konrad had also seen several completed VIs and V2s being transported across the site to the north-west of the power station, in the area they had identified as the development section. Between them they had also heard or seen at least ten V1 launches and a similar number of trials of the V2, one of which had spectacularly exploded shortly after take-off. They had also seen the high-altitude contrails of the successful rockets, which were referred to amongst the labourers as 'frozen lightning'. As a result, they had a pretty good idea of where the V1 catapults and the V2 testing and launch pads were situated. Between them they had managed to draw up a rough assessment of the V2's capabilities. It was nearly 50 feet long and about five feet in diameter. It was controlled either by a simple analogue computer or radio signals (both systems were being tested), guided by gyroscopes and propelled by a mixture of ethanol, water and liquid oxygen. It had a range of 200 miles and could travel up to 900 miles per hour. Such was its speed that it exploded on the ground even before it could be heard. The warhead contained over 2,000lbs of amatol explosive which would leave a crater 30 feet deep. Each weapon was capable of destroying a whole street and scores of people. It would attain a maximum trajectory height of 55 miles when fired at a target but could reach over 100 miles if fired vertically. They also discovered that a fully operational production line for the V2 was only weeks away.

They had uncovered a third, equally worrying area of research and production. Jet propulsion engines were also being manufactured, tested and fitted to a futuristic-looking design of fighter aircraft. Konrad had seen one such aircraft take off from the Luftwaffe airfield just a few hundred yards to the north of the power plant. He told Dominik what he had seen.

"It was shaped like a bullet, slightly smaller than a normal fighter but very sleek and menacing, with a sharply pointed nose, tapering forward from a single, streamlined and centrally positioned cockpit."

Dominik had heard many rumours about a jet fighter since they had arrived but he had never seen it, although jet engines were constantly being fired up and tested so he had become accustomed to the distinctive noises. His thoughts immediately flashed to someone who had not been too far from his mind in recent days: Danuta and what she had said about the best Luftwaffe fighter pilots being retrained. Now it made sense. They were going to be the ones to fly the new jets. Perhaps things were more advanced than he thought and so he asked, with rather more urgency, "How many engines has it got? Are they the same as they use on the rockets?"

"There's one engine mounted centrally under each wing and they're longer than a prop engine, shaped just like a torpedo and the wings are different too. They're raked back and turn up slightly at the ends, giving the whole thing a sense of speed, power and strength."

"What about weapons?"

"I couldn't see any weapons, so it was probably just a prototype being tested. But the really amazing thing was its speed. Once it had left the ground it virtually shot straight up, almost vertical. I've never seen anything like it. It must have been doing at least 500 miles an hour. It was amazing to see, even exhilarating and mighty impressive. But I'd hate to think of what effect it would have on our aircraft if it was heavily armed with cannon and rockets."

Dominik was also worried. "Just think about it, if they manage to bring the V1, the V2, and a jet fighter into full production, then we would lose this war." He needed to know more and quickly, "Did you see it land?"

"No, I had to get on with my work or somebody would have noticed me staring. I didn't hear it land either. Anyway from what I did see, I shouldn't think there was any chance at all that it could slow down enough to land safely while still under power. I suppose that once its fuel ran out, it would have just quietly glided back in. But I know one thing for sure: you wouldn't get me up in one of those things, not at any price."

For the next week they both concentrated all their intelligence-gathering efforts on the jet plane project, until they finally knew enough to satisfy their three mission objectives. The following day was Sunday, the day they had to make their escape. They knew the odds were against them but drew strength from their specialist training and confidence from their considerable combat experience. They talked through their final plans and tested their joint recollections of the escape route they had chosen exactly four weeks before. They each pictured the detailed map they had studied for hours when they were in the forest and alternately checked off the towns, villages, hamlets, crucial landmarks and road junctions along the whole route. Konrad had to be solely responsible for the first part of the escape plan because he was the only one with access to the critical laying-up position. Taking on this extra but unavoidable responsibility right at the beginning weighed heavily on him and so he was really anxious to be under way. So uncharacteristically nervous was he that he couldn't sleep. As he fidgeted he thought about the many problems they would face come morning.

Their options were limited by the tight time frame. They had to wait until after the morning appel and had to be clear of the prohibited area by the evening roll call, otherwise their absence would be discovered and the alarm raised. Once that happened, whether day or night, the whole north of the island would be sealed off and all normal activity would cease. All the prisoners would be locked up. Specialist elements of the garrison would be mustered and dispatched to predetermined locations or allocated specific search roles and communication functions. Any other person of whatever rank or position moving across the complex would be challenged and their documents and movements scrutinised. Every vehicle, military or civilian would be stopped and searched. There would be no exceptions. Dogs and SS guards would sweep across the open ground and extra roadblocks set up. A spotter aircraft would take to the air and two R boats (Räumboot – small minesweeper used for coastal patrol and in-shore defence, with a speed of twenty knots) and a much faster E boat (an allied term for the Schnellboot or S-boot with a speed of over forty knots), would take to the water. The local Nazi hierarchy had a detailed and comprehensive response plan to thwart any breach of security and it was practised and updated regularly. Both the Poles knew that if the general alarm was raised too early then their plan would certainly fail and they would either be captured or killed.

Konrad had planned to be at his start position at about midday. Along with twenty-six of his colleagues, he had been marched from the trenches outside of the oxygen plant along the track running round the southern end of a large lake known to the Germans as Kölpiensee, towards the power plant. This monumental facility with three massive chimneys had been built of red brick by a mixture of German tradesmen and foreign slave labourers between 1939 and 1942, but it was rather isolated in comparison to the rest of the complex, being situated on the north-western corner of the island. For easy access to vast quantities of water for the boiler and cooling process, and to facilitate an uninterrupted supply of coal (delivered by barge from the mainland), it had been positioned right alongside the shore. It also had its own small harbour about half a mile north of the village of Peenemünde.

With the numbers of slave labourers, both Jews and gentiles, growing by the day the scientists and administrators were becoming increasingly concerned about the foreigners' lack of hygiene and their close proximity. The food ration for a German was 2,500 calories a day but for the forced labourers it was less than 1,000. Their meals were not just insufficient but often putrid or rancid, with little or no nutritional value. It certainly couldn't sustain their high levels of labour. As a result of this, and the insanitary conditions of confinement, endemic disease and infection was already spreading and the German personnel were concerned for their own health and safety.

In an effort to limit the risk a dozen new 'prisoner-only' latrine blocks had been erected over the last six months, sited in the more remote areas. One was tucked away near the power station. It was hidden from general view by four black tors of stockpiled coal, a giant metal coal crane, a crusher and the roofed-in 100 yard conveyer drive that lifted tons of pulverised coal from ground level right to the top of the power station building. The various research and development systems on site soaked up vast amounts of energy and from 1942 onwards the power station was producing thirty megawatts of electricity. As a result the steam turbines had an insatiable appetite for coal.

Konrad was five minutes late when they arrived at the toilet block but was still well within his time frame. Diarrhoea and stomach cramps often caused a sudden sprint for the latrines once they came into sight, because they could only cater for eight at a time. These two German guards, like many of their colleagues, had soon become used to this mad, last fifty-yard dash. And so they regulated and controlled it, turning it into a form of entertainment, using the fear of punishment to hold them back until they signalled the 'off' with a cry of 'Scheiße!' Then they would stand there jeering and laughing at the desperate scramble, trying to guess which unfortunates would be too late and would end up soiled and stinking, and be ridiculed for the rest of the day.

At the shout Konrad was ready, critically sixth in line. He got a flying start and managed to hold his position. When he reached the portable wooden structure he carried on, straight past the now occupied sections. Instead of rushing in to take his place, precariously perching on the faeces-encrusted rail above the steaming trench, he ran on. Shielded by those still scampering and jostling for advantage behind, he dived to his right. He disappeared around the far corner of the traps and then crawled through the foot-high grass into the bushes beyond. He was taking a chance, but it was a calculated risk. Other than the SS, who concentrated their efforts on the Jewish labour outside and also enforced rigid security inside the production and research areas, many of the guards from the barracks were normal conscripts. Over time, quite a few had become bored by the monotonous routine and progressively more slipshod and dilatory, and although they always checked that the latrines were empty before they moved on, they often failed to count the prisoners out.

It was no real surprise, therefore, that on this particular day they were still too busy laughing and joking at the prisoners' antics to bother with such a mundane detail. No one ever tried to escape. It was certain death. These particular guards, like many of their colleagues, had come to accept that if things looked correct and relatively orderly, then that was good enough for them. After all, up to then it always had been! Their own military training and contemporary fascist practice had inculcated in them that these foreigners were inferior, sub-humans who passively accepted being herded around like cattle and humiliated. Five minutes later they moved off, escorting twenty-six prisoners, while Konrad crawled on through the trees towards his next position. When he arrived a few minutes later he watched and waited.

He was hidden from sight in a secluded corner within the trees, just to the north of the power station and over an hour passed by before he saw his opportunity. A military police officer (Feldgendarmerie) on a BMW R-71 motorcycle pulled up outside the back of an end-of-terrace house and disappeared inside. This row of cottages was used by the German technicians and managers responsible for the power plant and their friends and relatives. He took Dominik's dagger from his pocket and flexed his limbs to ease the stiffness caused by crouching in the same position. After ten minutes the rider returned to his machine and as he turned his back on Konrad's position to mount the saddle and kick start the engine, the Pole made his move.

There was no time to creep up and having already checked that all was clear, he ran flat out straight at the German, covering the 15 yards in a few seconds. The rider heard his footfalls and started to turn his head over his left shoulder, but he was too late. Konrad didn't slow down but ran on, heading to pass the machine on its nearside. As he closed he swung his right arm out and up, extending it as far as possible and tightly gripping the dagger. He then drove his fist downwards in a whip-like motion, using his full momentum and every ounce of his upper-body strength. He timed it to perfection, viciously stabbing the rider in the back of the neck as he came alongside. He kept a tight grip on the weapon and the force of the shuddering impact jerked his arm back painfully as he moved on by. Even so, he held on tight and his impetus pulled the rider forwards, dragging him off his machine. The blade sliced right through the left half of his neck and then on further, finally bursting out through his throat. Only then, accompanied by a sickening squelch and a hiss of escaping air, did Konrad's arm break free.

He took his jacket off and stuffed it into the massive wound to absorb as much blood as possible and then he stood the motor cycle back on its stand. He dragged the lifeless body into the woods and then ran back and wiped the blood off the bike with his shirt and cleaned up the bloodstain on the ground. Deep in the wood he stripped the German and covered the corpse with bracken and leaves. As best he could, he then cleaned the stains from the uniform with water from the lake, buried his own clothes and donned the uniform and the dead man's 'dog tags' (Erkennungsmarke). The jacket was rather tight across the chest and under the arms and the boots pinched his toes but all in all, it was just about passable. He examined the contents of his leather wallet. Along with the usual cash and a few photographs it contained a letter from his wife in Berlin and several photographs of Parisian landmarks. He kept it, along with his fourteen-page pay book (Soldbuch) which contained his brief military history, his photograph (taken in full uniform) and personal identification and medical history. Also tucked just inside the tan leather cover was his personal Peenemünde Prohibited Zone Entry Pass.

Konrad strode out of the woods towards the motorcycle and was suddenly struck by an idea that might improve their chances of success and made a quick diversion. He took the dead man's keys from his pocket and just as the rider had done so innocently a short while ago, entered the house through the back door. It was empty, but he saw from the photographs downstairs that he had killed the son of the house. His father was a Nazi administrator. Konrad quickly went upstairs and found his room. He collected his spare uniform and boots from a wardrobe and a Luger pistol, two stick grenades and ammunition from a chest of drawers and finally, a fistful of paper money from his bedside table. He loaded his finds into the leather panniers and kicked started his transport. When he rode away wearing the policeman's distinctive chain and crescent-shaped gorget, carrying his sidearm and with a breeze suggestive of speed and freedom on his face, his confidence and belief flooded back.

The island was two miles wide at this point and his rendezvous with Dominik was just over a mile away on the eastern side of the island, alongside the main north to south road. He reached the T-junction and turned north. After 200 yards, as the dusty road swept through 90 degrees to the west he turned left off the road into the entrance to the camp stores department (Arbeitslager Karlshagen Vorratslager). He parked the motorcycle behind a small outbuilding, pulled out his sidearm and then marched into the site where he knew Dominik had been working. He found him with a gang of labourers taking empty 100-litre containers from the store back to the water purification plant, some 200 metres away on the opposite side of the road. He called out for the supervisor and then approached the German guard, pointing his pistol directly at Dominik.

"This thieving bastard is under arrest. He's been stealing food from the other workers. We're going to find out who else is involved and then we'll probably shoot the lot. We've got to make an example of them otherwise they'll all be at it." He grabbed hold of Dominik's left arm, looked at a piece of paper in his hand and then at Dominik's tattoo. "It's him alright. There's no mistake." He pushed him roughly in the back, forcing him towards the road. "Come on, Polack and get a move on. You're going to be asked a lot of questions and you'd better give us the right answers."

The rest of the prisoners literally kept their heads down. They were desperate not to be noticed or associated in any way with the unfortunate accused man. The military police uniform itself had been enough to make them cower and then the arrogant threats drove home the German's absolute authority and ensured their continued submission. As Konrad had calculated, he was neither recognised nor challenged. The guard even shouted after them, "I bet you'll be back here for some more of this useless bunch before the day is out. They're all bone idle, you know and I reckon most of them are at it."

Konrad replied, "I might well see you later on then."

The guard set his prisoners back to work and reminded them of their value, "Come on, the show's over and now you're one light, so get on with it. Hurry up! You're all born as thieves, and then grow up to be next to bloody useless. You're not really worth looking after, seeing the small amount of effort you put into everything. Come to think of it you're nothing but a drain on the bloody rations."

Konrad smiled to himself; he had heard it all before. The same old refrain of contempt, across half a dozen countries and in as many languages. Without looking back, he raised his arm in acknowledgement and walked on with his prisoner.

When they reached the motorcycle Konrad gave Dominik the spare uniform and returned the dagger.

"Thanks for that. It's a beautiful weapon, so strong and sharp and it did its job. They certainly knew how to make them in those days and it hasn't lost any of its magic either." While Dominik dressed he quickly explained how he had taken the bike.

Dominik asked, "When do you think they're likely to miss him?"

"I'm pretty sure no one will stumble on the body, well not until they do a proper search or it starts to stink. As I said, he had just called in at his house so he might have already been off duty. If not, then it's anybody's guess, but I don't think they're likely to react straight away. They'll ask around first and his mates might even cover for him."

Dominik agreed, "That makes sense, so I should think we'll be alright for the rest of the day, well at least on that score." He checked the Luger and magazine and then put one grenade in each saddle bag, within easy reach of the pillion seat and said, "So far so good. We'll stick to the plan and make straight for the rendezvous. Let's hope they've managed to get everything set up at their end."

Konrad opened the filler cap on the petrol tank and said, "We'll soon find out," He shook the bike and listened to the sloshing petrol, "It sounds about half-full so it should easily be enough. It's nine miles to the end of the prohibited zone and then another twelve to the beach, but if they're not there, then we might not have enough for the fall-back plan."

"We can always steal some more. Anyway, don't let's worry about that now. Let's go!"

They mounted up, then turned left past an unmanned pillbox, rounded the right-hand bend and headed south. They ran into the first checkpoint two miles down the road at the entrance to Karlshagen. The post was manned by four soldiers from the local barracks, overseen by an SS Rottenführer, but it was obvious that their priority was incoming vehicles and personnel. The Poles and other southbound traffic were quickly waved on through, without any meaningful identity or security checks whereas all vehicles travelling north were stopped and searched and all papers examined. They passed through similar checks at Trassenheide, and Zinnowitz, but as they followed the road on out through the forest towards Zempin, they saw a line of roadside signs prohibiting vehicles from stopping on the highway and a column of guards at the side of the road. They were continually waving traffic on through and others were manning the entrances to three lumber tracks. Several dozen construction workers, accompanied by an assortment of military vehicles were being marched along one such track, deep into the woods. They both realised the significance of this activity.

They were stopped again at Zempin and this time the guard asked for Konrad's papers and said, "Where are you going?" Konrad gave his scripted reply.

"We've been allocated escort duty again today. We're picking up a delivery of new trucks at the ferry at Swinemünde. We've got to check out the drivers and the vehicles before we bring them on through. You can't be too careful when it comes to security."

The guard merely nodded and returned the papers after only a brief glance. Even so they could not relax because less than a mile ahead, at the narrowest point on the island, they would attempt to leave the prohibited area. The most rigorous of all the security checks took place at this choke point, where the road and the railway crossed over a spit of land only 300 yards wide. Here, they would be confined and at their most vulnerable, being trapped between the Achterwasser (an inland coastal lagoon formed by the Peenestrom River) on their right and by the 50 yards of silvery-white sand and the breaking Baltic Sea on their left.

A force of twenty, made up of a mixture of military police, Gestapo and crack SS troops was stationed around the clock at the two brick and concrete guardhouses that straddled the road. In addition, an armoured car and two machine-gun-equipped motorcycle combinations were permanently deployed on site. Metal posts, concrete beams and two earth bunds formed a security chicane on the south-eastern approach, designed to slow down approaching traffic and forcing it to comply with the 5 mph speed restriction. To complete the total military control and dominance of the site, a sandbagged and fortified heavy-machine-gun dugout was positioned on each knoll and the beach and surrounding heathland was heavily mined. The Poles had been carefully briefed on all these matters at Audley End House by Captain Wolak. So they knew only too well, that if they aroused the slightest suspicion at the checkpoint, there would be no chance for evasive action or a successful breakout. They had also agreed pre-mission, that they would not allow themselves to be captured and so in a matter of minutes they would either escape from the prohibited area or they would be dead.

Konrad slowed right down as they approached the barrier and stopped at the 'Warteschlange!' marker, cut the engine and waited. After a few seconds an SS officer emerged from the guardhouse and slowly walked towards them. When he had covered half the 15-yards distance, Konrad briefly held up his papers. Then, just as a staff car pulled up behind them, he looked over his shoulder, nodded his head twice and raised his hand as if in acknowledgement to the driver. He immediately kicked started the bike and slowly moved forward towards the SS man, acting as if the driver had signalled him to hurry up. The guard drew the same conclusion and not wanting to delay a senior officer more than absolutely necessary, he immediately switched his attention to the staff car and its occupants. He stepped back to the side and beckoned Konrad on through, hardly sparing him a glance. Once clear of the chicane he opened up the throttle and they sped along the mile-long, arrow-straight section of the Lüttenort towards the south-west corner of Koserow and the Streckelsberg beyond. This glacial moraine, just to the south-east of the village, formed the highest hill on the island, incorporating a 180-foot-high cliff. It had been afforested early in the nineteenth century to prevent erosion and to protect the village from the harsh sea winds and drifting sand.

The Poles passed through the Koserow checkpoint without being stopped and headed on towards Kölpinsee with the forest of the Streckelsberg on their left and encroaching right up to the roadside. At Peenemünde they had seen that the Bay of Pomerania had been used as a test range for the V2s, with the rockets being fired eastwards, parallel to the coast towards Gdansk Bay. The Germans had sited a string of observation posts along the whole flight path, designed to monitor, measure and record the tests. Because the Streckelsberg provided such an elevated location in an otherwise almost flat landscape, they had built a particularly large and robust observation platform within the forest. As they passed by Dominik saw it perched above the treetops like a giant fire lookout tower. He would later learn that at that very site they had also installed a prototype cinetheodolite for the optical tracking of the rockets. In the development of rocketry and associated technology the Nazis were years ahead of all their enemies and were using it to good effect.

Shortly after Kölpinsee they passed over the canal that dissected the island from north-east to south-west. As the throaty roar of the bike echoed off the restricting brick walls of the bridge Dominik wondered if his friends had already planted the explosives underneath. They had planned to destroy all three of the road bridges that spanned the mile-long waterway at 0200 hours, exactly one hour after the main diversionary action.

The motorcycle sped on, through the hamlet of Stubbenfelde with more woods off to their left and the smaller hill known as the Devil's Mountain, giving panoramic views across the island and out to sea. Years earlier, well before the Great War, steps had been carved into the cliff-face, giving access onto the beach, but the intelligence officer had told them that it had since been blocked off and the beach had been mined by the Germans. So the rendezvous had been fixed further along the coast where the cliffs petered out and were replaced by sand dunes. Just over a mile down the road they came to the village of Ückeritz and at the crossroads they turned left onto the Strandstraße and through a dappled tunnel of overarching trees towards the beach. When they reached the last Y junction, only 100 yards or so from the sea, they turned right, staying in the woods and running parallel to the shore. About half a mile later they came to a clearing on their right and Dominik drove off the road to their left into the trees, slowly manoeuvring the bike deeper into the woods. After about 70 yards, when they were satisfied that they were securely hidden from the road they stopped. Standing perfectly still, all they could hear was the singing of birds and the crashing of waves on the beach, 40 yards ahead.

They searched around for five minutes before Konrad found their five bags of supplies and arms wedged into the roots of a particularly large beech tree, where they had been left by their back-up team the previous night. They checked the weapons and then divided up the grenades, detonators and various explosives between them before repacking one bag each and adding the spare ammunition. Next, they changed out of their uniforms and dressed in the black fisherman's clothes that had been provided before cramming the German clothing and equipment back inside the remaining bags. They spent the next hour quietly reconnoitring their surroundings, concentrating on the area between the beech and the road. They finished their final preparations just before nightfall.

Twenty minutes later they heard the strident wailing of a dozen or more sirens from within the prohibited zone and they were both startled by the sudden noise despite the fact that they were half-expecting it.

Konrad said, "They must have just finished appel and now they know we're out. We had better get ready."

Dominik replied, "They probably haven't found the motorcyclist yet so hopefully they'll concentrate on sealing up the prohibited area and confine their searches within the base. They have no idea where we are."

"I doubt we'll be that lucky. Now they've started looking I don't think it will take them long to find him. Then they'll know exactly how we got out and they'll throw the net out very wide indeed. They won't wait until daylight either, because as of now we're right at the top of their most-wanted list."

Dominik started gathering up his equipment, "Then let's make it as hard as we can for them. You watch the beach and I'll cover the road." Before they split up, Konrad piled the discarded bags up against a tree and set a booby trap. Dominik couldn't resist a wry smile as he watched and imagined the gasp of utter surprise and fear that would be uttered by the first German unfortunate enough to find the stash and lift the top bag away. The last thing he would hear would be the unmistakable, predictive and fatal 'ping' of the spring, as the hidden wire pulled the pin on the instantaneously fused grenade, now securely attached to the bottom bag.

As they left, moving as quietly as possible in the pale moonlight, Dominik reminded his friend, "Don't call me until you see the signal from the boat. I'll watch the road at the junction right up to the last minute just in case we should have those visitors you're so worried about. In the meantime, I'll see if I can arrange a surprise or two for them and buy us a few extra minutes."

When Dominik reached the road he ran back to the junction and set about preparing his defences. He placed two rows of five mines (disguised by the SOE boffins as cowpats) diagonally but irregularly across the narrow road, starting about 100 yards on the village side of the junction. Each line covered a distance of some 40 yards across the concrete surface. He then placed another six at irregular intervals along each verge. Next he set shaped charges on the trunks of two trees, one on either side of the road about 50 yards closer to his intended position. He linked each detonator to a mechanical pull switch with a cocked striker and then he connected the two striker spigot rings to a length of thin wire which he suspended across the road about three feet six inches off the ground. Finally, he laid six trip wires, randomly spaced between trees on either side of the road, some attached to grenades and others to small anti-personnel mines.

He then withdrew back to the junction, prepared his own ambush point and waited. At 1am he heard the muted but unmistakable crump of explosions to the north and he knew that the back-up teams' diversions had started. He hoped that they had managed to blow up and destroy the first target, the railway line just south of Koserow, exactly as they had planned at Audley End House. His mind leapt back to those meetings: a time of comfort and safety which now seemed a lifetime ago. So much had happened since then, so much so that now the pressures of time, the stress of responsibility and the constant danger of being behind enemy lines all played tricks with his memory. However, as soon as he stopped reflecting and concentrated once again on his immediate surroundings, he realised that it was, in fact, only a few weeks ago that he had slept so soundly in his bed in England. Then he had rightly reckoned that, following any discovery of the escape, the Germans would immediately seal off of the prohibited area. He hoped that he was also right about the action at Koserow and it would achieve the objective of drawing off any enemy forces that still remained near to the rendezvous point. It was their only hope of securing an unobserved and unchallenged abstraction from the island. If it failed they could very quickly find themselves up against the deadly, fast patrol boats.

Aaron and Joanna had left the fishing boat just after midnight and rowed the lightweight canoe ashore. They made their way up the beach and over the sand dunes into the comparative safety of the woods. Somewhat surprisingly perhaps, they had chosen the most exposed and windswept course across the beach. But it was really the most logical route, because they knew that in such a remote area they were more at risk from stumbling into a minefield than being spotted by a patrolling sentry or even being discovered later, when they were further inland. They reasoned that the enemy were unlikely to place mines right out in the open, where they would be regularly exposed to sight by constant sand erosion, caused by the strong on-shore winds and frequent squalls that blew in off the Baltic. On the contrary, they expected that they would be concentrated along the gullies and buried in the sheltered paths and between the dunes.

En route they also discovered exactly why the locals sometimes referred to their home as 'the singing island'. The very fine, almost powdery, white sand squeaked and murmured underfoot as they traversed the beach and so they were forced to slow down and tread more carefully until they reached the grass-covered dunes. In the event, they made it safely into the woods, hid the canoe and then covered the 1,000 yards or so through the forest to the railway track in less than 20 minutes. Their chosen attack point was just inside the treeline on the apex of a long sweeping left-hand section of track where the line curved inland to cross under the main road. It then ran parallel with it, skirting around the south-western edge of Koserow before once more straightening up to resume its arrow-like path northwards. They had practised blowing up railway tracks many times during their training and so even in the darkness, they worked with a confident efficiency and the four separate charges, primed with their simultaneous timers, were quickly in place. Within the hour they were rowing back out to sea.

Marcin and Hannah had come ashore just over half a mile south of the other diversion team and their targets were the road bridges across the canal. They intended that all three structures should be demolished simultaneously, exactly one hour after the railway line was destroyed thereby confusing the enemy and temporarily at least, preventing any major movement south from the garrison towns close to the military complex. They had to climb the hill above the beach and then follow the eastern edge of Kölpinsee lake down to the south before they could cut inland towards target one, and this meant that they had twice as far to travel as the first team.

Once they cleared the reeds and marshland to the south of the lake they became far more exposed on the open pasture land. They deliberately passed well to the south of targets two and three as they suspected they would be guarded. They moved back into the trees to cross the country lane and the nearby main road before returning to the fields and heading back towards the canal. They were mightily relieved to find that the ample vegetation along its banks offered temporary concealment. In places the waterway was only about ten feet across but it was some five feet deep. It often opened out into small ponds and much wider sections, where the surrounding land was partially flooded or extremely boggy and very difficult to cross, sucking at their feet and slowing them down considerably. They ploughed on regardless, trudging towards their furthest target. It was situated just outside the fishing village of Loddin and only 100 yards from the western shore of the island where it meets the Achterwasser. Fortunately, there was no sentry on the tiny bridge which supported the single, unmetalled farm trackway and so they quickly but carefully set their charges. After one final check, they retraced their steps back along the canal, but this time they ignored the dog-leg and headed straight towards the main road.

Hannah spotted the sentry first. He was obviously bored, sloppy and lacking self-discipline. He was sat on the low wall on the top of the bridge with his helmet on the parapet alongside and he was facing away from them, smoking a cigarette. The red tip had immediately caught her eye when he carelessly brought it out to the side of his body to flick the ash off.

The third bridge that carried the nearby lane across the canal was only a further 30 yards beyond the sentry and so Marcin whispered in her ear, "Crawl closer until you can take care of him. I'll circle around and see if he's got company on the other bridge. Give me exactly five minutes and then kill him." They synchronised their watches before he moved off.

It only took Hannah a couple of minutes to move into position and a few more seconds to make ready. As she waited, the guard stood up and silhouetted against the ambient light of the night sky he turned to face in her direction, oblivious of any threat. She watched passively but fully alert as his discarded cigarette butt arched out from the top of the bridge and disappeared into the darkness of the canal bank. Then, feeling totally secure and unconcerned in the anodyne isolation of his familiar and uneventful comfort zone, the teenage conscript undid his fly buttons and started to urinate over the wall into the canal. She relaxed and smiled to herself in amusement at his naive stupidity when she heard the immediately recognisable splashing sound of him emptying an extremely full bladder into the still water, some ten feet below. She even stifled a chuckle at the loud, long and deep sigh of contented relief that accompanied his discharge. She checked her watch once again and then, right on time, she fired the crossbow. He was still in mid flow and boyishly swaying his hips from side to side, aiming his penis ever upwards, immaturely concentrating on gradually increasing the height and arc of spray when the bolt thudded deep into his chest. The force and sudden pain of the strike drove him down onto his knees. He opened his mouth in surprise and agony, but his cry was strangled in his throat as the second missile hit him square in the forehead, shattering his skull and ripping through his brain.

Marcin found no more patrolling sentries, indolent or otherwise. But he did discover a small vedette post alongside a well-trodden footpath between the two bridges. Slowly, on his hands and knees, he crept up to the door of the portable wooden building, which was more like a shepherd's hut on metal wheels than a proper military structure. He heard the sound of snoring inside and so he checked the position of the upright doorstops with his fingers to see which way the door was hinged. Satisfied, he then took his knife in his left hand so that it was ready and his Welrod in his right, before slowly lifting the latch and quietly pushing the door open inwards. His night vision was well accustomed to the low light level outside but even so, he struggled to see more than shadow in the almost pitch black interior. The air inside was fetid: an overpowering mixture of stale sweat, unwashed socks, rancid food, bad breath and flatulence. He recognised it as unique to the cramped sleeping quarters of slovenly soldiers in the field. He carefully shut the door behind him to avoid being highlighted in the doorway. Then for a moment or two he stood perfectly still just inside, holding his breath and allowing his eyes to readjust.

One soldier, asleep on a mattress on the wooden floor carried on snoring. But the other one was even more dilatory and unsoldierly and the Pole wondered just how on earth they could call themselves superior, when clowns like these were left on guard. Incredibly, he was seated on a wooden bench in the opposite corner to the snorer with his back towards the door. He was also asleep and slumped across a table which was butted up to the far wall and covered with half a dozen empty wine bottles. His head was cradled in his arms and Marcin noticed that both their rifles were propped up in the far corner in a small gap between the table and the left-hand wall. Then some innate instinct, or perhaps the movement of the air when the door had been opened and then closed, or maybe even the very close proximity of the Pole eventually broke through his alcoholic slumber and he started to raise his head.

Marcin reacted to the immediate threat and when the soldier's head started to turn towards him he placed the barrel of the Welrod to the nape of his neck and fired. He then half-turned to his right just as the snorer started to splutter awake – automatically responding to the audible phut of the gun's discharge and the squelch of the first bullet as it flattened out on impact. It had ploughed its way on, deep into flesh, muscle and bone before exploding out the other side and splintering through the table top where it became firmly wedged, its kinetic energy finally spent. The Pole then shot the second guard through the heart just as he came to his senses, realised the danger and leapt to his feet. Thirty minutes later the pre-prepared plastic explosive packs had been set and primed on both bridges.

Danuta was relieved when all four of the agents were back on the fishing boat and the canoes safely packed away. She had kept her weapon trained on the local, 63-year-old, German fishing boat owner throughout their three-hour absence. Although he had assured her that he was no Nazi or Hitler lover and just wanted to get on with his life, he simply could not be trusted. She should know, after all she was well aware of the Nazis' relentless iron grip that bent the will of the population and kept the vast majority fearfully loyal to the National Socialist Party. They controlled everything: the press and radio, the police, the judiciary, all communications, all cultural and religious institutions, travel, education (right from kindergarten through to university) and of course, all the usual organs and apparatus of the state.

Working in Germany, she had been bombarded daily by the political indoctrination that affected all aspects of everyday life, where even children at school were exhorted to denounce their friends, relations and their own parents too, for the slightest derogatory remark about their Führer, the Nazi party or its ideology. It was impossible for people to speak openly for fear of informants (doctrinal, paid or coerced), Gestapo agents, collaborators or even individuals or groups with a real or perceived grudge, or simple mischief-makers. Arrest and retribution were swift. Offenders were sent to prison or concentration camps or just disappeared. Enemies of the state were accused of political offences and brought before the Volksgerichtshof (people's court) where the death sentence was common for any 'crime' that was considered to undermine military morale or had that intention (Wehrkraftzersetzung). They were often little more than show trials held in kangaroo courts, presided over by Nazi-appointed judges. Some were over in just an hour or two, with no witnesses being called, little or no evidence being presented nor any arguments put forward by either side.

She hated every aspect of Hitler's regime and had dedicated the last few years of her life to the fight against it. But for now, she was just glad to be rid of her responsibility as a guard and was eager to return home. She had been ordered to take part in the seizure of the boat when the original operative broke his leg in an accident on the docks. The SOE was very anxious to limit the number of Home Army personnel involved, in order to maintain operational security. Because she had already met the team and was fully trained, she seemed the logical and best choice.

Dominik and Konrad heard the second round of explosions at 0200hours and knew that if all had gone according to plan then the boat would be offshore to pick them up within the hour. What they did not know, however, was that as a part of Peenemünde's defence plan, a rapid-response mobile patrol had just been turned out from their barracks at Stolpe Castle, some ten miles to the south and ordered to sweep the Baltic beach and the approach roads in their allocated five-mile sector from Bansin to Koserow. Their commander, Leutnant Schröder, and his 20 men had practised this as a drill many times and they were very familiar with the terrain. By experience and practice he had discovered the quickest and most efficient way to cover all the lanes, tracks and accessible sections of beach. With his men divided up into their transport of five Kübelwagens and two motorcycle combinations, they headed off in convoy for their familiar start point midway between the two towns. There they would split into two units, one clearing the designated area going north towards Koserow and the other travelling south towards Bansin. This starting point, right at the geographical centre of their designated search area, brought them down to the beach on the very road used by Dominik and Konrad.

The team's run of good fortune had come to a sudden and abrupt end.

Dominik heard the convoy approaching through Ückeritz, pulled his balaclava down over his face and checked his weapons and ammunition for the last time. He could tell from the approaching engine noises that the vehicles were motorcycles and Kübelwagens and although that was bad enough, he was relieved that there were no larger troop-carrying trucks or armoured cars. He was even more pleased when he realised that they had no idea that the Poles were there. The two leading motorcycle combination riders had their headlights switched on and unlike the rest of the vehicles, their slit mask, blackout covers had been removed so that they could light the way for the 'speeding', 25 miles per hour convoy.

The leading motorcycle hit the line of mines first and was blown ten feet into the air. The machine gunner in the combination was almost cut in two by the force of the detonation directly underneath his seat, only inches away from his feet. Dozens of pieces of ragged shrapnel punched through the metal of the sidecar, creating even more fatal shards with their passage. His clothes, equipment and boots were shredded by the force and heat of the blast and were stripped from his pulverised and smouldering body. The rider flew forwards through the air for another 15 yards, his initial speed considerably accelerated by the blast. His internal organs were ruptured, his skeleton dislocated and he was already dead when, some two yards off the ground, he hit a tree trunk head on. The force of the impact was sickeningly audible, even above the sound of revving engines and vehicles breaking heavily, as the drivers behind started to react in surprise and panic.

The second motorcyclist lost control as his machine was blown sideways by the force of the explosion. It careered off the road onto the right-hand verge and he desperately fought to keep it upright, whilst also trying to aim for a gap in the trees. He was partially successful and the front wheel and handlebars shot through a narrow opening between two huge beeches. The sidecar, however, took the full force of the impact when it struck the massive bole of the tree and collapsed inwards and crumpled to half its proper size. Even so, the resultant mangled mess bounced back a yard or more as it was ripped away from the motorcycle. The rider escaped injury and his bike was still serviceable but his passenger's neck was broken by the force of the whiplash, even before the tree demolished his face and shattered his skull.

The first two Kübelwagens were also destroyed. One before the driver was able to stop, meeting the same fate as the first motorcycle and the second when it drove off onto the verge in an effort to escape the trap and simultaneously set off several mines. So far, virtually half the vehicles and men had been neutralised and yet, not a single shot had been fired, but Schröder was no fool and he tried to recover the situation. Having travelled in the rear vehicle, he ordered his driver out and then ran to the vehicles in front and did the same. He had 12 men left and he was pretty certain that all those in the leading vehicles were already dead. He kept his driver and the one surviving motorcyclist with him and then sent the rest into the woods on both sides, telling them to keep off the road and verges and work their way forwards. He would summon assistance and then follow. They were to rendezvous on the beach. He figured that as the ambush had been so well prepared and being very close to the prohibited area, either the escapees or a support team were responsible and so they must be nearby. He had no radio; it had been with his Unteroffizier in the second vehicle. And so he wrote his report and ordered the motorcyclist to recover his machine from the trees and return to base. He was to inform the Peenemünde commander of what had happened, request reinforcements and suggest the immediate deployment of a naval gunboat.

Schröder had only just started to carefully pick his way forward through the intense darkness of the trees when the wood was briefly illuminated by the flash of another explosion as the motorcyclist rode over one of the mines on the verge. Then, just as he considered sending someone else back to base, the first trip wire was activated only 50 yards ahead of him. The screaming started. Several soldiers had received horrific injuries and one had lost both his legs above the knee. As their comrades struggled in the darkness and heat of battle to stop the bleeding with pressure and tourniquets, they moaned, screeched and wailed in unbearable agony. It was more than some of their comrades could take and three soldiers broke cover on the opposite verge and charged down the road. They drowned out the cries of pain with their own screams of anger and frustration and, none too soon as they saw it, with the belated but reassuring sounds of their own weapons being fired towards the unseen enemy. They, at least, were not going to be dictated to by a handful of rabble-rousers. So encouraged – but to the dismay of their officer – others started to emerge back onto the road.

The man leading the charge ran straight into the wire which was stretched at waist height across the road. In a fraction of a second the wire tightened, the rings were pulled free, the strikers engaged and then the air was filled with a thousand wood splinters. Some were the size of axe blades, as sections of tree immediately underneath the packed explosives disintegrated in a blinding, deafening flash. This lethal 360-degree volley of razor-sharp wooden missiles killed and dismembered men in all directions –cutting them down with a power and penetration that exceeded anything achieved by the best of England's legendary longbowmen.

And still Dominik waited.

Schröder gave the order to regroup, only to find that he had just five fit men left. At that point he realised that whatever the final outcome of the engagement, if he survived he was going to be impugned with a veritable storm of accusations, shame and ridicule. He thought he would be lucky to escape a court martial for negligence, incompetence or worse. Yet, he was confounded as to how it could have gone so badly wrong, so quickly. He was convinced that he had not been reckless or ill-prepared, but he instinctively knew that he could not retrieve the situation unless he killed or captured those responsible, and he was not going to do it by hiding in the woods. He made up his mind, gave his orders and then, accompanied by his driver and one other man, he started a flanking manoeuvre off to the left. Five minutes later, right on cue, the three remaining soldiers resumed the charge down the road.

Dominik waited in his concealed position until they were only 25 yards away before opening up with his Sten gun. One German went down almost immediately and the other two ran for the trees on Dominik's left. He fired another burst toward their entry point and then threw in two grenades.

When the noise of the explosions had passed Konrad called his name, "You're making a lot of noise back here. Far too much for our own good, I should think. And now that the boat's arrived I thought I should come and get you. The canoes will be on their way in very soon. So come on, let's get the hell out of here and secure the beach before any more Jerries turn up."

Dominik packed his kit, picked up his close-quarters weapon of last resort, the loaded trench gun, and followed his friend towards the surf. Konrad paused at the edge of the trees and listened intently. He had heard something carried in on the breeze, something that was out of place. Then they both heard it; sure enough, the distinctive sound of the singing sand. Unmistakeably it was footsteps, off to their left by the nearest dune. It would be another ten minutes before the canoes actually arrived and so it had to be the enemy. They waited for less than a minute and then two Germans appeared, clearly visible against the background of the sand dunes. The Poles fired together and both Germans collapsed to the ground. They went forward slowly and then Dominik bent down to check that they were dead, whilst Konrad stood and covered them with his Sten gun, just in case they had any fight left.

317

Schröder seized his opportunity and broke cover from behind the dune, firing his MP40 Maschinenpistole as he ran. Konrad, who was still standing over the Germans, was hit several times in the stomach and chest before Dominik could react. From a kneeling position and purely on reflex, he twisted to his left. Almost from ground level and with his left hand only, he fired his trench gun after blindly stabbing it upwards towards the German's torso. It tore away most of his right shoulder and he was poleaxed. Dominik then stood up, took the weapon in both hands, walked over to the German and in blind rage he slam-fired the weapon into the German's body until the magazine was empty and the weapon was dry firing. He then returned to Konrad and slowly fell to his knees beside his true friend and brother in arms.

He knew from the terrible injuries that he was already dead and at that moment, caring nothing for his own safety or the success of the mission, he cradled him in his arms and spoke gently of his regret and sorrow. The adrenaline and alertness of action were quickly driven from his body, firstly by the shock and impact of such a close personal loss and then by the realisation that his enemies and fate had once again conspired together to brutally rip away the very things he truly cherished. His hard defensive shell crumbled and he was overwhelmed by grief and remorse. So he let the tears flow, hugged his friend even closer and sobbed like a baby. He wept for his wife, Bogdana, his children Michal and Karolina, for Konrad, Adam and a disfigured Stan and for the dozens of friends and relations lost in his three wars. Now, as his personal list of the dead and injured grew ever longer, he thought the pain would never end. For the first time in his life he desperately wanted to give up and abandon the struggle altogether, just walk away and find a normal life, free from the horror and liability of war. In his anguish and anger he looked up to the heavens and screamed at his maker, "Have I not fought enough? Have I not suffered enough? Then he collapsed onto the sand, still embracing the man he respected and loved most in the world.

And that was how Marcin and Hannah found him ten minutes later.

Chapter Seventeen

THE NAZI GUILLOTINE

Swindon – 14th November 2009

I had spent the night trying to sleep on Stan's lounge floor, cramped up on a makeshift bed consisting of the cushion sections from the seats and the backs of the fireside chairs, covered in an old fashioned eiderdown. I woke up with a stiff neck, aching joints and a headache. It had been about 2am when he had finally reached the personally painful point in his narrative and told me how his father had died. Although over 65 years had passed, he still found the circumstances so difficult to deal with. Particularly because the team had been successful, achieved all their operational objectives and were at the very point of rescue and safety. And so I had joined him in a few shots of Polish vodka, just to dampen the emotions and as he put it, "Taste the true spirit and the warm fire of home." Anyway, following another hour or so of Stan's maudlin childhood reminiscences, I was in no state to drive home.

After a wash and brush-up and a couple of cups of coffee I was feeling much more human and almost fit to face the day ahead. Stan, who seemed to be totally unaffected by the alcohol or sentiment of the previous night, then joined me at the kitchen table. Without any preamble or small talk, he immediately and enthusiastically took up the story where he had left off.

"The information that the team brought out of Peenemünde swept aside all the doubts the Allies had about the scale, scope and immediacy of the horrendous threat posed by the German terror weapons and so they accepted Dominik's assessment and decided to bomb it, and they attacked with everything they had."

"Was it destroyed?"

"Well, they wanted to take out all the production lines and supporting infrastructure and the administrative support buildings which contained the records, plans and official documentation. They also hoped to kill many of the scientists, civilian staff and military personnel directly involved in the design, testing or production of the super-weapons and their critical components. Peenemünde had become the number one priority target."

I asked, "When was this exactly?"

"The team had only been back in England a few weeks when the first raid took place and it was massive. On the evening of 17th August 1943 Bomber Command sent in over 300 Lancasters, 200 Halifaxes and 50-plus Stirlings. Helped by a full moon they dropped nearly 2,000 tons of high explosive and incendiary bombs on three specific targets inside the Peenemünde complex."

"Was it a success?"

Stan scratched at his scar and gathered his thoughts, "Well, yes and no. The chosen targets included the scientists and workers living quarters, the rocket factory and the experimental works. Unfortunately, early on in the raid many of the bombs fell on the forced labour camp near Karlshagen about two miles away and 500 or more of our own people were killed: whereas the Germans lost less than 200 altogether."

"It turned out far more costly for us then."

"Yes, cruelly ironic, isn't it and on top of that we also lost 40 aircraft and their valuable crews as well: 245 men were killed or captured and it didn't end there."

He went on to explain that although reconnaissance photographs showed that significant damage had been caused on the three main targets, they were by no means destroyed and we had to bomb Peenemünde again a week later. The real problem, however, was that we had left it too late to inflict a fatal blow because the V1 was already in production near Kassel. To make matters worse, the V2 programme was also in the process of being moved. Almost everything had been transferred to the Mittelwerk underground plant deep inside Kohnstein Hill at Nordhausen, on the edge of the Harz Mountains. Initially, the slave labour workforce required for such a huge complex was taken from the Buchenwald concentration camp and when they arrived they were no better off. They were imprisoned underground in insanitary conditions inside unstable, claustrophobic and vermin-ridden tunnels where they were constantly deprived of daylight, fresh air, sufficient food and sleep.

The prisoners who became too weak or ill to work, and there were many, were sent to Auschwitz or Mauthausen to be killed. Later on, in an attempt to quickly replace the dead workers, save valuable project time and reduce the transport costs, the Germans built a new concentration camp at the site. It became known as Dora-Mittelbau. Some 25,000 of these overworked and abused 'inmates' died a terrible death from exhaustion, beatings, torture, summary execution, disease and starvation: all in the course of building the Nazi super-weapons. In twelve-hour shifts, working around the clock in the semi-darkness and choked with dust, they used pickaxes and their bare hands to widen the tunnels.

A massive slave army transported thousands of tons of rock or laboured on the construction sites or at the ammonia works or on the production lines of the armaments themselves, in the most dangerous of working conditions. Predominately they came from Poland, Russia and France and many had already been kicked, whipped and beaten by their previous guards and their Kapos. So they knew what to expect, but some were brave beyond belief and would still resist right to the very end. Over 200 were hanged for trying to sabotage the rockets or other weapons. These heroic souls were not to receive any recognition or medals for their tenacity but were anonymously incinerated in the crematoria. Most remain nameless to this day, their deeds long and readily forgotten by those who should be most grateful. So, all in all, the raids put back the deployment of the V2 by less than three months but did nothing to end the torment of Hitler's slaves.

Stan also pointed out the positive side, "Nevertheless, at that stage of the war just a few weeks delay in production probably hastened their eventual surrender and in the process must have saved thousands, perhaps even tens of thousands, of lives. And that doesn't take into account the fact that the Germans were secretly working on other weapons of terror and in time, they too would have been deployed."

There seemed to be no end to the suffering for the subjugated or limits to the Nazi capacity for contempt and inhumanity and I was sickened by it all. I tried to move him on, "So what happened to Dominik and the rest of the team? Losing your father like that must have hit you all very hard and I can't even imagine how you and your mother managed to cope with it."

"It was a difficult time, but the war went on and we all did what we had to do. Before I forget, there's something I would like you to remember about the rocket programme. This one thing above all else, and it's not commonly known either. Far more people died manufacturing the V2 than were ever killed by it exploding."

"Well, I certainly wasn't aware of that."

"I made it my business to find out. Every single one of the 4,500 operational V2s to come off the Mittelwerk production line cost five innocent and precious human lives. So there you have it, Mick: here's yet another bitter and scornful truth from the obscure corners of our long-forgotten Polish war. Well before the first missile was targeted against London in September 1944, that's throughout the whole research and development programme at Peenemünde and during production at Nordhausen, Hitler's dream weapon was already killing thousands. The very people he despised the most. Those he had labelled and condemned as sub-human."

"How many casualties were there when it was eventually used on the Allies?"

Stan really did know his subject well and replied straight away, "About 7,000, but there again, had it not been for people like my father, those brave Allied bomber crews and the undaunted slave saboteurs, who knows what the final toll might have been."

I let all this information sink in for a moment or two and it made me wonder just how close Hitler had come to developing a nuclear weapon. I remembered reading about their production and storage of heavy water, made famous in the film *The Heroes of Telemark*. I also knew about their failed efforts to produce a nuclear reactor (Uranmaschine) and their long-standing nuclear energy research project, which became known as Uranverein (the Uranium Club). I thought the generally accepted scientific view had always been that they were not even close to success, but Stan's comments made me think again. What if the V2s had managed to buy him a few more months, and what about a dirty bomb? Was I now being completely fanciful or didn't it bear thinking about? Uncertain, increasingly unsure of my facts and trying to avoid another long and hypothetical discourse, I brought him back to my original question.

"What happened to Dominik and the rest of you?"

He smiled at me, a broad knowing grin that spread deep creases across his whole face, wrinkled and knotted his scar and narrowed his eyes as they flashed mischievously. He rubbed his hands together in anticipation and then, this master of deviation and surprise, set out on yet another unexpected twist.

"Well now, just you listen. There will be time aplenty for that later on, but now it's definitely Urszula's turn to take centre stage. She was a remarkable woman and I think you'll need to know a great deal about her if you're going to achieve our final task."

It was no good me rising to the bait. At long last I was beginning to understand exactly how his mind worked. He would only tell me about 'the final task' when he was sure that I had all the relevant facts: the crucial details that would allow me to fully understand their reasoning and underline the importance, significance, and consequences of the request. Obviously, Urszula – whoever she was – had to come first and so I asked rather facetiously, "Am I right in assuming she was also a saboteur or a member of SOE or the Home Army?"

"Well done! You are a bright lad, but there's really no need to be frivolous, you know. In fact, she was a spy – one of the best and most active of all the assets controlled by the Home Army and the government-in-exile. The British had no idea of her existence and that was almost unique at the time. But her real value came from the fact that the Germans did know about her. The whole time she was in the field they were well aware that she was a secret agent but they thought they were running her, when in reality she was working for us."

"How on earth did that come about?"

Stan stood up and walked over to the sideboard, opened the top drawer and removed something, immediately hiding it in his hand. He came back to the table and with an elaborate flourish of his arm, put it down in front of me. It was a silk flower. A pure white rose. He said, "Her father was German and although her mother was Polish by birth, she had lived in Germany since she was seventeen and to all intents and purposes considered herself German. Although Urszula sometimes spoke Polish at home, particularly with her mother, she was raised as a loyal German citizen. Now, I'm sure you remember the White Rose file in the box. Well, it was this flower that first brought her to our cause and changed her life. Everything she did from that point on was because of it. I'll try to explain…"

In early 1942, Urszula Foerster was a postgraduate medical research student working at the Hamburg University Medical Centre at Eppendorf in the north of the city. There she came into regular contact with young students and soldiers. She was already vehemently opposed to fascism and as time passed she heard more and more stories of the brutality and harrowing descriptions of the horrors meted out to the civilian populations in the east. Then, in the summer, during the academic break, several of the male students were sent off to the Eastern Front for military service, where they were to act as medics. They returned four months later and corroborated the various accounts of mass murder and civilian suffering. When several more wounded soldiers spoke independently and graphically of their personal experiences in the

Warsaw and Lodz ghettoes she decided to act. She felt that she had to speak out and make a stand against the inhuman treatment of the Jews and other innocents.

Her opportunity came when she overheard two students talking about plans to distribute anti-government leaflets throughout the main university buildings. She cultivated their friendship and by explaining that she abhorred what was happening in Poland, partly due to the fact that her mother was Polish, she won their trust. She discovered that most of their small select membership came from middle-class backgrounds and they had grown up with friends or acquaintances who were Jewish. Many of these had been beaten, rendered homeless, persecuted, 'deported' or worse, on or immediately after the vicious watershed of Kristallnacht. She was invited to one of their secret meetings and was immediately inspired by their romantic bravery, their rebellious idealism and their objective of passive resistance to everything that the Third Reich stood for. She readily joined them.

In the following weeks she became more and more involved in 'die Weiße Rose' organisation until in January 1943, she was entrusted with the responsibility of meeting a courier from Munich who was to deliver 500 copies of bulletin No 5 entitled 'Appeal to all Germans!' for distribution across the city. Nearly 10,000 of these flyers had been centrally produced in Munich on hand-operated duplicating machines, with batches being despatched to eight other centres across Germany, including Berlin. The contents caused a sensation across the length and breadth of the country. The final lines in particular, struck a chord with many ordinary and war-weary Germans and supportive graffiti started to appear on the walls of universities and government buildings across the nation. The Nazi leadership were incandescent with outrage and indignation at what they saw as nothing short of treason. They immediately ordered the Gestapo to hunt down the publishers and smash their network. The order went out to all military and civil police that the hunt for the ringleaders was their top priority and to that end, anyone found in possession of the leaflets, just one copy or even a few lines, had to be handed over to the Gestapo for immediate 'interrogation'.

In fact, that short text on just one side of paper, which had sparked such an infuriated response, had been written by a young, devout Lutheran. He had also been a member of the Hitler Youth until he became disillusioned and then disaffected. He was horrified by the Nazi euthanasia programme, their complete lack of ethics and morality and their preposterous racial purity policies and laws. Yet years hence, after all the Nazi power and abuse had been swept aside, it would be his very words that would be enshrined in the principles of the new Western Europe, slowly emerging from the ashes of war. They may have been idealistic, somewhat naive aspirations, fearfully scribbled in secret at the time but today they remain the basis of all democracy.

At the beginning of February 1943 the news of the crushing German defeat at Stalingrad started to filter through the university and it also prompted the publication in Munich of the sixth leaflet. In many ways it was the most dangerous and inflammatory. It lambasted, indicted and ridiculed the entire Nazi regime, making a passionate invocation to the people to rise up and overthrow them. On the afternoon of 19th February Urszula was waiting at the crowded Hauptbahnhof (central railway station) to collect her group's leaflets from the courier. The train arrived ten minutes late, but none of the passengers emerged from the throng on the concourse to approach her at their rendezvous point, immediately under the western clock tower.

Initially, she was not too concerned about her security because the stations were regularly bombed by the Allies and public transport was becoming increasingly disrupted and unreliable and he could well have been delayed. But after another ten minutes, when the crowd started to thin and there was still no contact, she began to feel very conspicuous and uneasy. Some sixth sense told her it was time to move. She had only walked a few yards towards the exit, quickly picking up the pace, when she felt a hand take a firm grip on her left shoulder. She was forcefully spun around and her heart sank. She almost cried out in alarm before she heard the words, "Wait up! Everything's fine, I'm Karl, and I've got the delivery for you."

She looked up into the earnest face of a tall, blond eighteen-year-old. "You frightened me to death, you idiot. Why have you kept me waiting like this? For God's sake! I thought you were the police. Anyway I'm Hiltrude, so you can give me the package and let me get out of here. I've been hanging around for far too long already."

Satisfied with the agreed recognition code he said, "I'm sorry. Security's being tightened up back in Munich and in Berlin. We can't be too careful now and so I watched you for a few minutes, just to make sure I wasn't walking into a trap. We've even been told that the Gestapo have put a price on our heads. Apparently, they're offering huge rewards to anyone who will turn us in, so we must be making some real progress at last, to get them this fired up. All sorts of people are beginning to support us. I reckon that the Nazis feel that we're posing a real threat to their power base and this latest flyer will upset them even more. Let's hope it makes the whole bloody country sit up and listen. Anyway, good luck to you. I'd better be getting back." He handed the small leather satchel over to her and turned to walk away.

Relieved, she made straight for the exit. As she turned the corner onto the street, and walked towards her bicycle, she almost collided with a man leaning against the wall. She tried to side-step around him, but he grabbed her right arm, stepped in front of her and pushed her hard up against the wall, thrusting his left forearm across her throat so that she was trapped. Within seconds two other men arrived and one immediately grabbed at the satchel which she was still clutching in her left hand. She cried out in pain as he used both hands to straighten her fingers out and then bend them back, away from the handle so that he could wrench it from her grip. He took a quick look inside, "They're here alright! We've got the bitch. Let's get her straight down to headquarters and we can work on her all night. She'll tell us everything by morning."

Urszula tried to get away. She knew that once she was in the cells all would be lost and she was desperate to warn her friends.

When the man released his grip on her throat to take hold of her arms, she stamped down hard on his foot and then as he instinctively backed away, she used all her strength to viciously kick him in the groin. He dropped to the floor writhing and moaning and she seized her chance, turning to run. The one holding the bag, who was a relatively new recruit, was slow to react, but his more experienced companion had always anticipated such a move. He was the senior of the three, holding the rank of Kriminaloberassistent. He had learnt the basics in his pre-war role as a city detective and was well aware that the actual point of confrontation was the most critical time in the whole process of arrest, detention and interrogation. Having frequently worked on his own in the roughest of docklands, he had discovered through bitter experience that if you wanted to keep your prisoner, it was also the very time to control and totally dominate.

Additionally, Bruno Streckenbach, the pre-war chief of police in Hamburg, who had in turn been appointed the Gestapo chief, had forcefully impressed on all his men that it was also the time to be merciless. He had instructed that, from that very moment (the first laying on of hands on the prisoner), fear should be their weapon. The aim was to demoralise, disorientate and terrify; to soften them up so that the subsequent interrogators could quickly torture their way to the truth and obtain a confession naming their associates and accomplices. Before he had left on his appointment to command the infamous Einsatzgruppe1in Poland, he had taught all his subordinates that any resistance whatsoever must always be met with immediate and, if necessary, fatal force. Unlike some of his colleagues from the civilian police, this particular convert had always longed for the opportunity to punish without limits. He welcomed the concept of becoming accuser, judge, jury and executioner. Everything was now permitted, so he believed, but only in the name of the Fatherland and in service to Hitler. Yes, Streckenbach's pupil had admired his teacher and listened well and so he was excited, poised and ready when the cornered and desperate young traitor had made her move.

Before she had completed a pace forward he had grabbed her hair from behind with his left hand and yanked her back. He was fast and he was powerful. He twisted her locks around in his hand until his fist was tight against the roots and then he yanked her around to face him. It felt as if her scalp was on fire and she screamed out in pain, and he chose that moment to smile. Then he punched her square in the face with his huge right fist and he held nothing back. She immediately lost consciousness as the blow landed on her left eye and temple. They handcuffed her and with blood already pouring from her split eyebrow, she was dragged to their vehicle, receiving a few retaliatory kicks on the way from the one with the very sore and swollen testicles. With their prisoner secure, his colleagues laughed at his carelessness and stupidity. Careless, because he had left himself open to attack from a startled enemy collaborator. Stupid, because she could no longer feel any pain, yet every blow he landed aggravated his own injury and made him wince with the additional and unnecessary discomfort.

He became the butt of many jokes and jibes within the station over the next few days and this ridicule exacerbated his hatred and vengeful animosity towards the White Rose in general, and Urszula in particular. The other team from the combined police/ Gestapo operation had far less trouble in picking up the courier. Neither he nor Urszula had either the training or the experience to detect the surveillance operation at the busy station. They were also completely unaware that the Gestapo were already closing in on the whole movement. Two of the organisation's founding members had been arrested the previous day for distributing leaflets at Munich University. As the Nazi dragnet closed in on that city's entire membership, they had learnt the identity of two couriers and so they followed them, rightly expecting that they would lead them directly to other branches of the conspiracy. Unfortunately for Urszula, one of them was known by the code name Karl.

Urszula started to come round on the floor of the van just before they arrived at Gestapo headquarters on Stadthausbrücke and the first thing she heard was the driver laughing as he shouted out, "Hey Bernhard, how's your bollocks?" The third man immediately joined in the mocking laughter.

"There's bugger all to be funny about. It still hurts like hell and they're swollen to twice their normal size. It feels like I've got a couple of melons trapped between my legs."

The driver replied immediately, "Well, I reckon you must have a melon on your shoulders as well. You're a bloody fool and make no mistake. Fancy letting a woman do that to you. What do you make of it all, Aldo?"

Aldo was also enjoying Bernhard's humiliation, "Well it must surely be a watermelon that he's got for a brain, it would certainly explain the tears in his eyes," and they both burst out laughing again. Bernhard was miserable. He accepted that he had been careless, but he was already sick of the gnawing pain in his groin and the lack of sympathy from his comrades.

"Go on then you two, keep taking the piss while you can but I'm telling you now, as soon as we've got what we want from her I'm going to strangle the cow and very slowly with my bare hands."

Aldo spoke to the driver, "Don't go round the back, Lanzo. She's the first one of this lot we've brought in and it's so important that Berlin are bound to be all over us on it, so let's take her in the front and then all the staff can get a glimpse of her. Being seen in the limelight can't do us any harm either, as long as poor old Bernhard can manage to stand up straight for a few minutes."

"Sounds like a good idea to me, but we won't risk putting our 'poor wounded hero' on show. He can drive the van round the back and sneak in through the tradesmen's entrance after we've taken her inside," and with that Lanzo had added to Bernhard's embarrassment.

Urszula could hardly stand when she was dragged from the back of the van. Her left eye was dripping blood and completely closed up by the bruising and swelling; she was very groggy and had the worst headache imaginable. She was pulled upright just outside the five-arched entrance to the imposing five-storey, sandy/grey stone building that, until 1933, had been the Hamburg Police Department's headquarters. Despite some bomb damage to one corner of the building it was still fully functional. She glanced up towards the roof of the massive frontage and despite her limited vision, saw dozens of faces staring down at her from many of the 100-plus windows that seemed to stretch endlessly off to both sides. Some people were pointing at her and others were shaking their fists and making offensive gestures. They all appeared so animated and hostile and for the first time in her life she felt certain that her own death was close.

As they dragged her up the steps, she counted them out in her mind and for some inexplicable reason she just could not get the number out of her head, 'five steps – five arches – five storeys and she wondered how long she would last, five minutes – five hours – five days? She repeated those numbers over and over, focused in on them in an attempt to block out what was happening. They took her straight to the cells in the basement and she counted the steps down, ticking them off in her mind in groups of five.

A fat, uncouth and loud female guard was waiting for her outside the heavy steel door of the holding pen. She prodded Urszula inside with the handle of a whip and shouted, "Strip – take everything off! You're a traitor and an enemy of the Reich. You'll be thoroughly searched and then you will tell us everything."

She was forced to stand with her arms held high above her head and her legs spread wide apart. The guard's hands were thrust everywhere as her fingers explored and violated. Urszula, in an effort to detach herself from her shame, anger and embarrassment, tried to fixate on different mental images of steps, arches and buildings that she knew best. She pictured where they were, who she had been there with and what landmarks could be found within a five-minute walk. But with her attention focused elsewhere, she was too slow to respond to the woman's instructions to move or bend or stretch or kneel and so she was repeatedly hit over the head with the folded whip until she complied. All the time Lanzo and Aldo stayed in the cell, leering, threatening and making obscene comments and gestures. Finally satisfied, the female guard then left, taking Urszula's clothes with her.

Over the next three days she was left naked, deprived of sleep and food, beaten, repeatedly raped and humiliated by her interrogators and 'visitors' until she could stand it no longer. The final straw was when she was told that her courier contact Karl had died from his injuries following his 'fall' from a fourth floor window and she should expect the same. Exhausted, demoralised and desperate she gave in. After five days she had told them everything they wanted to know: first her life story and then details of her 'crimes.' The times, dates, locations and particulars of all her contacts and her interactions with the group at the university, even the minutiae of a typical working day. She held nothing back. She was signing her confession at exactly the same time that three of her compatriots from Munich were standing trial at the People's Court. They had established and led the White Rose movement and were quickly 'convicted' of treason and sentenced to death. All three were executed that same day – by guillotine.

Prussia had used a guillotine-like mechanism known as a Fallbeil (drop hatchet) since the seventeenth century and decapitation by guillotine was the usual means of execution in Germany until the abolition of the death penalty in West Germany in 1949. In Nazi Germany, the guillotine was reserved mainly for political crimes, including treason. Nevertheless, the Nazis' use of the Fallbeil, which was also called the Fallschwert (drop sword), a shorter, largely metal, redesigned German version of the French guillotine, was chillingly routine. It is estimated that some 16,000 people were guillotined in Germany and Austria between 1933 and 1945. The victims included resistance fighters and members of anti-Nazi youth groups both in Germany itself and in their occupied countries. They rationalised that these resistance fighters and radicals should be considered as guerrillas or terrorists because they were not members of a regular army and many individuals and batches of 'offenders' were transported to Germany and executed there. Decapitation was considered a 'dishonourable' death, in contrast to an 'honourable' end i.e. execution by a firing squad.

As his workload mounted, Johann Reichhart, the Nazis' chief executioner and a Nazi himself, who personally executed over 2,000 people, sought to drastically reduce the time taken during each execution. He removed the traditional tilting body-board of the Fallbeil and relied on a fixed bench onto which the condemned were physically held down by two or three assistant executioners. This development removed the time-consuming act of restraining the victim whilst buckling up the two straps (or in some particularly difficult cases three) around the condemned's body. This shortened the time taken for decapitation to only three or four seconds. He did, however, insist on wearing the traditional German executioners' uniform of black coat, white shirt and gloves, black bow-tie and top-hat. His macabre work also took him to many parts of occupied Europe including Poland.

There can be no doubt that the Third Reich's justice system was obscenely quick, medieval, brutal, an affront to common decency and anything but due process. Nevertheless, more trials of White Rose members followed and three more suffered the same cruel fate, whilst others were sentenced to between six months and ten years imprisonment. Six intelligent young people were decapitated simply because they possessed the temerity to attack the tyranny that was destroying their lives and their country. They did this, not with the deadly force of guns and explosives but with the subtle, corrosive power of their reason, their intellect and a few carefully chosen words.

Very early the following morning Bernhard entered Urszula's cell for the first time. Lanzo had decided that he could not risk giving him access until after a confession had been obtained because he was so vindictive by nature and intent on killing her. For the first time in days she had been left to sleep while the top brass conferred with Berlin to decide her official fate. Bernhard was disappointed that he was unable to drag her to her feet by her hair because it had all been shaved off as a part of the interrogation plan. Instead, he quietly knelt beside her and then slapped her several times across the face until she was fully awake and trembling with fear, anticipating more torture. He had again split open the cut above her eye and blood was streaming down her face as she cried out for him to stop. He sat astride her, his weight bearing down and pinning her to the flagstone floor.

"Oh, don't you worry my sweet little Polack, it won't be long now. It's time to pay for making a fool out of me. I told them what would happen and I always keep my promises," and then he started to throttle her.

At first she struggled with all her might, kicking out, thrashing her legs about, punching at his arms and body and scratching at his face and eyes, but her range of movement was severely restricted by his position and strength. He also managed to protect his head with his upper arms by hunching his shoulders and retracting his neck, pushing his chin down onto his chest. Soon she was using all her energy just trying to breathe but it was futile; she was already suffocating and the fight was gone. Her vision blurred, her chest felt as if it was on fire and she started to turn purple and lose consciousness. This was all far too quick for Bernhard so he released his iron grip and started to punch her in the face, so hard that his knuckles split and he was spattered with her blood. As the blows landed he screamed at her, "Wake up, you treacherous bitch! Wake up! Look me in the eyes. I want you to watch me when I squeeze the life out of your ugly, worthless and ungrateful carcass."

With his temper temporarily vented he stopped and waited. Almost immediately she started gasping for air again, struggling to fill her searing lungs and sucking in blood from her damaged face in the process. She was assailed by wave after wave of agonizing pain from her throat, chest and face, but her instinct for survival would not tolerate capitulation again and it forced her to face the threat and open her eyes. They widened as she refocused on his pitiless face and were full of pain, hate and defiance when his hands moved back to her throat. Then the door suddenly burst open and Aldo and Lanzo ran in and dragged him off. They rushed her to hospital. Berlin had made their decision and the order had been sent down the line.

All local traces of her arrest, detention, interrogation and confession were to be immediately erased and all her contacts, without exception, were to be left in place and not arrested. Their fate would be decided at a later stage. But all original documents were to be forwarded with the prisoner directly to Berlin. They made it abundantly clear that they wanted her alive and well because they had a plan that involved her full cooperation. The staff at the Hamburg District Office were instructed to ensure that she left within 24 hours under the escort of their two most experienced officers. The order, addressed to the district commander personally, stated that Berlin would not countenance any failure, hindrance or delay. Her safe transfer was to be his top priority.

Stan chose that point to break off to prepare lunch but just a few minutes later, once we had sat down at the kitchen table with our soup and bread rolls I asked, "What exactly did they want her to do and why did she go along with it?"

"Once they knew of her parentage and background and discovered that she was also fluent in Polish and Russian, which she had studied at school and at university for her first degree, they saw her real potential. You see, the Home Army had become a real military and political threat to them and since their defeats in Russia, they were worried about a possible uprising in Poland putting their supply and communication lines at risk. They dreaded the Russians and Poles acting in concert, so they needed someone on the inside."

It seemed like one hell of a risk to me. "How could they possibly trust her? What was to stop her simply disappearing?"

Stan broke his two rolls up into small pieces and dropped them individually into his dinner. He seemed to be concentrating hard, self-absorbed, as he stirred them around and repeatedly pushed them back down into the liquid with the back of his spoon, waiting and staring at his bowl. He didn't take a mouthful until he was satisfied that his bread sponges had absorbed every last drop of fluid so that his meal took on the consistency of thick, glutinous porridge. I ate mine while he slowly performed this indulgence and I then had to wait until he had noisily sucked in and consumed every last soup-saturated morsel.

He saw me watching, "Unlike you Mick, I know what it's like to go hungry for days on end and many has been the time that I've survived solely on watery potato soup, so when I have some like this – thick with meat and vegetables – I make the most of it. I've earned the right to enjoy these simple pleasures so I'm not going to apologise for the impolite slurping or the dribbles of culinary satisfaction down my chin."

I ignored the occasional spray, remnants of chewed mush as he spoke and I smiled at his homily and his honesty and then I repeated my question.

He finally finished licking his chops and answered, "Of course they didn't trust her, but they had her over a barrel. They had given her back the power to save her friends. Those she believed she had already betrayed. The pain and abuse had also stopped and she wouldn't have been human if she hadn't been terrified of it starting all over again. So she knew what refusal would mean, both for her and the others."

"But I still don't see why she couldn't just pretend to go along with them at first and then take the first chance to get away and try to warn her friends?"

"She had been told in no uncertain terms that if she tried to escape or go over to the enemy, then those she wished to protect would be immediately executed, as would all the members of her own extended family. Don't you forget that everything she had discovered from within the White Rose and since, had convinced her that they would have no compunction in following through on their threats. She felt vulnerable, trapped and alone and that's why she accepted their proposal."

"But from what you told me, she obviously did go over to the Poles at some stage."

For the first time Stan started to show signs of irritation towards my interruptions and he snapped right back, "Just you mind you don't get ahead of yourself here. The sooner you let me carry on, the sooner you'll know all the answers."

I put my hand up as a sign of apology and surrender and then he smiled in acknowledgement and continued, "Well, then they started her training and indoctrination."

He went on to tell me how she first met Klaus Schenker of the Abwehr, specifically Section III F – the Counter Espionage Agents Bureau. He was the man who was to become her instructor and handler. He had visited her every day and once her wounds had healed he had collected her from the Gestapo headquarters on Prinz-Albrecht-Straße which had until 1933, when it was requisitioned by the Nazis, been the School of Applied Arts and the Prinz Albrecht Hotel. These were once famous, hospitable places: haunts of comfort, culture, and happiness that will sadly now, always be remembered for their topography of terror, torture and murder. A micro-example of what Hitler created and what Greater Germany had become, all in less than a decade.

She was taken to a secret spy-school, safely hidden away from the locals and prying eyes, on a massive hunting estate in Bavaria. There she underwent intensive training in the arts of espionage, self-defence, weapons training and rather strangely, radio engineering. She also received one-to-one instruction on Polish and Russian culture and their complicated and often interwoven military histories. She was also shown a number of recent German Military Intelligence assessments of the organisation, deployment and objectives of the Home Army. She had no way of knowing if they were genuine, but she suspected that she would be tested in some way and the supply of false information to the enemy would be a likely starting point. Finally, on the 26th April 1943 Schenker issued her with several sets of identity documents and personal papers to match. He provided her with a pistol and a survival kit. Both were small enough to be easily hidden and ironically, the latter also contained a suicide tablet. He then briefed her for her first mission.

She travelled to Szczecin (Stettin) by train and then by bus to a nearby village in Kaszubia. As the countryside rolled by she tried to recall all she had learnt about her destination during her briefings. Her previous knowledge of the area had been somewhat limited, although she had heard that the people of Kaszubia spoke their own language and were fiercely protective of their history, culture and identity, having existed for centuries in a semi-autonomous relationship with both Prussia and Poland. Schenker had explained that, unlike the Poles, they were considered by the Nazi government as being of 'German stock or extraction' and were therefore deemed suitable for Germanisation. They had then been officially classified as 'third category Deutsche Volksliste' and therefore a structured, comprehensive and standardised process had been set in place to eradicate any remaining Polish sympathies or links.

However, what he had omitted to tell her was that the ethnic Polish minority had remained active prior to the war and many belonged to The Union of Poles in Germany. But because of discrimination and oppression by the German authorities between the wars, their numbers had gradually fallen to about 2,000. Then in 1939 all Polish organisations were disbanded by the Nazis and many professionals were arrested, imprisoned and executed. Others went underground or were hidden within the Kaszubian community. Therefore problems had started almost immediately after war commenced as most Kaszubians believed that 'there could be no Poland without Kaszubia and no Kaszubia without Poland'. These were the famous words of a revered nineteenth-century Kaszubian journalist and activist who strove to create a strong Kaszubian identity but only as 'one branch, amongst many, of the great Polish nation'. Resistance groups such as 'Gryf Kaszubski' soon sprang up. They rapidly expanded into the whole of Pomerania and soon became an integral and vital part of the Home Army.

The Nazis retaliated to this defiance by rounding up and killing thousands of civilians, many of them well-educated community leaders and representatives. So her handler had carefully and deliberately chosen this area for her insertion into the Home Army because of its mixture of German, Kaszubian and Polish communities with their conflicting loyalties, multilingual heritage and ethnic rivalries. He had also provided her with the bait.

The very next day she went to the address she had been given in Szczecin. It turned out to be a flat in a four-storey apartment building in the Old Town area with an impressive view of the Haymarket and St Jacob's Cathedral. There she had her first meeting with a member of the Home Army. Schenker had told her that he was a low-level, part-time messenger whom they had been watching on and off for some time but so far had not arrested. He was to be her way into the Szczecin section. The German reasoned that he was so low in the pecking order of the organisation that he would always be looking for a way to improve his status by impressing those up above. She had been told that this meant that he would certainly listen to what she had to say and then report the meeting to his boss without asking any difficult questions. He further argued that once she introduced herself, then the file would do the rest.

The meeting went as planned. Although the courier was suspicious and nervy when she first told him that she had vital information for the Home Army, he became intrigued and then astonished when she produced the official Nazi documents. They were stamped and embossed with the Gestapo seal. He made a few coded notes of some key dates and facts and then memorised her address. Two days later she was stopped on the street in her village by a young woman and taken to a house near the old Town Hall in Szczecin where she was interviewed by two middle-ranking Kaszubian officers from the Home Army. Other members were busy searching her lodgings and digging into her background.

She had first considered revealing all at this meeting when she had realised that Schenker's undertaking to protect her friends and family for as long as she cooperated was in fact erroneous. For a start, under her new circumstances, she would probably never know if anything did happen to them. She also reasoned that the best way to ensure that she had a regular stream of information to satisfy him was to get the Poles to provide it. That way, at least she could remain true to her principles and she might even achieve something worthwhile without increasing the existing risk to those she had left behind. But she had finally made up her mind to throw her lot in with the Home Army when she managed to hide one of the leaflets retained by Schenker. The evidence it provided made her feel confident that they would then believe and accept her.

So, after she had been 'patted down' to make sure she was unarmed, she told her Kaszubian interviewers the whole truth without embellishment or omission. She slowly talked them through everything that had happened since she joined the White Rose and she then handed over the documents that were concealed in her underwear. First she gave them the file given to her by her handler, the one she had shown the messenger, a heavily censored and mostly innocuous account of the existence and purpose of the Edelweiss Pirates. Then she handed over the genuine White Rose leaflet.

She held nothing back and they were both amazed and impressed with the story and surprised by the account of her own personal involvement and capture. The amount of detail and the obvious emotion in her voice convinced them that it was the truth. She confirmed the authorship and authenticity of the leaflet but could offer no such assurance regarding the other documents. Her detailed, repetitive and probing debrief took three full days and only ended when she had nothing left to reveal. Messages were then passed up and down the organisational chain, checks were made and follow-up enquiries initiated. Intelligence assessments were also completed until, nearly two weeks later, the Home Army were totally satisfied with her credentials and very excited about her potential. But prudence was not cast aside entirely and certain precautions were implemented. Nevertheless, a provisional plan was approved at the highest level to make best use of her skills, position and aptitude. They hoped to place her in a district where she could regularly feed misinformation to Schenker, whilst obtaining high-grade intelligence for the Poles.

In view of Stan's earlier tetchiness I waited for him to pause before I asked my question, "Did they do anything with the White Rose leaflet?"

"Yes, it was one of those found in her possession when she was arrested – bulletin number six – and it was forwarded to the British along with a fictitious account of its discovery and the Propaganda Department had a field day. The Allies edited it slightly and then airdropped millions of copies right across Germany. So you could say that the Gestapo and Schenker scored an own goal. In a roundabout way they managed to achieve maximum publicity, perhaps even saturation coverage for their own protesters' anti-government vitriol. They had unwittingly paved the way for their enemies to effectively pour further scorn on the Nazi regime and disenchant the German people: to a degree and intensity that the White Rose members could only have imagined in their wildest dreams. Quite a memorial to them I think."

"Perhaps you're right, but they paid a terrible price." I waited for a second or two to see if he was going to continue, but he said nothing, just stared off into space, deeply wrapped up in his own thoughts. So I asked, "At the risk of being told off again, what or who were the Edelweiss Pirates?"

He looked towards me rather vacantly, scratched hard at his scar and blinked twice as he refocused and then said, "That's not really that important for now, Mick. I'll gladly tell you another time but I'm determined to finish Urszula's story first. I'm already beginning to feel a bit tired, so we should crack on."

He told me that the Kaszubian Griffin underground network kept her at Szczecin for a while, until an Intelligence Officer came from Warsaw. He had been sent as a part of their precautionary plan to make the final decision as to whether or not she could be trusted and if she was mentally and physically capable of coping with the constant dangers of being a double agent. He was looking for certain personality traits and he was pleased with what he found. She was highly intelligent, spoke several languages fluently, coped well with isolation and was calm and stable under stress. Even when tortured she had held out for as long as possible and the process had hardened her and forced her to commit to the Allied cause. What convinced him of her real potential, however, was that she was sceptical, almost cynical, of the motivations of others and was not easy to manipulate, yet she was zealous about her own desire 'to do whatever it takes' to bring down the Nazi regime. She was also prepared to take great personal risks to do so. He found her to be naturally quiet and thoughtful, courteously careful with her behaviour and attitude, almost secretive with her opinions and he was in no doubt that she would take great personal pleasure in deceiving her German controller on an almost daily basis.

He concluded that she was clandestine by nature and would enjoy the constant deception for its own sake. He thought that with a little more training she could also take full advantage of her beauty and poise, to control, direct and deceive, almost at will. Satisfied, he helped her complete the first task that Schenker had set her. She had to build her own radio to keep in touch with the Abwehr. Then he acted as her handler, briefed her for her first mission and provided her with her new identity and false documents.

I couldn't stop myself. I just had to interrupt again. "That can't be right! Surely the Germans provided their spies with radios, just like we did with the SOE?"

"Not always. After all, this was an infiltration operation, so just think about it from their point of view for a minute or two. If the Poles accepted her, then she would be searched and so would her address. They would watch her or detain her and at the very least be suspicious of her for some time. She wouldn't be given much freedom of movement and she certainly couldn't have any contact with Germans during the acceptance stage. So the risks inherent in providing her with a radio were just too great and it wasn't as if she had other cell members to help her. As they saw it, she was entirely on her own in the viper's nest, especially in the beginning. It was far safer to let her build one when she felt she had enough time and space and it was by no means unusual for them to operate this way, after all they had taught her exactly how to do it."

"I suppose that makes sense, but it's still a surprise. It doesn't exactly fit in with this fixed idea I've got in my head, admittedly probably obtained from books, films and television, of how these agents operated." He tut-tutted in derision but made no other comment and moved on.

He explained that she had received further intelligence and briefing-cum-training from a local commander before she left on that first undercover, intelligence-gathering mission and I was taken by total surprise at what he said next.

"She went to Koszalin. She was sent there to find out exactly what was going on at the Freiherr von Fritsch Barracks and the country house where the pilots were staying. With her German background, her general bearing and beauty, backed up by her forged documents and cover story, she had no trouble getting a job as a waitress at the local Nazi bordello and she used all her skills and wiles to discover the facts. Well as much of the truth as was humanly possible in such a close-knit and secretive training establishment and perhaps I'll tell you a bit more about that another time."

As he spoke I had become convinced that this was no strange coincidence and suddenly I realised the full significance. "So she must be the woman who met Dominik and the others in the forest and briefed him about the rocket troops training programme, the Spartans and all the rest of it. Danuta is Urszula!"

Stan slowly and mockingly clapped his hands together several times. "I know you always get there in the end, Mick but sometimes you need a nudge or two along the way. Yes, Danuta was her Polish code name throughout the war, but the Germans knew her as 'Katze'. The surprise doesn't end there either because we need to explore the intimate relationship that gradually developed between her and Dominik."

He scratched at his scar again as his mind seemed to drift away to another time and place, probably long in the past and then he looked straight at me. "Yes, you definitely need to know all about that, but not today. I seem to be so tired all the time. I suppose that's just another cross I've got to bear. Anyway, I'm going to bed."

He stood up very slowly and made for the bathroom. At the door he turned and said, "I'm sure you don't want to spend another uncomfortable night on the floor either. Why don't you go home and have a proper rest. You can see yourself out and I hope we'll both feel much fresher in the morning. Who knows, tomorrow I might also have time to tell you about my part in the great escape from POW Camp 23." Then he laughed and locked the bathroom door.

He had this vexing knack of always springing revelations on me at the end of the day when I thought he was winding down and I was not at my most attentive, to say the least. Perhaps that explains, to some extent, why I suddenly became fixated on two words instead of thinking about the real implications of his disclosures. I was left undecided as to whether he was using the word 'waitress' euphemistically or not. Annoyingly, the thought stayed with me most of the way home, until a similar uncertainty crept in about his use of the word 'intimate'. These semantics seemed to take on a huge yet dubious significance in my tired and befuddled brain, to the exclusion of almost everything else. I too was in desperate need of an early night and all further thoughts of prostitutes, wartime relationships and prisoner of war camps would have to wait.

Chapter Eighteen

THE HONEY TRAP

Swindon – 15th November 2009

Stan was waiting at the door for me the following morning and the transformation from the previous night was amazing. He was bright, cheerful and eager.

"Come on in, Mick and please do hurry up. I've been thinking about how I can best tell you what happened to us all between the summer of 1943 and the end of 1944. I hope I've got the sequence of events straight in mind now, but it was a long time ago and they were strange and exciting times. Much of what I'm about to tell you I only discovered from the others long after the event, so you might need to check on some of the dates and places."

He sat down at the kitchen table, sorting through his notes and papers, talking to himself as he arranged them into two separate piles. Then, whilst he mumbled away, he started rummaging around in a small box of photographs, apparently looking for one particular item, telling himself, "It's here somewhere, I know it is. I found it only the other day. Oh, what have I done with it? Come on Stan get a grip!"

I left him to his impatient self-admonishment and made us both a cup of coffee, an arrangement that had gradually developed into an unspoken rite, to be performed before we settled down each morning for another instalment from Stan's astonishing chronicle. I was just about to return to the table with our drinks when he exclaimed, "Got you, you elusive little bugger!" and he held up his prize for me to see. It was a three inch by two inch black and white photograph showing a young Stan with his arm around the shoulder of another man and they were both in German army NCO's uniforms. The second man's face was also very badly scarred and he was wearing an eye patch. I said, "That's got to be you and Flight Sergeant Bernard Slawinski."

He smiled and pointed to the other two people sat in chairs in front of them and obviously posing for the camera, "That's Marcin and Dominik, but do you recognise the uniforms they're wearing?"

I took it from Stan and had a closer look, "Well it's the Free Polish Army, I can see the shoulder flash, but they could be from any unit. It's impossible to tell with such a small print."

"It's the 5th Polish Guard Company."

I was surprised and quickly compared the snap against the guards' group photograph that had originally been in the chest with all the other items and I was not mistaken.

"From what you told me I thought that you and possibly Bernard were going to act as plants but that Dominik and the rest were going to carry on working for the SOE. So why are they in guards' uniform in this photograph but neither of them appear on the official one?" Even as I said it I realised the obvious. They were still working for the SOE, but what was so important to keep them all in the UK when their defined role was in occupied Europe?

He tactfully ignored my hasty question and carefully put the photograph on top of one of the piles.

"Just a minute, Mick, I don't want to muddle these up and that belongs on there with all the prisoner of war camp stuff. But I really want to tell you about it in the order that it happened so I've got to start with the other pile. Then if we take it one step at a time, you'll eventually know about everything that happened to Dominik, Urszula and the rest of us."

I sat down, secretly wishing he would just get on with it and gave him his cup of coffee. Between sips he asked me rather earnestly, "What do you know about the Zamość Uprising?

I didn't have to think about that one, "Absolutely nothing at all. I've never heard of it but judging by your tone, I think that's about to change." Then he told me and although I thought I had become inured to the horrors of the Nazi regime, I was once again shaken by the depraved levels of calculated and inhuman cruelty.

Zamość, Poland – August 1943

I learned that the Zamość Uprising was a term generally used to describe the actions by the Polish resistance movement against the forced expulsion of civilians from the Zamość region of the General Government. Under the Nazi Generalplan Ost, the Polish population were to be replaced by German citizens. The Death Camps of Sobibor, Majdanek and Belzek were established in this area and during 1942 and 1943 up to 10,000 Jews a day were being murdered there. Belzek the nearest to Zamość, being only about a mile south of the town's railway station, was the first Nazi extermination camp created during the Holocaust as a part of 'the final solution'. It was established specifically for the implementation of *Aktion Reinhard*: the extermination of the Jews in the General Government area. From March 1942 to the end of June 1943, over half a million Jews and tens of thousands of Catholic Poles were 'exterminated' in this one camp. There were only a handful of survivors.

Following the decimation of the Jewish population in the Zamość district, the Nazis laid claim to the entire locality and declared it to be the 'First Resettlement Area' of the General Government. They ruthlessly evacuated over 300 villages, uprooting over 100,000 Polish peasants to make room for SS men and the Volksdeutsche to settle there. In many of these villages, the Germans organised mass executions and over 10,000 people perished in the course of the 'ethnic cleansing'. The survivors were sent either to Auschwitz or other camps or used for forced labour.

More than 50,000 Poles were deported to Germany from the Zamość region alone.

Even more Machiavellian, over 30,000 children were taken from their parents. Some died in Auschwitz or at other camps or in the course of the deportations. Others, while passing through the Zamość transit camp, were selected for their apparent Aryan racial characteristics and were considered suitable for 'reclamation' under a process called 'Eindeutschung'. They were screened for adoption by Nazi Party and SS members. The chosen were told that their parents were dead (often but not always true) and were inculcated with repeated xenophobic lies and distortions, all designed to make them reject their past and their Polish heritage. They were given German names and indoctrinated in the right and rites of Aryan supremacy in an attempt to make them proud of their new nationality and racial identity. Even after the war ended, very few of these kidnapped children were ever reunited with their real parents. This SS policy of mass murder, brutality, child abduction and expulsion of the Poles in the Zamość region was the spark that lit the fire of widespread popular resistance to German rule. Even the German administration commonly referred to the rebellion in their official reports as the 'Zamość uprising' and having set the background, Stan then explained the SOE involvement.

Virtually all the AK fighters had withdrawn from the towns and villages over the previous year or so to avoid the round-ups and persecution and had since set up operations from within the many large forests that existed throughout the district. They fought back fiercely, often attacking German convoys, bases and patrols with several hundred fighters at a time. The result of months of this guerrilla warfare was that the Germans concentrated their forces in the urban areas, but the Poles operated virtually unhindered in the countryside. Then in August 1943, the Zamość Commander of the AK sent an intelligence report to Warsaw concerning SS Gruppenführer und Generalleutnant der Polizei, Odilo Globocnik (nicknamed 'Globus'). This was the man hated and feared by the

Poles, who had been charged personally by Himmler to establish and oversee all the death camps in the Zamość and Lublin area and to take complete charge of Operation Reinhard. The report stated that Globocnik had recently fallen out of favour with Berlin because he had demonstrably failed to bring in sufficient numbers of German settlers and despite the Jewish slaughter and crackdown on the Poles, he had failed to pacify the area.

He was to be replaced by Dieter Kaufmann who was one of only twelve officers forming Himmler's inner circle and a regular visitor to Hitler's Berghof. He was something of a loner but a fervent, loyal and trusted Nazi, with a fearsome reputation as a military and police leader who was only called upon to deal with the most difficult and demanding of tasks, where speed, experience and audacity were required. In between missions he was kept in Berlin, always working on Himmler's own pet projects. The Reichsführer liked to treat him as his personal trouble-shooter, the man who could be relied upon to prevent disaster, so he kept him close at hand until he was once more required in the field.

In response to the Zamość slaughter the AK had hastily arranged a special operation to kill the mass murderer Globocnik before he left. Although this was primarily a revenge assassination attempt, it was also intended to shock and intimidate the replacement. Unfortunately Globocnik was not even in the German convoy they attacked, but they did capture a Hauptsturmführer (SS captain) who was wounded in the leg and refused to answer any questions. A live SS prisoner, especially an officer, was a very rare commodity in those parts and so the Divisional Intelligence Officer was immediately dispatched from his headquarters to personally take charge of him. Unfortunately, the AK never had a chance to interrogate him because he killed himself whilst being held in a cellar, awaiting his arrival. He slashed his wrists with a piece of shattered headlight glass that he had picked up from the road at the ambush site.

His briefcase contained little of significance except for one encrypted file addressed to Kaufmann which, together with a report on the captain's capture and death, was forwarded via

Warsaw to Polish Intelligence in London. The intelligence analyst receiving the report became extremely interested in the SS captain because he was apparently en route with a coded dispatch for a very high-ranking and politically influential senior officer. His actions also suggested that right from the point of capture he had planned to commit suicide rather than face interrogation. This meant he was certainly no mere messenger but perhaps someone very well connected to the Nazi hierarchy or privy to highly classified information, and so he preferred to die rather than risk being forced to give up his secrets. Alternatively, in view of the location, he also thought it possible that the captain was personally linked to Nazi war crimes and by killing himself he was trying to prevent any exposure of the facts. Either way, he was sufficiently intrigued to mark it 'top priority' for the codebreakers.

When the documents were deciphered it appeared that the file had been sent to Kaufmann from the commandant of the Sobibor Concentration Camp, Hauptsturmführer Franz Karl Reichleitner, who had seemingly added nothing other than Kaufmann's name and rank and the nine words 'as discussed – found on the body of the Jew,' all inserted above his signature on the front page. He was ex-Gestapo and had also been the commander of the Hartheim Euthanasia Centre during the Nazis Aktion T4. It is estimated that a total of 30,000 people, including hundreds of Polish priests, were murdered at this one location (there were five others) by using carbon monoxide poisoning. The whole operation was supervised by so-called 'euthanasia doctors'. Amongst those killed at Hartheim were the sick and the handicapped as well as about 12,000 prisoners from concentration camps. The official records attempted to hide their fate with duplicitous entries such as "sent on recreational holiday" or "transferred for more suitable work" or "moved to another hospital nearer home". The nature of their 'sickness' was often recorded on these documents as: German hater, communist, Polish fanatic, homosexual or workshy. Reichleitner was very experienced in mass murder, long before he went to Sobibor.

The file contained no other signatures, references or clues as to the details of the author/s and the papers consisted almost entirely of mathematical formulae, indecipherable results of wind tunnel tests, and lists of micro-measurements and specifications. The experts concluded that they related to jet propulsion and Wunderwaffen research and experimentation, but their initial heightened level of interest shot through the roof when they also managed to decode a few words included within the various sub-headings of the documents. There were references to 'Chronos (time), centrifuge, implosion theory, vortex motive power, Die Glocke (The Bell)' – and finally a link, something they had definitely seen before, just a few critical words at the end of the file, 'could be linked to the Leonidas project'. This provided the only concrete lead and as it had previously been encountered on the Peenemünde operation, Dominik and his team were sent straight back to Koszalin. Their instructions were to contact Urszula, bring her up to date and help her discover exactly what was going on at the Freiherr von Fritsch Barracks and the nearby country house.

Dominik was delighted to meet Urszula again. He had thought of her almost constantly since the Peenemünde operation and it was those treasured images that had carried him through the dark days after the death of Konrad. He had thought that was where she would always remain. As a beautiful, charming and passionate lover she could exist only in his most vivid of dreams. Despite his hopes and needs, he feared she would be unattainable, a never-ageing enchantment he would constantly treasure and take to the grave. Such thoughts often troubled him through the day because they made him feel weak and vulnerable but at night they comforted and sustained him, driving away the horrors of war and brutality. Then suddenly, another twist of fate had thrown them back together and he couldn't hide his boyish joy when he walked into the isolated barn on the outskirts of Koszalin to find her waiting inside.

He felt embarrassed by his obvious but unfamiliar clumsiness and naivety as he embraced her and kissed her cheeks, all with far too much squeeze and infatuated enthusiasm. She pushed him away firmly and now expecting to be rebuffed, he looked enquiringly into her face. She slowly raised her eyes to meet his gaze and her initial look of surprise and petty annoyance gradually melted away and was replaced by a broad smile of realisation and acceptance. High on sentiment and anxiety, he totally forgot his flowery and ardent speech, honed and perfected by numerous rehearsals. He simply blurted out his feelings for her, describing his dreams and hoping she would not see him as fixated or obsessive or be too shocked or offended by the detail.

Urszula waited for a moment, seemingly thinking through the consequences of what she would do next before she took a pace forward to occupy the space between them. She then pulled him in, stood on tiptoe and tilting her head back, she reached up and kissed him several times. She said very little, other than soothing words of comfort, tenderness and encouragement and just a few minutes later on the soft hay at the back of the barn, with all thoughts of the mission and danger temporarily put to one side, they became lovers.

The next morning, as he held her protectively in his arms, she slowly told him her story, explaining why she was dedicated to the Allied cause and how she had become a double agent. She also spoke of where she worked and why, leaving him to fill in the unsavoury but necessary blanks, but she assured him that although she flattered, flirted and teased to obtain facts, she was not a prostitute. Finally, she brought him right up to date with her latest intelligence-gathering operation at the brothel.

"I've found out they're creating a new Luftwaffe unit called Kampfgeschwader (Battle Wing) 200 or KG 200."

"What's it for?"

"It's going to be their special operations wing. It's intended to take responsibility for all long-distance reconnaissance flights, the testing of new aircraft designs and for operating captured aircraft to deliver saboteurs and agents behind our lines. A few of the selected pilots are on a special course preparing them for their new role. Some are billeted here at the camp, but most of them are staying at a requisitioned manor house about five miles away. It's the same one that they used to house the oath-taking pilots and most of the current crews use the facilities at our bar."

"How did you find out about this new unit?"

"One of them has taken a real fancy to me and luckily for us, when he's maudlin and has had too much to drink, which is virtually every night, he doesn't just let things slip; he talks to me quite openly as if I was one of his comrades. He's always bemoaning the loss of his brother and as he puts it, so many of his other fellow pilots who were just too young to die. When he passes out I also get the chance to listen to his troubled ramblings and go through his pockets. I think he's disgruntled and demoralised, that's why he's so careless and undisciplined. He's not at all security conscious. Apparently, he's the youngest son of a once powerful but eccentric baron from Lower Saxony. I think it's only his inherent and aristocratic sense of duty and honour that keeps him fighting for the Nazi cause, but by all accounts he is one of their most successful fighter pilots."

Dominik found it difficult to concentrate solely on what she was saying. His thoughts kept drifting back to their own relationship and whether they had a future together. He wanted to interpret her assurance that she was not a prostitute so that it would also mean that she didn't use sexual intercourse as a weapon to ensnare or beguile her targets. But he had seen enough of what war could do to warp and subvert normal morality. He doubted that even if she wanted to, she could maintain such a stance if she came under direct suspicion or simply needed to submit in order to get all the information she was after. He wondered how she would then cope and how it might affect them both.

For his own part he concluded that he would just have to accept the need for her to use her body in such a way. A part of him was certain that she already had, simply because it was necessary if the mission was to succeed. He only hoped that her considerable mental strength and experience of torture and abuse meant that she would be able to disassociate and rationalise her need to become a whore. All these thoughts rushed through his mind, not because he felt angry feelings of possession or jealously but because he needed to prepare himself for every eventuality. He did not judge her. He loved her and wanted to protect her. He realised that he had done so from the very moment they had met. As he mulled things over, he also came to accept that their relationship might be fleeting because the chances were that one or both of them would be captured or killed during the operation. Nevertheless, he needed to minimise the risks and he realised that to do so effectively and consistently, he had to be on top form: so he forced his mind back to the job in hand and the specific brief.

"Have you heard any more about the Leonidas or the Spartans?"

She came straight back, "I think it's all linked together. Hanna Reitsch, the glider champion from before the war, is now a top test pilot and she's visited the camp several times and addressed the pilots. Apparently, and as crazy as it seems to us, they're drawing up plans to turn the V1 into a manned aircraft by adding a small cockpit and flight controls. They're calling it the Fi-103r Reichenberg and Reitsch is convinced that she will be able to fly it and so will they once they've had the new training."

"How will it be used? Are they going to be suicide pilots?"

"Well, as far as I can gather they're supposed to line it up on their target and then bail out. That's the stated plan anyway, but they're already referring to it as the Himmelfahrtskommando, which literally means 'a trip to heaven mission,' so they must know that there's really no chance of survival."

Dominik made the connection. "So the Nazis think they can save Germany in the same way that Leonidas, the Greek king of Sparta stopped the invading Persian army at the Thermopylae pass. Just 300 elite warriors fighting to the last man, but instead of spears the Nazi unit will be armed with flying bombs."

She said, "I'm not really surprised, they always seem to harp on about the great and ancient historical legends. They're fascinated with all that military bravery and sacrifice, but they never learn the wider lessons of history and that could be their downfall. Well, let's hope so."

He was not surprised that she had learnt so much in such a short time. She was indeed an amazing woman and he was reluctant to put her in more danger. Then as he pondered what to do next, he thought he had hit upon the answer to both their problems. Yes, he had definitely made up his mind, but he felt that until his own mission was complete he couldn't act on it. Whatever the consequences for himself, he intended to take her back with him. Back to the comparative safety of England and the warm generosity of the people who had taken the Poles into their homes and their hearts. Blinded by his own affection for her and the thought that they had both done enough and sacrificed enough for the Allied cause, it never occurred to him, not even for a second, that she might not agree. Pleased with his own decisiveness he returned to their operation and asked, "Can you get into this pilot's quarters?"

"I don't know. I might have to work on him for a while, but he's here for another twelve weeks so it should be possible. What have you got in mind?"

He opened up his rucksack and said, "Hide this in his room or in a suitable communal area where we're most likely to pick up something really useful but minimise the risks involved as much as you can. If you can't find anywhere appropriate, somewhere it's unlikely to be found by accident then don't leave it at all. And don't forget, you've also got to be able to retrieve it without drawing any attention to yourself."

He then handed her the listening device supplied by Station IX. In comparison to the minute and sophisticated electronic wizardry of today it was both crude and very bulky. This was despite the boffins' best attempts to strip it back to the minimum of necessary components to reduce its overall size. In essence, it was simply a crystal microphone linked to a shoebox-sized wire recorder but it worked well enough and he showed her how to operate it and change the spools over. He spent some time explaining how best to avoid the common problems of massive knots and breakages and how to splice the wire. He gave her twelve spools, measuring 2¾ inches in diameter and ¾ of an inch thick. Each one held 7,000 feet of tightly coiled stainless steel wire, not much thicker than a human hair and could record continuously for up to an hour. She would quickly discover that working with such thin, springy and tangle-prone wire could be an absolute nightmare. He also gave her the headphones for use on playback and a few tips and ideas on how best to secrete the microphone and recorder.

He then asked if she had heard any mention of the words Chronos, centrifuge, implosion theory, vortex motive power or the Bell amongst the pilots' conversations. He was not surprised when she answered in the negative and he told her the little he knew before giving her the latest list of 'false intelligence' to be forwarded to her German handler. It was a mixture of lies, exaggeration and minor or irrelevant military and political truths: all packaged together to confirm her credentials and usefulness whilst simultaneously misleading the Abwehr. Finally, they agreed a location for a message drop and then said their lingering goodbyes. Much later she returned to her room at the bar/brothel and Dominik set out to brief his team at the safe house on the edge of town.

Over the next few weeks the Poles settled into an uneasy domestic routine. Although they were primarily waiting for Urszula to report progress they were well aware of the very high level of personal risk involved, exposing her to discovery or capture at any time. Furthermore, the longer they stayed in position themselves, the more vulnerable they would become and so they decided to give her no longer than eight weeks before they would be forced to act independently. They needed an alternative and so they all threw in ideas and proposals, some of which were more outlandish than others and crumbled under collective scrutiny but eventually they thrashed out the details of an alternative last-ditch option. Dominik then shared out the various reconnaissance tasks, making sure that everyone was totally involved in both the preparation and the collective ownership of the new scheme.

Six weeks later, having finally worked through all their what ifs, they were ready to break into the camp's administrative block and search for documentary evidence or other clues relating to the research, manufacture and deployment of the feared Nazi Wunderwaffen. Having virtually accepted the need for Plan B, Dominik was somewhat surprised and very relieved to find a note waiting for collection at the drop. After seven previous weekly visits to the graveyard that had left him empty-handed he was beginning to think the worst and the concern and dread for Urszula had been slowly eating away at his professional resolve. He had been seriously considering bringing the alternative plan forward, but everything changed again when he deciphered the message:

I passed on your gift to my friend a week ago and she is already delighted with the music. It sounds wonderful and she wants to thank you herself.

It was clear enough: the device was in place and she had something definite and promising to report. The use of the word 'herself' rather than 'personally' at the end, also told him that she would meet him at the alternative rendezvous point, three hours earlier than the previous meet. She was being extra cautious and telling him so.

Dominik had found the waiting intolerable and he ached for her company, but he also felt guilty that his concentration of effort and thought were constantly being pulled away from the operation to fixate on Urszula and her safety. Soldiering was in his blood and the warrior in him became increasingly concerned about their romantic involvement. He knew it would inevitably compromise the team's security, put all their lives in ever more danger and ultimately could jeopardise the whole mission. Being fully aware of what his duty and country demanded of him and well used to personal sacrifice, he chastised himself for behaving like a besotted adolescent. He resolved to talk things through with Urszula, but he could still see no obvious solution to the problem.

He loved Urszula as he had loved his precious Bogdana and having lived like a monk and denied himself of female company for far too long, he could not contemplate losing her to a war that had already taken everything he treasured. He had never felt so emotionally confused or ambivalent and he anxiously hoped that she would be more judicious and offer wise council. Such unaccustomed indecisiveness was leaving him moribund, but deep down he knew exactly why he was at such a total loss. At that subconscious level he recognised that he was in desperate need, not only of the gratification and solace of her body and her affection, but also for the adrenaline and clarity of purpose that only combat offered him.

They met in an outbuilding at the rear of a bakery owned by a member of the Griffin and before she could say anything he told her exactly how disconcerted he was feeling and then asked, "So, that's where we are as far as I can make out. What do you think we should do about it?"

She hugged and kissed him before replying, "Oh Dominik, I love you dearly. Surely we're both entitled to grab whatever happiness we can. I agree that the operation has got to take priority and neither of us must do anything to compromise it, but we're safe here and I think we should take full advantage of the opportunity on offer."

After they had made love she said, "I worry about you just as much and I don't think you need to stay here any longer. I'm sure you'll agree too when you hear what I've discovered."

He sat in silence as she told him. He heard about the massive research and development programme to produce modern super-weapons that the Germans hoped would halt and then decimate the advancing Russian armies and turn the course of the war back in their favour. He was amazed and stunned by the audacity and dreadful potential of her words as she summarised her analysis of the various conversations captured on the secret recordings. As he listened to the many examples of advanced, cutting-edge technology he became increasingly incredulous. Each incremental element seemed to be more farfetched, until the whole story sounded more like the wild imaginings of a science-fiction novel than a reliable breakdown of the enemy's military research programme.

She started with Professor Heinrich Focke's experimentation with Vertical-Take-Off-and-Landing (VTOL) and circular wing aircraft. The creation of the jet engine had enabled him to design a propulsion system known as the 'turbo-shaft' (which is still used in helicopters today), and in 1939 he patented a revolutionary saucer-type aircraft with enclosed twin rotors. The exhaust nozzle forked at the end of the engine, forming two auxiliary combustion chambers located on the trailing edge of the wing. When extra fuel was fed in they effectively became afterburners and provided horizontal propulsion. Control at low speed was achieved by alternately varying the power from each auxiliary combustion chamber.

Then she mentioned Dr Alexander Lippisch, the leading German aviation expert who had worked at the Gottingen Aviation Institute. In collaboration with experts at Darmstadt and Munich Universities he had built a series of small triangular aircraft using rocket propulsion, after which he began working on his most advanced design – the Lippisch Supersonic Flying Wing: a triangular, delta-wing aircraft that was light years ahead of anything else anywhere in the world. In addition, she told him about the Horten brothers who had also built several effective flying-wing prototypes incorporating a composite material made of laminated plywood, sawdust, charcoal and glue. Apparently, this absorbed radar waves, giving it a highly desirable and potentially deadly 'stealth' capability.

She moved on to a specialised team, established at a secret facility at Prague airport (Prag-Kbley) working with the blueprints of another, more complex and larger disc-like aircraft. It had been designed by the German aviation experts Schriever, Habermohl and Meithe, assisted by an Italian, Bellonzo. They had been experimenting there since 1941 and it was believed that the chosen prototype would be ready for testing by the end of 1944. Within the complex they called the aircraft 'the flying top' or 'the spinning top' because of its similarity to the child's toy, and the pilots had been told that it would fly at 1,000 mph at altitudes of up to 30,000 feet. It was described as a flat hoop or skirt that spun around a fixed pilot's cabin in the shape of a dome. It carried a crew of three, had a retractable undercarriage and incorporated steerable disc wings and remote nozzles to provide VTOL and horizontal flight.

Of the ten or so prototypes, the largest was some 40 yards in diameter and the project, which had originally been run by George Klein under the control of Albert Speer at the Armament Ministry, had recently been completely taken over by the SS. They were determined to move into production as soon as possible and it was rumoured that the new commander, SS-Gruppenführer Hans Kammler, had already selected the most suitable model. Interestingly, some of the preparatory fabrication and component testing for this design had taken place at Peenemünde. The propulsion, stability and guidance systems in the V2 and those in the flying-disc were also designed around the jet engines and gyroscopes that had already been tested on the island. That work had then continued at the Mittelwerk underground facility once the rocket programme had been transferred.

Swindon –15th November 2009

Stan was not in the least surprised when I butted in, "Come on Stan, I know the Germans were working on a whole range of fearsome weapons, like jet aircraft, rocketry, massive guns and stealth technology. I can even accept that they intended to use suicide pilots and develop nuclear weapons, but I'm sorry, I just can't entertain the idea of flying saucers! For God's sake! You must be mad!"

He laughed, "You've reacted just as I thought you would. Look, nobody called them flying saucers in those days; that name came along after the war in 1947 in America when it was used in the press to describe UFOs, and these certainly weren't alien craft."

"Exactly! And I don't believe in any of that crap about inter-stellar spaceships, UFOs, or the associated nonsense about visitors from other planets. It's complete drivel and should be consigned to history's dustbin, along with all the conspiracy theories concocted by educated nitwits with too much time on their hands."

He came straight back at me, "Have I told you anything, anything at all in all the time we've been meeting that has proved to be baseless or untrue?"

"Well, no, but you can't expect me to accept that the Nazi's invented flying saucers. Although we've moved on nearly 70 years in real time and light years in technological advancement, it's just as preposterous today as it was then. That should tell you all you need to know about flying bloody saucers. You'll be telling me about alien abductions and little green men next."

"Come on Mick, don't go right off at a tangent. All I'm asking you to accept is that they were building and testing prototype disc-like aircraft and flying-wings, some of which were jet propelled and capable of VTOL. Taken together, they posed a significant and mounting threat to the Allies. Especially so, when you consider that they had a nuclear programme including the Bell running in tandem and their best brains, technicians, pilots and arms experts had been siphoned off from other projects to speed things up. What's more, the whole enterprise was shrouded in the utmost secrecy and was being controlled and driven by the SS. After all, you're the only one who's mentioned flying saucers! So can you do that? Just bear with me on this?"

I knew that if I kept on resisting he would gradually wear me down and so still somewhat reluctantly, I nodded my acquiescence, "Okay, I'm listening but please, let's keep it all well within the bounds of reality."

He was just as serious and determined, "I have and I will. I can assure you that what you've heard is true enough and certainly no more outlandish than some of the other things I'll be telling you about. But for now, I think you've had enough for one day. We both have. You need some time to think about what you've heard and please don't dwell on thoughts of flying saucers. It just confuses the issue. You need to think more about the science and less about the fiction. Tomorrow we'll go back to Koszalin and hopefully carry on with Urszula and Dominik's story without you picking holes in everything."

Stan's attitude at calling an abrupt halt to the day's proceedings was rather a surprise to me. It seemed a bit over the top, even though he was becoming increasingly crotchety when challenged. Nevertheless, he was right insomuch as I needed more time to think things through and write up my notes and he needed his rest. I decided it was best all round just to do as he wished and so I thanked him and left for home.

Chapter Nineteen

CAPTURE

Swindon – 16th November 2009

Stan was most apologetic about the previous day. He said that he had felt on top form first thing in the morning but had later suffered from acid indigestion, and had then developed a throbbing headache. As the day had progressed the discomfort and pain had increased and the combination had gradually worn him down until he just wanted to 'close his eyes and rest in a darkened room'. He assured me that it was a one-off and nothing to worry about and that a good night's sleep had worked wonders. He insisted that he was now feeling fine and so we had our first cup of coffee of the day before he once again took me back to the Koszalin story. He immediately whetted my appetite by revealing that Urszula had deliberately saved the best information to last but she finally got around to revealing what she knew about the Bell...

She told Dominik that she had hit the jackpot.

"I also know what Die Glocke is. It's being used at a secret facility near to or inside the Wenceslas mine, close to the Czech border. The programme is also known as 'Chronos' and it's a centrifuge device forged out of a very hard, heavy metal with a ceramic outer skin. It's approximately 10 feet wide by 13 feet high with a hemispherical domed top giving it the overall shape of a large bell: hence the name."

Dominik could hardly control his impatience, "But what does it do?"

"Well, it contains two counter-rotating drums or cylinders which are filled with a mercury-like substance which they've code-named 'Xerum 525' and it consumes prodigious amounts of electrical power and glows when operated, even for very short periods. It's been described as a heavy particle accelerator or an artificial neutron source, whatever that is. Anyway, the director of the project is Professor Walther Gerlach who is the leader of or at least a very senior manager at the Nazi's Atomic Weapons Research Programme and about three months ago he also visited the training school here."

Dominik was really no wiser. "The only thing that's clear to me is that I don't really understand anything you've just told me about it. I still have no idea of how it works, but I've heard enough to realise that I don't like the sound of it and neither will our bosses. But are you seriously telling me that you got all this information from the aristocratic pilot's recordings? How do you remember it in such detail when I haven't even heard of most of the technical terms you've used?"

She smiled at him and then got up and stood behind him before bending over to kiss him on the forehead when he turned to look up at her. "I've got a photographic memory and so you should realise that I'll never forget your face or the way you stare at me with such wonder and lust, especially when you think I'm not looking." Then she laughed and he joined in.

Having lightened the mood, she went on to explain that she had already discovered that before his course the pilot was stationed at an airfield near Turnov. It was just inside the Polish border with Czechoslovakia and halfway between the Wenceslas mine and the Prag-Kbley site to the northeast of Prague. He had also told her that he had flown over both establishments many times and had once made an emergency landing at the Prague base. The two secret sites were only about 80 miles apart and so he had also managed to pick up a great deal of rumour and gossip. This was her main reason for choosing to hide the recorder in his room.

Dominik was genuinely impressed with her ability and he was momentarily tempted to take her in his arms again, but he immediately dismissed the idea as recklessly indulgent. He forced himself to pursue his question about her amazing memory.

"From what you've said I can understand how you would be able to remember and later recall a specific document or a poem or some other written material, but how did you cope with these voice recordings? I would have thought it needed a different process altogether."

She tried to explain, "I've been recording for ten days now and virtually the whole course has been in his room at one time or another and they're always drinking and talking about how they think things will turn out in the end. So while he's been sleeping off his exertions and the drink, I've pieced everything together by listening to hours of their incessant ramblings."

She explained that she had managed to tease out what was relevant by analysing all their discussions and arguments and disregarding the mass of masculine posturing and often meaningless and high-spirited jousting and inter-unit banter. She had gradually built up quite a comprehensive picture of the current state of their research programmes. Then she wrote it all down, carefully cross-referencing, evaluating and constantly re-playing and checking, searching for linkages. She did this time and time again, and during her visits to the airman she carefully probed for confirmation or clarification. Finally, she committed the pages to memory, destroyed her notes and hid the wire spools.

Then she made him laugh again, "Unfortunately it has also meant that I've had to wade through a mire of endless, gratuitously graphic and competitive accounts of their seemingly impressive, and often overly-athletic, sexual conquests. And most of them were with the girls at the bar who have been shipped in from southern Germany and France. The local girls keep well away, some because they hate the Nazis and the rest because they don't want to be labelled as collaborators or punished by the underground."

"Good for them, but I think we should quickly pass over the details of the airmen's sex lives. It was probably little more than wishful thinking or boastful exaggeration anyway. The military are made that way the whole world over. We need to get back to the serious business of the Bell. Have you any idea how it works or what they're going to use it for?"

"They say 'it breeds weapons-grade uranium'. I don't know what that means either, but it certainly sounds ominous. If you need any more proof then you should also know that they've uniquely given the project the Third Reich's highest known classification of secrecy and funding. That's priority category 'Kriegsentscheidend' which literally means 'critical to the outcome of the war'. The only other fact I could glean was that it emits strong levels of radiation whenever it's activated. Apparently, it has killed dozens of animals that they've deliberately exposed it to just to test the effects of the process. By all accounts they were liquefied and the pilots have also heard rumours that several scientists were killed during the early experiments. Of course, these reports may well be exaggerated."

Listening to her menacing account and remarkable powers of recall, Dominik began to formulate a plan to get her back to England and out of danger. He asked, "Have you removed the recorder from his room yet."

"No, I wanted to check with you first as to whether we have enough or if you wanted me to leave it a bit longer. I've got two spools left and I was going to give them all back to you the next time we meet."

Dominik did not hesitate as the final element of his plan dropped into place. "No, you've been magnificent already and we shouldn't push our luck. You've probably got far more than our masters could ever have hoped for anyway. So let me know when you've recovered the equipment and I'll make the arrangements to get us all out as soon as possible."

She kissed him and then stood back to look at his face. "I'm not coming with you, Dominik. If I disappear, even for a few days, I'll come under immediate suspicion. Your government needs me in place here and now that you've got a pretty good idea what they're up to, surely you of all people can see exactly where my duty must be. I can't possibly leave. We've all worked too hard and sacrificed too much to abandon such a rich seam of intelligence. I'll try to remove the recorder tonight and I'll let you have it back, along with the recordings and that should reduce any risk of discovery and I promise I'll be extra careful from now on."

Dominik was determined to see his idea through and he came straight back at her, "I'm sorry but no – you can't stay here. You've got to come back with us and that's an order. The information locked inside your head takes priority over everything else. It could change the whole course of the war and it needs to be heard by experts. I can't possibly remember it all and there's bound to be small details, perhaps even something critical, that you haven't told me. No, I'm sure they'll want an in-depth and comprehensive debrief from you personally when we get back, even if that means that you're finished as an agent."

She was not about to give up without a fight. "I disagree. There's really no need whatsoever for me to leave. You'll have all the recordings and I can write up my report and analysis in code. I'll give you everything I've got, in the minutest of detail, or I could even record it onto one of the spare spools for you to take back."

"Don't you see, Urszula? We just can't afford to write it down – and you will not record it onto a spool either. In fact, you've got to destroy the recorder and the tapes straight away. They've served their purpose and we don't need them anymore." She started to interrupt but he impatiently waved her off and spoke over her, "Look at me! The stakes are just too high and to keep them would be one risk too far. If they manage to find us with that evidence, it would give them all the time they need to cover their tracks, to move things around and to make their security virtually watertight. We would never get another chance so we simply can't take that risk, not with this grade of material. You have all the information we need. It's listed, tabulated and recorded inside your brain so you're coming with us and that's final. As much as I want you back home for myself, for the two of us: it's now become an operational necessity."

She knew his mind was made up and although she was beginning to see some merit in his argument, she was not totally convinced. She worried that his understandable focus on her personal safety was preventing him from being truly objective and it felt as if her mission as a double agent was being cancelled far too prematurely. She could not hide the disappointment in her voice when she answered, "I'm not sure about any of this, but you're the commander and, of course, I'll follow your instructions. I just hope that they'll see it your way when we're back in London."

Early that evening she destroyed the wire spools and then once again, accompanied the pilot back to his quarters and when he eventually fell asleep she took the opportunity to get dressed and silently carry his chair across from the desk and stand on it to recover the recorder and microphone from their hiding place. They had been tucked neatly behind the beautifully carved crest and surrounding tracery that formed the centrepiece atop the deeply arched cornice on the eight-foot-tall, antique oak armoire that dominated the whole room. She placed the equipment at the bottom of her overnight bag, underneath her toiletries and change of clothes. Then, without disturbing his slumber, she quietly slipped out the door and down the stunning, cantilevered marble staircase with its highly polished and sparkling gold-plated balustrade and solid brass rail. He had told her that the inspiration for such a rare and beautiful feature inside an otherwise run-of-the-mill country house was Madame de Pompadour's staircase at the Petit Trianon Palace at Versailles.

As she slowly descended in her stockinged feet, trying to avoid the slightest noise and being guided by the moonlight seeping through the massive windows, she recalled how he had spoken so enthusiastically and with such authority. His conversation returned to her, almost word for word and she distinctly remembered him telling her that the pattern on the panels between the balusters was 'a classical, swirling Vitruvian scroll motif', a term that she had never heard of before. He also emphasised, with no small degree of pride and respect, that the staff spent many hours every day polishing it to maintain the incredible lustre. She smiled to herself when she reached the cavernous, oak-panelled and carpeted entrance hall, satisfied that her considerable powers of concentration and recollection had not been adversely affected, not even by the highest levels of stress and danger. She slipped her shoes back on, feeling confident in her own ability and pleased with the success of the operation. She was even beginning to look forward to the escape to England and the inevitable opportunities and challenges that a happy and contented life with Dominik would surely provide.

However, the next thought that flashed through her mind was that 'pride cometh before the fall' and it was triggered at the very moment that she heard the ominous and echoing click of a wall switch. The hall was flooded with bright artificial light from the central chandelier and the half dozen, large, metal wall sconces. She had been taken completely by surprise and before she could react a voice boomed out, "Stay exactly where you are and you will come to no harm. Try to escape and you will be shot!" As soon as she saw him standing in the corner by the huge, iron-studded front door she knew she was in serious trouble. He was an SS general: tall, broad, supremely confident and dressed all in black, an imposing and intimidating figure, standing perfectly still, totally in command and pointing his Luger directly at her. He was flanked by three other soldiers armed with submachine guns and two men in civilian clothes. She had seen enough of their ilk in recent months to know that they were unmistakably Gestapo.

In those crucial seconds, just before she took the most important decision of her life, she had only two considerations. Firstly, the mere presence of such a high-ranking officer meant that this was not some routine security check or a speculative operation that she could talk her way out off. No, this was a well-organised and pre-emptive strike. They were definitely onto her. Her second thought was to escape or at least prevent them from taking her alive, but the former seemed impossible. She made her decision – and she hoped that they would all open fire as soon as she moved. The thought of further torture and brutal, repeated rape terrified her even more than death itself. She would not be captured.

She spun around, reaching into her pocket and taking hold of the tiny box as she did so and she ran straight towards the passageway that led past the drawing room and the library, to the rear door beyond. No one fired at her as she covered the first six paces into the corridor, shaking the cyanide capsule free from its container as she went, just managing to prevent it falling to the floor by juggling it into the palm of her hand. She uttered an audible gasp of relief, realising that she had nearly lost what was probably her last and only chance of true escape. So she held it secure and ready, silently said her final goodbye to Dominik and asked God to at least protect the man she loved. But then, just as she drew level with the drawing room door, a soldier stepped out from the library up ahead and blocked her path.

She stopped dead in her tracks and without a nanosecond's hesitation she popped the pill straight into her mouth. At that very moment another, unseen SS soldier, a Scharführer (sergeant) standing just inside the drawing room, reversed his rifle and punched the metal butt straight into the side of her head. She never saw it coming, not even a blur of movement and being exacerbated by the narrow width and concave curvature of the stock, the heavy blow was concentrated into two points of impact. It split open her cheek and smashed into the side of her forehead. She collapsed to the floor, bleeding profusely and rendered completely unconscious.

SS Gruppenführer und Generalleutnant der Polizei, Dieter Kaufmann walked purposefully towards her body issuing orders and carrying the bag she had dropped in the hall. The sergeant's police training and his operational confidence had been reinforced and heightened at the detailed and very professional briefing that had been personally delivered by the general. This very rare, probably unique occurrence, and the fact that all those taking part had been handpicked by him from the best units throughout the region, illustrated the critical importance of the operation.

They all knew what to expect and they had been warned that she would certainly try to escape and might even take a suicide pill or a 'kill-pill' as the general called it. He said that it would most likely be an oval capsule, about the size of a pea, consisting of a thin-walled glass ampoule covered in a rubber solution to protect it against any accidental damage. It would probably be filled with a concentrated solution of potassium cyanide or cyanide salts. He surprised many by explaining that the pills were never swallowed whole because they would simply pass harmlessly through the digestive system. Instead they had to be crushed between the user's teeth and only then was the fast-acting poison released. He emphasised to his men that death would follow within just a few minutes, much too quickly for any medical intervention. He told his troops several times throughout the briefing that she had to be taken alive and he finished with the same demand, banging his fist on the table in time to his words, just to reinforce the point.

Although the sergeant had been fully prepared and he was waiting, poised to strike, he had indeed reacted with incredible speed and awareness. As soon as he saw her raise her hand to her mouth he instinctively struck her violently on the side of the head in the hope that the impact or the whiplash would dislodge the pill. When that failed, he followed her to the floor and in one fluid movement he had her on her side and his fingers in her mouth. He hooked out the pill from under her tongue, along with a pool of blood and two of her teeth. He examined the suicide tablet and then, apparently satisfied, he crushed it into the floor with the heel of his boot, catching a telltale whiff of bitter almonds.

Before the general had reached him he had already examined her injuries and was applying pressure to her wounds to stop the bleeding. The general's words at the briefing were still ringing in his ears and he was absolutely delighted that he had managed to keep her alive for his boss. But he also wanted her fit enough for an early interview and so to avoid any further deterioration in her condition, he gave his report while still on his knees tending her.

"She didn't have time to swallow the pill and I got it out in one piece, Sir. I'm also pretty sure that there's nothing broken.

She's lost a few teeth and her face is badly lacerated, so she needs stitching up, but she should come round within an hour or so with no lasting damage. I should think that by then the dizziness, nausea and a blinding headache will be the least of her worries."

Kaufmann directed that the whole establishment be mustered outside and the commanding officer ordered to report to him in the hall. The prearranged search teams were brought into the house and their section leaders told to await his orders. Whilst they all gathered he wasted no time in boosting morale and reinforcing his own reputation as an outstanding leader by publically congratulating and commending the soldier who had struck her and brought her down. He then sent him and two others to take the prisoner to the military hospital.

He gave staccato and precise orders, "You will handcuff her and that's how she's to remain. All three of you will stay with her at all times. They will do nothing other than stitch her up. No other treatment whatsoever. If she comes to, she will speak to no one and you will personally vet the one doctor who treats her. She will not be seen by any other staff, medical or otherwise, not even a nurse. You will then take her back to our headquarters. There will be no diversions, delays or problems. Are my orders perfectly clear?" A chorus of "Yes Sir" was the only response expected and it was delivered with volume and enthusiasm.

When the commanding officer arrived, still half-dressed and dishevelled, Kaufmann wasted no time. He pulled the wire recorder from the bag and held it up for all to see before addressing the already sweating Luftwaffe Oberst (colonel).

"This establishment is a shambles and a fiasco and you are responsible for it. A spy has been coming and going at will and has been recording our secrets so that they can be delivered to the enemy. She has done this with impunity right under your nose. Your guards, your security measures and your personnel are a diabolical disgrace and an affront to the Führer and all our brave soldiers, sailors and airmen who risk their lives daily. While they are making the ultimate sacrifice you are drinking, whoring and behaving like clowns. Well, this is certainly a circus, but no more.

Colonel, you are under arrest for gross dereliction of duty and treason."

He ordered him removed from the premises and sent for his deputy who was already awaiting the summons and desperate to do anything asked of him in order to enhance his own position and limit the damage to the establishment.

Just a few days previously he had informed the SS that as he was walking past the pilot's room he had noticed that the door was ajar and could hear him inside having a conversation with a colleague. He distinctly heard words to the effect of 'they reckon that the Bell is a secret weapon that could end the war in days, but apparently it could also cost millions of lives. And what about our own families if they should retaliate in kind?' He had also discovered that the same pilot was regularly smuggling a girl from the local brothel into the house at night, contrary to standing orders, good discipline and common sense.

He had immediately taken his suspicions to the commandant who told him in, no uncertain terms, not to be so gullible and prudish because such unfounded and fanciful rumours were always circulating and, of course, the men would talk about them. He dismissed him out of hand with the words, "Secret wonder weapons – nonsense, you're just grasping at straws. What is important and compelling is that our flyers are likely to die in combat at any time. Their life expectancy can be measured in days and so I think they're also entitled to do a bit of whoring first. So don't bother me again with your melodramatics, just concentrate on your proper duties. Leave me to run this place properly, back in the real world where I do the worrying and decide what is really important, and you just do as you're told."

He was not deterred by his senior officer's stance, but before he could go over his head he thought he needed some more tangible evidence and so he decided to conduct an off-the-record room inspection. He waited until the pilot left for the day's training and then he went on his own fishing expedition. He could hardly believe his luck and his confidence soared when he found what he thought was a recording device hidden on top of the wardrobe.

Within a few hours of the report the information had already reached Reichsführer SS und Chef der Polizei, Heinrich Himmler, who immediately telephoned Kaufmann at Zamość demanding to see him the next day. On arrival in Berlin he was briefed personally by Himmler on his mission to Koszalin. There were to be no written orders, but he was told that he had been selected because of his proven track record in crushing organised resistance and in testing and pointing out the weaknesses in a number of security systems designed to protect their secret weapons establishments. Himmler thought that he had a rare ability to spot weaknesses that eluded others, even in the most thorough and complex of plans. He had already appointed Gruppenführer der Polizei, Frank Daecher to replace him at Lublin and Zamość so that he was free of all his other responsibilities.

Himmler summed up, "So, yet again, I'm putting my trust in your ability. While I ratchet up project security I want you to clear up this mess and make sure that nothing leaks out about the Bell. There will be no mention of this operation on your personal file and as far as everyone else is concerned, you're back in Poland sorting out the peasants' revolt."

As he spoke, Kaufmann thought for a moment or two about telling him of Reichleitner's recent telephone call concerning the documents hidden by the Jewish scientist. The commandant had told him that the prisoner had been sent to Sobibor from the Mittelwerk underground plant after he had been discovered hoarding food and the file had been found hidden in his clothes by one of the Ukrainian guards during 'delousing'. Unfortunately, the Jew could not be questioned because he had been shot and killed when he foolishly tried to snatch the papers back and kept shouting out, "The world must know about the Bell!" So to some degree or another, the secret was already out and Kaufmann had intended to launch an investigation once the file was in his possession and he knew exactly what he was dealing with. Nevertheless, he suspected it was indeed a major security breach because Reichleitner had said that the document was indecipherable, suggesting it was in code. So after quickly considering all this he decided against mentioning it, preferring not to send Himmler into a rage over the delay. He felt it was much better to deal with one threat at a time.

The Reichsführer SS concluded the meeting with the words, "Whatever else you do, just make sure you don't let me down. I'll be perfectly blunt so that there can be no room for any misunderstanding between us. You have served me well up to now, but if you fail this time it could cost us the war and it will most certainly cost you dearly. If you succeed I'll put you in sole charge of the whole Bell operation so that between us we can sew it up tight once and for all. This latest debacle has proved that I need my best man in the role, someone I can rely on to get the job done whatever the cost. I really can't stress enough just how important this is. So do your duty for the glory of the Reich."

On his arrival at Koszalin Kaufmann had immediately launched 'Operation Redline' to detain the suspects and hunt down all their underground contacts. He would not rest until the whole conspiracy had been wrapped up and the threat to the Bell eradicated. His career and his life probably depended on it. Reichleitner's file would have to wait a while longer.

From the moment that Dominik was summoned by the Griffin commander he feared the worst. Any lingering hope evaporated and he knew that Urszula must have been killed or taken when he was told that the Nazis had launched a major city-wide operation against the underground movement. In the first day alone sixty separate premises had been raided and over 200 arrests were made. A 48-hour curfew had been imposed and SS troops, roadblocks and mobile snatch-squads were everywhere. The whole town was under siege and notices were being hand delivered to every house and business. They called upon the occupants to identify and hand over all the terrorists and saboteurs. They said they were the ones solely responsible for martial law having being declared in the first place and also for the inevitable difficulties, shortages and hardships that it would cause for the whole population. Ambiguously but chillingly it concluded with the phrase, 'not a single man, woman or child is safe while they remain at large'.

Additionally loudspeaker vans toured the streets ordering people to stay indoors, cooperate with the authorities and denounce the terrorists and traitors. They warned that anyone found helping, hiding or associating with the culprits would be shot, and the same fate awaited those who withheld any information as to their identity or whereabouts.

Apart from Urszula, most of those initially detained were not fighters and had little knowledge of the organisation but a few were connected and could lead the enemy deeper into their ranks. They both knew that it would not take long for the SS to torture the information from them and the commander said as much. So worried was he by the size, extent and unprecedented coordination of the German action that he had suspended all active and planned operations and activated their own contingency plans. All their key players were ordered to leave their homes and escape into the countryside or to go into hiding.

He said to Dominik, "If you stay here I'm afraid it's only a matter of time before they find you. My recommendation is that your team split up and move out. I'll give each of you one of my best people as a guide and you should arrange for your extraction as soon as possible."

Dominik then asked the one question that was plaguing his mind, but he was dreading the answer, "Is Urszula dead?"

"I just don't know, not yet anyway but judging from the way they're attacking us I should think it's most likely. That would explain why they've been forced to try to find another way into our organisation."

Dominik could see his logic, but he knew something that the commander didn't. She was a double agent and she was very good at what she did. He desperately hoped that perhaps there was still a slim chance that she could manipulate events to save herself. While he was pondering on this, the commander filled the silence.

"I don't know what you've discovered and I don't want to know, but you've certainly got them well and truly rattled and they're in one hell of a hurry. So my official order to you is that you don't hang about here any longer. To be honest, I've got more than enough on my plate now without having to worry about your team's safety and so I want you gone. I'm sorry if that sounds ungrateful and brutal, but I've got to think of the whole organisation and we're by no means ready for a full-scale battle. "

While there was still a possibility that she was alive Dominik wanted to stay. He even considered ordering his team to leave and remaining behind himself, but he knew they would probably refuse to go without him. Even then, they could do little without the support and intelligence-gathering capability of the Griffin and in view of the commander's remarks that was asking just too much. It was also obvious now that any last-ditch appeal would just fall on deaf ears. On reflection, he decided that if the mission was to be anything other than a total failure, then the only realistic option was to return to England with the limited information he had. He would have to hope that if she survived, then some sort of rescue mission based on reliable and accurate intelligence could be planned from there. So he finalised the arrangements for his team to travel to their secondary extraction position just outside the village of Karsin about 75 miles to the south-east.

It took two weeks before they all met up again at the rendezvous where they found out that the Home Army had already arranged for them to be flown out on a Liberator which had been fitted with extra fuel tanks. This flight, from the recently formed all-Polish Special Duties Flight (Home Squadron) was not being used in its normal role to drop parachutists but was going to land to deliver its cargo. It contained weapons, spare parts and explosives, three replacement radio operators and two Polish officers from the 2nd Corps who had been training in Palestine before being sent on active service to Italy. They had been the most senior railway systems engineers in Warsaw before the war. Captured by the Russians in September 1939, they had been transported to the Gulag but had managed to escape with Anders army. They had now been 'volunteered' to return to provide technical advice and support to the AK.

In light of the Russian offensive the underground were planning a major operation to sever all west-east railway communications, to prevent the Germans from making any major troop or equipment movements, either to reinforce or resupply. The engineers, who were not parachute trained, would help select the most appropriate and vulnerable targets. The planners believed that their professional knowledge and experience was also necessary to fully exploit the ensuing chaos and maximise the extent and duration of the damage. They could also provide details of any reliable track engineers still working on the system who could then be recruited to help. So the aircrew had been instructed to take the extra risks involved in a rapid touchdown and turnaround.

In contrast to the relatively small deployment needed for a parachute drop, a major AK operation was necessary to ensure a successful landing and takeoff. A remote large field or meadow was a necessity. As was a defendable protective perimeter and limited vehicular access in order to make it easier to control the approaches and attack any enemy incursion before they could become organised. A reception team was still needed and additionally, a flare path detail, section commanders, spotters, good communications and adequate transport were all vital. In total some 200 fighters would be on the ground. In the event the prearranged identification codes were confirmed and the plane landed safely on the reduced runway in the stubble field. The unloading and exchange of passengers took less than seven minutes and the team were safely home by dawn.

Chapter Twenty

KAUFMANN'S WEB

Swindon – 17th November 2009

I knew there was something seriously wrong as soon as Stan failed to answer the door. He had always either been waiting for me or he would call out as soon as I rang the bell - but not today. I thought I had got to know him quite well and felt certain that if he had gone out he would have left a message pinned to the door. On my first visit I had noticed that there were several pinhole marks and pieces of old tape residue sticking to the door jamb. I looked through the letterbox, but there was no sign of him in the hall. I listened but there was only silence from inside. I called out several times, but there was no response and so I ran round to the back and looked through a small crack in the curtains in his rear bedroom window. I could see him collapsed on the floor between the foot of the bed and the door. The back door was also locked. I called an ambulance and then had a quick hunt around, just in case he kept a back door key 'hidden' in one of those favourite places which a burglar would no doubt find in a matter of seconds, but I drew a blank. Some detective I was in a time of crisis.

Then I remembered that both doors were fitted with deadlocks, security chains and bolts and so I smashed a pane of glass in the kitchen window and managed to get in. He was unconscious but breathing shallowly. I moved him into the semi-prone position, checked his airway and took his pulse. It was weak and thready and his lips were blue, his skin clammy and he was ashen grey in colour. It seemed fairly obvious that he had suffered a heart attack and so I made him as comfortable as I could, threw some essentials into a bag for him and waited for the paramedics.

They were great and their no-nonsense professionalism, thorough examination and constant reassurance without minimising the seriousness of his condition, filled me with some hope. They quickly wired him up to a monitor and administered oxygen as they wheeled him to the ambulance. When I glanced inside it looked more like a mobile emergency clinic, loaded with complex technology, lights and alarms. It struck me that these men and women were quietly and efficiently saving hundreds of lives up and down the country every single day. Almost unnoticed, they were using their considerable medical training and first-aid skills, well-rehearsed and sophisticated recovery techniques and procedures, and administering life-saving and painkilling drugs. I had no idea of how much they were paid but as we raced away, I knew it was nowhere near enough.

The driver had explained that speed was of the essence. The quicker they got him to hospital, the better his chances of survival and a full recovery. It was blue lights and sirens nearly all the way to the Great Western. We arrived just a few minutes later, having been through most of the traffic lights on red, almost continuously exceeding the speed limit, passing the wrong side of several keep-left bollards and travelling against the flow of traffic down a one-way street. As soon as we arrived he was whisked into casualty and I was asked all the usual questions about what had happened, what was his medical history, where were his relatives and his next of kin? I told them the little I knew, but as far as I was aware he had no family left, not in the UK at any rate. Then I waited, and as the hours ticked by ever so slowly, I waited and waited…

They eventually sent me home at 6 pm with the news that he had come round but had been moved into the Coronary Care

Unit where they were carrying out diagnostic tests before they could decide on any future treatment. The casualty doctor told me that I would be unable to see him until the next day at the earliest and she explained that the first 48 hours would be crucial. If he survived that period, then there was a good chance of a decent recovery. She assured me that they would let me know if there was any change and advised me to telephone in the morning.

When driving home I reflected on the increasing vulnerability of our old folk, particularly as they now lived longer, many finding it difficult to manage financially and some not seeing their relatives for months or years at a time. They have been left to cope on their own as everyday life becomes more of a struggle or they are moved into care homes. What a misnomer that had proved to be in too many infamous cases. I thought that in comparison Stan had been fortunate so far, but perhaps that had all changed now. I was sad that such an independent and fiercely self-reliant man had in just an instant become so helpless and dependant, and for the first time I realised just how much he meant to me. I had known him for only a relatively short time but he had so quickly earned my respect and admiration as an incredibly brave and remarkable man. He had endured so much, and along with the other members of Dominik's team he had been a linchpin in so many of the critical Polish and Allied wartime operations. He was larger than life, a modest and humorous hero who even in old age was driven by an inner force and determination that would have eluded most of us, even in our twenties.

I had come to regard him as a true friend and a mischievous father figure or perhaps a favourite uncle would be a more accurate metaphor. Having examined his life and character in such a close and personal way and having been privy to his innermost thoughts and emotions, it was hardly surprising that some of his attitude, enthusiasm and spirit had inevitably rubbed off on me. I was convinced that I was a better and more compassionate person for knowing him. Yes, he was an old man who had already had a long, eventful and fulfilling life, but I desperately wanted him to survive and for the first time in many years I found myself praying, even though it felt hypocritical for such a lapsed Catholic. It was just that he really was too good a man to lose so suddenly and at that moment I could do nothing else to help him. I also felt guilty. Judging from his increased touchiness he had obviously been unwell for a few days and yet I had simply accepted his assurance that it was just dyspepsia, migraine and general tiredness: nothing to worry about. What would I have discovered if I had taken the trouble to ask him just a few searching questions? Perhaps I would have become concerned enough to insist on him seeing his doctor. If I had taken him straight away would it have prevented the heart attack? I didn't know the answers, but I felt certain I had failed him. I should have realised that he wouldn't want to worry me and would play it down and I should have been more aware of the potential consequences.

Then I started to think about the things that he had already requested of me and the hints he had dropped about what he had yet to ask me to do. I found myself solemnly promising to see it all through, whether he continued to be there to help, tease and guide me or even if I had to go it alone – I would be honoured to do it in his memory. I certainly owed him that much. No sooner had these thoughts formed than I found myself changing tack as I tried to convince myself that I was worrying needlessly. Of course he was going to be alright. He had been a fighter all his life and that was hardly likely to change now, especially when he had unfinished business, but I still had a very restless night, finally falling asleep just before dawn.

When I was able to speak to a doctor shortly before ten o'clock, he told me that Stan was fully alert and responsive, but weak. The results of his initial blood test had shown that there was only minimal damage to the heart muscle. The ECG and angiogram had confirmed that the cause of the heart attack was atherosclerosis. He explained that his coronary arteries had become narrowed over many years by a build-up of fatty deposits known as plaques. Following the tests they had successfully treated him with thrombolytic therapy, an injection to break down the clot that had formed when the plaques had broken away from the artery wall and partially blocked the blood flow, which had caused the initial heart attack. He added that despite his age, his chance of making a full recovery was now much better. They could also reduce the risk of him suffering another heart attack or a stroke by a combination of medication, a low-fat and high-fibre diet and regular but approved exercise. He then rather pointedly made it clear that, for the time being, he needed plenty of rest to allow his heart to recover and that, 'This doctor's strict orders are no demanding visitors, no anxiety, no stress and no return to his flat until a full home assessment has been conducted by the occupational therapist'. He would also have to be seen by a member of the cardiac rehabilitation team.

I finally got to visit him on Mercury Ward on the fourth day after his admission. He was looking more like the feisty Stan I'd come to know. I was also relieved to see that he wasn't covered in tubes, he wasn't sleepy and he hadn't lost his sense of humour. He smiled straight away and although his voice sounded weaker, he started talking as soon as I sat down.

"Hell's bells, Mick, I've got to go back to school you know and this is what they're going to do. So listen carefully or you'll miss something really important." He then rattled off a missive, mimicking a teacher's voice, with authority and gravitas. "'We will assess all your coronary risk factors and then give you a full and comprehensive but personally tailored exercise and education programme, with regular reviews and attainable short- and long-term goals, and even advise you about your lifestyle, habits, medication and recommended living aids.'" He added, "Now I really am out of breath and guess what, I didn't even know I had a 'lifestyle'. Up until yesterday I thought I was just a boring old fart and my habits were unmentionable. Now, it'll all be out in the open, laid bare for you and the whole neighbourhood to see and what's more, I'll have a different topic to cover every week. Homework as well I expect."

"Oh Stan, I do hope you're taking some of this seriously. You've had a very close shave, so they're right, and you need to do everything you can to stop it happening again."

"Of course I am, all of it, but it is daunting. On the one hand, I don't want to lose this new-found 'lifestyle' when it holds so much promise. But on the other, we both know I might not make it next time anyway. I am 86 after all and I can't go on forever. I suppose this uncertainty is just another cross I've got to bear. Anyway, I learnt all that hospital-speak stuff and almost word-perfect too, from one of their leaflets, just to impress you on your first visit."

"But what have you really learnt so far?"

"Too many pizzas, pies, chips, crisps, pasties and beer, that's where the real blame lies. But why is it that everything that's supposed to be bad for you always tastes great and everything that's good for you always tastes like shit? I suppose that's another of life's unanswerable questions, just like how does a snowplough driver get to work?"

I had to laugh at his efforts to lighten the mood and I stood up and held his hand, "Stan, you don't need to quote leaflets at me to make an impression. You've always amazed me, you know and despite your odd jokes and chronic flippancy, you must have been listening to some of what the staff have said because on the way in the nurse told me the good news. They are satisfied enough with your progress to allow you to go home tomorrow or the next day at least."

He looked at his watch, "Okay, you've made your point so I promise there will be less levity here from now on, at least for today. So let's get down to business then. We've only got an hour left before Sister will come over and throw you out so she can tuck me in for the night." He chuckled to himself at the very thought and said, "Get your notebook out then and I'll tell you what happened next."

I didn't argue. It was far less stressful all round just to do as he suggested, and so I listened as he took me back to Koszalin and continued on with the story of Urszula's arrest...

Kaufmann filled the cells with prisoners and left the woman to stew in her own pain and apprehension. He was a great believer in the sobering and tongue-loosening power of extended solitary confinement. He had decided not to interview her until he had most, if not all of the facts. When the pilot's room had been searched they quickly found the recorder's hiding place. A perfect physical fit was clearly visible, forming an outline in the dust on top of the armoire. The pilot was arrested straight away, as were his three immediate neighbours, one opposite and the two either side. They were joined by the officer in charge of security at the manor house, the duty officer of the watch and the commanding officer who had been under house arrest since the raid. They were kept separate and interviewed over three days, during which they were all threatened with the firing squad.

Although his questioning was aggressive and accusatory to say the least, he had kept an open mind as to their culpability right from the very beginning. Before very long he was totally satisfied that none of them were, in fact, spying for the enemy, but he was equally sure that several of them had been duped into giving away state secrets. So he interviewed them all, time and time again, finding out who had been in the pilot's room since the woman had first been seen in the building. After a few hours they all began to cooperate and as more names were mentioned, they too were arrested. Gradually, by constant cross-referencing and re-interviewing, always seeking corroboration and building up a timeline, he developed a pretty good idea of what had been leaked and by whom.

He knew she was an enemy spy. The recorder in her possession proved that, but he wanted to find out just how deep and wide the conspiracy went and who exactly now knew of the Bell's existence. They searched her room and found nothing incriminating. Enquiries at the bar revealed that she came from Berlin, was highly recommended and had supplied impeccable references, but no one really knew anything else of consequence about her. His experience was that these 'serving girls' lived in each other's pockets and often shared everything, even their most intimate thoughts. She was obviously an exception and she was also overqualified for the work. Such a profile supported his case and it was not altogether unexpected, but he was always thorough and so he had her referees interviewed.

He discovered that the letters were not fakes as he thought probable but genuine correspondence from her previous employers. Naturally, the woman in custody was not the person to whom the references were given. She was about the same age and similar in appearance, but there was a three-inch disparity in their height, they had different coloured eyes and the real owner was apparently still working in Berlin. Of course, the letters of introduction could have been stolen but what was surprising and a real gem of a lead was that one of the referees had told the Gestapo interviewer that he had heard that she was already working again, long before she had asked for the open reference. When the referee had queried the point at the time she had said, rather mysteriously and pompously, that she really couldn't speak too much about her current job because it had to do with important military and intelligence matters. Kaufmann immediately knew that he was on to something.

He went with his hunch and used his influence and contacts in order to bypass inter-departmental red tape and tight security restrictions to conduct a comprehensive search of all intelligence service personnel records (Personalhauptbüros), including the SS, SD, Gestapo and the Abwehr, looking for the real owner of the references. Low and behold, she was eventually flagged up as an Abwehr employee: a typist in Section III F. He knew that was their counter-espionage bureau so now he was pretty sure of what had been going on right from the start and exactly who was responsible. If he was right then the Abwehr in general, and Canaris in particular, would be incensed when they found out what he was about to do.

Himmler had always thought that Admiral Canaris, the head of the Abwehr, was politically unreliable. In fact, he had never really trusted the old-school, military man whom he derided as 'an archaic officer and a misguided gentleman with no Nazi party affiliation or anti-Semitic sympathies'. He suspected that the admiral had supported Hitler in the thirties only because he saw him as the one person with the political organisation and muscle to defeat the spread of communism, which he loathed. The SS commander became even more concerned as Canaris continued, year after year, to preside over a burgeoning Abwehr, relentlessly increasing its power, influence and operational capability.

Meanwhile, a shrewd and politically skilful Canaris, aware of the hostility and rivalry, openly sided with Hitler and Himmler but was already convinced that their plans and policies would lead to certain disaster. He started to secretly work against them to undermine the regime while appearing to cooperate with the SS and SD. Once he had seen first-hand what was happening to the Poles and Jews at the hands of the SS Einsatzgruppen in occupied Poland he was reported as saying 'The Abwehr will have nothing to do with the persecution of Jews'. Later, as details of more massacres and brutality poured in from Abwehr agents across Europe he even opened direct contact with MI6 and asked for details of the Allies' terms for peace if Hitler was removed. He was not particularly surprised when Churchill replied 'unconditional surrender'.

This mutual antipathy, suspicion and intrigue that so divided the leaders of the Abwehr and the SS formed the breeding ground for an intense rivalry and mistrust that spread its tentacles into every level and every facet of the two organisations. To a certain extent this was aggravated and encouraged by Hitler, who consistently distrusted his generals and was often displeased by them. Therefore he tended to rely too heavily on his own instinct. He had an incredible memory for detail and demanded that every point they made had to be correct and consistent with his previous briefings and decisions, but he lacked their military experience and strategic caution. Subsequently, his frustration with them and his desire to be in total control led to him continually meddling in affairs that would have been best left to them. Often dissatisfied, Hitler played one general off against another, sometimes even initiating or sustaining rivalry and antagonism as a means of 'keeping them on their toes'. This, in turn, caused further tension as they then saw themselves in competition with each other, both for his approval and the allocation of scarce resources. Such internecine feuding became a prominent feature within the German high command and a major factor in the downfall of the Nazi Third Reich.

Kaufmann was working towards a position where he could totally discredit Canaris and his whole organisation and give Himmler the excuse he had long been looking for to seize control of the Abwehr and fully assimilate it into the SS. It could then be forced back under rigid Nazi discipline and doctrine where anything less than total loyalty and commitment could be rooted out. So he thought it was time for drastic intervention for which he would need the highest authority and clearance so he telephoned Himmler. He listened to Kaufmann's proposal in silence and then replied, "Do exactly as you suggest. In the meantime I will make some discreet enquiries at this end and prepare for the opportunities and dare I say it, the repercussions if you are mistaken. I'm sure you clearly understand that if it should go wrong, then you will be the one sacrificed as a rogue element. I will not have the SS lose another battle with the Abwehr. Good luck and keep me informed."

The first thing Kaufmann did was send for the Scharführer who had prevented Urszula from killing herself.

"You and I are going to interview the spy. I have chosen you to assist me because you are smart, quick thinking, shrewd and loyal. My orders are: one – nothing that is said between the three of us must be repeated to anyone else, ever; two – you will take notes of the interviews but will say nothing at all, unless I expressly invite you to; and three – she will not be assaulted, tortured or abused in any way. Now repeat those orders back to me, word for word. There must be no mistakes; our mission is far too important to countenance failure."

The sergeant did as he was told.

Kaufmann could see that she was frightened and immediately tried to reassure her that there would be no violence.

"You will not be harmed and for the time being I have only one question for you. It is not a trick question and there is no reason whatsoever why you shouldn't tell me. Who is your handler from Section III F of the Abwehr? You may know it as the Counter-Intelligence Unit, and that title tells us all we need to know."

Her mind raced. She had imagined all sorts of horrors that might well occur in her cell and had considered her response to many different scenarios, but this was altogether different and totally unforeseen. She wondered if it was some kind of test. They must know she was an enemy agent. The recorder proved as much and they wouldn't have arrested her for working for the Abwehr, but then again, he obviously knew she was doing that too. He could have found out who her handler was at any time with just one telephone call, so why not? And why hadn't he bothered to interview her before now? She tried to make sense of it all, but she had too many questions screaming out for answers. Was there something else entirely going on here? Perhaps there was an angle that she could work with, an opportunity that would give her even a slim, outside chance of survival. Alternatively, perhaps the situation was much simpler and she was over complicating it because she couldn't think clearly and logically. Had they begun with such a simple question, one that they already knew the answer to, just to get her talking, hoping that she would then continue to cooperate and answer all their questions? She decided that she needed much more information before she could decide what they were really after and so she quickly stifled the brief germ of hope and kept silent, waiting to see how matters would progress.

Kaufmann waited too. He knew she would be thinking it through and he wanted her imagination to be working on overdrive. The more mental stress and confusion he could create now, the more likely she was to agree to his offer later on. He followed up, "We both know that his job is to protect and guide you. He's probably out there now even as we speak, wondering why you've disappeared and using all his considerable resources to find you and sooner or later he will. You must know that. So let's save us all some time and effort shall we. What's his name?"

Why was he making such a big issue of it? Then it suddenly occurred to her that he wanted to find her handler before he managed to discover where she was. That meant that Kaufmann had no idea of who he was because he hadn't made that telephone call to the Abwehr. So there must be some serious problems between them and she guessed that left her even more vulnerable and defenceless, caught right in the middle. She also believed that protecting the Abwehr was certainly not worth being tortured or dying for and anyway, as she was in the possession of the SS, they were the greatest and most immediate threat. Unless Kaufmann was keeping her for another purpose entirely, she could be shot at any time, on any pretext and that would probably be far more likely in the near future if she continued to stay silent. So she tried to buy some more time to give herself the chance to think it all through more rationally.

For once she relied on her instinct rather than her training, and told him, "Klaus Schenker." He thanked her politely and the Nazis immediately left the room. She was returned to her cell and she pondered on what she had learnt from the short interview and the way Kaufmann had conducted it.

Inwardly the SS general was very relieved that he now had the first piece of concrete evidence to support his theory and he was anxious to press on with his plan while he still had momentum and the element of surprise. The clock was now ticking and once he made his next move he had to expect the Abwehr to react both quickly and robustly. He would need to keep one step ahead and focus on firstly proving the Abwehr's link to the Polish underground and the British. Then he could corrupt the truth to prove that they had conspired against Germany using MI 6 and the woman. If only he could keep control of events he would show that the Abwehr, the so-called premier military intelligence service in the Reich, was passing details of their most secret and deadly weapons systems on to the British. There could be no greater case of treason. But the end game was to prove that the crime was orchestrated at the very top and so he also had to establish a direct conspiracy between Schenker and Canaris. That would not be so easy, but he had a plan that he hoped would culminate in Himmler delivering the coup de grâce.

But first, to make his plan totally convincing he needed another piece of information that he knew he probably wouldn't be able to get from the girl – certainly not in time. So he started to review all the arrest and interview reports of the dozens of underground prisoners and the additional written statements of those who had preferred to cooperate rather than be sent off to a concentration camp. After several hours of sifting and searching he found what he was after. Satisfied, he then issued the orders that sealed the fate of all those arrested in the raids.

The half dozen that had been identified as middle-ranking AK members were to be shot that day and the rest, the underlings and sympathisers, were sent to Neuengamme concentration camp in Hamburg where they would be worked to death in the brick kilns. The aristocratic pilot and four of his colleagues were just too valuable a resource to dispose of. So they were immediately transferred to where they were needed the most: the squadrons operating in defence of the shrinking Eastern Front where there were already insufficient fighter pilots to meet the escalating attrition rate. Here demand for new aircrew had spiralled way out of control. In response, the Nazis started to rush the recruits through a truncated training programme in an effort to quickly plug the massive gaps, with the inevitable result that the quality of their pilots deteriorated rapidly. The vicious circle was then complete because these novices were nowhere near a match for the resurgent enemy and were quickly lost in combat. However, the commander at the manor house and the other officers arrested with him were expendable and they appeared before a hastily convened military tribunal, charged with gross dereliction of duty, subversion of the war effort and undermining morale (Zersetzung der Wehrkraft). They were all convicted and hanged the same day.

The SS general, his sergeant and two Gestapo officers waited inside Schenker's home in Szczecin until he returned from work that night. As he stepped unsuspectingly through his own front door he was quickly and quietly arrested on suspicion of espionage. They then searched his house and vehicle thoroughly, seizing a mass of documents and surveillance photographs before taking him and his wife away in handcuffs, all under the cover of darkness to avoid any public scrutiny. He was outraged – full of bluster and indignation – but he was certainly no fool and immediately recognised a classic set-up when he saw one. His greatest worry was for his wife's safety. She was of a fragile constitution and started crying hysterically as soon as she was forced from her home.

Before they had travelled more than a mile or two in the eighty-mile journey, she had already been slapped several times across the face by her escort in an attempt to shut her up. Each time he hit her, he increased the severity of the blow until she was bleeding freely from the mouth and nose and her constant wailing had been reduced to a mere whimper. Her husband's increasingly loud and impassioned pleas for her to be left alone had been completely ignored, and as the miles passed by his feeling of dread and isolation increased. No matter how much he racked his brain he just couldn't work out what he was being set up for or why it was happening. Who was giving the orders? He took little comfort from the realisation that he probably wasn't simply going to disappear. If they had wanted him dead they would have done it quietly, back at the house. So he was obviously part of some bigger plan, but he had a bad feeling that gnawed away at his diminishing resolve with each passing mile.

Long before they reached their destination he was convinced that it would not end well for either of them. She was obviously brought along as a hostage, an insurance policy to make sure he 'cooperated' whenever they decided to make their demands. When they arrived at the SS headquarters in Koszalin nothing happened to raise his spirits or ease his troubled mind. On the contrary, he was greeted with silence, separated from his wife, stripped naked and thrown into a cell. His shouts and frantic banging on the cell door went unanswered, as did his demands to telephone his Head of Section and even Canaris himself.

First thing the next morning Kaufmann interviewed the woman again. In the stark interview room he was calm, pleasant, quietly spoken and reassuring as he pointed out that her facial injuries were healing well and that she was looking far better. He even apologised for starting so early, removed her handcuffs and offered her toast and coffee but she refused. The sergeant sat alongside him, silent and expressionless, giving nothing away with his note book and pens to hand on the metal table positioned between them. At first the general's tone was conversational, "I think you must have been wrestling with your problem all night, trying desperately to find a way out of your precarious situation. You are obviously an intelligent and gifted young woman and you must have proved that many times so you also know that you are within days, perhaps even hours of facing a bullet, the guillotine or the hangman's noose."

She started to reply, "I've done nothing—" but suddenly he spoke out more sharply, raising his voice and banging his fist down on the table, cutting her off.

"No rehearsed protestations please. We are way past that point and I don't want the sergeant here wasting his valuable time and getting cramp by writing down pages and pages of meaningless nonsense about your innocence and victimhood. No, let's get back to the matter in hand. What are we to do with you? How exactly will it end?

Then he waited for her response and she did not disappoint.

"I'm well aware of what your sort can do. I've seen it all before many times and I'm always horrified and sickened by the brutality and inhumanity that comes so naturally to you. But we both know that you need something from me before you kill me. That's the only reason I'm still alive. So why don't we talk about that. Like your poodle sergeant here, I don't want to waste any of my even more precious time."

He laughed and then looked sideways at the sergeant who remained impassive, carefully writing down her cutting reply. "I would say he's more like a Dobermann Pinscher or a German shepherd than a poodle, very Teutonic and loyal, but we might both see exactly which one he is later on. Nevertheless, you do have a valid point and I agree with the main thrust of your reply, so I think you're ready now. The time to surprise you has definitely arrived, a little earlier than I expected, but I hope that it will also destroy your stereotypical and bitter view of us, dedicated servants of the state that we are."

She felt she had nothing to lose because the veiled threat of setting the brooding sergeant loose convinced her that he had already decided upon her destiny. So she went on the attack.

"You're so good with words, I'll give you that but you're also overconfident, condescending, pompous and arrogant. Coincidentally, the very things I really hate in a man so I'm afraid we won't be able to build up that nice comfortable relationship you're working towards here. You're just not my type, and by the way, the uniform does absolutely nothing for me."

He didn't bite back at her. He simply ignored her remarks and carried on. "But you can survive all this. I don't have to kill you, even though we both know you're a double agent working for the Poles and the British and definitely not for us. But that's all over now so I think you can still see the war through and then go back to happier times: a little more weary and cynical maybe but still young enough to carve out a new life and career. You could get married, have children and once again embrace freedom and replace this deathly nightmare with the power of your dreams."

His unctuousness turned her stomach, but she still encouraged him to throw her his lifeline, knowing full well that it would probably turn out to be just smoke and mirrors.

"And what do I have to do to find this redemption?"

Slowly and deliberately he set it all out for her and she could hardly believe what she was hearing. It was so unexpected and seemed completely illogical. She asked questions about the detail and the assurances he was offering and then he talked her through it once more. Afterwards, in her presence and hearing, he dictated his demands and the conditions of the agreement to the sergeant, who wrote it all down.

Finally, he gave her the two sheets of paper and said, "Take it with you back to your cell and study it. I'll see you again tomorrow for your answer."

She said nothing as she was led away. She was totally focused on trying to rationalise what had just happened and she was anxious to get back to her cell to analyse every single word and phrase. Her mind screamed at her that the proposal was just another Nazi ruse with hidden and fatal consequences for her, but her heart wanted it to be a genuine reprieve and dare she believe it, a way back to Dominik.

At 5am the following morning Kaufmann was roused from his bed by a messenger who told him that his female prisoner had been found unconscious in her cell. He rushed down to the basement and found the duty officer and his sergeant already in attendance. She was coming round as he walked in but looked very pale and was groggy, disoriented and totally uncommunicative. The general immediately demanded to know what had happened. She was so crucial to his plans that he had to keep her alive for a few more days at least, and this was a worry he could well do without.

The duty officer assured him that, in accordance with his instructions, she had not been assaulted or punished in any way and that the guard had simply found her collapsed on the floor. He added that there was no sign of any additional injuries and nothing to indicate that she had attempted to take her own life. He was also satisfied, bearing in mind his considerable experience in cell duty, that she was not faking an illness and in his opinion she had probably just fainted from dehydration and a lack of proper nutrition. He pointed out that she had been refusing most of her drinks and had eaten next to nothing since she had been detained. Kaufmann thanked him for his rapid response and clear and concise report and then ordered his sergeant to make her comfortable, call the duty doctor immediately and wait with her until he arrived. He was not going to risk a recurrence.

Just over an hour later the sergeant reported back. She had indeed fainted from a sudden drop in blood pressure, caused by a combination of her recent poor diet and the early stages of pregnancy. She was, in the doctor's estimation, about eight weeks gone and he had told the sergeant, somewhat tongue in cheek, that he was confident she would safely reach full term, provided her captors fed and watered her properly and did everything possible to reduce her stress levels. Kaufmann was not in the slightest displeased; on the contrary, he left to interview Schenker with a real spring in his step. He had just been handed an extra, totally unexpected and decisive bargaining chip that meant that she would comply.

The guards had been given orders to keep Schenker awake all night, treat him with utter contempt and to rough him up before morning. He was no coward and was quite capable of dishing out his own punishment from time to time, but this was different. Nothing had been done reactively or in the heat of the moment. The abuse was cold, calculated, impersonal and relentless. In their minds he had already ceased to exist as a trusted and relatively senior member of the security services and no longer was he even seen as a sentient human being. Now he understood first hand why so many members of the Abwehr loathed the SS and Gestapo, often provided a safe harbour for their enemies and conspired against them at every opportunity. It was much more than professional rivalry; it was a clash of opposing politics and principles. It was almost undeclared warfare: the old, traditional, plodding and yet reassuringly safe, versus the new, young, reckless and arrogantly strident.

He was also cold, hungry, demoralised and mystified by his sudden and dramatic change in circumstances. Throughout the night he had been driven almost crazy by the sounds of his wife suffering, screaming and calling out to him for help from her cell along the corridor. His desperate pleas to the guards to stop hurting her were mostly ignored, but occasionally they responded with jeers and taunts as to what they would do to her next. His imagination spun out of control, looping a vivid kaleidoscope of the horrors being inflicted on his gentle, innocent and delicate wife. He recognised that their behaviour of detached indifference one minute and cruel and sadistic treatment the next was designed to wear him down and prepare him for interrogation. Make him ripe for the plucking. He wanted to fight it. He wanted to be a hero, rescue his wife and bring these brutes to justice, but he was not made of such stuff. As the night wore on every ounce of resistance was beaten out of him. He gave up when he realised that the only reason the guards ever entered his cell was to give him another beating. So it was the terror of anticipation that was the ultimate and deciding factor.

Schenker was dragged, still naked and handcuffed, into the interview room where he was none too gently strapped into a metal chair. The guards had been rather overzealous in complying with their instructions and although fully conscious, he looked badly beaten about the face and torso. Kaufmann came round the desk and bent over him, but he was already a broken man and he literally shook with fright. He strained so hard against his restraints in a futile attempt to shrink back, to cower away from the dark intimidating presence that the leather straps chafed through the skin on his wrists.

Initially, the general spoke quietly, almost whispering, "You have already been condemned to death. There are only three things left to decide. When and how you are disposed of and what we do with your wife. I and only I will decide on the first two, but you, and only you, can save her. Do exactly as I tell you and she will be released and cared for. She will receive your pension and retain your house. But I can assure you that you are in no position to bargain, delay or refuse. In a moment I will explain why, but firstly I need to know that you have fully understood what I have said so far. You are, after all, in a somewhat distressed and injured state. So have I made myself perfectly clear?"

Kaufmann took a pace back and coldly stared at his prisoner, waiting for a response. Schenker tried to speak but his mouth and throat were so dry from the fear and trauma that he could only croak. He averted his eyes in shame and nodded his head submissively.

The general pulled his own chair round from behind the desk and sat down, just a couple of feet in front of him and the sergeant took out his note book as his boss started, "Well, now we move on and this is what I know to be true. You recruited a female agent, a German national and gave her the code name of Katze using the real identity of a secretary in your own department and you then issued her with authentic identity documents which were also obtained by the same employee in her own name. It was very sloppy and amateurish, even for the Abwehr and that's what first gave you away."

Schenker tried to speak again and this time he managed to utter a few words, "She was ideal for what we wanted—" before Kaufmann screamed at him, "Wait until I've finished! You were going covert within your own organisation because you intended running a rogue agent for private purposes and you were hiding the fact from both your peers and your superiors. There would be no reports, no authorisations, no checks, no supervision and no expenses. She would be working exclusively for you. The question I then asked myself was exactly who were you working for. The British obviously, the Poles perhaps, but who within the Abwehr controlled you? You didn't have the experience, the resources or the connections to set it all up. No, it was the arch-traitor, the man who promotes himself as Mr Convivial but who is really a Janus figure, the snake Canaris!"

Schenker finally realised what was happening. He was just a pawn in an elaborate scheme to topple the head of the Abwehr. He was horrified and despite the warning, he managed to pluck up enough courage to immediately refute the accusation.

"It's nothing to do with Canaris. You've got it all wrong. Her mission was legitimate. She infiltrated the Polish underground—"

Kaufmann punched him once in the face, a backward flick of the wrist but hard enough to reopen the splits in his upper lip and make his nose bleed again. Then quite calmly he stood up, pushed his chair back and leaned over the prisoner, so close that Schenker could smell the garlic sausage that lingered on his breath as he threatened, "You will not speak until I tell you to. You will concentrate on me and listen carefully and then you might, just might, save your precious wife and your own posthumous reputation."

He then collected a towel from the drawer in the desk and dabbed at the prisoner's face, soaking up the blood until he had staunched the worst of the flow. "I know it all, you see. You sent her into the airman's quarters, here in Koszalin, where she planted a recording device provided to you by the British MI6 so that you could obtain our military secrets and hand them to the enemy. We have the evidence, all of it and the woman's signed confession to back it up and prove the whole conspiracy." He paused to allow him to take it in. "Now you can speak, you traitor!"

Schenker could see the noose tightening every time the General piled on the accusations, but after he had cleared his throat and spat out the globules of blood that had been draining there, he tried to defend himself.

"She had penetrated the Polish underground and would have led me to their senior command. They trusted her, she was working her way in for us and she had been giving me authentic and reliable information and I can prove it. We're spies for the Reich, not traitors. I won't, I can't be a part of your perversion of the truth."

"Oh don't you worry. I've sorted out the so-called Griffin, and in just a matter of days. Smashed their organisation and arrested dozens of them, but whatever you two gave them they've already handed it over to the British. It's gone and we can't do anything about that now, so we're into damage limitation. But I'm really not interested in the few amateurs who are left and anyway none of them are going to confirm your account so you're totally on your own." He then said to the sergeant, "Tell the guards to break his wife's legs and then drag her in here so he can see what he is responsible for." He cupped Schenker's chin in his left hand and forced his head up so that he was looking straight into his eyes, "That will be just round one and we can keep it up for days, perhaps even weeks. We won't let her die either but before today is out you will both wish we had."

As the sergeant opened the door to leave, Schenker's tormented voice cried out, "Stop. No more please. She's had enough, you bastard. Leave her alone and I'll say whatever you want. I'll even sign a statement, but I hope you rot in hell for what you're doing. You're a cold-hearted murdering shit." Then he lost his flash of loathing and broke down completely, his head collapsed onto his chest and he sobbed uncontrollably.

Two hours later, once Schenker's signed confession was safely in his hands, the general had him and his wife taken out into the courtyard at the rear of the building where they were blindfolded and shot by a firing squad for treason. He deemed that no trial was necessary, just his signature. With their removal he continued his witness-eradication policy, drastic and immediate action to bury all possible links to the truth. The cover-up had started with the 'disposal' of the Griffin fighters. He wanted to offer up Canaris's head on a platter in the certain knowledge that the 'evidence' could not be challenged. He then telephoned Himmler and they exchanged information before he went off, keyed up and buoyant, ready to interview the woman he now knew to be Urszula Foerster.

He reverted to his friendly, polite persona and asked how she was feeling before placing Schenker's full statement in front of her and telling her to read it before she gave him her answer to his previous day's proposal. As she started to absorb the content she was stunned and he could see it.

"It's genuine – made in front of witnesses and in the true tradition of all written confessions obtained by talented detectives, it contains information that only the offender could know." He took the sheets from her and indicated, "Here on page 2, the name of the MI6 agent that Canaris and Schenker met in Spain in 1942. And again look, at the foot of page 3 the name of Schenker's contact in the Griffin who introduced him to the foreign agent known as DOMINIK!!"

He watched her face closely and could tell immediately from the barely perceptible flash of shock and distress in her eyes that he had pulled off a masterstroke. It was definitely the right man and he now had another name for Himmler. The only name, and mentioned just the once, that he had subsequently been unable to account for or cross-reference in the hundreds of pages of paperwork connected to the Griffin arrests. Neither was he to be found in any official German intelligence records or informant files and he was not known to the local police or prison contacts. Now she had confirmed what he had suspected: he was not just an outsider but a British or Polish spy.

He hammered home his advantage by telling her, "Even if you were not so worried about your own life yesterday, things have now changed dramatically. So much so that our previous agreement of your life for your statement is now off the table. The only option you have left is to save the life of your unborn child and you have to do exactly what I say. You must see that there's nothing else left for you now because I'm holding all the cards. So I'll send the sergeant in and he'll show you where to sign."

He picked up all the papers and left, not waiting for or expecting an answer. The first thing she did was to say a prayer for Dominik, hoping that although they were on to him, he might have already escaped and was safe. Then she wept with frustration and wretchedness, accepting her own total helplessness as she lost even the will to resist. Kaufmann had won and she had no choice. She signed the statement that condemned her.

When Kaufmann had first realised that the Poles had found out about the Bell he had promised himself that one day he would have his revenge on the agent concerned. Now that he had a name, a basic description and reflex confirmation by his accomplice he felt closer to achieving it. As he sat in his office relishing such a moment he also thought about the woman. Suddenly, it occurred to him that her brief but spontaneous reaction when his name had been mentioned was charged with far more emotion than just surprise or concern. Then he realised why. It was passion. They must be lovers and the unborn child was his! The insight gave him the germ of an idea and as he thought it through, a plan began to form in his mind that would resolve two difficult problems.

The following day after a meeting between Kaufmann, the doctor who had treated her and the sergeant, Urszula was sent to the only major concentration camp for women – Ravensbrück near Fürstenberg. It was 40 miles north of Berlin and 55 miles south-west of Szczecin. Uniquely, she had her own SS guard, Kaufmann's sergeant, who delivered her personally to the commandant, SS Captain Fritz Suhren. He also gave him a hand written letter from Kaufmann who cited Himmler's personal authority for the additional document entitled, 'special instructions for this prisoner's detention and treatment'.

At about the same time that the Schenkers were being murdered, Admiral Wilhelm Franz Canaris marched into Himmler's office at Gestapo headquarters at 8 Prinz-Albrecht-Straße in Berlin. He was a small, enigmatic, somewhat frail man who lived on his nerves, but he was very intelligent, well read, sensitive and normally quiet and reserved. He had a very hard, almost impenetrable shell and was a very good listener who was truly at home and came alive in the world of political and military intrigue. He was a master of deceit and subterfuge, as slippery as an eel and as wily as a fox. Wherever he went he sowed mystery and confusion and everyone he met thought they had told him too much but had learnt next to nothing in return. In the First World War he was a celebrated hero, a U-boat captain who quickly progressed to become Germany's top military spy. He was a man with years of espionage experience and he had cultivated hundreds of sources and reliable contacts right across the world. He believed he was more than a match for Himmler and he had come well prepared.

He immediately accused Himmler of trying to undermine his authority with the Führer to satisfy his own personal and long-held lust for the cachet and military veneration that he believed only the Abwehr could bring. He launched into an all-out verbal attack, accusing him of conducting a criminal enterprise to murder his agents and of deliberately sabotaging a major operation where an Abwehr agent had not only successfully penetrated the Polish Resistance but had also talked her way into the very heart of a British spy ring, operating in Poland and Germany.

Himmler was also prepared and he had learnt a great deal from his previous skirmishes with Canaris. This time he did not underestimate him. He pulled a file from his drawer and threw it across the desk at his visitor. He shouted at him that he didn't covet the Abwehr; on the contrary, all he wanted to do was make it work properly. The file contained a catalogue of Abwehr criminality, incompetence and treachery that he had personally prepared for the Führer. It listed the accusations and provided pages of supporting evidence, including proof of the widespread fiddling of expenses and the invention of phantom agents to illegally obtain and siphon off state funds. Then there was the currency racketeering that his organisation was masterminding right across the world with the vast profits being used to run unauthorised and anti-Nazi operations or disappearing into the pockets of certain favoured individuals. It also detailed the non-existence of intelligence evaluation systems with an over-reliance on rumour, gossip, garbled and nonsensical reports and diplomatic chatter, all leading to the deliberate overloading of the system. Because of the gross incompetence of the Abwehr, so the report said, critical intelligence was constantly being lost or overlooked. It was also accused of being a haven for dissidents, Jews and misfits, more interested in political intrigue and the defeat of Nazism, than the destruction of Germany's real enemies. The file concluded with an indictment of Canaris himself for treason against the state. The prosecution facts were laid out clearly and concisely, this time supported by written statements from Kaufman and his sergeant and their star witnesses, Schenker and Urszula.

Canaris never batted an eye, merely suggested that they both see Hitler immediately and present him with the facts and let him decide who was to be sacked or shot. Himmler hesitated, having expected an immediate string of denials and counter-charges he was temporarily wrong-footed. Canaris then followed up by pointing out that Kaufman and the sergeant were obviously

Himmler's men and he suspected the other two 'witnesses' were already dead. Both murdered to prevent them from telling the truth and retracting their statements. He added that he had a file of his own proving that the SS had, for reasons of petty departmental jealousy, deliberately ruined the best chance Germany had of penetrating British Intelligence and had murdered Abwehr staff in the process. What he asked, would Hitler make of that?

He finished by pointing out that he had a copy of Himmler's appointment diary showing the very significant times and dates that he had personally briefed Kaufmann in the last month or two. He threw Himmler's file back at him and allowed himself a smile, and as he turned to leave he pointed out, rather smugly for once, that not all the Abwehr's agents were incompetent. In fact, some were the best in the world, many were known to him personally and they were everywhere, including within the ranks and officer corps of the SS and the Gestapo.

As soon as Canaris left the building Himmler telephoned Kaufmann and called him back to Berlin for a full debrief and reassignment. A week after that meeting, having listened to his protégé's advice and having thought carefully about his options, he raised the subject of the Abwehr and Canaris at one of his regular meetings with Hitler. He never presented his file but started to provide solid evidence of mismanagement, incompetence and lost opportunities within the organisation and constantly questioned Canaris's reliability and loyalty. Over the following weeks he drip fed more information, gradually building the case for the removal of Canaris. He did so without gross exaggeration or claims of treason that would undoubtedly have caused the Führer to fly into a rage and confront the elusive Canaris in circumstances outside of Himmler's control. This softly-softly, incremental and reasoned approach was far more successful and finally Hitler was convinced that he should go. On 12 February 1944, he ordered Canaris to stay out of Berlin and German intelligence was put under Himmler's direct command.

Chapter Twenty-One

DEVIZES PRISONER OF WAR CAMP

Swindon – 24th November 2009

Stan was back at home and I was staying with him, just for a few days while he settled into his new routine. He told me that suffering a heart attack was a life-changing experience and he didn't want to be one of the 10% of patients who would have another within a year of leaving hospital. He said he was determined to stick to his rehabilitation plan, at least until he knew I was committed to complying with his final demand.

He laughed, "That could turn out to be true in more ways than one!"

I assured him that I was resolute, but he didn't seem convinced. "You think so now, but you might well change your mind when you know exactly what it is. It won't be easy and it could prove extremely dangerous. Anyway, don't worry yet because you need to know a bit more of the story first."

I pressed him to tell me what he really wanted, but in typical Stan style he refused to budge an inch reminding me, "I've got to avoid stress and confrontation if I want my heart muscle to heal properly and that's going to take from six to twelve weeks. And don't forget you're supposed to be here to help, not to provoke." I held my hands up in mock surrender but he jokingly pressed the point, "I'm pretty sure that in my weakened state, if you were also to become difficult and give me yet another cross to bear I'd just collapse under the additional burden and would probably never, ever get up again."

He then told me what had happened to the team when they arrived back in England from Koszalin...

During a lengthy and sometimes acrimonious debrief Dominik revealed everything he could remember of Urszula's Wunderwaffen findings. The Polish operations officer saw the mission as a total failure. He was far more concerned about the loss of a valuable agent and keeping her existence secret from the British than delving much further into the supposed potential of Hitler's latest weapons. He was also worried about the considerable damage done to the local Griffin network and he was reluctant to accept the existence of the flying wings or discs, even as prototypes and was completely dismissive of the Bell. Without the additional evidence of Urszula's oral testimony, the powerful authority of the wire recordings or any photographic or written confirmation of what she knew, Dominik's impassioned warnings went virtually unheeded. He stressed that that the enemy would now be working flat out to cover their tracks, to hide or move whatever they could and to improve and increase their security and physical defences. He thought the window of opportunity for the Allies to launch an attack was running out and he urged them to strike before it was too late.

After much debate at the highest level a compromise was reached. Bombing raids were approved for the Freiherr von Fritsch Barracks, and the Manor House, which had previously been flagged up by British Intelligence as possible targets. They also authorised reconnaissance missions for Prague Airport and the Wenceslas mine, but they were not given a high priority and would have to wait for a suitable slot in the schedules. Dominik was told that the D-Day preparations held primacy and considerable resources were being concentrated there. The final response of the top brass to Dominik's recommendations was quoted as: 'We have done all we can, but we simply don't have the assets for speculative multi-site raids where the intelligence is based on unconfirmed and questionable information, some of which is little more than tittle-tattle. However, we recognise the potential dangers and so the file will be kept open for review – pending secondary source clarification.'

The operations officer had also told Dominik that the local AK commander had since discovered that Urszula had been captured in a joint Gestapo/SS operation code named 'Redline' commanded by the SS General, Dieter Kaufmann. Although initially mightily relieved to hear she was alive Dominik was soon devastated to learn that she had been sent to Ravensbrück concentration camp and that there was to be no rescue attempt by either the resistance or the SOE (Polish Section). It was considered to be just too risky, especially when they had no confirmation that she was still alive. A few days later the whole team was thanked for their efforts by their commanding officer at SOE and then stood down for an extended period away from active duty.

Nevertheless, they were not left moping and idle for too long and in early April 1944 they commenced a lengthy period of intense training, including joint commando field exercises in preparation for their planned deployment in Operation Dunstable. Following the intended Allied invasion of France in the coming summer or in the event of a sudden German collapse, a cadre (nearly 150 men and women) of German-speaking agents was to be dropped near prisons and labour camps (those holding Polish nationals) right across Germany. Their orders were simple – free the prisoners and cause mayhem at the very heart of the Nazi powerbase. Dominik's team were allocated to operational area Hamburg–Kiel where they were to organise and prepare the Polish workers to defend themselves. They also carried out local reconnaissance to identify suitable economic and military targets that could then be sabotaged once the Allies had landed.

Much to his surprise, Stan was also selected for a vital mission that autumn: Operation Foxley. He took great delight in telling me about his part in the plan to assassinate Hitler! The first idea was to bomb his special train (Führersonderzug) because the SOE had extensive experience in the use of explosives to cause derailments. The plan was quickly dropped as Hitler's schedule was much too irregular and unpredictable, with stations only being informed of his arrival a few minutes beforehand. Another plan was to poison the drinking water supply on his train but after initial discussions it was considered too complicated and certain to fail without an inside man. The planners finally decided on the sniper option. In August 1944 a German, who had once been part of Hitler's personal guard at the Berghof, had been captured while fighting in the Falaise pocket in Normandy. He revealed that at his mountain retreat in Bavaria, Hitler took a 20-minute morning walk at approximately 10am every day and that he preferred to walk alone. An examination of his favoured route showed that he was relatively unprotected for just a short period before he reached his destination – the teahouse. This occurred while he was simultaneously out of sight of the static sentry posts and the mobile security detail that Hitler insisted should discreetly follow on, some distance behind. The prisoner also told them that when Hitler was in residence, a Nazi flag was flown on the building and it was clearly visible from a cafe in the nearby town.

It was decided to kill him during his morning exercise. The British intended to parachute in two snipers (one a German-speaking Pole and the other British) both wearing the correct German army uniforms (mountain troops) into the area surrounding the compound. They would then infiltrate the Berghof grounds before moving to a secluded and camouflaged position in the woods, well within effective rifle range (up to 300 yards) which also had a good view of the relevant section of the path used by Hitler. An inside man was also recruited. He was a fervent anti-Nazi who lived only 20 miles from the Berghof who would hide them until Hitler visited and then guide them into their position.

Stan and his partner practised for hours at a time and for weeks on end, by firing at moving targets with an accurised Kar 98K, the standard Wehrmacht rifle, under conditions which simulated the actual assassination. They also rehearsed an alternative plan just in case they were unable to reach the firing point or Hitler survived the initial attack and arrived at the teahouse unharmed. They would then divert to a second preselected assault position and destroy his car with a bazooka when, as customary, it left the teahouse to take him back to the Berghof.

Although there was some resistance to the plan from within SOE, it was supported by the head of the German Directorate and Winston Churchill. Stan's chest still swelled with pride when he told me that in November 1944 the Prime Minister visited them on the firing ranges, produced a bottle of Johnnie Walker Red Label Scotch Whisky and toasted them. Such an impression did he make that nearly 70 years later my friend had no trouble reciting Churchill's departing words:

> You have been given the task that will make you the envy of the free world. When you succeed, as I know you will, you will have cut out the heart of the Nazi malignancy that has murdered millions and threatened our very existence. Overnight half the globe will shake free from the tyrant's iron shackles knowing that their deliverance from suffering is at hand. Finally, the elusive and precious prize of peace will be within our grasp.

I was impressed and said as much, "I bet you dined out on that a few times over the years, but what happened to make them call it off?"

He walked over to the sideboard drawer, took out a photograph and handed it to me. It was a wartime snap of Churchill sat at a large desk smoking his trademark cigar. I turned it over to find that the great man had signed it underneath his own endorsement: 'I'm sorry my Polish friend, but I have been told that our arrangement has been cancelled. Perhaps we will both rewrite history in other ways! Good luck with the special guard duty.'

As I examined it Stan told me, "You're the first person outside of our team that I've told about this, and other than Dominik and Jan, I've never even shown that picture to anyone else. The operation never happened because we were just too late." He explained that Hitler left the Berghof for the last time on 14th July 1944, never to return. That was well before they had even started training for the assassination.

He added, "It was typical of so many joint operations during the war – some good intelligence and inspired planning – but lousy timing. Anyway, half the war cabinet had already come to the conclusion that Hitler was, by then, so incompetent and irrational that it was better for our cause to leave him in place rather than risk someone more capable taking over."

I took another look at the photograph, "Well, he certainly showed a personal interest in what you were doing."

"Yes, the Prime Minister had been told that our whole team had been remustered and Dominik was taking us all to Wiltshire. So he obviously knew exactly what we were going to be up to." With that Stan started to work his way through the second pile of photographs and documents that were still sitting on the kitchen table, exactly where he had left them before he had collapsed. He showed me several photographs and a sketch map of the Prisoner of War Camp Number 23, situated just off the London Road at Devizes and he told me what had happened there...

In the beginning it was just a transit camp, some called it a 'cleansing camp', in the days when that word simply meant to wash or to free from unpleasantness, long before it had taken on today's negative and murderous connotations. The Germans arrived by train, at first some 500 at a time from Southampton and other south coast ports. They were mostly undernourished, poorly clothed, unshaven, filthy, lousy and hungry. They were escorted from Devizes railway station by armed soldiers with fixed bayonets and some of the locals were astonished by the large numbers involved and the look of complete defeat and dejection on most of their faces, many walking along with their hands raised in surrender.

The exceptions were the real Nazis – the SS and other political and specialist units –many of whom still strutted about, arrogantly issuing orders to their countrymen and talking of Hitler's final victory, yet to come. Their allegiance and belief in their superiority and destiny was unswerving and there was no doubt about who ruled the German roost, both outside and then subsequently inside the camp. At first they only stayed a day or two, just long enough to be searched, cleaned up and deloused, showered, examined by a doctor, fed and given clean prisoners' uniforms. They were also separated into military subgroups, such as Air Force, Army, Navy, Engineers, Parachutists etc, before being moved on to permanent camps and Devizes had finally received that status itself in November 1944.

I examined the photographs and tried to imagine what it must have been like. "So when it changed over to a regular establishment, how many prisoners did it hold?"

"Roughly 7,500 and it held all three categories."

I was at a loss again, "What do you mean, categories?"

Stan then clarified that before they arrived each POW had been interviewed and graded by a colour-code system. They were all issued with a patch to be worn on their uniforms. White patches – category A – were for prisoners with no suspected loyalty or affiliation to the Nazis. A grey patch – category B – meant that the prisoner was probably not an ardent Nazi, showing no obvious strong feelings either way. Hard-core Nazis and all Waffen SS and U-Boat crews wore a black patch – category C. Camp 23 held prisoners from all three of these groups and while the biggest category by far were the greys, the smallest were the whites, leaving about a quarter wearing the black patches. They were all housed in thirty large Romney Huts and a variety of tents, but the latter were gradually replaced by the addition of forty Nissen Huts, and by the time the Poles arrived all the prisoners were housed in permanent accommodation. The camp was surrounded by a double ring of wire fencing with rolls of barbed wire at the top and bottom and protected by perimeter watchtowers.

He explained that his team had been urgently recalled from Germany to be sent to the camp, and only later did they learn that it was connected to the Battle of the Bulge, the surprise German counter-offensive through the Ardennes which began on 16th December 1944 when they launched one final Blitzkrieg. They punched a hole in the Allied line deep into Belgium, aimed at splitting the invading armies and retaking the major port of Antwerp, thus cutting the Allies supply lines. As General Heinz Guderian, the renowned Panzer Commander who fully developed and advocated the strategy of blitzkrieg said, 'Man schlägt jemanden mit der Faust und nicht mit gespreizten Fingern', (one should punch with the fist and not with an open hand). Hitler had hoped to drive a huge wedge between the British and the Americans and then sue for a separate peace in the west. He would then be free to turn all his resources, including his new terror weapons on the Soviets.

Devizes – November 1944

During the early part of the month several German prisoners had been captured whilst trying to escape and there were rumours flying around that other attempts would be made. This was confirmed when guards also discovered that holes had been cut in the perimeter wire, but immediate roll calls had found no prisoners missing. This added to the general atmosphere of tension and unease. It was understood by the camp commander that about six to ten hard-line Nazi NCOs were ruthlessly running the camp, inciting violence and retribution against any perceived defeatism or lack of loyalty to the cause. He felt that these men posed a serious risk to their less militant countrymen and to the general security of the camp. He also suspected that at least one tunnel was being excavated, but despite several intensive searches nothing had been found. At the time the guard duties were conducted by a mishmash of Pioneer Corps companies, mostly men deemed unsuitable for active service or those who had been wounded and could no longer return to the front.

On the pretence of responding to the British camp commander's request to beef up security in order to contain any serious trouble, the 5th Polish Guard Company (3 squads of 36 men each) was selected to take over. They arrived in the last week of November, after the Polish Section of the SOE had secretly arranged for their deployment as cover for their own mission. Dominik, Marcin and Aaron were each assigned to one of the squads so that they could maintain cover throughout the twenty-four-hour period. As far as their guard colleagues were aware, they were just routine replacements. They had been fully briefed on the company's standing orders, operating procedures and personalities. With their considerable undercover experience they blended in straight away.

Posing as nurses, Joanna and Hannah were to coordinate and manage the operation from a commandeered office in the American 128th General Hospital, which had been set up earlier that year in the Waller Barracks on the opposite side of the London Road. On arrival, the Poles discovered that when the camp had been built a number of secret microphones had been buried within the fabric of the walls right across the site (as was the case in many of the POW camps in the UK). They had never been wired to recorders and so, rather foolishly, the Pioneer Corps had never used them, simply because they couldn't spare the men to monitor them. The feed was quickly extended across the road to Dominik's temporary control room where the two women happily shared the additional responsibility.

The operation was up and running five days later when a fresh group of German prisoners arrived from Southampton. They had been captured during the last few days of the Battle of the Scheldt in northern Belgium and across the border into Holland. Two of the prisoners were Stan and the ex-pilot Bernard Slawinski and they certainly looked the part: a pair of decorated, combat-hardened and battle-scarred Nazis. Captured but by no means defeated. Their uniforms, equipment, units and backgrounds had been thoroughly researched and their war records, identities and supporting documentation would all withstand detailed scrutiny. They had trained for months for such an opportunity.

A great deal of care had been taken during their insertion into the group of prisoners at the forward prisoner reception unit in

Middelburg. The Germans always had misgivings about Polish soldiers, knowing that many of them spoke fluent German and had even previously served alongside them in their armed forces before switching sides. So to minimise any early suspicion of Stan and Bernard being Polish stoolpigeons, they had been 'captured', roughed up and delivered to Middleburg by a small contingent of the Black Watch (from the 2nd British Army fighting on the Poles right flank) rather than soldiers from the 1st Polish Armoured Division, who were deployed in the centre with the 1st Canadian Army on their left. The Scots had become very friendly with a group of Polish Commandos who had been stationed near Kirkcaldy before D-Day. Although they were given no details of the mission, they were only too glad to help when approached by the Polish liaison officer attached to the British field headquarters.

Since their first moment of detention the two Poles had completely transformed themselves. They spoke nothing but German, they thought only in German and they became completely immersed in German military life and culture, rapidly learning and imitating the natural behaviour, idiom and attitude of their fellow captives. Their role, the key element in what was a major Polish operation, had been authorised after high-grade intelligence had been received from agent Knopf.

A group of about fifty staunch SS officers, many posing as ordinary Wehrmacht officers or NCOs, had allowed themselves to be captured or had deliberately surrendered to British Forces in order to organise major unrest and to coordinate mass escapes from several POW camps across the UK. Their audacious mission was to mobilise tens of thousands of prisoners, seize military weapons, vehicles, tanks and planes, then join together and fight their way to London. This was by no means as crazy as it first sounds. At the time the UK was denuded of front-line troops because virtually all combat-ready forces were already fighting on the continent. The German plan, therefore, was to tie down the limited Allied forces that were available, cause panic amongst the population and instigate the withdrawal of aircraft and ground troops from

414

France, Belgium and Holland to deal with the 'uprising'. Knopf had confirmed that the mass escape was a diversionary plan aimed to coincide with a major German counter-offensive. The problem was that, as yet, he had no idea where that was to take place. It could have been anywhere across thousands of miles of front.

The pressing task for the Polish moles was to find out, and they couldn't tell the British authorities about the mass escape plan until they had – not without the risk of revealing that Knopf was still providing them with exclusive intelligence. Quite naturally, they were most concerned about events in the east and what would happen to Poland post-war. The Allies, on the other hand, were already drifting away from their previous reassurances and it looked increasingly likely that Stalin would seize control of their country. Quite bluntly, the Poles felt that they could no longer rely on the intelligence being provided by the British because of the conflicts emerging within their respective national interests. So as far as the war in the east was concerned Knopf was their only guarantee of genuine, top-grade intelligence and they needed to maintain their direct link. There was also a chance that the British, not having the same long and fruitful association with the German agent, wouldn't have believed him on this occasion anyway because the plan seemed so ludicrous, daring and foolhardy.

In view of all the information of escapes and Nazi influence that had come out of the Devizes camp, it had seemed sensible to SOE Polish section to base the operation there. Stan and Bernard were both assigned to hut 8, which already contained over 200 prisoners. It had a concrete floor and double wooden bunk beds were laid out in neat rows, running the full length of the building with walkways in between. The Polish guards would patrol through the huts on night inspection, randomly turning back the blankets, to ensure that the prisoners were not wearing their uniform or boots, in preparation for an escape bid. The two spies soon discovered that hard-line Nazis tried to control everything inside the camp by the use of their 'Rollkommando' – a group of brutal, self-appointed enforcers who terrorised and punished the other prisoners for the slightest contravention of their rules and regulations. Offenders were brought before the 'Ehrenrat' or prisoner's council and there had been several suspicious 'suicides' as a result.

Although prisoners deemed trustworthy by the prison authorities were regularly allowed to work outside the camp, those designated 'black' were always held inside and treated with the utmost suspicion. Despite the increase in perimeter security, in many ways the problems inside became worse not better with the arrival of the Poles. Stories were coming out of Poland about the mass murder of thousands of civilians by the Germans as they brutally crushed the recent Warsaw uprising. Some of the guards had wives, children and relatives in the capital and suspected the worse. They made it perfectly clear that they hated the Nazis with a passion and would not hesitate to shoot, given the slightest provocation. They openly called the prisoners, particularly those they saw as Hitlerites, Nazi bastards, pigs and shits. They pushed them around, threatened and goaded them, constantly reminding them to watch their backs because they would have their revenge. Tensions were therefore running high and with potentially lethal danger all around, the two Poles were quick to manufacture and hide a number of crude weapons made from everyday items such as toothbrushes, tin cans and wood. They needed to defend themselves – from both sides.

Life in the camp was always hard for the Germans too. They were woken at 5am by a bugler and they paraded outside, often left standing for up to an hour in the biting wind, pouring rain and latterly sleet, frost and snow. In the winter they were always cold and hungry. For example, breakfast consisted of just a watery and tasteless porridge with two small, thin slices of bread, washed down with a mug of weak tea. Three embossed tokens made out of old tin cans were issued every day and had to be handed in at meal times to prevent anyone from obtaining extra rations. If they were lost or stolen then the unfortunate would not eat that day. The sheer number of prisoners meant that toilet arrangements were wretched, even by the standards of the time. Large, malodorous buckets festered in the latrines until the despised morning ritual of 'shithouse punishment'. With two prisoners to each bucket, it was suspended in the middle of a pole braced between them, and carried high on their shoulders. As they walked gingerly, watching every footfall, towards the septic pit, they shouted loud and clear warnings to any approaching prisoners. At that time of day the cry of 'Achtung Scheiße!' rang out across the camp. In the accommodation blocks, frothy night pails gurgled, bubbled and splashed out their intermittent tune throughout the hours of darkness, always overflowing by morning. But there was ever the weekly shower to look forward to.

For those confined around the clock the biggest problem by far was the mind-numbing boredom and with so much time on their hands, escape inevitably became the focus for many and for some it developed into an obsession. A camp industry grew out of it. Rations were hoarded, documents forged, civilian clothes and tools made or stolen and plans drawn up, refined and amended on an almost daily basis. Tunnels were started, ingenious hiding places created and rough-and-ready weapons prepared. With the creation of an escape committee the whole process was coordinated, improved and accelerated. Lookouts, runners, printers, forgers, tunnellers, a quartermaster, a command structure and even an armourer were all appointed under their patronage but briefed and controlled by the Rollkommando.

In addition to the camp newspaper, the 'Wochenpost', the Nazis started issuing secret 'Daily Orders' reminding the prisoners of:

> ... *your unswerving duty to the Führer. The time to fight as an army of brothers is again rapidly approaching. Be warned, our victory is only days away and our incarceration will end in glory. We will be free. Free to fight and free to defeat our enemies for the greater good of the Fatherland.*

These documents also included the passwords to be used by the twenty hand-picked men who would start the breakout by overpowering the guards and seizing their weapons. At Camp

23 a worrying number of escapes had already been made, but all the prisoners had been recaptured within a day or two. This small group of die-hard Nazis were on a venture to change all that and cause bedlam for the British.

Within days the Polish moles had identified Sergeant Fürst from Hut 6 as the ringleader of the Rollkommando and 'the voice of the escape committee' and had passed the information on to Aaron. Unfortunately, there was no microphone in that particular building. Hannah and Joanna had also discovered that the microphones fitted inside the accommodation huts were virtually useless, revealing little of value because their range was limited by their fixed positions and the large amount of background noise generated by so many prisoners. However, those fitted in the two offices used by the senior NCOs and in the sickbay were much more effective. Joanna had listened in to a conversation in the Stabsfeldwebel's office (he was a 25-year service volunteer sergeant major who was the de facto administrative and organisational link between the camp authorities and the prisoners). He was discussing an escape being planned for the first week in December. It was to be the final reconnaissance mission for the mass breakout later in the month. Apparently, they wanted to revisit nearby RAF Yatesbury (four miles away) and observe it in daylight to see if there were any operational aircraft stationed there, other than light trainers. A couple of weeks earlier four escapees had managed to penetrate the perimeter during the night and remove two such aircraft from a hanger, but they were unable to start the engines. They had also managed to exit the base undetected and later that morning 'allowed' themselves to be captured so that they could report back.

A week after arriving Dominik heard from London that Knopf had discovered that the German High Command had recently put together a special parachute unit – SS Panzer Brigade 150 – unusually, entirely made up of 2,500 volunteers drawn from all ranks and services across the Third Reich. It also contained a special English-speaking commando unit of about 150 men known as 'Einheit Stielau'. Polish Intelligence feared, quite wrongly as it turned out, that this Brigade might be parachuted into England to support the prison escape. This added further credibility to the Nazi 'great escape' conspiracy, putting even greater pressure on the mission. The Allies were now desperate to know where the attack would take place. Dominik was suddenly told that he had only three days to achieve the objective and so he had to modify his plans and Stan and Bernard had to be told of the changes.

Dominik knew from their long and close association exactly how his team operated and so at lunch time, along with several other guards, he conducted a random spot check for weapons in one of the two mess huts. He was not surprised, just very relieved, when he discovered a sharpened toothbrush handle hidden in Bernard's boot and it gave him just the excuse he needed to talk to him without arousing suspicion. He was immediately arrested, along with three other unfortunates also found to be carrying makeshift weapons, and they were all taken in for questioning. Once on their own, Dominik told him that they could wait no longer.

"If anyone in here knows the answer it'll be that jumped-up sergeant, the bastard who runs the Rollkommando. You'll need to get close to him and pretty damn quick so here's what I've got in mind..."

An hour later the four prisoners were returned to their huts, all carrying signs of having being assaulted for their trouble. Bernard was sporting a bloody nose and a cut above his good eye. After he and the others had told their stories, the tension ratcheted up another notch. The Germans did not take kindly to the Poles beating them up and they were particularly enraged by the injuries caused to a defenceless, unarmed and shackled, one-eyed man who had been so badly scarred fighting for the honour of the Fatherland. Bernard later briefed Stan on the scheme that he had agreed with Dominik and they made their own preparations.

Dominik received a message to contact Hannah urgently and when he arrived at her office he saw the look of excitement on her face before she blurted out, "I've just found out that one of the prisoners actually worked for Kaufmann. He was talking about it in the sickbay to another prisoner called Kurt who broke his ankle playing football. He told Kurt that he would make sure that he wouldn't be left behind because the escape committee would do as they were told. He said that he could sort it out because he was still working under the orders and protection of General Kaufmann and he wasn't going to abandon any of his SS colleagues. I'm absolutely certain that I heard the name correctly. It was definitely Kaufmann."

Dominik took a moment to react, "I don't suppose they said enough for you to identify him?"

"All I know is that Kurt called him Golo and that's usually short for Gottfried or something similar beginning with g-o-t-t. He also said that if he had to, he would carry him out himself."

Dominik thought it through before responding, "It shouldn't be too difficult to find out who he is. I'll get on to it straight away. It also tells us that the breakout isn't far off so we're running out of time anyway. From what you heard it also sounds as if Kaufmann is behind this whole escape operation and I'm not going to let him beat us this time. Thanks Hannah, keep your ears open for anything further on Golo and let me know soonest."

Dominik had only just got back to the prison when he heard more troubling news. Two newly appointed American 'interrogators' had been visiting the prison that day to practise their techniques on real prisoners. When they walked into hut 6 one of them overheard two prisoners speaking and before they had realised they had company, one of the Germans had said, 'Everything hinges on the armoury key. We must have it or none of us will get out of—" Then he broke off abruptly and the Americans pretended they didn't understand and just asked a few innocuous questions in English to cover their presence. They knew that a raid on the armoury meant that the prisoners were intent on a major and violent breakout. They immediately informed the camp commander who passed it up the line and an urgent meeting was called at Salisbury Plain District Headquarters to thrash out a coordinated plan to identify, isolate and arrest all the main conspirators and simultaneously increase security and institute comprehensive search operations at all POW camps across Britain.

With that news Dominik realised that he didn't even have three days; he had to act straight away before the reinforcements were called in and the plotters arrested. Once that started to happen there was no predicting how it could affect the Polish guards. Stan and Bernard could well be left without any backup and there would be so much activity that panic could set in and then they would stand no chance of finding out where the German attack was to take place. As he ran to find Marcin he thought that he probably had a few hours at most before he lost all control of the operation and things were already starting to fall apart. They had to improvise.

Half an hour before evening roll call Aaron and Dominik entered hut 6. The lookout had warned his colleagues of their approach and ten or so prisoners rushed around in those few precious seconds grace to hide anything incriminating. As they walked in Dominik immediately recognised Golo from his photograph in the camp records where he was recorded as Corporal Gotthard Drescher. Seeing him in the flesh, the Pole had no doubt that he was SS and Kaufmann's man just as he claimed. Despite the basic and austere surroundings, the stained and worn uniform and his stubble beard, he still retained an arrogant, defiant and superior look. He was sat on a bottom bunk alongside the leader of the Rollkommando, Sergeant Markus Fürst, but Dominik was certain that he too was using a false identity.

They later learnt that Drescher was really Obersturmführer (SS lieutenant) Gotthard Schwarz, having been promoted twice since the Koszalin operation and Fürst was Sturmscharführer (SS warrant officer) Markus Hahn. Stan and Bernard were sat at a table a few yards away where several games of chess were taking place. At exactly the same time on the other side of the camp Marcin was entering the sickbay to see Kurt. He was not the Wehrmacht Obergefreiter (corporal) that he pretended to be either. He was in fact Untersturmführer (SS second lieutenant) Kurt Lange. Within the hour the Poles would know whether or not their plan had worked.

Aaron walked straight up to the two SS men and shouted at them in German, "Stand up when a guard enters the room you Nazi shits," and he prodded Drescher in the chest with his rifle. They stood slowly, exchanged a glance but said nothing. Aaron continued, "We have received information that you two are in possession of forbidden articles. Turn out your pockets you murdering bastards and be very careful because if you so much as twitch, I'll shoot you where you stand and then go and have my dinner. Kosher, of course. And I think I'd be doing the world a favour by ridding it of Kraut scum like you."

They did as they were told, but the exchange had drawn an audience and a group of about fifty angry-looking prisoners started to gather, mumbling and quietly uttering their own threats at the guards.

The search revealed nothing of consequence so Aaron ordered, "Take your clothes off, we'll do a strip search and also make sure nobody's circumcised. That really would be difficult to explain away in this Aryan shithole and I'd give anything to see you at each other's throats."

The muttering and brewing discontent grew louder and the crowd inched forward. One or two found their voices, "Leave them alone, you Jewish pig," and "You're both big men with guns in here but crap on the battlefield," and then the hut wit shouted out from the back, "Why don't you piss off back to Polackland. Oh, you can't because we are still there, looking after your wives and sisters no doubt. Making sure they don't go without." Several prisoners laughed but most just strained forward to see if there was a reaction.

Excitement was a rare commodity in the camp; tedium and routine ruled their lives, but now many were enjoying the tension and the dangerous air of expectation.

Drescher spoke for the first time. "It's alright men. We don't want any trouble today so cut out the stupid taunts and let them have their fun. They won't find anything."

Dominik had seen enough to spot the weakest link and so he upped the ante. He leaned in closely to Fürst, just as he was taking his trousers off and whispered in his ear, "We know all about your escape plan. You've got an informer. A Nazi rat." He then pushed him violently in the chest. Caught off balance with one leg in his trousers and the other out, he fell over backwards and crashed onto the floor to the side of the bunk. Aaron cocked his weapon as the crowd pushed against the front row to see exactly what had happened but Drescher never moved. He calmly called out, "Everything's fine. Now just take it easy and don't any of you even think about making matters worse."

Dominik bent over and picked up the small pair of wire cutters that he had furtively dropped inside the prisoner's trousers when he had whispered to him. He held them up for all to see and said to no one in particular, "Not even very good at hiding things are they, but they can both have a night in solitary to think about it and then it'll be up in front of the commander in the morning."

Fürst pulled himself up and started to protest his innocence, "They're not mine. You plant—"

Drescher cut him off dead with just a withering glance and a brusque command, "Shut up!" There was no longer any doubt whatsoever as to who was really running things inside.

The two Germans were marched off towards the cells with their hands on their heads, but en route they were suddenly barged in the back and forced into the gap between the two Nissen huts that were used as the chapel and the camp office. This dark narrow strip was not penetrated by the sweeping beams of the guard tower searchlights and was one of only two such blind spots on the whole camp. It was patrolled regularly, but the guards couldn't be everywhere and the Poles knew the regular patterns. Before the prisoners could recover from being sent sprawling, their captors quickly retrieved the items they had left there earlier and gagged and blindfolded them. Then they tied up their hands, punching and kicking them into submission as they did so. Using a brief flash of a diffused torch Dominik checked his watch many times over the next eight minutes. Being so close to the final roll call of the day he was pretty certain that they wouldn't be disturbed by another guard carrying out an additional random patrol. They would all be too busy, but nevertheless every second spent hiding away, waiting for the designated time, seemed like an hour.

Exactly two minutes after the headcount had started they heard the sound of footsteps approaching and the Poles tensed up, ready for immediate action. They exhaled and relaxed somewhat when Marcin whispered his name before turning into the tight passageway to join them. He was carrying an unconscious Kurt over his shoulder. Three minutes later they walked out from the other side of the Nissen huts just as an army lorry backed up. They bundled the three prisoners into the back and Dominik climbed up to join them. Marcin headed off to report to the guard commander at roll call and Aaron marched away towards the detention cells, already a few minutes late for his night shift.

Hannah drove the US army truck towards the two large, wooden gates at the entrance. She handed the guard the signed delivery order for the weekly shipment of extra supplies, rations and treats so kindly donated to the Polish guards by their neighbours, the well-supplied and generous staff at the US Hospital. He gave the document a quick glance to make sure that it now bore a receipt and signature, but he didn't bother to check the proffered identity document and vehicle pass. He had seen them only 15 minutes earlier when the same vehicle had entered the camp. He then used his torch to check underneath the lorry and take a cursory look over the tailboard, but he didn't bother to climb aboard to look behind the four crates stacked towards the front. He felt there was no need because they were on their sides facing out and he could clearly see that they were all empty. He assumed that, as usual, they were the ones from the previous week's delivery and were now being returned ready for the next supply. Everything appeared correct and he didn't have any feelings of suspicion or unease so he waved the driver out and she turned right onto the main road. A few hundred yards later she took another right into Horton Road, making for Stanton St Bernard where Joanna was waiting at an isolated farmhouse that had been recently acquired by the SOE. The three of them unloaded the passengers, checked their restraints and then locked them in the cellar.

Dominik was impressed with Hannah's disguise. In the dull artificial light in the kitchen she looked just like a man. Although thin and short, these features had not been obvious when she was sat in the lorry's cab. Her hair had been cut short and she was dressed in a reasonably well-fitting American army uniform with cap and gloves. Her breasts had all but disappeared and she was wearing theatrical stage makeup that thickened her eyebrows, eliminated her high cheekbones and gave her the suggestion of a five o'clock shadow.

She saw him staring and said, "I know, I probably wouldn't get away with it in proper daylight, but it was good enough for tonight. Anyway, when you ran out of manpower you looked mightily relieved when I told you that I could handle the driver's job." She had also reminded him that she had taken the specialist camouflage and disguise course at Audley End House.

He carried on looking at her, genuinely surprised at the transformation until she suddenly winced with discomfort, "I'm sorry but I've got to get out of these things right now. The binding is so tight that it's killing me and I can hardly breathe." As she rushed out he laughed with surprise and embarrassment at the vivid mental image conjured up by her departing words, "I'll have sore nipples and tender tits for weeks after this torture." Still shaking his head he left her to get changed and went outside to the truck. He returned it to the US hospital and retrieved their own guards' lorry, which he then hid inside the barn before making the final preparations for his night-time foray.

Chapter Twenty-Two

FINAL DISCLOSURE

Devizes – December 1944

Timing was crucial and so once the Germans had been loaded onto the lorry, Marcin quickly marched all the way across the camp. He had to ensure that he delivered the arrest and detention certificate to the roll call commander while the count was still being made. It indicated that the three prisoners had been taken to the isolation cells where they would be held overnight to appear in front of the CO in the morning. The document showed that they had been charged with possessing a prohibited item and conspiring to escape. He then rushed back across the camp to the cell block, having already swapped shifts to ensure that he shared the night duty with Aaron. Once the camp had settled down after lights-out they made ready, hoping the alarm would sound before morning.

Stan and Bernard had witnessed the consternation amongst the prisoners when Drescher and Fürst had been detained. Everyone wanted to know if the Poles had discovered their plans. Several men asked the Stabsfeldwebel if the escape would now be cancelled altogether. When the additional news of Kurt's arrest filtered through it immediately caused another stream of questions and speculation as to exactly what it meant for the prospects of their breakout. All thoughts of security seemed to have been jettisoned as those involved in the plan clamoured for instant assurances and information from the one man left who should have the answers. Both the Poles made a great effort to remember the faces, and where they could the names of those showing the most concern and interest. By the time the Stabsfeldwebel called a halt to the commotion by announcing that he would be holding an emergency meeting of the remaining escape committee members, the two spies had a mental list of about thirty prisoners.

The three Germans struggled to sit up in the pitch darkness of the cellar. They were lying on their backs at the foot of the ten concrete steps which led up to the double-locked steel door. Their hands were still tied behind them and their feet were also tightly bound with sash cord. Although they had been relieved of their gags and blindfolds Kurt was additionally hampered by the heavy plaster cast that encased his left leg from his toes to his knee. Using his heels to dig into the stone-slabbed floor and lifting his backside clear, Fürst gradually pushed himself alongside Kurt. Drescher did the same on the opposite side and then working together, they managed to drag themselves and Kurt backwards until they were all backed right up against the wall. Kurt badly needed a painkiller, the burning and stabbing sensation in his ankle was excruciating and he could feel it swelling up and pressing into the plaster. He gritted his teeth and asked, "What's going on? Where are we?

Fürst replied, "Someone's betrayed us and now they know about the escape. I've no idea where we are, but it's not too far from the camp because we were only in the truck for about ten minutes. Anyway, we've got to get out of here so we haven't got time to go into it now. Let's get these ropes off and then we might be able to fight our way out."

Speaking in whispers they then spent the next hour or so taking turns trying to undo the knots in their bonds. They found that working behind their backs by touch only, with such a limited range of movement in their fingers, was almost impossible. The fact that the Poles had used lengths of cord that had been soaked in water added to their problems. The harder they pushed and strained against them the tighter they became until they broke through the skin on their wrists and ankles and the pain became almost unbearable. Their nails bent backwards and split as they tried to work their fingers into their colleagues' knots and they too bled and throbbed. The harder they tried, the deeper the cords bit into their flesh until their hands and fingers became numb. Although this eased the pain somewhat, by the time they eventually gave up, more constricted than ever, they had totally lost the little dexterity and strength that they originally had.

Kurt asked, "Can one of you now please answer my question. Why on earth have we been kidnapped by our own guards? It doesn't make any sense at all."

Fürst agreed, "If they know we're involved and the extent of it, then why haven't they just split us all up and shipped us off to other camps? From their point of view that would be problem solved – for a while at least."

Drescher thought he might know, "These aren't ordinary guards. Just look at the way they operate and interact and then compare that to the rest of them. They're professionals – Special Forces or commandos, something like that. But they seem to know exactly who we are and I think their job is to take us out of the equation without our comrades knowing anything about it. Then they can deal with the rest without any organised resistance. After all, without us three there is no mass escape. Nobody else knows the plan after stage 1 or the rendezvous points or the radio frequencies and codes."

Fürst began to fear the worst. "You're right, without us they're bound to fail and it gets even worse because we weren't marched off to solitary or out through the front gate for transfer as I would have expected, but we were smuggled out like contraband under cover of darkness. So somebody's gone to a lot of trouble to set this up. It doesn't look good for us, does it?"

Kurt caught up, "Surely they couldn't get away with killing us? That's ridiculous! I'm sure they stick to the Geneva Convention, don't they?"

Fürst found a crumb of comfort, "Of course they do and they're proud of it, and anyway, it's not a total failure I suppose. They'll still have to bring in extra troops and tie up transports, escorts and guards to ship out 7,000 men right across the country to new prison camps. Then they'll have to use dozens more to tear our camp apart to look for our documents, equipment, supplies and tunnels."

Drescher corrected him, "Don't be so bloody naive. We don't stick to the international rules so why should they? And you're wrong about the rest as well because they won't do all that. They'll just move through the camp systematically, block by block and hut by hut. They might arrest a dozen or so connected to stage 1 if they find the maps, documents and other evidence, but that will be about it. Life would quickly go back to normal for the rest"

Fürst was becoming increasingly agitated, "Far from normal, I think. You mustn't lose sight of what this was all about in the first place. Unternehmen Wacht am Rhein (Operation Watch on the Rhine) is our best chance of winning the war in the west and it has got to succeed. It's the only thing that matters and back home they're depending on us. Their attack and our breakout are supposed to be two sides of the same coin. But now we've let them down by getting ourselves stuck in this hole. We're totally buggered before it even starts."

Kurt joined in, "You're absolutely right, Markus. We've failed completely and we all know it really. I don't think we can do anything about it either. It's just fate: we're bottled up here by these Polish bastards just like our panzers will be contained in the Ardennes by the Americans and all because we haven't managed to tie down a few divisions like we were supposed to."

Kaufmann's sergeant was quick to react, "For Christ's sake watch what you're saying and keep your voices down." But he also knew that if he was to stand any chance of turning the tables, then he would certainly need their help and so he offered some late encouragement, "Look we're all still alive and we've got a duty to fight on right to the end. We're SS officers and sworn to die for the cause. So please stop the bloody whining and make sure you're both ready. If we get half a chance then we'll make our move. I'm not letting myself be strung up by a couple of degenerate Polacks. We just might get out of this yet and bring our own plans back on track. If not, then we'll die trying. That's our duty and don't either of you forget it."

Above ground Joanna listened in to their conversation, magnified by the powerful earphones connected to the microphone hidden behind the metal grill on the air vent in the cellar. She ignored the insult and smiled with a deep sense of relief and satisfaction. They had done it. The plan had worked and now they were sure. The attack was coming through the Ardennes into the American sector and she also had the German code name for the operation. She set up her radio and sent an emergency encrypted message to SOE Polish Section in London and then waited for the others to return.

Both the British and Americans had already received some snippets of intelligence to suggest that a major German counter-offensive was being planned. Additionally, fragments of radio traffic and information from Ultra indicated a build-up of men and equipment on the German side in the Ardennes and this was confirmed separately by local residents. In fact, several middle ranking Allied officers predicted exactly the right location, but their warnings were dismissed as implausible and misleading, being unsupported by any conclusive evidence. The senior commanders believed that the Germans were preparing defensive positions only and that if an attack was to come, then it would be further north against the British line. They were convinced that the Ardennes was a quiet sector. The Polish information when it came arrived almost too late and was greeted with some scepticism. By now the weather had closed in, the whole area was cloaked in thick fog and all aircraft were grounded. No aerial reconnaissance could take place to confirm or disprove the intelligence. Less than 48 hours later the panzer tanks were rolling forward against sparsely defended positions.

Dominik was blacked up as he crept silently along the northern bank of the canal in the sudden downpour, keeping well clear of the towpath, heading for the perimeter wire on the south-east corner of the camp. He crept through the wood that took him to within 50 yards of his target and then he stopped and listened. The silence was disturbed only by the dripping rain and the shrill calling of two sentinel screech owls as they tried to outperform each other. He got down on his stomach and started to crawl forward through the soaking wet grass. He stopped dead when he heard the distinctive metallic clinking of military equipment as one of the guards in the corner watchtower 60 metres off to his right started to climb down the ladder. Up until that point Dominik was reasonably confident that if he was really quiet, then he would succeed because the guards would naturally focus their attention on the inside of the camp. However, once on the ground and patrolling on foot, a sentry would instinctively look in all directions as he walked and that made him much more of a threat.

He watched him take about twenty paces in each direction along the path between the two lines of wire as he stretched his legs and fought the creeping tiredness that had bedevilled bored sentries throughout history. He repeated his stroll several more times before climbing back up to join his colleague. Dominik crept forward again and undetected he reached a spot roughly halfway between two towers. He took the cloth from his pocket and used it to muffle the noise as he slowly and cautiously cut a two-foot-square hole in the wire. He repeated the manoeuvre on the inside fence and then took an extra minute or two to bend the cut edges slightly outwards making it look as if the strands had been cut from the inside. He then snagged a small piece of material onto one of the points. Marcin had ripped it from Kurt's uniform jacket when he had been unconscious before he was loaded onto the lorry. Finally, before crawling back across the field, he scraped the heel of his left boot backwards right across the path between the holes in both fences. He made quite a gouge in the rain-softened ground. He hoped that it would later be interpreted as the trail made by Kurt's plaster cast as he had been dragged through by his comrades.

Dominik had just reached his bicycle, hidden in the hedge at the junction of the Horton Road and Chandlers Lane when the alarm sounded. He took a quick look at his watch and confirmed the time. The 'escape' through the wire had been discovered just before 4.30am, probably by one of the patrolling dogs and its handler. He pedalled as fast as he dared in the darkness, keeping right in the centre of the lane, making for the farm near Stanton St Bernard about four miles away.

At the same time, chaos and pandemonium descended on the camp. The alarm sounded, the guard were turned out and as if by magic, reinforcements arrived. The darkness and shadow of the camp buildings was suddenly bathed in bright light, not just from the fixed lamps and the searchlights but also from vehicle headlamps and spotlights as the perimeter fences were encircled by army trucks, armoured cars and Bren gun carriers. Engines were revving, orders were shouted and troops poured from the vehicles to take up their prearranged positions. It was an impressive show of speed, force and discipline and taking place in darkness, it also created a tense atmosphere of high drama and menace. The prisoners came rushing out and at first they just milled about, taking in the extraordinary scene, assessing the situation and chatting to each other. Then slowly the shouting, chanting and jeering started: just a few emboldened individuals at first, encouraging and empowering others until it had spread right across the camp. Then they started singing their marching songs full of brash, triumphant jingoism, stamping their feet and working up a fatalistic bravado. Suddenly, despite the presence of armoured cars and lines of armed soldiers, a group made a rush for the fence. They were unaware that one of the units deployed was B Company of 8 Parachute Regiment and a few short bursts in front of the charging Germans from a couple of their Bren guns was enough to stop them in their tracks. Had they not relented, then the consequences would have been dire.

Those four empty magazine cases were the only evidence of shots being fired during the 'Great Escape' attempt at Devizes, although it was reported at the War Office that 'tanks had to command the streets to put a stop to the incredible plot that came very close to succeeding'. So close in fact that the War Cabinet decreed that the affair had to remain a closely guarded secret. Many years later a national newspaper finally printed the story and the byline included this summary 'the amazing twists and turns of an endeavour that makes the plotting of Allied POWs as detailed in bestselling books like *The Wooden Horse* and *The Colditz Story* look insignificant by comparison.'

The prisoners were forced back into their accommodation huts, but in the commotion Stan and Bernard managed to declare their true identity to the guard commander stating that they had vital information on the plotters. At first he was not convinced and questioned them at gunpoint, but after their continued insistence and a close examination of their Polishness they were taken in front of the colonel. They provided him with the relevant telephone numbers and names of those who could vouch for them at SOE Polish Section. Nothing was said of the rest of the team. As far as the colonel was concerned, they were simply spies inserted by Polish Intelligence to identify and report on Nazi war criminals. An hour later, before they were issued with civilian coats and told to leave the camp for their own safety, they gave him the details of those they suspected of being involved, starting with the Stabsfeldwebel. They were added to the few names the colonel already had from his own sources. Then, as the night moved towards dawn, they were singled out and removed from their huts by teams of heavily armed paratroopers. They were transferred, under close escort, to the guardroom at the neighbouring Le Marchant Barracks to await transport to the London Cage for interrogation. It was obvious to the guards and camp authorities that no mass breakout had occurred, but the hole in the fence indicated that someone had succeeded. Although their priority was the arrest and separation of the organisers and planners, a full role call was arranged for 0700 hours. Meanwhile, the Police, Home Army and local authorities were notified and search parties sent out to scour the roads and countryside.

Stan and Bernard made contact with London as soon as they had reported to the Polish guard commander and asked for his help. They were told by SOE to wait at the temporary control room on the American camp until the others returned. The captain, having been told the same story as the colonel, was left shaking his head in amazement at the fortitude, ingenuity and audacity of some of his fellow countrymen. However, he was not so impressed a few minutes later when Marcin and Aaron reported to him and also declared themselves as part of the clandestine Polish operation. As they disclosed their plan to abduct the three Germans and their own cover-up he became increasingly angry that they had deceived him and his men and also disappointed that they had not taken him into their confidence at the very beginning. However, he calmed down once they had apologised and made it clear that time had been rapidly running out because the British had become aware of the escape and they couldn't take the slightest risk of the abduction being prevented.

They revealed the entire operational plan to him and pointed out that the original idea of infiltrating the Rollkommando had to be abandoned because of the sudden time limitations and so they had switched to the kidnap strategy. They explained that the ringleaders had to be removed from the prison, away from where they felt reasonably comfortable and powerful, to be placed under conditions of extreme stress and anxiety. They needed to be totally controlled and restricted, not allowed to do anything other than focus on their own danger and apparent hopelessness. Only then, so the Poles reasoned, might they make a fatal slip. Marcin emphasised that in any case, the three Germans were still being kept under close guard and would be returned relatively unharmed later in the day, whatever the outcome.

Somewhat resentfully, the captain agreed to destroy the arrest and detention certificate, show all three as being present at the evening roll call and ensure that his men kept silent about what had really happened. He assured them that, despite his irritation at being marginalised, his duty and that of his men was clear and that the stance of the guard company would be unanimous. They would report that the Nazis were last seen in their accommodation at lights out and nothing suspicious had been noticed until the hole in the fence had been discovered. At the 0700 hours roll call it would then become obvious that they had escaped through it, acting as some sort of advance party well before the cordon had been put in place to stop the threatened exodus. Marcin and Aaron then checked in with SOE and were told to regroup at the farm as soon as possible and so they took off in one of the guard jeeps 'borrowed' from the Americans.

At 7.15am, back at the farm with mission accomplished, Dominik cut the prisoners free while Joanna and Hannah stood guard. He made Drescher and Fürst carry Kurt up the steps and then lift him onto the back of the canvass-sided army lorry. He retied their wrists with fresh cord and Joanna climbed up to join him. It was their intention to take them back to the POW camp and claim that they had found and recaptured them on the Horton Road. The Poles sat on the nearside opposite the prisoners on the bench seats. Joanna was holding a double action Webley Mk IV .38/200 revolver, a model that had been officially adopted for the British military and identical to those issued as a side arm to the guard officers. The standard issue rifle was just too unwieldy and cumbersome for vehicular escort duty, whereas the compact Webley was ideal. Dominik had his favoured trench gun. Hannah drove off, carefully making her way up through the gears, as she travelled along the country lane towards Horton.

Drescher asked, "Where are we going now?"

Joanna saw no reason not to tell them. "Back to prison. We don't need you anymore because the escape has been prevented and all your fellow plotters will have been rounded up by now. I imagine they will send you somewhere very special and it will be a long time indeed before you get back to Koszalin. Perhaps we will decide to shoot you anyway. What do you think, Dominik?"

The blood drained from Drescher's face as his chin dropped and his eyes widened. It was a spontaneous and involuntary reaction but not in response to the threat. He was dumbstruck because the realisation suddenly hit him like a punch in the face. He made the connections – Dominik – Koszalin – Urszula, or Katze as the Abwehr had called her. Dominik was a Pole and the British agent – and he was sat opposite him! This man, the very enemy that Kaufmann had sworn to hunt down, the one who was still responsible for disrupting the vital plans of the SS stared back, coldly taunting him with his quiet confidence and composure. Somehow, the devious Polack already knew who he was and must have made the connection back to the SS general.

Drescher boiled over. His violent reaction was triggered by a combination of factors: the unrelenting frustration of confinement as a POW; the months of pent-up tension while planning the escape; the ignominy of the painful incarceration in the cellar; and finally, this astonishing appearance of their nemesis. He launched himself across the gap, springing off the soles of his feet with every ounce of his strength. A split second later all the others in the back started to react to the sudden movement. Both Dominik and Joanna managed to fire off one shot before all three Germans crashed into them.

Hannah automatically reacted to the sudden gunshots. She ducked down and hit the brakes hard, far too hard. At that precise moment the truck was approaching a narrow humpbacked bridge over the canal, where the road then dropped away with a sharp turn to the right. Here the Kennet and Avon waterway turned back onto its easterly course after taking a huge meandering loop northwards around the village of Horton. Forty miles an hour on the approach was slightly too fast, but under normal circumstances, steady braking, careful steering and a clear road would have seen them safely across. However, the road surface was wet, the wheels locked up and there was no traction or steering as Hannah lost all control. She took her foot off the brakes, but it was already too late. The arch of the bridge acted like a ramp and the wheels left the road surface completely. They crashed back down to earth at the mouth of the rough track alongside the towpath on the nearside of the roadway. Hannah braked again, but the vehicle was still travelling too fast and the wheels wouldn't grip on the gravel. They skidded straight across the track, crashed through the wooden rail fencing on the far side and dropped four feet into the adjacent pasture where the lorry rolled onto its offside. Its weight and momentum shot it across the damp grass on the 90-foot-wide band of turf. Still travelling at about 30 miles per hour it then crashed head-on into the eight-foot-high buttressed wall that surrounded the neighbouring farmhouse.

Aaron and Marcin heard the high-revving and whining engine and the crunching impact as they approached the bridge from the opposite direction. On arrival, Aaron saw that the front of the lorry had punched a hole clean through the wall and the bodywork had been crushed right back into the engine. A huge pile of rubble had collapsed onto the nearside wheel arch and bonnet and shattered the windscreen. Chunks of masonry had fallen through into the cab half burying the driver. The whole vehicle was quickly becoming shrouded in a cloud of brick dust and vented steam from the fractured radiator. They pulled across the road and parked on the gravel track and as they sprinted across the field they heard shouting from inside the body of the truck.

They had covered about half the distance when a man suddenly appeared inside the rear of the truck, standing to the side of the now vertical tailboard. They heard a gunshot and he slowly toppled over and fell to the ground. When they reached him he rolled onto his side and unsuccessfully tried to stand up. Marcin recognised him as the German prisoner Fürst. He had been shot in the right shoulder and he saw that his hands were still tied together behind his back. The Pole pinned him to the ground, planting his right boot firmly on his chest, "Keep still and stay down there. I'll see to you in a minute."

The German was losing a lot of blood and was already in shock, but he immediately recognised the Poles and spoke through gritted teeth. "You've got a lot to answer for today, you bastard, but at least you haven't had it all your own way. Take a look inside."

Aaron had already run to the front of the truck and looked into the cab. He only needed a glance to see that Hannah was dead. The force of the impact had thrown her forward and the flying glass and lumps of brick and mortar had pulverised her face beyond recognition. The fatal injury, however, had been caused by the steering wheel which had crushed her chest, the spokes and rim collapsing as it did so. Spear-like, the central column had then been driven further on as the cab was crushed. It punched right up through her heart, impaling her to the seat. Death would have been instantaneous. When Marcin saw Aaron coming back shaking his head to indicate that Hannah was dead, he left Fürst where he was and said, "Keep an eye on him. He's not going anywhere in that condition but see if you can stop the bleeding. I'll check inside."

Joanna's head and shoulders protruded from a tangle of arms and legs wedged between the benches. She was facing the rear with her gun in the classic two-handed grip, pointing down at the other three passengers jammed underneath. Her hands and the weapon were covered in blood. The others were not moving, but her pale, severe and blood-spattered features managed the briefest of smiles when she saw Marcin. She tried to stand up, but Dominik's torso was lying across the back of her legs pinning her knees to floor and as she moved he moaned.

She stayed still and said, "I think they're all alive, but both the Krauts are hit and Dominik's got a head injury. You'll have to be careful with him. I think it's quite bad. His hair is full of blood. I shot the other one when he tried to run away. He didn't give a damn about his so-called mates. What about Hannah? I've called out several times but she's said nothing."

"Let's get you and Dominik out of there and then we can worry about everything else." As he spoke he heard the bell of an approaching ambulance and he guessed the farmer must have telephoned for them.

Aaron gave him a hand and they managed to get the two Germans who were nearer the rear of the truck than the Poles out first. Both were conscious, but Drescher had received a shotgun blast in the side and was barely aware of his surroundings, certainly in no state to offer any resistance. Kurt had started screaming as soon as they moved him. The knee on his broken leg was now badly dislocated and he had a 'through-and-through' bullet hole in his other thigh. They compressed the wounds and made the Germans as comfortable as they could and then turned their attention to Dominik. He was breathing slowly and drifting in and out of consciousness, sometimes groaning and muttering incoherently. He was still holding on to his weapon and Marcin had to prise his fingers open to remove it. Apart from the three-inch laceration to the back of his head, they only found cuts and bruises on the rest of his body. A Home Guard mobile patrol which had been out searching for the escapees had arrived and with their help all the casualties were taken to the American Hospital and the Germans were kept under constant armed guard.

En route Joanna had told her colleagues what had happened.

"They must have planned something in advance because it was so quick and they all acted together. Even though we were both armed and alert I never saw it coming. Drescher sprang at Dominik, but he managed to duck sideways and shot him in the side."

Bernard asked, "Was that before the crash?"

"Just, and the other two were onto us straightaway as well. Kurt kicked out at me with his plaster cast and caught me in the chest, but I managed to shoot him at about the same time as his foot made contact."

Stan asked, "What was Fürst doing?"

"He headbutted me in the face a couple of times, but Dominik who was already on his feet, must have seen what was happening and grabbed him from behind and pulled him back. That's when the lorry turned over and we all fell into a heap. Dominik must have hit his head when he was thrown backwards and Fürst fell on top of him." (This was confirmed later that day when the Military Police investigator found traces of blood, hair and scalp on the metal drop-side of the lorry).

Bernard asked, "What about Drescher?"

She said, "He went down as soon as Dominik shot him and he rolled under the seats out of the way. As far as I know he never managed to get back up. Anyway, after the impact everybody was left dazed and shook up. We were all slow to react to the new situation. Fortunately, I still had hold of my gun but Fürst was uninjured and was on his feet first. My legs were stuck firm and Drescher was wedged under the seat by Kurt, who had probably fallen on top of him when the lorry rolled over. Fürst said nothing at all and barely glanced at us before he tried to get away. So I shot him before he disappeared from sight. You know the rest."

All four injured men underwent immediate surgery. None of the Germans' injuries turned out to be life-threatening, but Dominik's prognosis was far less promising. He had a fractured skull and had since fallen into a coma. His chances of recovery were given as fifty-fifty. Stan sat at his bedside and thought about all they had lost in their fight for Poland. His own father was already dead and now Hannah had gone as well. His godfather and friend, who had already lost his whole family and his new love, was now also fighting for his life. He and Bernard were scarred beyond recognition and they had all lost count of the friends and brother soldiers that had been left behind, scattered across Europe and beyond. He was sick of war and he prayed for it all to end. He prayed for Dominik and he longed for peace.

Swindon – 29th November 2009

I could tell from the tone of Stan's voice and the fixed look on his face that this was not going to end well, but I had to know.

"What happened?"

"The military doctors were great. They had been repairing bodies around the clock for months on end, dealing with the most horrific of injuries and all forms of battlefield trauma. But despite several operations and many hours in theatre they just couldn't save Dominik. The blood clots caused a series of strokes and he died a week later. He never regained consciousness and I never got the chance to tell him all the things I wanted to say."

"I'm sorry. He was a remarkable man."

"He had survived so much, you know. All the wars, all the battles: the hardships, the trenches, the treachery and the losses. So many losses – so much violence that he could have died at any time. But the bitter irony is that he was killed in a single-vehicle road accident in a quiet country lane, miles from the front lines and the action and he still had so much left to do in life."

His eyes filled with tears and I tried to reassure him, "I'm sure he already knew how you felt. You two were like brothers."

"No, he didn't. I had spent days at his bedside, hour upon hour thinking about what we had achieved and what we all meant to each other. I had promised myself that when he recovered the first thing I would do was tell him that he was the most honourable, loyal and inspirational of friends. I can honestly say that he was also a leader like no other: fearless yet sentimental, compassionate yet ruthless, resilient yet vulnerable and intelligent yet physical. It's strange, but his incredible record as a soldier and a human being was forged by his contradictions and his resourcefulness. Losing him and Hannah so soon after my own father was a harsh blow."

I waited a moment and then asked rather expectantly, "But I bet this isn't the end of his story, is it?"

"No, not quite Mick and now we're getting to the bit where I'll be asking you to take over. There's one thing left that you've got to do for Dominik, something that his friends couldn't."

We had been here before, so I said, "I think it's high time you told me. Then I'll do my best. I promise you that much."

"In many ways telling you what happened to us all has been harder than the experience itself. I'm already worn out by the responsibility I've been carrying and this heart attack was the last straw. I'm sure I haven't got too long left now so we had better crack on. Anyway, about three months after the crash when the rest of us were back in London waiting for our next orders, I was contacted by one of the interrogators at the London Cage who told me that Drescher (now known by his real name, Lieutenant Gotthard Schwarz) wanted to see me about Dominik and Urszula."

That did surprise me. "That seems a bit irregular, to say the least. Why on earth would the authorities agree to that sort of request, especially from a card-carrying Nazi? He'd already proved what a nasty piece of work he was."

Stan said, "Things had changed dramatically for him and his cronies. The Battle of the Bulge was over by the end of January and even the most ardent Hitlerites could see that complete defeat was only months away. Their thousand-year Reich was being bombed into oblivion and Schwarz's wound had become infected and wasn't healing very well, plus he had been charged with murder."

"What had he done this time?"

"Within weeks of arriving at his next camp he had presided over a kangaroo court and 'the accused', whom they suspected of being a camp informer, had then been found beaten to death in the latrines. Schwarz had admitted ordering the killing or, as he insisted on calling it, the legitimate sentence of the court martial and was himself facing the death penalty. He said he needed to see me before he died and as he probably intended, I was intrigued."

Stan then told me about their meeting at the London office of the Combined Services Detailed Interrogation Centre, known colloquially as the London Cage. He set the scene by explaining that today Kensington Palace Gardens is one of the most exclusive and expensive addresses in the whole world and its stately row of 170-year-old mansions, built on land owned by the Crown is home to ambassadors, billionaires and princes. But between July 1940 and September 1948, one of the country's most secret military establishments was based at numbers 6, 7 and 8, three of the most magnificent residences. He met the Nazi, not in one of the grand rooms of the luxurious mansion house but in the rather less salubrious but functional surroundings of the basement. The interview was conducted under the watchful eye of one of Colonel Scotland's interrogators. They conversed in German and the Nazi spoke first.

"I have some information for you, my scar-faced Polish agent and I wish nothing in return. I am telling you of this thing because I believe that I owe no loyalty to a man who abuses the power directly entrusted to him by our Führer and then corrupts officials to comply with his selfish will, contrary to their sworn oath and binding duty."

Stan interrupted, "Look Corporal Drescher or SS Lieutenant bloody Schwarz or whatever your real shitty German name is, I'm simply not interested in your warped sense of duty or your sudden indignant righteousness. If you've got something to say just get on with it. I haven't got all day."

"I do not understand why you find it necessary to be so abusive, but I will not pretend to you either. I am glad that the man known as Dominik is dead. I wish that I had killed him myself when I had the chance, but like you and me, he was a soldier and that I do understand. The woman, Urszula –alias the double agent Katze –was pregnant with his child when I captured her."

Now he did have Stan's attention. "What happened to her?"

"I think there will be no more insults now. Suddenly, you are very interested in what I say and so you will listen. She was sent to Ravensbrück concentration camp and the commandant was given special instructions, personally by Kaufmann. She was to be properly looked after until after the birth of the child and then allowed to nurse it for three months. Then she was to be shot and the child would be collected by Kaufmann."

The interrogator, who was already used to enquiring into some of the most horrendous of war crimes and knew what was happening at Ravensbrück and the other camps butted in. "If she was sent there she probably wouldn't have survived long enough to have had the baby, even if she was under some sort of SS protection. Although it's run by an SS captain called Fritz Suhren, he has his evil quotas to fill. The women die every day."

The German was insistent, "Kaufmann told Suhren to keep her alive and that's what he would have done. I'm sure of it."

The interrogator said, "I'm afraid it's not that simple and you know it. The place is vastly overcrowded with about 50,000 women incarcerated there. They're kept in the most primitive of sanitary conditions and epidemic diseases, particularly typhus, are common. Food rations were poor right from the start but are even worse now, what with the terrible shortages and many women simply starve. Once they become too weak and are no longer capable of work they are killed at the camp. Tens of thousands of others are shipped out to special killing centres where they're gassed and every day others are murdered at the camp and their bodies disposed of in the crematoria. Even Suhren couldn't guarantee her survival in such a place."

The prisoner shouted, "That's not true. It's all propaganda and lies. We are soldiers and we don't murder thousands of women and children."

Stan tried to get him back on track, "But why would Kaufmann want his enemy's child."

"I'll tell you exactly what he said. He told me that it was his destiny. The mother was half German and had shown herself to be brave, strong and courageous. The father was a clever, elusive and resourceful spy. He admired these attributes even though they were his enemies and he believed the child would probably inherit them. He was unable to have children, the result of having mumps when he was 14 years old and his wife was desperate for one."

The interrogator asked, "Did she know where the child was coming from?"

"He was going to tell her that it had been officially adopted under the Nazi Eindeutschung scheme. But he told me that he didn't really want to get a child that way because they were often much older and had already developed their own personality and behaviours and would resent the change. In which case he thought they might not respond well to the Germanisation process, whereas Urszula's baby was young enough and sufficiently unsullied to be nurtured and moulded to his own design and image. He saw it as the ideal answer and he could also claim it as his own without having to worry about any meddlesome officials or the fear of future contradiction by the child."

Stan was amazed at the delusional reasoning and he also tended to agree with the interrogator about her bleak prospects. "Do you know what happened to Urszula or the child, if there was one?"

"When I left Koszalin she had given birth to a son, so I expect that she was already dead or very near her time of execution. We SS are sticklers when it comes to obeying orders. Well, most of us are, but Kaufmann is the exception. I told him then that I didn't agree with what he was doing and that he should go through the proper channels and the next thing I know I've been sent over here. I suppose he saw me as a threat to his plans and was hoping that I would be gone for good." The German crossed his arms, sat back in his chair and said, "There, that is all I have to say before you hang me for fulfilling my legal obligation to the Fatherland and killing the traitor. What a crazy world we live in. Make of it what you like for my war is over."

Epilogue

THE DEBT

Swindon – 26th November 2009

Stan brought me up to date. After the war Aaron had decided not to go back to Poland, and instead he joined a Kibbutz in Israel. He wanted to be there at the birth of a free and democratic home for all Jews or as he put it, 'a refuge from the tsunami of hate, repression and bigotry: the Shoah that so nearly destroyed us all.' They kept in touch for ten years or so and he knew that Aaron had married and had a son. Then early in the 1960s his letters suddenly stopped. Marcin had gone back home to France in 1947 and Bernard, still bemoaning Poland's loss of his treasured city of Lwów, went with him. They had become great friends after the deaths of Dominik and Hannah, and disfigured Bernard wanted to make a fresh start. To him, France seemed as good a place as any and he was reasonably fluent in what was his fourth language. When Stan had last seen them on a trip in 1956 they had set up a business together, running a small farm and a local taxi service just outside of Laon, in Picardy.

Stan and his mother had settled in Swindon after the war as it wasn't safe for them to return home. Anyone who served in the Free Polish Army or the Home Army was often viewed as a traitor by the new regime and they were liable to harassment, arrest and imprisonment. If the authorities even suspected that they were Cichociemni or had been in the SOE then they faced far more severe consequences. So they stayed, and for a long time they tried to find out what had happened to Urszula. They wrote to the Red Cross and the International Tracing Service, which had been set up in 1948, but there was no record of her anywhere, not even under her real name. Numerous letters of enquiry about her and Kaufmann sent off to the MoD, the Polish government-in-exile and the communist regime in Poland all met with negative responses. It was as if the two of them had never existed. Stan gave up after five years of fruitless effort. He explained that he had lost heart when his mother died in 1951, after struggling for several years with cancer.

"I think it was just the hope of finding the boy that had kept her going for so long. The disease was killing her slowly and I marvelled at her inner strength and acceptance. At the end she was skeletal thin and in so much pain, it made me cry, but she was never demanding and she never complained. When I lost her – my wonderful brave Mum who had fought all her life and deserved better – well, it really knocked me back for a very long time."

We sat quietly for a moment or two, immersed in our own thoughts and sorrows. Then, just as I was about to ask him if he had any idea why they hadn't been able to find a trace of the German or Dominik's son, he took yet another file from the sideboard drawer. He placed it on the table and asked me to read it, explaining that it had been sent to him in 1985 by the interrogator who had supervised his interview with Schwarz alias Drescher at the London Cage. Stapled to the front sheet was a small card on which the correspondent had neatly written:

Stan,

along with thousands of others this document is about to be released under the thirty-year rule. I'm sorry I couldn't let you see it

*any earlier. If you still want to find out what happened to the child
then you really should start with DIN. See the attached translation.
Best of luck,
John Brent.*

There followed several pages containing a full profile of SS
Gruppenführer and Generalleutnant der Polizei, Dieter Kaufmann
and I was to be surprised once again. He had also been captured
and held in the UK. At the top was a photograph of him in uniform
bearing the caption KAUFMANN B112516 (his British Prisoner
of War identification number). His date of birth was given as 24th
August 1903 in Düsseldorf. His SS number as 3-612 (joined 1st
December 1931). It stated he had been captured in Germany near
the Dutch border on the 1st May 1945. I skimmed through a full
list and description of his promotions, postings, responsibilities
and decorations (including the Iron Cross 1st and 2nd class),
but what caught my eye was the handwritten note scrawled right
across the last page of the file. Hanged - Warsaw 21st March 1955
and an ink stamp: 'PWIS (H) LDC/WO 317/3184/65-63' at the
foot of every page.

I examined the letters on the stamp for a few moments and then
it clicked. Even before I met Stan, I already knew something of the
wartime MI19 Prisoner of War Department having read about the
background and exploits of the talented Chief Interrogator, Lt. Col.
Alexander Scotland. As a police interviewer I had been interested
in the ground-breaking questioning techniques employed at
their facility in the capital. The first eight letters of the acronym
stood for Prisoner of War Interrogation Section (Home) London
District Cage. Therefore, I had no doubt that Stan was right and
this was indeed a genuine file. The subsequent letters and numbers
on the stamp were case reference identifiers. During 1944-45 Col.
Scotland had been responsible for interviewing all high-ranking
Nazis suspected of mass murder. Presumably, that was the reason
for Kaufmann's lengthy detention and execution, but why would
the British have handed him over to Poland then under Russian
communist rule, rather than have him tried at Nuremberg? And

what had happened to him after Koszalin and in the ten years between his capture in 1945 and his death in 1955? By any stretch of the imagination, such a long period was extraordinary in such cases. War criminals sometimes only waited hours after they had been convicted before they were executed. There was no appeal procedure but even so, a delay of a few weeks or even months was possible but not ten years! Intrigued, I read the file in detail.

He was a protégé of Himmler and quickly rose through the SS ranks, even achieving appointments as a highly paid Gauleiter (regional Nazi party leader with dictatorial powers) and also as a Special Assignment Officer, an Inspector of the Secret Police (Gestapo) and the Security and Intelligence Service (SD). In 1941 he was posted to Poland as an SS district commander and chief of police, where he oversaw a number of ruthless counter-insurgency operations and Jewish round-ups. He had inspected a group of concentration and labour camps in the Lublin area to ensure that they improved their efficiency by speeding up their work and death rates to meet centrally approved targets. He had personally presided over the execution of the whole population of three villages, in reprisal for partisan activity. In 1943 he was transferred back to Berlin. Strangely, there his record suddenly ended. There was nothing further, nothing at all until his capture. I told Stan what I was thinking.

"It's obvious from this that when you were writing your letters and asking your questions they all knew where he was because he was in custody. Yet, even after all you had done for the Allied cause they still wouldn't tell you. Not the British, not the Poles or the Communists: nobody lifted a finger to help you. That tells me there's far more to it and they were hiding something really big. Whatever it was, they were trying to keep a lid on it and it must have happened after 1943 because that's where his record ends so abruptly. By handing him over to the Russians to dispose of – well strictly speaking it was to the Polish government but at that time it meant the same thing – they ensured that there would be no leaks or revelations. Having said that, I don't have a clue as to what it's really all about."

"Neither do I and there's another thing: I've never really accepted Drescher's explanation of why he told us about the child either. It sounded too orchestrated and rehearsed and it was so out of character for such a fanatical Nazi, one who was literally going to die for the cause. He wouldn't have been worried about a bit of self-serving child abduction and bribery because that's what the SS did every day. So I'm sure that whatever his motivation was, and it must have been pretty powerful, it wasn't that load of crap he gave us."

I thought about it for a moment, "I think you're probably right. It was just a bit too glib and convenient. But there was certainly nothing in it for him personally – as you said, he was going to hang anyway."

Stan moved us on by giving me another sheet of paper. "This is the DIN translation that John Brent sent me with the Kaufmann file. I think it's pretty self-explanatory, as far as it goes."

It was handwritten:

The Eye of Revenge (Translation)
Declaration and statement of intent:
Shall we not avenge the six million? Of course we will. We must. It is our duty to each other, to the survivors, to everyone lost and to the future global generations that will now never be born. A million children that will never be parents, whole communities that have been eradicated: shtots, shtetls and dorfs and all destroyed by malevolent hatred and poison, spat like venom from the fangs of the Nazi monster. We will not let them walk away from their heinous crimes. Jews will not be impotent in the face of this horror. We will not stand idly by. As they struck, so we shall strike. As they terrified, so will we terrify and as they slaughtered, so we shall slaughter. As with us, it will be men, women and children: none shall be spared the sword of retribution. The greatest evil ever unleashed against the human race will be avenged. All must be made equal and this is our judgement. This we solemnly swear and so be it.
Augsburg – November 1945 DIN

The threats were cold, clear and menacing, but as no such atrocious and retaliatory actions had been made I dismissed them as theatrical sabre-rattling. I had absolutely no inkling of who or what DIN really was, but I had a good idea of where this was leading. I told Stan, "Come on then, I think we're finally there so spit it out. What exactly do you expect me to do?"

"Write Dominik's story as I've asked, and find his son. He would be 65 now. If he's still alive then give him the book and the parchment scroll and the dagger. It is his heritage and his destiny after all. If he's already dead then find his children. If there are no descendants then give it all to the new World War II Museum in Gdansk. It opens in 2014, so there's your deadline. That's what Dominik would have wanted so it's what I want, and it's what you must do. History has a habit of repeating itself and I suspect it won't be long before Poland needs her heroes again. Dominik has shown the way. He must never be forgotten."

"Even if his son is still alive he will almost certainly believe his father was Kaufmann. He will consider himself to be German. Hell, he will be German. That's all he will have ever known. Why on earth would he be interested in any of it, and even if he is, why should he have custody of such precious objects? Whatever he is, he's certainly not Polish and they are!"

Stan was determined, "Kaufmann's wife may have fled abroad with the boy at the end of the war. She brought him up and he would have believed she was his mother. He may or may not have been told that Kaufmann was his father, but he certainly wouldn't have known him nor had any memories of him. He would only know what she told him."

"Where would they have gone?"

He had thought it all through. "Hundreds of Nazi families went to South America or the Middle East. She would have changed her name, perhaps many times, after all her husband had been hanged ten years later as a mass murderer. She probably adopted a different nationality and he may have been brought up as an Argentinean or a Brazilian. In fact, they could have settled anywhere if they had the right documents but whatever happened, his true father was

Dominik and so I disagree with you. The boy was – the man is – and he always will be – Polish. Whatever happened to him it wasn't his fault. He must be told about his father and all his antecedents."

I followed his logic but life as post-war fugitives must have been very difficult, so I asked, "How would they have lived? What would they have done for money and security?"

"She would have had access to ODESSA and the other organisations and individuals who were helping Nazi fugitives. They had millions in looted art, gold and treasure. She would have been well looked after and protected."

The more he told me, the more daunting the task appeared and I said so but he persevered. "Just take it one step at a time, Mick and who knows, perhaps along the way you'll also find out the real explanation for Drescher telling us about him. Anyway, you're the detective so follow John Brent's advice. He had remembered me, Urszula and Dominik's son over all those years so he must have had his reasons. Yes, investigate DIN first. I'm sure you'll find something and then go wherever the evidence takes you."

"Do you know anything about this DIN person, group, movement or whatever it is?"

He walked round the table a little breathless, leaning on it for support and said, "Nothing at all. When I got the file from the interrogator I didn't know where to start and I was on my own with no one to turn to for help. There were no computers for people like me or internet search engines then and nobody I asked had ever heard of DIN, and believe you me, I asked everybody. I tried the library, the schools and the local college and all the obvious places, but people looked at me as if I was daft. They saw me as a regular nuisance and in the end I just got too old and weary, I suppose and so to my shame I gave up again. But then I met Jan and between us we managed to put a plan together to get you and your computer involved. You're our last hope. You will do it, won't you?" He sat down and leaned across the table waiting for my answer, looking rather anxious, grey and uncomfortable.

I agreed to do as he asked and then he said, "There's one other thing. I've got some money put aside and I'm going to give it to you. It's not a fortune by any means, but it should cover your travelling and living expenses for a year or two. I don't want you to be out of pocket while you're working for us." He then stood up very slowly and held out his hand, "It's time you made a start. Go and find out about DIN. The talking should end now. I've performed my last duty to my small band of fighters and friends so you must now take over the reins and drive the story on. None of us knows where it will end but we, and that's the living and the dead, are all depending on you."

He shook my hand, hugged me close and then with the future settled he finally felt unburdened. Freed from the duty and self-imposed constraints of his past, he broke down completely. He collapsed into my arms and wept like a child. Tears of relief and painful remembrance streamed down his knotted cheeks, tracking down the scar, and his chest heaved and was racked with the distressed sobs. I held him close, trying to sooth and console with kind, soft words, waiting for him to recover – but he never did. He had decided to let go. With his last victory secure he knew his fight was finally over and the lion's heart of this battle-scarred and heroic fighter fluttered for the last time and was still.

As his tears stopped, slowly mine began to flow. Not just for Stan: a truly decent, honourable and proud man and a modest, amusing and single-minded companion of whom I had become very fond. I would miss him like a lost brother. Not just for Dominik, whom I had come to know and understand through his own graphic and compelling written words and those spoken by his devoted friend. Not just for the rest of the SOE team, whose gallant and courageous story had drawn me in and so inspired me. I had never met them, but I pictured their faces as I imagined them to be. Adam, the adventurous aviator – lost and abandoned in the ruins of a Nazi dungeon. Faithful Konrad, Stan's father and husband of Joanna – killed on a beach near Peenemünde. Hannah, Aaron's sister, who had been with them almost from the start – died in the army lorry crash near Devizes and tragically so close to the end of the war. I remembered Dominik again – he too died there – and his wife Bogdana and their innocent young children, Michal and Karolina, brutally murdered by an NKVD psychopath. Finally, his second love, Urszula, the mother of his stolen child – she was almost certainly killed at Ravensbrück. Why did they have to pay so heavy a price? Dominik had so vividly and succinctly warned us of the mind-shattering consequences of the horrors of the trenches saying, 'There is no honour or glory in any of it. That is war!' Yet he and his friends had fought on into the map-changing campaigns against Stalin's Soviets and Hitler's storm troopers and their secret police forces and death squads. Both regimes committed mass murder and ethnic cleansing on an unimaginable scale: an industrial slaughter that included millions of women, children and babes in arms. That was not war. That was genocide.

Then I thought about the others who had survived the war but had carried the mental and physical scars of their suffering for the rest of their lives. There was Stan's mother, Joanna, who sadly suffered again and never saw old age, Aaron from Lwów and Marcin from the French underground. Last heard of in France was Stan's pilot friend and latter-day spy, Bernard, who had survived the most horrendous burns and still found a way to battle on. I also remembered my own father and his brothers-in-arms. There seemed to be so many and now they had all gone. Hooked on such high and powerful sentiment I also wept for their whole generation who had collectively endured so much, taught us so much and lost so much through those terrible years. I asked myself why so many of these heroes when in their eighties and nineties had been forgotten. Why had they been lost in plain sight, invisible to the busy, the important and the indifferent? I lamented the fact that even when glimpsed – as a group or individually – then they were viewed by many in the modern world and sadly so often, even by society itself, as an exacting encumbrance, an escalating waste of costly and limited resources. Where had I heard that before?

It made me wonder whether my generation and those that followed had learnt anything at all from their achievements and sacrifice.

I called the doctor and waited with my dead friend. I promised him that I was going to pay my debt. Knowing that I had a book to write and a missing person to find, I dried my eyes and hoped that I too would not let them down or tarnish their memory. Then I remembered the lines from Rupert Brooke's poem, Clouds. *'They say that the dead die not, but remain near to the rich heirs of their grief and mirth.'* I smiled as I whimsically imagined Stan's shrewd spirit already *riding the calm mid-heaven in wise majesty, watching the moon and raging seas* and hoping that we mortals would do the right thing. Only time would tell.

⋐⋐⋐

Historical Annotations

Battle of Vienna – 1683

This conflict was fought between the forces of the Holy Roman Empire in alliance with the Polish–Lithuanian Commonwealth (Holy League) commanded by the King of Poland, Jan III Sobieski, against the armies of the Ottoman Empire and its fiefdoms, commanded by the grand vizier, Merzifonlu Kara Mustafa Pasha. It was, as described in Chapter One, a battle of huge military and political significance, a turning point in European social and religious history and Sobieski was lauded as the architect of victory. It is also true that the king became isolated during the battle and was rescued by his loyal forces.

The significance of this victory is reflected in the honours heaped upon the king. For example, the Austrians erected a church on top of the Kahlenberg Hill, north of the city in his honour. The constellation Scutum Sobieskii (Sobieski's Shield) was named to memorialise the battle and pay tribute to the king. It is the only constellation bearing the name of a non-astronomer who was still alive at the time of the appellation. The train route from Vienna to Warsaw is also named after him and an Austrian composer honoured him in his *Partita Turcaria*, sub-titled, 'A Musical portrait of the Siege of Vienna by the Turks in 1683'. Because Sobieski had entrusted his kingdom to the protection of the Blessed Virgin (Our Lady of Czestochowa) before he left for battle, Pope Innocent XI commemorated his victory by establishing the worldwide feast of the Holy Name of Mary. It is celebrated on 12th September.

In addition to the legends emanating from this battle concerning the origins of croissants and coffee, it has also been alleged that the first bagel was a gift to King Jan Sobieski to commemorate his victory over the Ottomans. It was apparently made in the form of a stirrup, to commemorate the victorious charge by the Polish cavalry. It was also said that when the Ottomans were driven away from Vienna their military bands abandoned their instruments on the field of battle, allowing the western world to acquire cymbals, triangles, and bass drums.

Polish Army in France – 1918

Known variously as Haller's Army, the Blue Army or the Polish Legion in France, this significant volunteer force which eventually totalled 100,000 men, consisted of both infantry regiments and armoured units (equipped with Renault FT 17 tanks) and a fervent and potent Air Corps. Some 23,000 men were volunteers from North America, mostly recent immigrants from a non-existent, impoverished and occupied Poland who had not yet become American citizens. An assembly centre and training facility was established at Niagara-on-the-Lake in Southern Ontario, Canada. They were later joined by released German and Austro-Hungarian prisoners of war being held in France and Italy, Poles already serving in the French army and other exiles flocking in from around the world. They all saw the Great War as a once-in-a-lifetime opportunity to fight to free Poland and establish her independence. Their leader was the highly decorated and well-respected General Jozef Haller de Hallenburg, a great soldier, leader and statesman who was central to Poland's struggle throughout the first half of the twentieth century. After WWII he settled in London where he died on 4th June 1960 at the age of 87. He was buried in Gunnersbury cemetery, West London. His ashes were returned to Poland on 23rd April 1993 and are now kept in a crypt at St Agnieszka's garrison church in Krakow.

The Lwów Eaglets

Originally the term was applied exclusively to the young volunteers who fought within the city from 1st November 1918 to 22nd May 1919 following the Ukrainian seizure of power and during the subsequent siege by the Ukrainian army. However, over time the term's meaning has been broadened to include all the young soldiers who fought in the area of Eastern Galicia in the defence of the Polish cause during the Polish-Ukrainian War and the Polish-Bolshevik War. The Lwów Eaglets were interred in a portion of the Lychakiv graveyard that became known as the 'Cemetery of the Defenders' and it holds the remains of both teenaged and adult soldiers, including foreign volunteers. The cemetery and its memorial were designed by Rudolf Indruch, an Eaglet and student at the Lwów Institute of Architecture. Among those buried there was 14-year-old Jerzy Bitschan, the youngest of the city's defenders and six-year-old Oswald Anissimo, who was executed together with his father by Ukrainian soldiers. Sadly in 1971, under Soviet governance, the graves and monuments were destroyed and the Cemetery of the Defenders of Lwów was turned into a municipal waste dump and a goods vehicle depot. When the communist regime finally fell, restoration work on the memorial was started and following Polish support for Ukraine's Orange Revolution in 2004, the cemetery was officially reopened in a Polish-Ukrainian ceremony on June 24th, 2005. The last surviving Lwów Eaglet, Major Aleksander Salacki died on 5th April 2008.

The Kościuszko Squadron

The name was chosen for the reason given in Chapter Three. Andrzej Tadeusz Bonawentura Kościuszko – 4th February 1746 to 15th October 1817 – was a Polish/Lithuanian and American General. He remains an outstanding national hero of Poland, Lithuania, the United States and Belarus. He led the 1794 Kościuszko Uprising against Imperial Russia and the

Kingdom of Prussia as Supreme Commander of the Polish National Armed Forces. He also fought in the American War of Independence as a colonel in the Continental Army. In 1783, in recognition of his dedicated service, he was brevetted to the rank of Brigadier General and became a naturalised citizen of the United States. When he had first arrived in America he realised that the Declaration of Independence embodied everything he personally believed in. So moved was he by the document that he sought out and met its principal author, Thomas Jefferson, the influential Founding Father and the third President of the United States. They became close friends. The Pole was held in such high esteem by America and her leaders, who were truly appreciative of his efforts in their cause, that several towns across the United States and a county were named after him. So too was the highest mountain in Australia and the surrounding National Park. Statues and monuments have been erected in his honour around the world and hardly a large town or city in Poland exists without a street bearing his name.

Captain Merian Cooper, the famous American aviator, adventurer and film director/producer saw service as a bomber pilot in WWI, was shot down and captured. In July 1919, when he was an Allied adviser and observer at Lwów, he proposed that American and other foreign flyers should join the Poles in their fight against the Bolsheviks. In October, five American, three French and two British pilots met in Warsaw and signed their contracts to join the Polish Air Force arriving in Lwów on the 17th October. The 7th Combat Squadron 'Tadeusz Kościuszko' went operational in December. They fought for Poland in the war with Soviet Russia under the command of Major Fauntleroy and were first used during the Kiev offensive. Merian Cooper was shot down on 13th July 1920, but he survived and was taken prisoner by the Cossacks. Budionny had placed a bounty of half a million roubles on his head, but he managed to convince his captors that he was only a corporal, no one of any significance. Nevertheless, he had to endure near starvation rations, humiliating treatment, forced labour and typhus. Nine months later, weak, thin and barely recovered from his illness he managed to escape from the Gulag and after a six-week trek he arrived at Riga in independent Latvia. He was hailed as a hero, decorated with Poland's highest award and promoted two ranks to Lieutenant Colonel. Such was the squadron's contribution to the war effort that nine of the seventeen American pilots were awarded the Virtuti Militari. The name of the squadron also lived on in WWII with the famous all Polish 303 'Kościuszko' Fighter Squadron, the most successful RAF squadron in the Battle of Britain.

Stalin's Role in the Polish-Soviet War

The command and communication problems which embroiled Stalin, the Political Commissar on the Red Army's South-Western Front, are central to events in Chapters Five and Six and even today, historians debate his motivation. It has been argued that he was acting under Lenin's orders to take Lwów, so that the communist revolution could be extended into Romania and Germany but others are not convinced. What we do know is that Stalin was in part blamed for the war's failure. In August 1920 he was called before the Politburo to explain his actions. He resigned his military commission, something he had previously threatened to do on several occasions when his views had been challenged or disregarded, and then he attacked the entire campaign strategy. At the Ninth Party Conference on 22nd September, Trotsky openly criticised his war record, accusing him of insubordination, blind personal ambition and military incompetence. He claimed that Stalin had focused exclusively on enhancing his own reputation by recklessly striving for victory at Lwów, thereby jeopardising critical operations elsewhere. Nobody at the meeting challenged these assertions. Neither did Stalin, he simply restated his earlier position that the war itself was a mistake, something that, in hindsight, they all agreed on.

Semyon Budionny

This famous cavalry officer led the Konarmia as described. Despite becoming bogged down at Lwów and being defeated at Komarow he emerged at the end of the Russian Revolution as a lionised Soviet hero. He continued to receive Stalin's support and this probably explains how he managed to survive the various military purges of the 1930s. In July 1941 he was the commander-in-chief of the Soviet armed forces facing the German invasion of Ukraine during Operation Barbarossa. He operated directly under Stalin's inflexible order not to retreat under any circumstances. Consequently, his forces were surrounded and suffered one of the greatest routs in military history, with one and a half million men being killed or captured.

True to form, Stalin made him the scapegoat and sacked him as commander-in-chief, but he received no further punishment and was later reappointed to several command and honorary posts. Despite being blamed by Stalin for some of the Soviet Union's most catastrophic defeats he still seemed to benefit from the leader's patronage. After the war he was allowed to retire as a Hero of the Soviet Union and he died of a brain haemorrhage in 1973.

Nazi Wonder Weapons

There is little doubt that Hitler's scientists and weapons designers were amongst the very best in the world and they developed some of the most sophisticated and advanced armaments of the age. As the war progressed, they became involved in a desperate and frantic race to bring their most sophisticated and technologically demanding ideas, programmes and prototypes into production. Towards the end of 1944, their Wunderwaffen of rockets, missiles, massive guns and much more became their only hope of staving off imminent defeat. In this way Hitler hoped to buy enough time to produce even more advanced weaponry and thus turn the tide of the conflict, leading to his ultimate victory. The Allies were aware of the exceptional talent and the ground-breaking potential of this army of scientists and became involved in their own desperate race to capture them in the dying days of the war. As the Cold War approached the superpowers knew that many of these men and women already had the plans and the ability to give them the advantage in the arms race that would last for 50 years. A great deal of research has been undertaken in recent years and more evidence of these secret weapons has come to light, particularly following the break-up of the Soviet Union. Books have been written, films and television documentaries made and other serious investigations conducted, all with a view to leaving us better informed. With regard to the Bell, flying discs, atomic weapons and others I have not mentioned, the debates, claims and counterclaims still rage and so the reader must choose how much to believe.

German Resistance to Hitler

Although the Nazi regime proved popular with most Germans, there was always a degree of organised opposition which ranged from simply ignoring Nazi regulations to attempting to assassinate Hitler. There were over forty documented plots to kill him, some of which never progressed beyond the planning stage and seventeen occurred during the period of WWII. They varied greatly and apart from those planned by the Allies, they included attacks by lone gunmen, numerous bomb attempts including placing a device on his plane, military ambush and the flooding of his Berlin bunker's ventilation system with gas. The most famous was Colonel Claus von Stauffenberg's July 1944 bomb plot at the Wolf's Lair.

Most resistance, however, targeted Hitler's regime and his forces of oppression. The politically active socialists and communists were the first to show concerted and open hostility, but they were ruthlessly crushed by the Security Police and the SS. Some young people resented being forced to join the Hitler Youth and others were politically and morally opposed to fascist extremism. They created the youth movements such as the White Rose and the Edelweiss Pirates. The truly courageous and

Most important of all are the veterans who have spoken to me of their experiences. I have been privileged to listen to so many incredible wartime memories. Some have been awe-inspiring, others dark and heart wrenching, but all have been told to me with a mixture of compassion, regret, hope and fear. Almost to a man, their desperate and overriding desire has been that their suffering and the sacrifice of so many of their comrades, family, friends and innocents should not be forgotten. We all owe it to them to remember – and to learn the bitter lessons of history.

principled struggle of the former movement is outlined in some detail in Chapter Seventeen, but the subject deserves further explanation.

It was formed by students at the University of Munich in 1941 following the Archbishop of Munster's well-publicised sermon in which he condemned the Nazi euthanasia programme (the killing of those labelled as 'a drain on the rations' because they were considered to be genetically unsuitable).

The early membership included Hans and Sophie Scholl, Willi Graf, Christoph Probst, Alex Schmorell, Traute Lafrenz, Katharina Schueddekopf, Lieselotte Berndl, Jürgen Wittenstein, Marie-Luise Jahn and Falk Harnack. Most of these prime movers were people in their early twenties, although a professor was also sympathetic and assisted their cause. The group, horrified by the brutal, tyrannical and murderous policies of the Nazis, adopted a strategy of passive resistance and published leaflets calling upon the German people to reject Hitler and all he stood for. These flyers were sent anonymously to people all over Germany, taking addresses randomly from telephone directories. They also left quantities of the leaflets in public buildings and communal areas and sent them to educationalists, university lecturers and business leaders. The extracts quoted in this book are accurate and six of the leaders were indeed executed as described.

After the fall of the Nazi regime the members of the White Rose, especially Sophie, became icons of post-war Germany. Within the cleansed German psyche they came to represent the epitome of organised, moral and selfless opposition to tyranny and were lauded as heroes.

There is a black granite memorial to the White Rose Movement in the Hofgarten in Munich and the square outside the central hall of the city's university is called Scholl Siblings Platz and one of Germany's major literary prizes also bears their names. Many other public buildings, spaces and streets right across Germany carry the now famous names of its various members.

The Edelweiss Pirates, only referred to in passing in this book, also deserve similar recognition. It was mostly an informal,

loose-knit and city-based organisation that grew and expanded its activities as the war progressed. They started by just being a nuisance to the authorities, refusing to conform and seeking an alternative lifestyle by rebellious dressing, sleeping rough and playing jazz: anything that was contrary to Hitler's view of a good German. Their name was taken from the emblem of the edelweiss, which they wore as an ironic representation of the Führer's favourite flower. But theirs was not a highbrow, well-educated organisation, propounding lofty moral and ethical principles; they were ordinary young working-class people who knew the difference between right and wrong and wanted to strike out at fascist brutality. Many progressed to painting anti-Nazi graffiti on walls or throwing bricks through factory windows or pouring sugar water into the petrol tanks of military vehicles or simply distributing anti-government propaganda.

They offered shelter to army deserters and escapees from concentration camps or labour camps, and in groups and gangs they regularly attacked members of the Hitler Youth. Their acts gradually became bolder until they were carrying out armed attacks on military depots, derailing ammunition trains and sabotaging war production. Pirates who were caught faced serious consequences. At best, they were threatened, beaten and humiliated by having their heads shaved. Others were sent to prison or psychiatric hospitals where they faced euthanasia, or to labour and concentration camps. Some were executed by hanging.

Even though a number of their members were honoured in Israel in the 1980s for 'their humanity and courage in saving Jews from the Holocaust' such recognition by German politicians and historians came much slower and with reluctance. This was partly due to the mass amnesia and indifference that dominated post-war society in West Germany and also, unlike the White Rose movement, because of the observed lack of national cohesion within the organisation. This unresponsiveness was also reinforced by the absence of any definitive documents listing their aims or formulating a shared ethical standpoint. Only recently, as their membership has been drastically whittled away by the years,

has Germany officially recognised their considerable contribution to the fight against Hitler and everything he represented.

Perhaps the most famous group was that which included the aristocrats, Prussian and conservative military officers, diplomats and disgruntled Nazis. They plotted to kill Hitler, hoping that his sudden and violent demise would lead to an anti-Nazi uprising. There was also a degree of antipathy by the Church locally, particularly when the Nazis suppressed and defamed the Ministry. At great personal risk individual members of the clergy spoke out and sheltered and aided Jews, but overall there was little organised or coordinated religious opposition. On the contrary, the concordat of 1933 between Hitler and the Vatican sparked immediate controversy, initiating widespread accusations of Papal cooperation with the Nazi regime and Roman Catholic complicity in the persecution of the Jews. The breadth and severity of these charges have only increased with the passage of time and the emergence of further evidence of collusion, such as post-war escape lines for SS officers being established and managed by senior clerics.

The Pomeranian Griffin

This secret military organisation was a wartime Catholic-based, anti-Nazi resistance movement set up in Pomerania and East Prussia. It takes its name from the legendary creature featured on the Pomeranian coat of arms. It was formed in July 1941 by the amalgamation of three smaller groups, the Kashubian Griffin, the Military Organisation for Independence and the Zawisza Partisan Unit. It had over 500 active fighters, most but not all of them based in the forests and up to 20,000 non-combatant members who provided all manner of assistance and intelligence. Although they claimed regional autonomy, they mostly cooperated with the Home Army and answered to the government-in-exile. They carried out acts of sabotage, distributed anti-Nazi propaganda and conducted intelligence-gathering operations, notably regarding the V1 and V2 rockets at Peenemünde. In 1943 it was partially

infiltrated by the Gestapo, but the organisation regrouped and survived the war. When the Soviets took over, its members were persecuted and hunted down because of their religious convictions and their nationalism. Many were sent to the Gulag alongside the very same Nazi officers and Gestapo agents that they had fought against. Others were executed.

Special Operations Executive

Right from its very inception in July 1940 this organisation has been enmeshed in controversy, rivalry and resentment and the basic dispute over its importance and worth has continued to this day. Winston Churchill ordered it 'to set Europe ablaze,' its mission being to encourage and facilitate espionage, sabotage and reconnaissance behind enemy lines. To those few people who knew of its existence it was variously referred to as 'the Baker Street Irregulars', 'Churchill's Secret Army' or 'The Ministry of Ungentlemanly Warfare'.

What has never been in dispute is the courage of the men and women agents, many of whom became a legend in their own time. Casualties among them were heavy and many of those captured by the Gestapo were savagely tortured and executed or sent to concentration camps. The full extent of their individual contributions to the final victory has only recently emerged and is still not widely known and appreciated. Even less so are the exploits of the Polish Section. I have tried to shine a light on the type of operations that were undertaken by those trained at Audley End House and the following two documented and true-life examples prove once again that fact really is stranger than fiction.

SOE supplied and supported an AK guerrilla force operating in the forest and hills south of Warsaw, between Radom and Kielce, in the heart of Nazi-occupied territory. Their leader was betrayed, but he survived and escaped. Later, dressed as an SS officer he held up a troop train and seized all the weapons from the German soldiers. Another SOE-sponsored operation enabled two agents and eighteen men dressed as SS soldiers to raid the prison

at Pinsk. They killed the commandant and a sentry on the main gate and released forty prisoners including three captured agents.

For all these Polish saboteurs and spies operating inside France, their home country and elsewhere in occupied Europe, and the aircrew who dropped and supplied them, daily existence was tough and dangerous. Their life expectancy was exceedingly short. So we must hope that the historians and military analysts will one day be able to agree their closing arguments as to the overall effectiveness of the SOE. Only then will the jury of history be able to return a conclusive verdict. Either way, the memory of the agents deserves to be honoured for all time. Some 500 such volunteers passed through Audley End House and over 300 parachuted into Poland. More than 100 made the ultimate sacrifice. Of a total of 500 drops made, nearly 200 were into Warsaw during the two months of the Uprising. Over 70 aircraft were lost on Polish operations. Every year at the Saffron Walden Remembrance Service, a wreath bearing the Cichociemni badge is laid in memory of the Polish Agents.

SS Panzer Brigade 150

SS PB 150 (Brandenburger) was, in fact, used in Operation Grief (sometimes referred to as Operation Condor) during the German breakout at the Battle of the Bulge on 16th December 1944. The small English-speaking subsidiary unit was used to spearhead a bold 'false flag' operation said to have been Hitler's own brainchild. They were issued with American uniforms, documents, weapons, equipment and dog tags and deployed in jeeps. They penetrated the American lines, having been tasked to capture vital bridges over the River Meuse. Once in position, they were to be immediately reinforced by the rest of this armoured commando formation using captured American tanks and transport. Although they failed to secure and hold their targets, they did manage to cause maximum confusion and chaos by spreading misinformation and changing the road signs. They also misdirected the retreating defenders and the Allied reinforcements

being pushed forward. When the Americans discovered the ruse they responded aggressively and increased their security measures and a number of the infiltrators were captured. Even then, a few continued the deception by claiming that they were on a mission to assassinate General Eisenhower. This caused him to increase his personal security and accept strict limitations on his freedom of movement in theatre. Those captured still wearing the American uniforms were later executed by firing squad.

The Devizes POW Camp Escape

In his book *The London Cage* (first published in 1957) Lieutenant Colonel A.P. Scotland devotes a chapter to 'The Great Devizes Plot'. He revealed that a group of zealous and ruthless Nazis had been devising a master plan for a mass breakout with the intention of forming a fighting phalanx to march east and join up with more escapees from other camps. The fanatical scheme he details is almost identical to the story later printed in the national press. One of the prisoners interrogated confirmed the conspiracy and thirty-two 'ringleaders' were taken to the London Cage to be interrogated. Some recent research, however, indicates that although there was indeed a genuine escape plan, it did not involve 'fighting columns' or a march on London. Many now accept that the plot had quickly gathered its own fanciful momentum by embellishment, confusion and subterfuge amongst the plotters and later with hyperbole by the press.

In many ways the real aftermath was just as shocking and dramatic. Following questioning in London, the prisoners were sent to a maximum security 'black camp' (POW Camp 21) in Comrie, Perthshire. One of them, Feldwebel Wolfgang Rosterg, who had been a camp interpreter at Devizes, was suspected by the rest of being the traitor who had revealed their plans to the enemy. On the evening of 23rd December 1944 in Hut 4, eight of the POWs from Devizes viciously beat him before dragging him semi-conscious to the bath house building where he was hanged.

Six months later all eight were sent to London to answer for his murder. The court martial took place in the large drawing-room of No. 8 Kensington Palace Gardens. They all pleaded not guilty and were represented by solicitors: Captain Roger Willis (later His Honour Judge Willis of Bloomsbury County Court) and Major R. Evans. Two were acquitted and six, all in their early twenties, were convicted and sentenced to death. At 8am on the 6th October 1945, after one sentence had been commuted to penal servitude for life, the other five were marched to Pentonville Prison in North London and there hanged by Albert Pierrepoint. Their victim was interred at the German Military Cemetery at Cannock Chase in Staffordshire.

Nazi War Crime Trials in Poland

In the epilogue we read of the fate of my fictitious Nazi SS officer Kaufmann, but in reality, his long convoluted path to justice was not that unusual as it fell within the terms of The Moscow Declaration. This was signed during the Moscow Conference on 30th October 1943. The formal name of the agreement was the 'Declaration of the Four Nations on General Security'. The final section was entitled 'Statement on Atrocities' and having been largely drafted by Winston Churchill, it was signed by the U.S. President, Franklin D. Roosevelt, the Soviet Premier, Joseph Stalin and the British Prime Minister himself. It commented on 'the evidence of atrocities, massacres and cold-blooded mass executions which are being perpetrated by Hitlerite forces in many of the countries they have overrun'. It went on to state that German offenders would be sent back to the countries where they had committed their crimes and be 'judged on the spot by the peoples whom they have outraged'.

In consequence, a Supreme National Tribunal was set up in Poland in 1946 and seven major war crimes trials took place. Perhaps the most notable was held between 27th August and 5th September 1946. SS Hauptsturmführer, Amon Leopold Göth, commander of the Kraków-Płaszów concentration camp stood

accused of tens of thousands of murders. It was further alleged that he had personally killed over 500 Jews. As he strolled through the camp he would shoot men, women and children in the head with his pistol on a whim or for crossing his path or just glancing at him. His mere appearance sent dozens of terrified prisoners running in all directions across the open ground, just like startled rats. This was the monster so vividly portrayed by Ralph Fiennes in the 1993 film, *Schindler's List* and he could also kill randomly and at will, without even stepping outside. Göth was the depraved commandant who so callously, sadistically and brutally took pot-shots at the prisoners, carefully aiming his rifle from the balcony of his house inside the camp. He was hanged near the former site of the Płaszów camp on 13th September 1946, aged 37. The executioner, perhaps nervous and agitated by the solemnity and symbolism of the occasion, miscalculated the length of rope necessary to hang him on two occasions and so it took three attempts to successfully carry out the sentence.

After 1947 alleged war criminals were tried before the ordinary courts in Poland. Prosecutors identified over 12,000 Nazi war criminals living abroad that it wished to put on trial and eventually about 2,000 were extradited, most but not all before 1949. Including people detained in Poland and those extradited, some 2,500 were convicted and 630 sentenced to death. These included SA Gruppenführer Ludwig Fischer, governor of the Warsaw district who was executed in 1947; SS Obersturmbannführer Höss, the first commandant of the Auschwitz death camp. He was also hanged in 1947 on a gallows outside the infamous camp's gas chambers: the scaffold is still there as a memorial to his crimes.

According to unofficial statistics, Polish tribunals (including those held during the occupation by The Home Army) dealt with a total of 40,000 defendants accused of Nazi crimes. This counted both Germans and their collaborators and trials were still taking place well into the 1950s, including that of SS Gruppenführer Jürgen Stroop, suppressor of the Warsaw Ghetto Uprising. He had already been put on trial at a U.S. Military Tribunal at Dachau for the summary executions of Allied airmen shot down over

Germany. On 21st March 1947 he had been sentenced to death. However, that sentence was not carried out; instead he was extradited to Poland. There he was convicted of mass murder and on 6th March 1952 he was hanged. SS Gruppenführer Jakob Sporrenberg, responsible for the Majdanek death camp had also been convicted in Warsaw in 1950, but he was not executed until December 1952. Interestingly, he too had been interviewed by Colonel Scotland in England in 1945. He was also linked to Globocnik's notorious activities in Lublin and connected to the top secret Die Glocke project. Scotland described him as the vilest creature he had ever met, and he had encountered many a foul murderer.

Acknowledgements

This is my opportunity to thank the numerous individuals and organisations that have assisted in the research and publication of this novel. Without their time, enthusiasm and expertise I doubt that the project would have succeeded. There are too many to list here and I fear that I would inevitably overlook someone's contribution, but I am truly grateful to them one and all.

However, I would particularly like to mention Paul Bechler of Devizes who was a member of the 5th Polish Guard Company at the Prisoner of War Camp. He proudly but modestly told me his story, providing both inspiration and a wealth of firsthand background knowledge.

Thank you to Lisa Webb and the staff at The Wiltshire Heritage Museum at Devizes. They were particularly helpful and kindly allowed me access to a recently acquired and fascinating 'diary' of an unknown German soldier who was imprisoned at the camp. Cleverly written in rhyming couplets and illustrated with beautiful watercolour drawings this booklet provided me with a unique, contemporary insight into the camp, its inmates and their daily lives.

I also owe a huge thank you to Lynn, Claire my editor, and the whole team at Indepenpress for their patience, hard work and encouragement. They have made it happen.